The Lombardi Family Saga

Book I:
French Legend–
The King
of Rohan

Joe-Ming Cheng, Ph.D.

Andrew Benzie Books
Martinez, California

Published by Andrew Benzie Books
www.andrewbenziebooks.com

Printed in the United States of America
First Edition: November 2019

10 9 8 7 6 5 4 3 2 1

Cheng, Joe-Ming
The Lombardi Family Saga
Book I: French Legend—The King of Rohan

ISBN: 978-1-950562-22-0

Senior Writer: Joyce Krieg D.J. Foley
Cover Painting: Seth D.J. Foley
Cover and Book Design: Andrew Benzie

Acknowledgements

My gratitude to those who taught and enlightened me: Ms. Dan Hsia Hsi, my primary school master teacher; Mr. KM Cheng, my middle school master teacher; Mr. SC Tang, my high school master teacher, teacher Ms. Helen W., Dr. Glenn Lee, my Dentist. They taught me Chinese classics and in concordance with western science, humanity, and renaissance. Dr. Virgil Elings, Professor at UC-Santa Barbara; Dr. Glen Landon and Dr. David Huffman, professors at UC-Santa Cruz, taught me be exploring-minded and to formulate the findings and discoveries in greater simplicity. Great thanks for the encouragement and support of my father, Mr. SC Cheng, my wife Pying, daughters Shannon and Audrey; classmates MM Chen, Theresa Ma, and friend Gary Whitley; for Seth Foley's front cover drawing; the extended and elaborated effort of my designer/publisher Andrew Benzie; and, last but not least, Ms. Krieg, the senior writer of this book.

CHAPTER ONE

Golden sunlight flooded the kitchen of a typical French suburban home in the countryside near Dijon as Gilbert Rohan burst through the door and placed his schoolbooks on the counter. "Mama, guess what!" he exclaimed.

"What, *mon cherie?*" Antoinette looked up from the stew she'd been stirring and replied with a smile. Her youngest child was 18, a man, and would be going off to university in the fall. But today, with his brown eyes dancing and round face bubbling over with excitement, he was still her little boy.

"The most exciting thing! I've been chosen out of all the students at school for a free luxury tour of a wonderful castle."

"That is exciting news! Which castle will you be touring?"

"Rohan! Isn't that interesting? The same surname as ours. Do you think that's why I was chosen?"

"Could be just a coincidence. After all, you are smart and well-mannered—who wouldn't want a young man such as you in their castle?" Antoinette did her best to keep her tone light, to encourage and support her son, but a tiny seed of doubt began to sprout deep inside. *Rohan! My husband has always been so secretive about his family. What does this mean for us—for the future?*

Gilbert continued to babble on. "This is one of the most prestigious castles in all of Europe… if they still had a king, he'd have as much power as the Pope… so much history and heritage…" Then his eager face fell. "There is just one thing…"

"I thought so," Antoinette said. "As the Americans say, there's no such thing as a free lunch."

"I can't go by myself. I have to have a chaperone, and it's expensive." He handed a sheet of paper to his mother.

Antoinette reached for her reading glasses. In her early sixties, her face only had a few fine wrinkles, her figure was still girlish and slender, and her dark brown hair hung glossy and smooth down her back. Reading glasses were the only concession she made to age. Now she took in the details about the trip to Rohan Castle, the guided tour of the Duke's inner quarters, the four nights the students would stay on the castle grounds. Then she reached the part about the cost for the chaperone.

"Forty-five hundred Euros. That is expensive," she said. "We're not a wealthy family, you know."

Gilbert gazed at his mother, his eyes pleading.

"Well, when your elder brothers and sisters graduated from *lycée* and went off to university, we gave them special graduation gifts. We do have some savings. Perhaps we can call this your graduation gift and I can go with you after all."

"Really?" Gilbert's face light up at this hopeful sign.

"We'll talk to your father about it tonight at dinner."

"Thank you, Mama. This is the most exciting thing that's ever happened to me!" He gave his mother a hug and Antoinette could feel her youngest child's heart beating hard against her own.

*　　　　*　　　　*

Dr. Tom Rohan, the owner of a small chain of drug stores and CEO of a drug development lab, arrived home for dinner at 6:45, just as he did on every weekday. His advanced age had been a carefully guarded secret, as had been the ill health he suffered with during much of Gilbert's childhood. His strong will, healthy eating and dedication to exercise had restored him to his robust and energetic self for the past five years.

Even though only three individuals were left in a household that had once held nine, the Rohans continued to gather for their evening meal in the modest home's formal dining room that Tom himself had built. This was a plain and rustic room, with a trestle table, wooden chairs, a fireplace in one corner, and a simple china cabinet. The only distinguishing feature was a carved, wooden sculpture of a dragon hanging from the coffered ceiling. It glowered over the dining table, almost three meters long, painted brown and with small wings. The creature's mad eyes and protruding tongue, 30 centimeters long, seemed to stare at the diners with menace. When guests would ask about such an unusual decoration for a dining room, Tom would only say that it was an old family tradition to invite a dragon to dinner.

Now as the family began to partake of the chicken stew, crunchy bread and fresh salad that Antoinette had prepared, Gilbert repeated the story he'd told his mother that afternoon, the astonishing and breathtaking news that he'd been chosen for a luxury tour of a famous château. "I heard the current Duke just passed away," Gilbert finished. "He has no heirs. No uncles, no brothers, no male or female offspring. The old family line has ended."

"And which castle would this be?" Tom asked.

"Rohan!" Gilbert said. "Isn't that exciting? The same surname as ours. Do you think that's why I was chosen?"

Tom's hand paused in spooning stew into his mouth. *Château du Rohan. So… they have found me at last.* For decades, he'd been in hiding, hoping he could live a simple, ordinary life with the family and work he loved, far away from the stress and strife of royal life. He gazed up at the dragon as if gaining strength and wisdom from the mythical beast. Another thought brought a smile to his lips. *So, if they want to bring us out into the open, then let's do it!*

Antoinette's words interrupted his thoughts. "I just don't know how we can afford it. They require each student to have a chaperone, and it costs forty-five hundred Euros. I just checked the budget and we've got maybe half that amount. Remember, we've been having cash flow problems lately."

Tom ignored his wife and turned to his son. "You must go, of course."

"What about paying for the chaperone?" Antoinette said while Gilbert broke into a cheer.

"We'll all go," Tom said.

"You mean you'll come too?" Antoinette said. "But we don't even have the money for one chaperone. How can we possibly pay for both of us?"

Tom waved off her concerns as if they were no matter. "I said 'we'll all go.' You, me, Gilbert, and his six brothers and sisters." He watched as the expressions of his wife and son showed astonishment, delight and concern.

"But that would cost almost forty-thousand Euros," Antoinette said, shaking her head. "Where would we ever come up with that kind of cash? The bank would never loan us that much money."

"You just let me take care of that," Tom said.

"But—but—" Antoinette sputtered. "Even if you can raise the money, what you propose about bringing the whole family is simply impossible. Have you forgotten about our oldest son, an army general, commander of the 7th District? And what of the others? A banker, a lawyer, a teacher and two housewives with families of their own to take care of. Every one of them has important jobs or duties. You expect them to just drop everything and come along on this trip? This plan is not even a dream." She pushed her plate away and threw down her napkin in disgust.

"If I raise the money, will you convince our children to come along on the trip?" Tom asked in a calm, even voice.

"But this is insane," Antoinette continued in her same scoffing tone. "You are not going to pawn our business or our family home to pay for this trip. Not when we worked so hard for so many years to earn these assets. I won't allow it!"

Tom and Antoinette rarely fought, and Tom could see Gilbert was close to tears at this downward turn in the discussion and the imminent destruction of his dream trip.

"I will get the money and I pledge to you I will not touch our shops, our business, our home or our savings. Now, will you convince our children to come along on this trip that means so much to Gilbert? Think of what a wonderful graduation gift this will be for our last child?"

"Well…" Antoinette said, her voice softening. "You really can raise that kind of money without endangering our assets?"

"You have my word of honor." Tom reached across the table to place his hand over hers.

"I suppose it would be fun to have the entire family together again," Antoinette said.

"Say yes, Mama. Please?" Gilbert said, sounding like a little boy begging for candy.

"I can't hold out against the two of you," Antoinette said with a little smile. "Yes, let's do it."

So the die is cast, Tom thought, telling himself it was all worth it just to see his youngest son so happy.

Chapter Two

Antoinette stared out the passenger side window as the countryside of the Burgundy region sped past. As the time and kilometers ticked by—two hours, then three—and their destination drew nearer, the landscape changed, becoming industrial and urban, the motorway more and more congested.

Paris! Antoinette could not even remember the last time she and Tom had visited the City of Lights. It must have been their first wedding anniversary, she decided, when they treated themselves to a three-star hotel and an evening at the Moulin Rouge, before the babies began to arrive and made such luxuries of time and money impossible. These days, they had no need to visit Paris, the small city of Dijon more than adequate when it came to shopping, services, and occasional "date nights."

When Antoinette had questioned Tom as their journey began early that morning, he only smiled enigmatically and said, "Well, I did promise to raise the money for Gilbert's trip to the castle—and for the whole family to come along—didn't I?"

Antoinette knew that sly look and teasing tone all too well. She'd heard it for the first time when she was a young university student and Tom was a member of the faculty. Now, some forty years later, she still loved Tom and placed her trust in him.

The couple entered the city and Tom maneuvered their ten-year-old Renault sedan through the narrow cobblestone streets until he reached Rue Vivienne in the Paris Opera district. He found a place to park and as Tom assisted her out of the passenger seat, Antoinette studied the storefronts, the names, the windows with shiny round objects in glass cases. Some of the stores even had armed guards at the entrance, and all came with strong steel gates or roll-up doors for security after hours. "Coin shops?" she asked. "You drove all the way from home to Paris so we could go shopping for old coins?"

"Not shopping," Tom replied. "Selling." He reached into his pocket and pulled out a small velvet bag. He undid the drawstring and held out the receptacle so Antoinette could see the contents. She gasped when she saw the unmistakable glitter of gold.

"You said no one could ever touch, open or even see your fifty antique gold coins or your land deeds," she protested.

"I told you I'd figure out a way to pay for the trip without touching our savings, our shops or our home," he said, still in his light, teasing tone.

"Do you think this one coin is worth forty thousand Euros? Enough to pay for the trip?"

"Actually, I'm hoping to get fifty thousand Euros for it, not forty," Tom said.

"Fifty thousand? You must be dreaming." Still she allowed Tom to lead her to the entrance to Maison des Numismatique. No uniformed man guarded the front of this shop, but Tom did have to press an intercom button, identify himself, and wait for a series of complicated locks to disengage before he and Antoinette were permitted to enter.

A short, wrinkled man with a pair of reading glasses sliding down his pointed nose introduced himself as Alain Marchand, the shop owner and chief evaluator. He took the coin from Tom and studied it first with the glasses, then squinting through a magnifying glass. "In fifty-five years in the business, we've never seen a coin quite like this," he said politely, "but we have heard about it. Do you mind if I have my brother take a look?"

"Not at all. Do what you must do," Tom said.

Alain summed a man from the back of the shop and introduced him as his brother, Barry. Barry wore the same reading glasses sliding down a pointed nose, but he was obviously older than Alain, age-spotted and stooped.

Barry peered at Tom's coin under a microscope, placed it on an assayer's scale, and hurriedly paged through the yellowed pages of a large, heavy book. Then he said, "You do realize what you have, Monsieur Rohan, don't you?"

"Why don't you tell me?" Tom said. "After all, that's why we traveled all the way from Dijon to Paris."

"This could very well be one of the most treasured coins in all of France," Barry said. "It could be worth as much as one-hundred fifty thousand Euros."

With that pronouncement, Antoinette had to clutch Tom's hand to keep from falling to the floor. One hundred-fifty thousand Euros? For one little gold coin? And Tom had another 49 hiding back home! Her emotions cascaded, making her dizzy with confusion.

"We will need to have this examined by a team of experts," Barry continued. "We will give you our decision in two hours. Is that acceptable to you?"

Tom replied calmly, as if he were expecting this answer, that yes, this would be acceptable and that he and Antoinette would return to the shop in two hours.

*   *   *

The Hard Rock Café with its noisy and cluttered homage to American pop culture was not the place for lunch that Antoinette would have chosen for such a momentous day, but as Tom pointed out, it was convenient, right around the corner on boulevard Montmartre. She pushed around the ingredients on the plate of her California Cobb salad, barely tasting the grilled chicken, lettuce and avocado, so overcome was she with nervous anticipation. Tom, she noticed, had no problem with his appetite, diving into a huge bacon cheeseburger with gusto.

Finally, she spoke the thought that had been pounding on her mind ever since the coin dealer had mentioned 150,000 Euros. "We worked so hard for forty years to build up what little we have. We scrimped and saved and did without, and yet we were never able to save more than five thousand Euros."

"I understand, *ma cherie*," Tom said. "This must be very shocking and confusing for you."

"All this time, you've been sitting on a treasure," Antoinette persisted. "You could have sold just one of those gold coins and it would have changed our lives forever. Not to mention the lives of our children."

"Sudden wealth does not necessarily make people's lives better. Just look at all the unhappy lottery winners all over the world."

"You could have at least considered it," Antoinette said, tension in her voice. "You could have at least asked me."

"Perhaps I should have," Tom said, cleaning his sticky fingers carefully with his napkin. "But perhaps it is a blessing that we had to work hard, and that we created our lives with our own skills and our hearts. Our children have all turned out to be happy, productive, fulfilled adults, wouldn't you say?"

"Yes, but..." Antoinette tried another tactic. "What do you know about those so-called experts in that coin shop? They say your gold coin is worth one-hundred fifty thousand Euros. But what if it's actually worth one million? Two million?"

All Tom would say in response was, "We'll find out one day, perhaps not too far in the future."

On the way out of the restaurant, they passed by the Hard Rock Café's gift shop, with its collection of logo pins, keychains, glassware and tee shirts. "Gilbert would like one of these, don't you think?" Tom said, pausing in front of a shelf filled with tee shirts with the classic circular logo, PARIS printed in large letters underneath.

"Of course, he would love it, but..." Antoinette paused to study the price tag. "Thirty Euros just for a tee shirt? We can't afford—"

"Sure we can," Tom said. "Trust me. Now, what size is Gilbert wearing these days?"

*   *   *

When Tom and Antoinette returned to Maison des Numismatique, they were ushered into a small, secure chamber that reminded Antoinette of a vault in a bank where safe deposit boxes are kept. Alain Marchand invited them to seat themselves around a conference table. Also in the room were Barry Marchand and the three additional experts: a middle-aged man with the curly side locks and fringed shawl of an Orthodox Jew, a dark-featured woman with an Italian accent, and a young man whose fresh, eager face reminded Antoinette of Gilbert.

"We all agree the coin is genuine and worth at least two-hundred fifty thousand Euros," Barry Marchand said. "We are prepared to offer two-hundred twenty."

"Is that the best you can do?" Tom asked.

Barry nodded. "Yes, and that's pooling all of our liquid assets. You might find a better offer in London or Rome, or perhaps Dubai, but this is the best offer you'll find in Paris."

Tom turned to Antoinette, his voice low so the others could not hear. "What if we accept two-hundred thousand, with the proviso that we receive eighty-thousand immediately?"

Antoinette could only stare, her eyes telegraphing the message: *But this coin is worth so much more! Why settle for so little?*

"Think about it," Tom whispered. "Eighty-thousand up front means our children's families can come on the trip too if they want."

Before Tom could respond to the Marchands and their team of experts, Antoinette spoke up. "You are just dealers. You must be representing someone else. Who is the actual buyer of my husband's antique coin? What does this person plan to do with it?"

The expressions on the faces of Alain and Barry Marchand and their three associates, up until now casual and pleasant, turned serious.

"This coin could be worth a million dollars, two million even," Antoinette continued. "And you expect us to settle for two-hundred twenty thousand. Plus, we have no idea who the actual buyer or buyers might be. What is their intent? Could they harm our family?"

Whatever smiles that might have still remained on the faces of the five coin experts vanished. They huddled and whispered, stumbling over their words, and the voice of the female appraiser rose in anger.

"We cannot divulge the name of the buyer," Barry Marchand finally said, his voice tinged with hostility. "That's standard business practice. As to whether someone intends to harm your family, we have no answers."

"Now, now," Tom interrupted. "There's no need for this negotiation to become unpleasant." Turning to Antoinette he added, "Why would anyone want to harm our family? We are simply the owners of a small chain of pharmacies and a lab, nothing more."

Then back to the Marchands, he declared, "The offer stands. Two-hundred twenty thousand Euros, eighty-thousand transferred immediately to my bank account."

Before Antoinette could quite process what was happened, contracts were signed and hands shaken. Tom turned over the coin in its velvet bag to Alain Marchand, who immediately locked it in a safe. The Marchands made the financial transaction on their computer. Tom logged onto his bank account from his phone and only when he was satisfied that the eighty-thousand Euros had truly been deposited into his account did he say his farewells and escort Antoinette back to the Renault.

"I sure hope you know what you're doing," Antoinette said as the small sedan wove its way through the streets of Paris back to the motorway.

"Have I ever let you down?" Tom said, the smile back in his voice.

"But this is all so sudden and so confusing. Yesterday Gilbert came home with a bit of exciting news from school. And now this!"

"I know. But don't you think you should be concerned about something much more important?"

"And what would that be?"

"Using your charms, convincing all of our children to join us in a big family reunion. And packing a suitcase for yourself, of course," Tom said, leaning over at a traffic signal to give his wife a kiss.

CHAPTER THREE

Gilbert could barely contain his excitement as the Renault sped along the A36 motorway, taking him away from his home and school in the suburbs of Dijon, and upwards into the lush, green foothills of the Vosges Mountains. Each mile brought him closer to his destination—Rohan Castle, and the luxurious visit he'd been promised at school.

His father had invited him to sit in the front passenger seat—"We Rohan men need to talk," he'd told Antoinette—another unusual occurrence that made this trip extra-special. His mother seemed happy enough to relax in the back, with the unused seat next to her occupied by the luggage the family couldn't fit into the trunk of the small economy car.

"You do know where we are, correct?" Papa said.

"Of course," Gilbert said. He'd done little except study up on the history and geography of the region ever since he'd heard the exciting news the previous evening that not only had Papa raised the money to make the trip, but that his six brothers and sisters—and their families—would be joining him. "We're on the A36 heading east and we just passed through the town of Bescançon," the boy said, proud of his knowledge.

"No, not that," Papa said with a gentle laugh. "Where are we in history, what is the significance of this region?"

The answer popped immediately into Gilbert's mind. "We're in Bas-Rhin, one of the original *departements* established during the French Revolution."

"And Bas-Rhin is part of..." his father prompted.

"Alsace," Gilbert responded. "One of the most fought-over

regions in all of human history. Germany, France and Italy have all claimed this territory at one time or another."

"More blood has been shed in Alsace over the centuries than on any piece of land on the planet," Papa muttered to himself, his expression turning temporarily serious. Then to Gilbert, he said more cheerfully, "Can you tell me what was going on in this place during the ninth century?"

"Sure," Gilbert said. "The Carolingian Empire. Charlemagne." He felt a tingle of excitement just saying these legendary royal names out loud. "The Carolingian dynasty ruled as kings of the Franks since the mid-700s and kings of the Lombards of Italy since the late 700s. And then Pope Leo III crowned Charlemagne emperor of the Roman Empire in 800."

"Excellent. And what happened after that?"

"A civil war broke out in 840 to 843 after the death of Charlemagne's son, Louis the Pious," Gilbert said, glad he'd re-read his history book the previous night. "Then the empire was divided into thirds, with the king of Rohan still recognized as the ruler of the middle section."

"Did you know they called it Mitteleuropa?" Papa said. "Middle Europe, extending all the way from the Netherlands to Lombardy and Tuscany in Italy, and taking in huge portions of today's France and Germany. All ruled by one powerful king."

Gilbert shook his head, trying to imagine such vast land holdings. "And then it all just fell apart," he said.

"Well, that's what the history books would lead you to believe," Papa replied. "Deaths and in-fighting among the descendants of Charlemagne. Corruption and weakness. The usual." He paused to navigate a sharp turn in the mountainous road. "But the king of Rohan was still recognized as the emperor, even though he had little power outside his own kingdom. And the unity of the empire and the hereditary rights of the Carolingians continued to be acknowledged."

Gilbert turned this over in his mind. "So, if there were a king of Rohan alive today, someone who could trace his bloodline all the way back to Charlemagne…?"

"That really would be the stuff of legends, wouldn't it?" Papa said with an affectionate smile toward his youngest son.

*   *   *

The road rose steeply and the Renault maneuvered around another sharp turn. The conversation between Antoinette's husband and son in the front seat halted. All three passengers simply stared in wonder. For there before them was their first glimpse of Castle Rohan.

It rose majestically out of the dense pine forests of the Vosges range and appeared almost as if carved by nature rather than by man. Red sandstone formed Medieval turrets and battlements that stood high and proud, lording over all it observed: Alsace, the Black Forest, the Rhine and beyond. Antoinette found herself shrinking in the back passenger seat, overcome with a combination of fear and awe at this sight, both beautiful and yet disturbing. It was if the foreboding structure somehow sensed the arrival of a family that bore its name and was trying to decide whether to welcome them or turn them away.

All misgivings vanished from her mind when the car pulled into the centuries-old Bavarian-style village that stood just outside the castle gates. The students and their chaperones from throughout France who had been selected for this special trip would be staying in hotels and guest houses the first two nights. For the third night, they would stay in the castle itself and on the fourth day take part in an exclusive VIP tour of the castle. Tom had reserved an entire small hotel to house his wife, his seven children, and their spouses and offspring.

Antoinette unpacked, dressed for dinner, and hurried to the first floor dining room. When she entered the country-style room with its white tablecloths, wooden chairs and fresh flowers, and saw her husband, all seven of her children—and their children—ready to greet her, she was overcome with emotion. She tried to remember the last time all seven of her offspring had been in the same place at the same time, and decided it must have been Gilbert's christening—eighteen years ago.

Antony, the eldest, looked stern and handsome in the full uniform of a one-star French army general, complete with pillbox hat covered with gold braid. Her second eldest, Julia, had always been the smart and serious one. Now a successful attorney, she appeared in a chic business suit and carried a polished designer briefcase. Antoinette just hoped Julia would be able to relax sufficiently to enjoy the next four days.

Next came Ronald, who had followed in his father's footsteps into the field of education, on track to achieving a full professorship while still in his early thirties. He was followed in birth by Phillip, a banker with ambitious plans to amass both wealth and power. Adele and Louise, at 27 and 24 respectfully, had both married successful businessmen and were happy to stay at home, raising small children of their own. And finally came Gilbert, always and forever her baby, the boy whose good fortune at school had started the chain of events that led to this warm and heartfelt family reunion.

The hugs and kisses finally over, at least for the moment, Antoinette turned to Tom. With a trembling smile and fresh tears spilling onto her cheeks, she said, "This is the most wonderful gift you could have ever given me. I am so sorry I ever doubted you. Of course you were right to sell—"

Tom placed two fingers gently on Antoinette's lips to prevent her from mentioning the sale of the gold coin. "Best not to speak of that just now," he whispered. Turning to his family, he said, "The important thing is that the Rohan family is all together once again. To the Rohans!"

The assembled sons and daughters, their spouses, and their sons and daughters broke into loud cheers and applause. What followed next was an hour and more of sharing, reminiscing and catching up. Old family stories came to the surface, usually starting with "Remember that time when…" Though careful to watch his budget, Tom had always been able to treat the family to a skiing vacation in winter, and a summer holiday on the Côte d'Azur. One memorable year, he surprised them all with a weekend at Disneyland Paris. These excursions created some of the happiest memories now making their way around the room.

Amidst the laughter and lively conversation, a voice rose in song. Adele, launching into another Rohan family tradition, the old Frère Jacques nursey song, but with the name of each sibling substituted for that of Jacques. Thus it became, "Are you sleeping, are you sleeping, brother Antony, brother Antony…" Soon the rest were joining in, verse after verse in the round, naming each of the seven offspring of Tom and Antoinette from Antony to Gilbert. They finished with one last rousing chorus while their own children looked on with bewilderment and amusement.

When the laughter and cheers finally died down, Gilbert burst out impulsively, "You are the best Mama and Papa in the whole world!" This was followed by another round of hugs.

"Now, now," Tom finally said as the final heartfelt embrace faded away. "Settle down, and I will let you in on a little secret."

The room hushed, and Antoinette wondered what would happen next.

"You see," Tom said. "Whatever I know about being a good father and husband I learned from my own dear mother and father. They taught me the importance of offering support while also setting fair and firm limits. From them, I learned how to be strong and how to be tender, and when to use each. Even more than that, they showed me by example the importance and the power of unconditional love. Above all, love."

Antoinette would have given all the money in the world to freeze this moment in time forever, to simply bask in the glow of family togetherness. But the spell was broken when a bell tinkled and a butler announced that dinner would be served.

With a scraping of chair legs, flutter of cloth napkins and rattle of cutlery, they seated themselves around the dining tables. The kitchen staff began serving heaping portions of fragrant, flavorful *coq au vin*, accompanied by salad, bread and an excellent Burgundy wine.

Just as the cheese course was being served and Antoinette felt that she would burst from a combination of the delicious, plentiful food and sheer happiness, the concierge approached her husband and whispered into his ear. Tom excused himself, muttering something about an important phone call.

He returned perhaps ten minutes later, a serious look behind the wire-rimmed glasses that he always wore. To Antoinette he said, "It seems I have been called to Paris on urgent business. I must leave tonight."

"Tom, no!" Antoinette cried out. "We just arrived. You've been driving all day. You can't be serious."

"But I am, *ma cherie*. The very future of our pharmacies and lab could be at stake."

"Surely it can wait until morning."

"I'm afraid it cannot," Tom said.

"But what of our family reunion? What of the tour of the castle?"

"Not to worry, I'll be back before you've had time to even miss me." And before Antoinette could raise further objections, he grabbed his coat and was out the door.

CHAPTER FOUR

It was past midnight when Tom finally arrived on the outskirts of Paris. He found an inexpensive hotel at one of the exits of the motorway, checked in and immediately collapsed onto the bed, overcome with sheer physical exhaustion and consumed with worry about the future of his business. The telephone call had been from his bank, insisting that he appear at the Paris headquarters first thing in the morning. What could be so important? Twenty-four hours ago, his business affairs had been in perfect shape. What had happened?

Sleep refused to come. As Tom tossed and turned, a new, more disturbing concern crowded into his mind: what if this had nothing to do with his pharmaceutical business, and everything to do with his family history.

He revealed his true name—Maximal Oto Thomas Rohan—to no one and went by the plain and simple name of Tom. He lived quietly on farms and in small towns as he pursued a career in the pharmaceutical industry and did his best not draw attention to himself or his family.

Then came the invitation extended to his youngest son to tour Castle Rohan. That couldn't have been a coincidence—could it?

So be it, he finally told himself. *If this is my destiny, then I shall do it for the good of the Rohan heritage and for all humankind. The farms and the countryside hid and sheltered me for many years—now I shall plant the seeds of benevolence.*

With that comforting thought, his eyes finally drifted shut and Tom was blessed with the sleep he so desperately needed.

* * *

The next two days were a whirlwind of activity for the Rohan family. For Gilbert, mornings were spent in classroom lessons with the other students throughout France who had been selected for the exclusive tour of the castle. There they learned more about the fascinating history and rich culture of the Alsace region. From Professeur Pelletier, Gilbert discovered how Lothair, Charlemagne's eldest grandson, was designated the heir of the great and legendary leader. However, the other male descendants immediately disputed this, citing the tradition of the Franks that the land be divided among all the male offspring. Thus, Lothair found himself at war with his own father and brothers.

Gilbert raised his hand, "But Professeur, Lothair hardly sounds like a French name to me."

"Very good," Professeur Pelletier replied. "You are correct. That is precisely why Lothair, or Lothar, took an addition name. Do you know what that name was?"

"No sir," Gilbert said, shaking his head.

"Rohan!" Professeur Pelletier said. He was a small man with a ruddy complexion and a ready smile who obviously loved history and loved teaching. "Lothair became Lothair Rohan. And Rohan has been the family name ever since."

Rohan! Gilbert felt his cheeks growing as pink as Professeur Pelletier's. While the boy enjoyed school and had a special fondness for medieval history, he was a bit shy and felt uncomfortable with too much attention heaped upon him. So he pretended to bury himself in his textbook while the Professeur went on to describe how the kingdom of the Franks became divided throughout the decades and centuries, as each king needed to make sure each son inherited at least some land. Gilbert was reminded of the comment Papa had made on the drive to this place, of deaths and in-fighting, corruption and weakness.

"By the time Napoleon arrived in 1800, the Holy Roman Empire was composed of more than 300 kingdoms," Professeur Pelletier said. "Even though their combined armies would have been three times as powerful as Napoleon's, he was able to conquer them because they were so less organized. This allowed Napoleon to impose severe penalties. He took over the fertile land and expelled Prussia and Austria, reduced the 300 kingdoms down to 24 and put his own brother in charge of them."

He continued, "In 1805, Austria joined forces with other European powers to oppose Napoleon, but he was able to defeat both the Austrian and Russian armies at the Battle of Austerlitz. Then in 1806, he formed the Confederation of the Rhine, which included sixteen German states in an alliance with France—in essence, a French vassal state. Napoleon named himself a 'Protector' of the Confederation. All its members agreed to support him if war broke out again."

The young teacher raised his arm and jabbed a finger to emphasize his final point. "And that is how Napoleon was finally able to announce that the Holy Roman Empire of the German nation no longer existed!"

The formal classroom activities concluded at the noon hour. In the afternoons, the students and their families enjoyed the many recreational and cultural activities in the region: hiking in the dense pine forests of the Vosges mountain range, shopping at the many farmers markets and crafts fairs in the area, and touring the lush and colorful gardens at nearby estates.

For Antoinette, the most precious aspect of these two days were not the activities, as entertaining and enriching as they might be, but simply having her entire family together in one place. Her heart warmed as she watched the numerous cousins get to know each other better, and beamed with pride as Gilbert took charge as an elder to the generation of grandchildren. He patiently organized games, took them on walks in the woods, and in the evening, regaled them with tales of long ago, of brave knights, fierce battles and beautiful princesses.

If only Tom were here! The presence of her husband would have made Antoinette's happiness complete, a full circle of family unity and love.

Why had he left so abruptly? Is our business really in trouble? And where is he now?

*   *   *

While the Rohan family—minus the patriarch—enjoyed their time together, some 100 of the world's most powerful men and women gathered in an exclusive hotel in Strasbourg, the ancient city next to the border with Germany, only 55 kilometers from Castle Rohan. These were leaders of secret millionaire's societies, financial syndicates, royal families, Vatican officials, all coming together for one purpose: to keep a watchful eye on the future of the Rohan family line.

For this would represent more than simply the fate of a few family fortunes or royal treasuries—much, much more. Trillions were at stake, trillions of Euros, dollars, yen, riyals and rupees. The Rohan land holdings truly were that vast and valuable: prime real estate in southwest Germany, in and around Milan, Italy, and the entire Alsace region of France. Currently, much of these lands were being managed in a trust by the Vatican. Complications of mega proportions would result if the Rohan bloodline were truly extinguished. Every single one of hundreds of centuries-old deeds of trust would need to be reviewed by the courts to determine the rightful owners. The legal labyrinth could take years to untangle and the outcomes uncertain, landmines that could explode the financial industries and markets.

And so these powerful 100 waited. Paced, argued, fretted and waited. Voices rose and fell in dozens of languages. More than one delegate could be seen discreetly sending text messages to a broker with orders to sell or buy, or to an attorney to change the terms of a will or trust.

Gabriel Monet mingled in their midst, a Bluetooth device connected to a cell phone clamped in one ear. "What?" he demanded, his voice rising above all the rest. "The mission has been aborted?" A string of loud curse words followed.

"Really," muttered the president of the Bank of England. "Who allowed such an uncouth lout to set foot in here?"

"There is nothing to be done about it," answered a man wearing the flowing robe and keffiyeh headdress of an Arab sheik. "Gabriel Monet is a violent thug who has seized control of Strasbourg and most of the Rohan lands in eastern France. He owns this very hotel we find ourselves in."

"But how could one gangster amass such power and control such wealth?" the banker asked.

"Gambling," came the reply. "He and his gang started out by organizing the gambling, both the legal casinos and the underground dens. Once he had the gaming industry under this thumb, the rest was easy."

Before the Bank of England president could make another comment about ejecting the "uncouth lout" from the elegant old hotel, Gabriel Monet solved the problem by slipping into a small conference room next to the grand hall where the delegates had gathered. Inside, he found the three men whom he had invited: a billionaire from one of the Caribbean island nations that specialized in tax shelters, a short, squat, balding man from an oil-rich nation from the former Soviet bloc, and an Asian wearing a gray Mao-style jacket and trousers.

"This could be our golden opportunity," the Caribbean islander said. He was dressed in a conservative business suit, but his sun-streaked hair and deep tan gave away a lifestyle of beaches and golf courses.

"Da," replied the man from the "Stan" country. "With that imposter out of the way, we can consolidate our holdings, become the most powerful financial group in the world."

"I assume the mission succeeded?" the Asian man asked Gabriel.

All three men—among the wealthiest in the world, who wielded tremendous power behind the scenes—turned and look at Gabriel Monet for an answer.

"There has been... shall we say... ah... a slight delay," Gabriel mumbled.

Six pairs of eyes glared at him with menace.

"Nothing that can't be taken care of easily," Gabriel said, returning to his usual demeanor of ruthless control. "It will all be handled in due time, trust me."

Meanwhile, the details of the phone call Gabriel had received were beginning to ripple through the ornate meeting room, the astounding news of an assassination attempt on the streets of Paris, and the mysterious rescue. For some, this was a positive development. For others, the worst possible outcome.

But one fact all could agree on: the fate of the Kingdom of Rohan, for better or for ill, would have earth-shattering impacts on the world's financial markets, from Hong Kong to New York, Tokyo to London, Dubai to Buenos Aires. No nation or principality, no matter how small or far-flung, would escape.

CHAPTER FIVE

At last the moment came that Gilbert had anticipated for so long—the students and their families were leaving their hotel rooms in the village outside the castle gates and actually moving into the immense fortress itself! At the end of the second day's lessons and activities, everyone—students, teachers, chaperones, and the entire Rohan family—climbed into comfortable motor coaches for the short but challenging drive, while porters stowed their luggage into the baggage compartments. Gilbert and his new friends chattered in excitement as the conveyances slowly made their way through the woods and up the steep, narrow road, coming to almost complete stops at the many hairpin turns.

At last, the busses halted. The drivers assisted the passengers in disembarking and Gilbert finally had his first close-up look at Castle Rohan. He had to crane his neck to see the tops of the battlements and he gazed in amazement as an eagle circled the pointed peak of the uppermost turret. A clanking sound drew his attention to the foreground. Could it be? An actual drawbridge was slowly lowering, immense iron chains easing the thick wooden planks of the bridge until it landed with a loud bang on the opposite side, spanning the moat. Gilbert felt as if he had just stepped into a movie about the knights of the Middle Ages.

A bearded man wearing a belted tunic, breeches and knee-high boots stepped from the arched entryway to the castle and strode boldly across the drawbridge. Even though Gilbert knew the fellow must be only a costumed actor, he still felt a thrill of excitement. "Welcome!" the man said in a booming voice. "Welcome to Castle Rohan!"

With that invitation, the assembled students, teachers and family—all 180 of them—made their way across the drawbridge and took their first steps into Castle Rohan. There they found more staff members, all wearing historically accurate medieval attire, at the ready to assist them with their luggage and to get them settled in their assigned rooms. As Gilbert made his way along the winding corridors, he stared in fascination at the ancient stonework, the many carvings of beasts both real and mythical, and beautiful stained glass windows. And this was only the outer wing of the castle! He could only imagine the wonders and marvels that would await them during their tour of the innermost rooms the following day.

Once settled in their rooms, the visitors gathered in a vast dining hall for a sumptuous dinner. As they were finishing, a man wearing a business suit rose from the head table, clapped his hands to bring the assembly to order, and introduced himself as Victor Monet, the chief superintendent of Castle Rohan.

Gilbert had never seen this man before, but he somehow seemed familiar. He appeared middle aged, anywhere between thirty-five and fifty-five, with a shiny bald head and deep-set eyes. For some reason, Gilbert was reminded of his father, even though this Monsieur Monet did not resemble Papa in the least.

"Tomorrow you will be privileged to have a unique and unusual experience, total immersion in daily life in a medieval castle," Monsieur Monet announced to the assembled students, chaperones and teachers. "You will enter the innermost sacred places of the duke's living quarters. You will see how this grand edifice was built and defended through the centuries and learn about the art behind the design of its coat of arms, and much more. You will experience life as it must have been for the lord of the castle over one thousand years ago and through the centuries. Prepare yourselves for a once-in-a-lifetime experience that you will never forget."

He paused to let this sink in, and finished with, "Therefore, I would advise all of you to retire early so that you will be rested and fresh for the activities of tomorrow."

Gilbert promised himself he would do exactly as he was told. After spending an hour or so after dinner entertaining his cousins with card games and reading aloud from tales of the King Arthur and the Knights of the Round Table, he dutifully retired to the small sleeping chamber to which he'd been assigned, climbed into the bed, and pulled the soft down comforter up to his chin. But sleep would not come. Gilbert was simply too excited, too overwhelmed with what he'd already seen and experienced and what he anticipated when dawn arrived.

He climbed out of bed and donned his robe and slippers. Just a bit of exploring, he told himself. Just walk down a few corridors in this outer wing, maybe find a balcony where he could peer out at the stars and at the lights of the villages of the Alsace. He crept down the dark, silent corridor, feeling more than seeing the immense size and power of the castle. It was as if these ancient stone walls were actually whispering to him. Was it an invitation—or a warning?

Gilbert rounded a corner and saw soft light spilling from an open door. Taking one step through the doorway, he found himself inside a small chapel with an altar, two burning candles on tall wrought iron pillar holders, and a stained glass window.

As his eyes adjusted to the light, Gilbert realized he was not alone in this sacred chamber. A female figure knelt at the altar, her hands clasped in prayer. Gilbert quietly moved closer and realized the woman was his dear mother, and that tears were rolling down her cheeks.

"Mama?" Gilbert whispered, doing his best not to startle her.

She turned and a smile quivered on her lips when she recognized her youngest child. She rose to fold him into an embrace. "You're supposed to be in bed, aren't you?" she chided him gently.

"Couldn't sleep."

"Neither could I," she admitted.

"But Mama," Gilbert said. "Is something the matter? You're…"

"I know." She dabbed at her eyes with a tissue. Then in a rush of emotion she said, "I'm just so worried about your father. I've heard nothing from him since he was called away two nights ago. That's just not like him. For one thing, he would have called to let me know that he'd arrived safely in Paris and that everything is in good order with our business and the bank. So I came in here to pray for him."

"I'm so sorry, Mama."

"He worked so hard to bring the family together," she said with a small sob. "This reunion meant everything to him. It would break my heart if he were not here tomorrow for our tour of the castle. I just can't help but think that something terrible has happened to him."

"I wish there was something I could do," Gilbert said.

"You already have," she said, taking both his hands in hers, "just by being my dear sweet son. Stay here with me for a while, and we'll both pray for the safe return of your father."

*   *   *

At 7:30 the following morning, Antony Rohan peered in a mirror and inspected himself in the full dress uniform of a general in the French Armée de Terre. Like Antoinette and Gilbert, the eldest son of Tom Rohan had found it difficult to surrender to slumber the previous evening. Something was up—his finely honed military instincts had him on high alert. His little brother just "happened" to be chosen for this special luxury tour of Château du Rohan. His father just "happened" to find the money to treat the entire family to this lavish vacation. Then his father just "happened" to be called away to an important business meeting in Paris… and hadn't been heard from since.

Antony did not believe in coincidences. Things didn't just "happen." His distinguished career in the military had made him well versed in the history and tactics of warfare. He'd been thoroughly trained in anti-terrorism techniques, both in ferreting them out before they had the chance to strike, and stopping them once they were in position to do great damage on French soil.

Something was about to happen. The question was—what?

Antony took one last look at himself in the full-length mirror, from the traditional *kepis*—the pillbox-style hat with gold braid and a small visor—to the beige jacket with the gold epaulettes and chest full of ribbons above his heart, down to the black boots gleaming with polish. Satisfied that he would pass the most rigorous of inspections, he hurried to the hall where the visitors had been served dinner the night before.

No matter what danger presented itself on this day, he told himself he would protect the family, or die trying. Because family always came first.

*   *   *

After a traditional light French breakfast consisting of croissants, *tartines*, butter, assorted jams and jellies, fresh fruit and *café au lait*, the students, their families and their schoolmasters were divided into smaller groups for their docent-led tour. Anticipation buzzed through the air—at last, they were going to see the inner sanctuary of the duke! Antony, however, swallowed any excitement he may have felt and kept himself at the ready, alert for the slightest hint of trouble. The Rohan family was so large, they made up one entire tour group. Their docent, like the others, was dressed in a long medieval gown with a girdle made of links of lightweight metal that encircled her waist just above the hips, and a *hennin*, the traditional conical hat with a filmy silk scarf that drifted from the pointed top.

She led them down a long hallway and through a wide, arched doorway. "We are now entering the innermost and oldest section of the castle," she informed them. "You could say that this is the very living heart of Château du Rohan. Because of the private nature of the rooms and items you are about to see, and the extreme age and rarity of many of them, we do request that you refrain from using flash photography. Some of the rooms, the most personal and private, will be roped off. You may look inside, but please do not enter. And of course, do not touch any artifacts or artworks."

As the tour proceeded, Antony noted the extreme opulence of many of the chambers, the rare books with their gilded covers and the ancient parchment manuscripts in the library, the heavy, intricately carved furniture in the bedroom, the magnificent tapestries in the drawing room. In his military career, he had visited many fortresses and government palaces throughout the world, but this was clearly the most impressive. Still, he did not allow himself to be distracted by this priceless luxury and kept a steady watch on the rest of his family, ready to spring into action at a moment's notice.

The tour groups were spaced so closely together that he could easily hear footsteps and conversation from both ahead and behind him, but thus far all he heard was the informative material being recited by the docents and the questions posed by the students. He did make note of the guards holding their posts at regular intervals throughout the tour. Like the docents, they were attired in medieval costumes—belted tunic, knee-high boots, cowl and hood—and appeared to be armed only with a stage prop spear. Antony was willing to lay odds, though, that these men were not merely actors, and that underneath their costumes they were outfitted with utility belts featuring the latest gear of a modern security guard: two-way radio, truncheon, handcuffs and Taser.

The group reached the next stop on the tour, the castle armory. In this large, vaulted hall were arrayed weapons and military gear from every epoch since the castle's existence, from the crossbows and spears of the Middle Ages through the early muskets of the Renaissance era, 19th century cannons, and even a machine gun from World War I. A dozens suits of armor and chain mail lined one wall. From the eager and animated chatter from the students, especially the boys, Antony judged that he was not the only visitor who found the armory to be fascinating.

The docent led the visitors onward and stopped at a doorway where a red velvet rope prevented entry. Guards stood at both sides, their spears held vertically. "This," she said, "is the duke's private dining room. When he did not have vast numbers of guests to entertain and impress, this is where he, his family and his closest advisors and friends took their meals."

"Mama, look!"

Antony tensed at Gilbert's boyish exclamation and pointed finger. Even though the young man did not sound afraid, Antony began to elbow his way to the doorway. Other family members were now craning their necks and standing on tiptoe to peer into the dining room, and each was echoing Gilbert in their cries of astonishment.

When Antony finally reached the doorway, he, too, let out a shocked, "Oh, my God!"

Before the awe-struck Rohan family was an exact replica of the dining room that the patriarch had built back home in the Dijon countryside: the trestle table and heavy wooden chairs, the fireplace in one corner, the simple china cabinet. And of course, the dragon, the carved, wooden sculpture hanging from the coffered ceiling. Just like at home, the mythical beast glowered over the dining table, almost three meters long, painted brown and with small wings, mad eyes and protruding tongue. Antony glanced over at his mother and saw the same look of wonder and confusion on her face that he was feeling inside. *All seven of us siblings had our meals in this exact same room in our modest family home. Did we have the blessing of Emperor Lothair Rohan and all the descendants of the Carolingian kings?*

Before he could even fully finish the thought, another commotion broke out at the doorway, more urgent and confusing than even the discovery of the dragon in the dining room. Tom Rohan was back! He appeared seemingly by magic, though Antony knew this could not be, concluding that his father had arrived too late to join the start of the tour, and had been whisked to this position at the entrance to the dining room through one of the secret passages that Antony felt sure must exist throughout the castle.

Tom put his hand out to remove the red velvet rope that prevented entry into the private eating chamber. One of the guards laid his own hand atop the barrier. Antony assumed this was to prevent Tom from entering. Instead, to his astonishment, the guard said, "Allow me, sir," clicked the hook that held the rope in place and allowed Tom to enter. Both Antony and Antoinette attempted to follow, but the guard immediately snapped the velvet rope back into place and shook his head.

"But he can't go in there! This is not permitted!" This protest came from Professeur Pelletier and was quickly joined by similar sentiments raised by the other schoolmasters. The two guards did not say anything, but each raised a palm to indicate both "stop" and "silence."

By now, the other tour groups had been drawn to the entrance to the dining room by the chaos. Out of the corners of his eyes, Antony spotted two other newcomers: swarthy men dressed all in black, one as large as an American football player, the other of average build but appearing diminutive next to his outsized companion. Antony had no idea who they might be, but they did remind him of the old saying about not wanting to run into either of them in a dark alley.

Tom Rohan was dressed conservatively in a dark suit, crisp white shirt and tie, just as he usually attired himself for business meetings. Yet to Antony, there was something different about his father. He stood tall and proud, exuding confidence and charisma. Antony groped for the right word to describe the new Tom Rohan. Regal. That was it—this simple, unknown pharmacist appeared downright regal.

Tom locked eyes one-by-one with each of his seven children and with Antoinette. When it was his turn to withstand that steely, blue-eyed gaze, Antony felt as if he were receiving an important message: *Trust me. Everything is going to work out as it should.*

The crowd of students, family, teachers, docents and guards packed themselves tightly at the doorway and whispered among themselves as they watched Tom stride with purpose and determination to the head of the table, bow slightly, and seat himself. He then dipped his head, shut his eyes and clasped his hands in prayer. The throng grew silent out of respect for this sacred moment.

After several minutes of contemplation, Tom sent a signal with his hand to the guards. One of the men in the medieval costume clicked open the hook, lifted the red velvet rope, and gave Antony a slight tap on the shoulder, indicating that he should enter. *Me?* Antony was so shocked he found it difficult to put one foot in front of the other. *Shouldn't it be Mama who is invited into this room with Papa?*

As if anticipating this objection, Tom turned to his family and smiled. "We will all be together soon. But first, I require a moment of private consultation with my eldest son." He hugged Antony and indicated that he should take the seat to his right at the table.

"Do you have any idea who General Miliot might be?" Tom leaned forward and asked in a low voice.

Of all the things that his father might have said to him, this was a question Antony never could have anticipated. "General Miliot?" he said, his nerves tensing just at the mention of the name. "Of course, I know who he is. He is the highest commander in the army, my boss's boss. What's this all about?"

"General Miliot will be calling my cell phone, but he will want to talk to you," Tom said. "This is very urgent. Our entire family is in danger."

"Danger?" Antony was about to utter another demand for details when Tom's cell phone chose that moment to beep, signaling an incoming call. Tom answered, identified himself, then turned the device over to Antony. "You keep it," he said to Antony, gesturing toward the small, glowing rectangle of electronic wizardry.

Antony kept the phone clasped tightly to his ear. In his tense state of hyper-vigilance, he concentrated both on the words being spoken by General Miliot and on scanning his surroundings for the danger his father had warned him about. But he saw nothing from the assembled students, teachers, family members and castle staff that raised an alarm.

"Listen quickly and pay attention," General Miliot was saying from the other end of the cell phone connection. "Time is of the essence. You can trust the Carolingian Sacred Heart and the Lombardi syndicate. They have both been dedicated to the protection of the Rohan dynasty for centuries. Do you understand?"

"The Carolingian Sacred Heart and the Lombardi family. Trust them. Yes, sir," Antony responded.

"One of the top managers of the Rohan corporation is a core member of the Carolingians."

"Who, sir?"

"That is for him to reveal when the time is right. Understand?"

"Yes, sir," Antony said.

General Miliot ended the call. Antony watched his father make eye contact with those two dangerous-looking men dressed all in black. They were clearly exchanging signals. A few moments ago, Antony's sense of caution would have been on high alert. Now, with the reassuring message he'd received from General Miliot, he relaxed slightly. No matter how menacing and unsavory these Lombardi thugs may first appear, he would put his family's safety in their hands.

Chapter Six

Antoinette's head swam with a dozens of questions she wished she could pose to her husband. Chief among them: *Where were you for two days? Why didn't you call? Are you well? Is our business still in good shape? Our retail pharmacies and the lab?* And even, *How could you? I was worried sick!*

But she was too well-bred to make a scene in front of her children and grandchildren, let alone dozens of strangers. So she swallowed her words and comforted herself by recalling the moment when Tom stood in the dining room, gazed into her eyes, and sent a message of trust and safety. And love. Above all, love.

Still absorbed with her own thoughts and emotions, Antoinette followed mechanically as the docent ushered the group on the next stop on the tour, the portrait gallery. This long, wide hallway connected the family dining room with the main hall. The docent explained, "What you see before you are portraits of the descendants of the Emperor Lothair Rohan from the Middle Ages to modern times. These are priceless works of art, many of them created by legendary masters, and coveted by museums throughout the world."

The docent stopped in front of the most recent of the paintings. She gestured toward a serious-looking man with black curls. "That is the current Duke Michael, who died just this past year at the age of forty. He left no children, so his passing marks the end of the Rohan line." She strolled to the portrait to the left. "This is his father, Gomel, and this," she took another two steps and paused under the painting of another distinguished gentleman with a serious expression, "is his grandfather, Pierre."

She made another few steps, the tour group following like a line of ducklings behind their mother, and stopped in front of an oil painting of a young man with a pale face, thick brown hair, and the similar severe expression of the other men in the portraits. Unlike the others, though, he was not attired in formal dress but in a simple, open-collared shirt and appeared not much older than a boy.

"This is Pierre's elder brother, Maximal Rohan," the docent said. "He is the fifty-fourth direct descendant of King Rohan. You may be wondering why he has the Italian name of Maximal. That is because he inherited a great number of lands in Italy. His full name is Maximal Oto Thomas Rohan—Italian, German and French—as the family crown holds land in all three countries. If he could be found, he would be as important as the Pope in Europe."

The docent paused to let this last fact sink in. Many of the students began raising their hands and blurting out questions. "*If* he could be found? What do you mean by that?"

The docent smiled as if she anticipated this response to the intriguing fact she had revealed. "The fifty-fourth descendant was a genius in the fields of chemistry and biology. He earned a doctorate in pharmaceutics at age 27. He lived very modestly among farmers, none of whom knew he was the son of a duke. Two years after earning his PhD, he joined the faculty of a great university and became a full professor when he was only 35. Then, one year later, he embarked on a journey to various foreign nations—and was never seen again."

This brought more raised hands and questions from the students and many whispers of wonder from the teachers and chaperones.

"That was 65 years ago," the docent continued. "If Duke Maximal Rohan could be found and were miraculously still alive, he would be 101 years old."

While all 180 visitors found this story intriguing and fascinating, Antoinette felt as if she might faint. She looked around at her children and saw the same shock on their faces. *It can't be—it just cannot. These things are not possible!*

For the face of the 54th descendant of the Emperor Lothair Rohan that stared down at them from the wall was a younger version of the man they knew as a husband and father. Tom Rohan—a man who appeared to be no older than his mid-60s.

Antoinette barely had time to process this latest revelation as the docents were herding the tour groups into the duke's Great Hall. "This truly is the heart of Chateau du Rohan," the docent in charge of Antoinette's group said as she led them out of the portrait gallery and through the portal to the Great Hall.

Despite the many surprises she'd already encountered on this trip, Antoinette was once again overcome with wonder and awe. She found herself in a vast space as beautifully designed and appointed as any of the famed cathedrals of her country: Notre Dame, Chartres, Saint Etienne. The portal featured the traditional *tympanum*, a semi-circular decoration with carved figures of medieval knights on foot and on horseback. Enormous stained glass windows filled the hall with a rainbow of light. The chairs and other furnishings were of dark wood polished to a high sheen, while massive blocks of red sandstone formed columns and arches. The curved ceiling soared far overhead, while underfoot a soft carpet partially covered a floor of marble. At the altar she saw two massive chairs as intricately carved as thrones. In back of them stood the traditional reredos, a screen that appeared to have been fashioned of solid gold and encrusted with the most precious of jewels. Everywhere she looked, her eyes soaked in beauty, reverence and refinement.

Just as the docent was explaining how the Great Hall had been so cleverly designed acoustically that a whisper at one end could be clearly heard at the other, Antoinette became aware of other persons entering the hall joining the students, chaperones, teachers and castle staff. At least a dozen men, all impeccably dressed in dark suits and each wearing a discreet communication device in his ear, positioned themselves strategically throughout the Great Hall, with special emphasis on the entrances and exits. She'd seen men like this on the TV news, guarding the premier and other political dignitaries, foreign and domestic: the DGSI, *direction générale de la sécurité intérieure,* or General Directorate for Internal Security. The French secret service.

But what were they doing here?

Antoinette had no time to pursue an answer to that question, for a commotion broke out at the portal. Craning her neck to see above the crowd, she saw her husband and eldest son entering the hall. With the excellent acoustics of the Great Hall, she could clearly hear several of the schoolmasters urging Tom and Antony not to enter. She also sensed increased tension and agitation among the secret service agents.

Her eyes followed as Tom ignored the objections and strode down the center aisle, back straight and head held high, exuding grace, elegance and dignity. He paused when he reached Antoinette and, with a gentle smile, held out his arm.

She hesitated and glanced around as if looking for permission or direction. Tom hooked his arm around hers and with a whispered, "Trust me, *ma cherie*," coaxed her from her spot on the sidelines and to the center aisle. Antoinette had never felt so nervous in her life—at least 200 pairs of eyes must be watching her at this point—but drew strength from the nearness of her husband and let him lead her toward the altar.

When he reached the spot in front of the two thrones and the golden, bejeweled screen, he stopped and began to unbutton his suit jacket. Antoinette felt her jaw drop in astonishment. *What was he doing now?* With a gesture as gallant as that of any medieval courtier flinging down his cloak to protect the dainty feet of milady, Tom lay the jacket on the cold marble floor and began to lower himself. Now Antoinette understood. He was about to kneel in prayer and expected her to follow along.

Before Tom could complete the movement, two of the men from the secret service rushed forward, each carrying large rectangular pads covered in red velvet and edged with gold cord and tassels. The pads were placed on the floor in front of Tom and Antoinette. With nods of thanks for this kind and thoughtful gesture, the pair lowered themselves at the foot of the altar.

Excitement and confusion continued to buzz through the Great Hall, as the Rohan offspring, the other students, and their teachers and chaperones traded theories as to what might be going on. Was this a normal part of the tour? Special entertainment just for them?

Who were these two people who were so bold to kneel at the altar? Just more actors? Or... was something momentous in the works, a development that would change the course of history?

Antoinette's thoughts had drifted far away from the confusion in the Great Hall. The last time she had knelt next to Tom in a sacred place was on their wedding day. She'd been just nineteen, shy and serious, and still was having difficulty believing this distinguished university professor and scientist would take an interest in a lowly student such as herself. But not only did he take an interest, he actually asked for her hand in marriage. That was four decades ago, and she'd thought she knew everything there was to know about her husband. Now she realized how wrong she'd been—he was obviously still full of surprises.

Another thought came to her, almost as if it were being whispered in her ear by one of the angels whose images were carved into the altar screen. *He has stayed by your side for seven children, and has always provided for you. He created a successful retail pharmaceutical business and lab. No matter what might happen, you can trust him. He will always take care of you.*

With that, Antoinette realized that the vows she had exchanged with Tom Rohan the last time they had knelt together at an altar were stronger than ever.

While Antoinette's thoughts were otherwise occupied, Tom bowed his head and clasped his hands in silent prayer, seemingly oblivious to the excitement that threatened to boil over in the Great Hall. The secret service agents hovered nearby, while the costumed guards and docents positioned themselves around the sides of the altar. At last, Tom made a barely audible "amen" and stirred slightly. One of the secret service agents asked if he would like to sit in the King's chair.

Tom said nothing, just rose and walked past both thrones and made a bow. Then he moved to a bench that faced the altar and sat down. He motioned to the empty spot on his right, inviting Antoinette to seat herself next to him. Antoinette obeyed, still uncertain and overwhelmed. *This cannot be happening to me—can it?* She felt as if she were an actress on a stage following a script, no longer a simple wife and mother. The only problem was, she had no idea how the play was going to end.

While Antoinette was arranging herself on the seat next to Tom, he leaned toward a wooden chest that sat against the wall. The symbols carved on the lid and sides were clearly ancient, yet the wood still gleamed brightly as if it had been carved only yesterday. Tom lifted the lid and pulled out a purple velvet robe trimmed in luxurious white ermine. Slowly he placed the cloak around his shoulders and fastened the gold cord loosely around his neck.

He stood so all could see him in his royal finery, then spoke. "Dear Brigitte, where is my belt and knife?"

By now, all chatter in the vast chamber had halted. All 180 visitors, plus the staff and secret service agents, waited, frozen with anticipation, as if collectively asking themselves the same questions. *What belt and knife? And who is Brigitte?*

An older woman emerged from the throng. With her gray hair in a perfect pageboy and dressed in a black designer dress and pearls, she personified the chic and elegance that only French woman possess. "Duke Maximal!" she exclaimed in a voice choked with tears.

A ripple of astonishment flowed through the bodies packed tightly in the Great Hall, Antoinette feeling it the most keenly. Something momentous was obviously unfolding in front of their eyes—but what?

"My Lord," the woman continued, still weeping. "King Maximal Oto Thomas Rohan!

Antoinette shivered from the top of her head to the tips of her toes. *Thomas Rohan—her husband! Who was this strange woman, and what was she talking about?*

"Could that really be you?" the woman exclaimed as she hurried down the aisle and stood before Tom. From a Louis Vuitton satchel she withdrew two objects: a thick leather belt carved with the same symbols as those adorning the chest, and a silver knife with a handle encrusted with jewels.

Tom uttered thanks, put the belt around his waist so that it cinched the robe, and slipped the knife between the belt and the cloak. Then he embraced the woman. "Brigitte, it is so good to see you again," he said.

The elderly woman could only nod helplessly as she continued to dab at her eyes.

"The last time I saw you, you were just a girl," Tom said. "Sixteen years old, as I recall. That was 65 years ago."

He turned to Antoinette and lowered his voice. "I know this must be confusing and overwhelming. But try to understand. My birth name is Maximal Oto Thomas Rohan."

Antoinette shook her head as tears spilled past her lashes and slid down her cheeks. "I just don't know what to say," she said in a trembling voice.

"I understand *ma cherie*," Tom said. "But here's a little riddle that may help you understand. Maximal Oto Thomas. Take the first letters of each name and put them in reverse order..."

"T-O-M," Antoinette said slowly.

"Exactly," Tom said, placing a kiss on her forehead.

The couple had been speaking in whispers, yet with the excellent sound quality in the Great Hall, everyone could easily hear every word. The visitors edged closer, not wishing to miss a moment of the drama. Brigitte, meanwhile, had burst into a second round of tears and sobs.

The seven Rohan offspring crowded as close as they could to their parents and exchanged words of their own. "Now we know why Papa was so insistent on all of us coming along on this trip." "This is a family reunion we won't ever forget, that's for certain." "I always wondered why we have a dragon in our dining room back home. Now we know—Papa was copying the same room in home of his ancestors."

Ten uniformed police officers now strode into the hall and positioned themselves around Tom and Antoinette, guarding them as if they were the highest ranking King and Queen of all of Europe.

Tom spoke to Brigitte. "Look in the chest, and find the cloak for Madame Rohan."

The elderly woman did so, presenting another red velvet robe trimmed in ermine. Tom took it from her outstretched hands and placed it tenderly around Antoinette's shoulders, taking great care to tie a perfect bow with the gold cord. Then he requested to Victor Monet, in his role as chief superintendent, that the castle staff prepare the Great Hall for the opening prayer.

Victor Monet directed the staff members did as requested, hustling to bring in 180 chairs and place them in rows so that each and every student, teacher and chaperone could comfortably observe the proceedings. Tom kept himself busy bringing his seven children and their families to the front, making sure everyone was seated together.

Antoinette did her best to make herself comfortable while wrapped in the heavy cloak when she became aware of another burst of commotion from the back of the hall. After all of the surprises of the morning, she thought nothing could upset her now. Then she realized the source of the arguing and jostling. At least twenty members of the news media, both print and broadcast, were attempting to invade the sacred space. Antoinette felt her heart drop. *My husband—my children—have done nothing to deserve all this unwanted attention!*

A moment ago, she had thought Castle Rohan had presented her with all of the possible surprises at its disposal. Now she realized with a sense of growing dread and dismay, this was only the beginning of the shocking events about to unfold.

CHAPTER SEVEN

Tom Rohan was surrounded by some 200 souls, including his beloved wife and children, yet he had never felt so alone in his entire life. The arrival of the news media pack finally threatened to break the calm, quiet resolve he had exhibited all morning. He could hear the reporters and photographers arguing with the security guards, demanding to be let in and given access. Others were more brazen, simply elbowing their way into the Great Hall and snapping away with their cameras.

A flock of vultures, he thought, circling to swoop in for the kill, picking over the Rohan family until there's nothing left but bone. *Just like they did to poor Princess Diana.* The thought of his and Antoinette's images splashed across the front page of one of those lurid supermarket check-stand tabloids made his stomach churn.

That unsettling thought unleashed a flood of memories and emotions from the past three days. First, the phone call summoning him to Paris for an alleged emergency with his business and the bank. Five hours of driving at night after an already exhausting day, and then hurrying to make his appointment at the bank as soon as it opened the following morning. Instead there came the near-miss of the assassination attempt. Tom was still connecting the dots, putting things together, but he knew one thing for sure—they wouldn't stop at one botched attempt. They'd stalk him until they succeeded.

That had been followed by the rescue—or was it a kidnapping?—by those thugs calling themselves the Lombardi family. They had referred to Tom as King Rohan, claimed they'd been watching over and protecting his family for generations, and treated him with kindness and respect. But could he trust them? Or had he innocently walked into an elaborate trap that was about to be sprung? Tom noted with unease that even now, two of the Lombardi were roaming around the Great Hall with the rest of the throng.

Tom paced in front of the altar, trying to block out the dozens upon dozens of voices echoing throughout the Great Hall and to calm his jittery nerves. The Lombardi had told him their mission was to protect the dynasty of Emperor Lothair Rohan and that their members' identities must be kept anonymous. They claimed to be part of another ancient organization, even larger and more powerful and more secretive. Its identity must never be disclosed upon pain of death.

Like something out of Hollywood, Tom thought. Secret societies, blood oaths—things like this do not exist in 21st century Europe, do they?

Even more disturbing, the Lombardis had informed Tom he was being targeted by a crime syndicate led by one Gabriel Monet—and that his twin brother, Victor Monet, was not only a director of the Rohan holdings, but was actually the chief superintendent of this very castle. Now, how was he supposed to deal with that? Two men who looked exactly the same, and one of them was determined to see him dead.

Tom rested against the stone wall, his mind and heart filled with despair. It was one thing for him to narrowly escape being killed on the streets of Paris. But now he'd brought his wife and his children and their families to this place. How could he have been so careless? Just one man with a high-powered assault rifle—or a cleverly placed bomb—could wipe out everyone crowded in this space within minutes. Would any criminal gang, no matter how ruthless, really mow down all those children, all those innocent bystanders? Tom knew the answer to that all too well.

Panic rose as he looked around, desperately searching for an escape route. Maybe he could gather up Antoinette, and their seven children, and their offspring, and somehow spirit them out via the way they came in before anyone noticed they were missing. A mad dash through the portrait gallery, the private apartments and the outer wings, and across the drawbridge. Freedom! But then what? They couldn't run forever.

He felt the walls of Castle Rohan supporting his back and shoulders and took a degree of comfort from the solid strength of the rough stonework. A moment ago, he'd felt as if there was no one he could trust outside of his immediate family. Now he realized that those that he loved the most were better off staying here, that they could rely on the ancient fortress for protection.

Still, there remained the daunting task of fully informing his family as to what was going on. Guilt washed over Tom as he thought of his dear Antoinette, so sensitive and shy. One more shock and she would surely drop to the floor in a dead faint. As to his children, and their families—hadn't they already had enough surprises for one day?

Far beyond his royal background, Tom was first and foremost a scientist and a researcher. Now he drew on that background by reminding himself of the cornerstone of the scientific method. Reliable information. Unimpeachable data. Observable results. With a new sense of resolve, he stood tall and squared his shoulders. If information is the key, then information he shall find!

He spotted the two Lombardi men first, the bear-like giant and his smaller companion. With eye contact and a nod, Tom made his instructions clear: find Antony and bring him to the altar.

Then he turned to Antoinette and placed his hands gently on her shoulders. "The other night, when I was called away to Paris, it turned out there was no business emergency."

"I rather thought as much," Antoinette said with a small smile.

"You probably aren't going to believe this," he began.

"Oh, but I will. Nothing would surprise me at this point."

"Some of what I'm about to tell you, I didn't find out until later," Tom continued.

"I already told you, I believe you," Antoinette said with tender mocking.

And with that moment of friendly, familiar give-and-take between husband and wife, Tom told his tale…

While he was tossing and turning in his hotel room by the motorway outside of Paris, other men in and around the City of Light were finding it difficult to sleep that night. Telephones rang and cell phones pinged with text messages. One-by-one, members of the notorious Lombardi crime syndicate received the same coded message: "Protection." Without having to be told, each set his alarm to awaken before dawn, laid out an all-black wardrobe, and double-checked his weapon to make sure it was loaded and at the ready.

Gabriel Monet was likewise busy on the telephone. He dialed the number of the kingpin of the Lombardi gang whom he knew would carry out orders without question. "The target will be arriving at Crédit du Nord on Rue du Louvre first thing in the morning," he said. "You know your assignment, don't you, Carlo?"

"Yes, sir," Carlo Alfonsi replied. "Remove the target. Permanently."

At 8:45 a.m. the following morning Tom was on his way to the bank on Rue du Louvre, ready to deal with the supposed emergency involving his retail drug stores and pharmaceutical lab. Alfonsi had also arrived as assigned, his handgun with its silencer stuffed into the waistband of his pants, ready to be drawn the moment he spotted Tom walking up to the doors of the bank.

A large, bear-like man approached him. Alfonsi recognized Roberto "Big Bobby," Lombardi, a fellow member of the Lombardi syndicate.

"Change of plans," Big Bobby said. "The target will be arriving by Metro."

"I only take orders from Gabriel Monet," Alfonsi said.

"You do want to complete your assignment, don't you?" Big Bobby said.

"What do you think?"

"Well, then, you'll take my word for it. The target decided not to drive into Paris this morning. Too much traffic." Esposito waved his arm to indicate the narrow streets choked with commuters. "Monet ordered us to stake out his hotel. We followed the target from there, watched him drive to the nearest Metro station, park and get out. His train should be arriving any minute now. You wouldn't want to miss him, would you?"

Alfonso grunted an affirmative response and began to jog in the direction of the nearest station of the underground rapid transit system.

Meanwhile, Tom parked the Renault as close as he could to Crédit du Nord and cautiously approached the imposing gray bank building at precisely 9:00 a.m., just as the doors were opening for business. He'd been anticipating trouble for so many hours that his nerves were frayed passed the point of logic or reason. When he felt a heavy hand on his shoulder, he wasn't even surprised or shocked, just filled with dread over his inevitable fate.

"This way, sir," a surprisingly gentle voice said. Then with more urgency, "No time to waste. Just do it!"

The next thing he knew, Tom found himself being hustled into the back compartment of a long, black limousine with darkened windows. The beefy man who had stopped him in front of the bank jumped in behind him, and with the roar of a powerful engine, the car sped through the morning traffic of the narrow streets of Paris.

The man sitting next to Tom leaned forward and spoke to the driver. "Alex, I assume we're being followed?"

"You assume correctly. Alfonsi just figured out we gave him the slip and got into his car. He's right behind us."

The big man turned to Tom. "Better fasten your seat belt. We may be running into a bit of turbulence." He chuckled to himself at his attempt at humor.

"Who are you people, and what do you want with me?" Tom demanded. He fumbled with the door handle, thinking that perhaps he could open the limousine and leap out before the car picked up even more speed. But the handle was locked tight, wouldn't budge.

"We intend you no harm," the man seated next to him said. "As to who we are, my associate in the driver's seat is Alex Capelli and I am Roberto Lombardi. My pals call me Big Bobby. We are at your service."

Then he took a deep breath and finished with, "Your majesty."

Tom could only stare in astonishment. No one had ever addressed him with the royal honorific before. "But how... why...? How do you know who I am? You're just gangsters, common thugs... what is going on here?"

Big Bobby flashed a grin, displaying a gold-capped front tooth. "Maybe you've heard of the Kingdom of the Lombards."

"Of course," Tom said as the limousine continued to take the cobblestone streets of central Paris at top speed, blasting through traffic signals. "An early medieval state established by a Germanic people on the Italian peninsula. Charlemagne was known as the King of the Lombards." He couldn't believe he was discussing history from a millennium and longer ago with these tough street criminals.

"Everyone thinks we're just a bunch of uneducated gangsters," Big Bobby said as if reading Tom's thoughts. "But what you don't know is that for centuries, we Lombardi have had a secret alliance with the Carolingian Sacred Heart."

The Carolingian Sacred Heart! Tom had heard rumors of this most legendary of secret societies all his life, but this was the first evidence he'd had that it actually maintained an existence here in the 21st century. Not only existed, but seemed to be thriving.

"Our mission is to protect the Rohan kingdom," Big Bobby said. "And to restore the rightful king." With another chuckle and glimpse of the gold tooth, he added, "That would be you, your majesty."

Tom couldn't help giving a tentative smile in return. During that sleepless interlude in the early hours past midnight, he had told himself he would embrace his destiny and do the best he can to use his power and wealth for just and righteous causes. He never could have dreamed that the first person to acknowledge him as the rightful heir to the Kingdom of Rohan would be a common street thug and that it would take place in a gangster's limousine speeding out of Paris.

"There never was a business emergency that required my presence at the bank this morning, was there?" Tom asked Big Bobby.

"What do you think?" Answering his own question, he continued, "Fortunately for you, we've been watching over you for years. When we saw you head back to Paris after delivering your family to the hotel in the village outside Castle Rohan, we knew something was up."

"That phone call," Tom said. "I suppose it came from Gabriel Monet, or one of his associates."

"I'd put money on it," Big Bobby agreed.

"But why the subterfuge? Why not just assassinate me at the castle?"

"Because it would look too suspicious," Big Bobby said patiently, as if Tom were a somewhat dim-witted student. "But a random act of street violence in the middle of a big city? Happens all the time."

With that unsettling image, and the realization of how narrowly he had escaped certain death, Tom settled back into the plush leather seat. While no one could see inside the darkened windows of the limousine, Tom was able to peer out and did so to distract him from worry over the danger that might be in store for him next. The large, armored vehicle had left central Paris and the suburbs behind, and now hurtled through farm country.

Now he watched as a vast field of lavender flitted by, almost as if it were moving and the car standing still. He was reminded of his early years on farms in Provence amidst the fields of lavender and mustard, and he recalled how much Antoinette loved lavender, both for its medicinal qualities and its lovely color and fragrance. He vowed that when this ordeal was over, his dear wife would never long for lavender again. She could surround the house with acres of lavender and hang bunches in every room of the house, sleep on a bed of lavender if she so wished—he'd make sure of it.

After another hour of driving, the limousine turned down a narrow, dirt road and came to a stop in front of a farmhouse that appeared deserted. The Mercedes AMG screeched to a halt behind it. Big Bobby assisted Tom in exiting from the luxurious vehicle. Tom had just finished straightening himself and stretching after the long journey when Carlo Alfonsi and two other men leapt from the German muscle car and reached for their guns.

"Not so fast," Big Bobby said. Before he had even finished speaking, some twenty Lombardi, all dressed in black and carrying weapons, emerged from the farmhouse. They formed a circle around Tom, Alfonsi and his two henchmen.

"Take him to the barn," Alfonsi ordered, jerking a thumb in Tom's direction.

Tom felt his insides turn to ice. So, this was to be his fate after all. Executed inside a barn like an American gangster in the 1920s. All that nice talk from Big Bobby about the Lombardi and the Carolingian Sacred Heart had been for naught, just a distraction to keep him calm during the drive.

"I said, not so fast," Big Bobby said.

"What are we waiting for?" Alfonsi growled.

"Aren't you forgetting something?" Big Bobby said. "Our vows to the Carolingean Sacred Heart—above all else, to protect the King of Rohan and his family."

"That's just a fairy tale," Alfonsi protested. "I'm under orders from Gabriel Monet."

"We take our orders from a higher source," Big Bobby said.

"Protection is just a code name," Alfonsi said.

"Protection is our sacred duty," Big Bobby said. "Don't you get it? When we hear 'protection,' it means just one thing—protect the King of Rohan."

With twenty men and their guns trained on them, Alfonsi and his two associates slowly lowered their weapons.

"Take them to the barn," Big Bobby said to Alex, slashing his hand across his throat to make his order clear.

Tom had been leaning against the limousine, observing the drama and slowly coming to realize that he was not to be executed after all, and that these Lombardi thugs really did intend to protect him. With that knowledge came a growing sense of power and resolve. He thrust himself between Big Bobby and Alfonsi and spoke one word. "No!"

Twenty-five gangsters simply stared at Tom.

"I will not permit bloodshed," Tom said.

"But your majesty, the penalty for disobedience to the sacred vows—" Big Bobby began.

Tom raised his hand for silence. To Big Bobby he said, "If I am to assume the royal throne to which I seem to be destined, then my first act shall be one of mercy, not vengeance." To Alfonsi and his two associates, he said, "Go, and do not involve yourself in the lives of the Rohans or the Lombardi ever again. Say nothing. Just go and do something good with your lives."

Big Bobby shook his head, as if thinking that Tom would regret the decision. Finally he waved his arm at Alfonsi and his men. "You heard him. Get out of here!"

Now Tom came to the conclusion of the story of his missing two days, telling Antoinette, "While you and the children were enjoying your holiday, I was hiding out in a farmhouse with Big Bobby and Alex." He gestured with his arm for the two Lombardi to draw closer so he could introduce Big Bobby and Alex to Antoinette.

Antony dogged their heels and Tom realized his eldest son must have overheard most of the story he had just told Antoinette of the failed assassination attempt and the rescue by the Lombardi. He said to Antony, "I suppose you think I made a big mistake, letting those three would-be assassins go free."

Big Bobby and Alex both nodded and traded looks that said, "No duh, big mistake." Antony, however, surprised Tom by saying, "You did what you thought was right at the time based on the information you had," while Antoinette stroked his hair and said, "You wouldn't be the man I love if you had not shown mercy."

"But never forget," Antony said, his face creased with concern, "your life is in grave danger from the very men whose lives you spared."

CHAPTER EIGHT

All eyes were now focused on Antony. The eldest Rohan son presented a figure of strength and security in his uniform of a French army general. If anyone had the knowledge, training and connections to keep the family safe, it rested on the firm, square shoulders of Antony.

"What do you advise?" Tom asked. "Stay where we are, or get out while we can?"

"Stay here," Antony responded immediately, his tone indicating that fleeing would be the utmost folly and danger. "The family is together. The Lombardi and the French secret service are both here to protect you. There is no safer place in all of Europe."

"It seems that my circle of trust is growing wider," Tom observed. "Now—that phone call you got from General Miliot. Anything you'd care to share with your father?"

Antony's stern face bore a flicker of a smile. "He tells me you can trust the Lombardi, and that there is a member of your board who is likewise on our side."

"Excellent!" Tom said.

"General Miliot also tells me that he is sending his most highly trained troops to the castle. Our equivalent of the American Navy SEALS."

Tom felt his strength and confidence resurging. Maybe this will all work out, he told himself, and his family will be safe after all. "And I've got not one, but two, secret societies watching over us," he said with a nod toward the Lombardi men.

"Eh, watch what you say," Big Bobby said. "Especially with outsiders within hearing distance."

"Oh, right," Tom said with a nervous chuckle. "Blood oaths, secret identities. How could I forget?"

A few giggles rippled through the gathering. Antoinette, who had remained silent from the time Tom had finished his tale of the Paris assassination attempt, now surprised Tom by speaking up with great courage and determination in her voice. "With all the land holdings in France, Germany and Italy, and all the Rohan business assets, it seems we have inherited not only great wealth, but also great vulnerability."

All eyes were on the shy, petite Frenchwoman, urging her to continue. "There is no turning back now," she said. "We're all here and safe, at least for the moment. Antony is right. To try to escape would put us in far more danger. We should stay where we are. Say nothing to the rest of the children. Not yet, anyway. And you know what else I think we should do?"

"No, what?" Tom, Antony and the two Lombardi demanded in unison.

"I think we should all enjoy our family reunion. Finally!"

Then she turned to Big Bobby and Alex, and with tears in her eyes, she embraced the two Lombardi strongmen. *"Grazi, grazi,"* she murmured. "You saved my husband's life. For that I am forever in your debt. *Grazi."*

At Antoinette's mention of the family reunion, Tom let out a sigh of relief and a surge of warmth and love swept through his being. His quiet little wife had just risen as a tower of strength and wisdom.

His mind now clear of all doubts and worries, Tom now took charge. He beckoned to Brigitte to come forward and said, "I will permit the news media to have access, but only on the left side of the hall."

"Yes, your excellency."

Tom hesitated momentarily, still not used to being addressed by the royal honorific. "My family shall sit at the front on the left side. Set up the chairs so that there are two aisles leading to the king's podium, one to the right and one to the left," he told Brigitte.

"As you wish, sir." The woman appeared puzzled.

"What I have in mind is a situation similar to two side-by-side balconies in a theater. Both can see the stage, but neither can see each other."

Brigitte thought for a moment, then said, "Clever, my lord. The paparazzi will be able to take all the pictures they want of you, but they won't be able to aim their cameras at your family."

"Exactly," Tom said, relieved to be understood. "I'm putting you in charge. Make sure there are plenty of guards around my family and that not a single one of those media vultures gets anywhere near my wife and children."

"Consider it done, excellency." Brigitte turned, but instead of departing to carry out her assignments as Tom had expected, she ushered a stranger into the inner circle. The man was middle-aged, dressed in a business suit but with no tie. He had hooded eyes and a shiny dome completely devoid of hair. Tom felt a flicker of recognition, but could not recall ever meeting this man before. *Why was Brigitte allowing this stranger into his tight family circle?*

"My lord," Brigette said, "Allow me to present Victor Monet."

Tom recognized the name as the superintendent of the castle. But he realized he'd heard the name before, long ago, from his own father. Rumors of a family scandal, an affair, illegitimate brothers, twins...

While these thoughts raced through Tom's mind, Brigitte continued with her introduction. "Monsieur Monet is one of five directors of the Rohan corporation and is head of both Human Resources and Public Relations. Each year, the board chooses a Director General, and this year, the honor goes to Monsieur Monet."

The man made a small bow in Tom's direction and said, "It is an honor to welcome you back to Castle Rohan, my lord."

Tom recalled that General Miliot had told Antony that one of the Rohan board members could be trusted and would reveal himself at the right moment. Tom introduced Monet to Antoinette and Antony and repeated the directions he'd given Brigitte as to the seating arrangements for his family and the news media.

Tom stood at the front of the Great Hall as the castle staff continued to set up rows of chairs for the 180 students, chaperones and teachers. The police and secret service were busy getting themselves into position. Tom was pleased to see that the reporters and photographers had calmed themselves now that they knew they would be permitted access, and behaved more like a pack of well-trained puppies than a flock of vultures.

The students were beyond themselves with excitement as the journalists were ushered in with their cameras, tripods and lights. They squealed with excitement as the host of the popular French morning news program *Télématin* made his entrance, pulling out their cell phones and eagerly snapping photos.

Victor Monet spoke in a stern voice to the students. "Have you no respect? You will turn them off your mobile phones and put them away immediately. If we see or hear one phone during the ceremony, it will be confiscated."

Tom gave a nod in appreciation in Victor's direction, relieved that the Rohan corporation board member had eliminated another avenue by which his family's privacy would almost certainly have been invaded. Then he heard the groans of disappointment and dismay coming from the section where the students were seated, and experienced a pang of sorrow for having ruined the teenagers' fun. He was reminded of the line from Shakespeare's *Henry IV:* "Uneasy lies the head that wears the crown." He wished he could do something to make these young people happy as he gazed out at their glum faces.

A new idea popped into his mind: *What do teenagers love even more than their cell phones?*

He summoned Brigitte and Victor Monet. "Just wondering," he said. "How long would it take for the kitchen staff to set up a buffet table in back and fill it with *macarons au chocolat*, baguettes, *saucisson et fromage*, pizza, hamburgers, frites, crisps, Nutella… you know, stuff teenagers like."

Tom watched with satisfaction as the castle staff scurried around to carry out his instructions. Delectable foods began to arrive, their tempting aromas soon filling the Great Hall. The students rushed to the buffet tables, their mobile phones forgotten and their voices bubbling over with cheers and laughter. The chaperones and teachers weren't far behind, piling their plates almost as high as the teenagers with the savory and sweet treats. Even the police officers and secret service agents were temporarily deserting their posts to snatch a slice of pizza or a chocolate macaron. The paparazzi didn't even bother to be discreet, stuffing their mouths and filling their pockets with extra bread and cheese for snacking later on.

"This business of being king isn't half bad," Tom said to himself with a smile.

Contented that peace and frivolity reigned supreme in the Great Hall, Tom turned to his family. He gathered Antoinette, his seven children and their offspring in a circle at the front of the hall. As he expected, they were bursting with questions. "Royal blood? Really?"... "You're *that* old? How can that be?"... "The dragon in the dining room? How did you know about that?"

Tom raised his palm for silence. "All will be revealed in due time," he said. He beckoned to Victor Monet and instructed him to set up a buffet table just for the Rohan family. Victor and his staff had the task finished within minutes, a long table set up in the narrow passageway between the seating and the altar. It contained pitchers of soda and milk and platters of pizza and hamburgers for the children, and for the adults, carafes of wine and *ratatouille*, *confit de canard*, *soupe de poisson* with crisp toast, *café gourmand*, and other dishes dear to the heart of the French soul.

Once everyone had filled a plate, their eyes gazed upon Tom with curiosity and expectation. They trusted their father to be true to his word, that he would take them into his confidence, reveal the family secrets, when he deemed the time to be right and not a minute before. Still, they knew the *pater familias* had something planned for this special moment. But what, exactly, they had no idea.

Tom cleared his throat and began to speak. "Now, what did we all do at every single family dinner when you were growing up? Surely you must remember."

The seven Rohan offspring looked at each other with smiles as they recalled the simple ritual. After saying grace and as dishes were being passed, each child took a turn in sharing one new thing they had learned that day. In that way, Tom had fostered family unity and impressed upon his sons and daughters the value of life-long learning.

"Now that we are all together at last," Tom said, "I propose we do just that, return to our old family custom. Each of you shall share with the rest of us the most important thing you have learned these past three days on this special trip." He nodded toward Antony, as the eldest, to begin and sent him a signal.

Antony immediately picked up the silent message. It wasn't time yet to share the truly important thing he had learned—that the family was in great danger, and that he would have to play a role in protecting them. Instead, the stern-faced army general looked almost boyish when he said, 'I learned all about medieval weapons and armor. Especially the suits of armor the knights had to wear. I had no idea how heavy and uncomfortable those things were. I'm very glad I only have to wear this." He finished with a gesture toward his dress uniform and pillbox hat.

Julia spoke next. "I discovered that work isn't the most important thing in the world. I learned that I can leave the law office behind for a few days and the world will not come to an end. I now know I don't have to respond to every text and email immediately, and that it is permissible to relax and as the Americans say, chill out."

Ronald, the university professor, said, "This wonderful trip has reminded me that the most valuable lessons come from outdoors, being in nature. From these majestic mountains I absorbed so much wisdom by simply observing the plants and animals, soaking in the beauty of the moment."

When it was his turn, banker Phillip spoke similar sentiments as his elder brother and sister, the value of slowing down and the simple pleasures of nature over the demands of a high-pressure career.

"I learned so much at the local farmer's markets," enthused Adele. "The men and women of the village demonstrated to me the importance of using fresh, local ingredients. I discovered it's actually not that difficult to prepare simple, healthy meals for my family. I can't wait to try it at home!"

Her younger sister, Louise, balanced a baby on one knee and her plate on the other as she said, "I have had the pleasure of discovering what a wonderful uncle Gilbert is. He has grown up to be a kind and generous young man. We're all so impressed at how he has taken charge of his nieces and nephews and helped us watch over them these past three days."

A round of applause followed as Gilbert ducked his head and blushed.

"And you, Gilbert?" Tom said to his youngest son. "It is thanks to your achievements at *lycée*, being chosen for this trip, that we are here at Castle Rohan. You must have learned many new things from your time in the classroom and on the castle tour to share with us. What's the very biggest lesson you have learned?"

"Well… I—I—I…" the crimson color deepened on the teenager's cheeks. "If you must know, I learned the right way to kiss a girl."

Outbursts of surprise and giggles greeted this confession. Two of the younger nephews looked at each other in disgust and said, "Uncle Gilbert kissed a girl? Yuck!"

"Her name is Gabrielle," Gilbert stuttered out. "Gabi. She's from Lyon and was chosen by her school to make this special trip, just like me. She's very smart and, well… she knows a lot about kissing."

"And you just met her three days ago? You work fast, *petit frère*," Antony said with an admiring look.

Hoots of laughter erupted from the two other brothers, while Louise protested, "Stop making fun of him. I think it's sweet."

"You were very brave to share that with all of us," Antoinette said, giving Gilbert a hug, then adding more seriously, "As long as all you're doing with this girl is kissing."

A commotion broke out, interrupting the warm scene of family bonding. The two Lombardi men were in a heated argument with loud voices and much waving of arms with a pair of local gendarmes, who in turn were exchanging tense words with one of the secret service agents.

From what Tom could tell, the police from the nearest village considered Big Bobby and Alex to be thugs, common criminals, and wanted them ejected not only from the premises, but from all of Bas-Rhin. The secret service agent, meanwhile, was trying in vain to explain that the two Lombardi were here to protect the Rohan family and that their presence had been approved by the highest authority, General Miliot.

Before Tom could intervene, Antoinette spoke up. "These men saved my husband's life. They may stay here as long as they wish. They are honored guests of our family. That goes for Big Bobby, Alex, and any other members of the Lombardi."

The two uniformed gendarmes may have been able to stand up to the secret service agent, but little Antoinette created too powerful a presence. Mumbling apologies, the pair slunk back into the crowd.

Antoinette turned back to her family. "You have just seen an example of the most important lesson I have learned these past three days. Never judge a person solely by his appearance or reputation. Look inside. That is where you will find the true character."

Tom allowed himself a sip of the excellent Bordeaux and surveyed his family. He knew this relaxed, joyful moment could not last forever, and that a supreme ordeal awaited him. He only hoped that he could spare his family from most of it, and that these precious people would never experience the worst of the danger.

He felt all eyes upon him as his offspring waited for him to share his lesson. He took a deep breath and began. "I have learned that moments such as this are the most valuable of all. Worth more than money... more than land... more than power and prestige. What matters most are the people you love, and the time you spend with them."

CHAPTER NINE

S ome fifty-five kilometers away in the ancient imperial city of Strasbourg, the powerful men and women who represented the world's largest financial markets and institutions, as well as the Vatican, waited nervously for news from Château du Rohan. Rumors and speculation ran rampant throughout the elegant meeting hall. Already, the news channels were airing reports of an unknown man, appearing to be in late middle age, donning the imperial cloak and requesting the belt and knife of the Rohan royal family. Who was this man? Was he just the father of one of the students engaging in an elaborate bit of play-acting for the amusement of the crowd? Or could he be the real thing, the heir whom the world had assumed had vanished decades ago?

Judging from the intense interest being shown by the news media as the story unfolded on the large television monitors mounted high on the walls, this was no mere prank. If this stranger really was the lost king of Rohan, what did this mean not only for their personal fortunes, but to the economic structure of the entire planet?

In one corner of the ornate room, three men surrounded Gabriel Monet. "You're telling us we no longer deal directly with the Vatican?" the Caribbean beach boy billionaire wanted to know. "You mean to say we're going to have to negotiate directly with that little pipsqueak calling himself the King of Rohan?"

"Too soon to tell," Monet said calmly. "He still must pass the tests and trials. Even if that unlikely event were to happen, the courts will have to decide whether the Rohan trusts are still valid."

"If you ask me, all deals are off," muttered the short, bald man who controlled the oil fields of one of the former Soviet bloc nations.

The Asian wearing the gray Mao-style jacket said, "This is preposterous. If this imposter really is who they are saying he is, he would be over one hundred years old. Yet look at him." He gestured toward the nearest television monitor. "He appears to be in his sixties and acts like he is in his fifties. Such things are not possible."

For that, Monet had no answers. Instead, he told his confederates, "If you want my advice, I would tell you to lay your hands on as many Rohan coins as you can. Beg, borrow or steal if you have to. They will be very useful for leverage later on. Trust me on that one."

While Gabriel Monet presented an image of strength and control, inside he seethed with anger, his thoughts and emotions churning. Who was this anonymous druggist, this nobody from the countryside, to suddenly appear and upset all of his plans to take over the Rohan trust? A complicated scheme taking years to put together, decades of sacrifice and secret deal-making, was now turning to ash before his eyes.

This man calling himself Tom Rohan had to be an imposter, Monet told himself. In the tests and trials that were to come, he would for certain be exposed as a money-hungry fraud. Disgraced in front of his family and in front of the nation's news media, hauled away in handcuffs. And then everything could go back to normal, Monet's plan for ultimate control and power still firmly in place.

But … the voice in Monet's head would not be stilled … but what if he were *not* an imposter, a fraud and a cheat? What if—as impossible as it may seem—this mild-mannered pharmacist with his round, owlish glasses passes all of the tests and proves to be really and truly the direct descendant of Emperor Lothair, heir to vast lands and uncountable riches? Then what?

Monet folded his arms and considered the situation while his three collaborators continued to stare at the TV monitors. There was always more than one way for a clever, ambitious man such as himself to worm his way into a position of power. Take blackmail, for one. This druggist must have a secret or two to hide—doesn't everyone? If that didn't work, kidnapping was always an option. That teenage son, the brat who started all this by winning a prize at school, would be his first target. An evil little smile formed on Monet's lips as he imagined Tom Rohan's reaction when he received an ear or a finger from his precious Gilbert in the post. He'd pay anything, give up all power, just to prevent more violence to his youngest son.

And if that failed to unseat this upstart calling himself the King of Rohan—well, there was always the tried-and-true. The assassin's bullet. Or the knife. Or the poison. It worked in the days of Julius Caesar, and it was still remarkably effective today.

His operatives had bungled the job two days ago on the streets of Paris. Next time, Monet vowed there would be no room for error, even if he had to do the job himself.

Conversation in the meeting hall suddenly came to a halt, a silence so profound Monet was reminded of the old expression of being able to hear a pin drop. He'd never actually believed that maxim before, but now he realized that if someone actually were to let a single straight pin fall to the floor, it would echo like a shot from a cannon. All eyes—all 100 pairs of eyes of the most powerful men and women from the world of finance—were riveted to the nation's all-news channel, France 24, on the television monitors.

What Monet and the rest of the gathering saw was an old woman, in her seventies at least, elegantly and properly dressed and groomed. The presenter, business editor Stephen Carroll, was saying, "Joining us is Duchess Marie de Courcillon. Duchess, you are willing to confirm that the man at Castle Rohan, the man calling himself Tom Rohan, is actually the long-lost heir to the Rohan dynasty. Is that correct?"

"Yes, that is correct," the old woman said in a voice strong and steady. "He is Duke Tom Maximal Rohan."

"And you say you were married to him when you were just sixteen?" the news presenter continued.

"Yes, that is correct," the woman repeated. An image appeared on the television screen of a much younger woman wearing a classic Paris ball gown and her hair in a popular style of the early 1950s. "I was sixteen and he was forty-seven. This was a tradition of our two families, that the eldest Rohan son would marry the eldest Courcillon daughter. It was a union on paper only, you understand."

"In other words, the two of you did not have a physical relationship?"

The older woman's face was back on the screen as the live interview continued. "That's a bit of an impertinent question," she said with a little smile. "But if you must know, we were not intimate as a man and wife, and the union bore no children. We dissolved this marriage-on-paper ten years later."

"And then thirteen years later, Tom Rohan married one of his students," Carroll said. "He was sixty then and she was only twenty."

"A brilliant girl," the duchess said. "But shy, terribly shy. Unable to function in any sort of social situation. And so they retired to the countryside outside of Dijon and opened a chain of little druggist shops."

"We've received reports in our newsroom that Tom Rohan had been ill for many years. Yet he appears to be at the peak of health, remarkable for a man of his advanced years."

"I have heard that too," the duchess said. "I understand he brought his health back with his advanced research in pharmaceutics, plus a healthy diet, exercise, and his strong will. He always was a bright and determined man, so who knows?"

"Your family and the Rohans have had strong ties for decades, even centuries," Carroll said, continuing to hold a microphone near the duchess's lips. "Is there anything else you can share with our viewers?"

The old woman thought for a moment, then said, "I think Tom has always had contact with his parents, and that his parents are the ones who arranged to have Tom protected by the secret service all these years."

"Really," the news presenter said. "That's very interesting. But tell me, how are you, or any of us, going to be able to verify this man's claim to be the king of Rohan? Anyone could make that claim. He could easily be an imposter."

"Ah but you see, Monsieur Carroll, there are simple and strict qualifications," she said with a smile.

"Go on," Carroll said eagerly. "The entire nation—the entire world—is waiting."

"First of all, take into consideration the fifty Rohan coins. Each has a unique marking that certifies the coin as genuine. The de Courcillon family has a record of all of those distinguishing marks."

"Anything else?"

"There exist at least a dozen land deeds over 500 years old. Each bears the Carolingian seal. Produce the deeds with the proper seals and you produce the heir to the kingdom of Rohan."

"Fascinating!" Carroll thanked the duchess for making herself available to France 24 and prepared to turn the newscast over to the next presenter. Once again, the finance ministers, bankers, land owners, oil sheiks and billionaires from around the world began to trade theories and speculations, their voices rising throughout the hall.

Gabriel Monet, meanwhile, sprinted to the entrance of the hotel and demanded that the valet bring his car around. If he pushed his Citroen C6 to the limit, he should be able to make it to Castle Rohan in just under a half hour.

CHAPTER TEN

Excitement and anticipation filled the Great Hall at Castle Rohan. The ever-efficient staff had cleared away the buffet tables and assisted all of the students, chaperones and teachers in seating themselves. By now, the story had reached every occupant of the hall that this 101-year-old man who looked unbelievably young—and the father of one of the students, no less—was actually Maximal Oto Thomas Rohan and was entitled to bear the title of Prince or King. Everyone from the youngest student to the eldest of the docents in their medieval costumes waited eagerly for the surprises that would unfold next. Even the castle historian, seated in a place of honor at a desk and surrounded by ancient books and ledgers along with a laptop computer, appeared to be bursting with wonder.

The electrifying buzz of conversation slowly hushed as Brigitte, always elegant in her black designer gown and simple strand of pearls, strode to the front and took her place at the podium. "Dear ladies and gentlemen," she said. The acoustics in the Great Hall were so perfect she needed no help from a microphone. "Château du Rohan has the great joy and honor to announce that our long-lost fifty-fourth descendant, Maximal Oto Thomas Rohan, has returned to his ancestral home. Dr. Rohan will be making his public prayer and speech, and Lady Antoinette Rohan, Doctor Antoinette Rohan, will accompany him."

Husband and wife, each wrapped in a royal velvet cloak trimmed in ermine, approached the altar. Tom wore the belt and chains of authority, the Rohan knife still stuck in the belt, while Antoinette was adorned in gold necklaces befitting a queen. The pair eased themselves down onto the soft purple kneeling pads in front of the altar.

Tom Rohan clasped his hands and began to recite the ancient words of respect and reverence. "Dear father, Raymond, King of Rohan, the descendant of Charlemagne... dear mother, Elizabeth, the daughter of King Orschwil... your elder son, Maximal Oto Thomas Rohan, and his wife, Dr. Antoinette Rohan, do humbly present ourselves in front of you."

He spoke in a normal tone, but his voice resonated with courage to every corner of the vast chamber as he continued to pray, for his parents and Antoinette's, for their ancestors, and for all those who came before them. "For the kingdom, the land, and the people of the kingdom. For the wind, the trees, the air, the sun and the stars..."

Tom rose from the kneeling position and assisted Antoinette in doing the same. The castle staff quietly and with great efficiency placed two chairs in front of the King's and Queen's thrones. Tom and Antoinette seated themselves.

"A week ago, the news reported that the Rohan dynasty had ended," Tom said. "But as you can see, we are very much alive. Antoinette and I are the proud parents of seven children, three daughters and four sons. Antoinette, will you do me the honor of making introductions?"

"It would be my pleasure," she said with confidence, her shyness seeming to have completely evaporated in the wake of the amazing events of the past four days. "But to preserve the privacy of our family, I shall introduce them by first name only, and they will not show their faces."

She then proceeded to name Antony, Julia, Ronald, Phillip, Adele, Louise, "And our youngest, Gilbert, whose exemplary academic and citizenship record at school is the reason we are all here today."

Sensing that the audience craved more information, she continued, "We're no different than all of you. We live in a simple home in the countryside outside of Dijon. We run a small chain of four drug stores and own a small pharmaceutical research lab. There is nothing glamorous about our lives, I can promise you that."

A smile crossed her face as she recalled, "When our first child arrived, Tom decided to build a home for us with his own hands. He planned the dining room to be an exact replica of the private family dining room here at Castle Rohan. All of our children had happy growing-up years in that kitchen and dining room as it had the blessing of the Rohan ancestors—and of course, the protection of the dragon."

Tom beamed his pride and approval at Antoinette and said, "My birth name was Maximal Oto Thomas Rohan. But—" and here he paused to make sure everyone was paying attention. "—I am *not* the prince of Rohan!"

Shocked silence greeted this statement, followed by loud whispers that echoed throughout the hall, bouncing from students to news presenters, from the secret service agents to the castle docents, the historian and the Lombardi men. They had all heard moments ago that Tom was the heir to the kingdom of Rohan. Now he was flatly denying it. How could that be?

Tom took it all in with peace and a calm demeanor. As the commotion diminished, he locked eyes with the audience, the media, the historian, Brigitte, Antoinette, and each of his children and their families. "I *was* King Maximal Oto Thomas Rohan," Tom said firmly.

Once again, voices filled with shock and surprise rose in the Great Hall.

"You see, it is very simple really," Tom said with an amused smile. "I was the 54th King of Rohan on paper for three days. Three days only!"

With that, his smile turned into laughter. The gathered students guests, media, security and castle personnel looked at each other, unsure what to do. This man who might or might not be the king of Rohan was laughing. Were they supposed to—or even allowed to— laugh along with him? For a few moments, Tom's chuckle was the only sound in the huge chamber. Then a few nervous giggles erupted from the area where the students were seated. The teachers and chaperones joined in, then the castle staff and finally the security guards. Soon the Great Hall was filled with the sounds of chuckles, giggles and guffaws from all of those present.

Tom waited for the joyful din to abate, then locked eyes with the historian and nodded slowly. The elderly, bearded man returned the nod and began to quickly enter instructions into the keyboard of the laptop computer that shared space on his desk with the antique books and ledgers. As he worked busily, one of the docents pressed buttons on a wall panel, dimming the lights in the Great Hall and causing a large projection screen to descend from the ceiling at the front of the altar.

Slowly an image began to appear on the screen of a handwritten decree, complete with signature and numerous stamps and seals. Gasps and murmurs of wonder filled the hall as the 200 occupants read the words and the significance began to sink in: King Raymond Rohan was ceding the kingship to Maximal Oto Thomas Rohan.

"My father issued and signed this decree shortly before he passed away," Tom said.

The historian pressed a key on his computer, causing this image to fade and a new one to appear. It seemed to be another sheet of royal stationery and with the same handwriting, signature, seals and stamps as the previous decree. On it, King Raymond had written, "This I decree and ordain because I dearly hope Maximal Oto Thomas will return one day. The day Maximal returns, he is the King, not a prince, not a candidate. He is the true and only King of Rohan!"

At this, the 200 souls packed into the Great Hall could contain themselves no longer. The roar of questions and declarations was like a volcano of emotion about to erupt, threatening to burst out of the castle and hurtle down the sides of the mountain, eventually engulfing the entire world.

Through all this turmoil, Tom remained an island of calm, projecting nothing but dignity, brotherhood, civility and charisma. He waited patiently until the assembled crowd finally realized they would learn nothing more from Tom until they calmed themselves.

When Tom deemed it was quiet enough for him to continue speaking and be heard, he said, "Yes, it is true—I disappeared from public life for sixty-five years. But... I never disappeared for a single moment from my parents."

Tom smiled to himself, thinking of the shock waves that this statement would be creating in the world's financial markets. Along with everyone else, he'd seen the news footage of the interview with Duchess Marie de Courcillon on France 24. She'd said she always assumed Tom had continued to keep in contact with his parents, and that they had arranged for him to have secret service protection even as he worked in obscurity in the pharmaceutical industry. Turns out, she was absolutely correct.

Turning now to Brigitte, Tom said, "Dear Brigitte, do you remember how my father used to talk about seeing a secret messenger? Two or three times a year?"

Brigitte's wrinkled face reflected shock. When she was able to speak, she said, "Yes, Lord Maximal. Those were the happiest moments your mother and father ever had. They always cleared the entire castle and the whole surrounding area and met entirely in secret. They were always so happy in the days before they expected the messenger to come, and then actually meeting with him, and then so very sad when the messenger left."

Brigitte began to speak rapidly, her voice rising, as she recalled, "We were never allowed to see this messenger, or even come close. But I did hear that on a few occasions, there were two of them, not just one."

Tom's eyes filled with tears and his voice shook with emotion when he said, "You see, dear Brigitte, that messenger was how I was able to stay in communication with my mother and father. They used hand signals to pass messages. And those times when you saw more than one messenger?"

"Yes?" Brigitte asked in a hoarse whisper.

"That second messenger was me."

Tears were streaming down both faces now, and for several moments Tom and Brigitte could only hold onto each other and let their feelings flow while the occupants of the Great Hall watched in stunned silence.

The ever-helpful Victor Monet discreetly handed a box of tissues to Tom and Brigitte. Tom composed himself, feeling as if a great burden, secrets kept for decades, had finally been released. "The meeting I remember the most was when I told my mother and father that Antoinette was expecting, and that they were about to become grandparents. That was the happiest and most intense moment of all."

He paused for a moment to allow his mind to wander back to that joyous time so many years ago. "I told my father that we could no longer live in an apartment," he said, "and that I would build a proper home for our new family. Papa insisted, practically demanded, that I build a dining room that would be an exact replica of the one at Castle Rohan. He always said the dining room is the true heart of the home."

"I remember that, too!" Brigitte exclaimed. "The old Lord Rohan had access to the castle dining room sealed off so that our best craftsmen could make detailed measurements. Your father personally made the blueprints on three large sheets of paper. They were taken away by one of those messengers."

Brigitte burst into a fresh round of weeping. "One year later, the messenger delivered a photograph. A young woman holding a baby in her arms and standing in a dining room with a dragon peering down from the ceiling. There was a man standing behind her, but you could only see him from the chest down. It was the old king's most cherished photo. He kept it on his bedside."

The historian made more keystrokes and a new image appeared on the screen. It had the look of a photograph taken with a Polaroid camera some four decades ago. The colors had faded and the edges blurred, giving it a dreamy, underwater look. A young woman holding a baby peered at the camera, where a man's figure from the chest down was visible in the background—the very photograph Brigitte had just described in her tear-choked voice.

Now it was Antoinette's turn to be overcome with emotion. "My lord!" she choked out between sobs. "That young lady—that was me! That dining room is in our family room in the countryside of Dijon. That baby—" She halted, unable to continue. Wiping away tears, she turned to Antony. "That baby—it was you. My firstborn, my Antony! The man standing behind me—that's Tom. Now I know why we have a dragon on the ceiling. The dragon is bringing us all the blessings of all the kings since Emperor Lothair Rohan!"

By now, Antony and all the other offspring of Tom and Antoinette were swept away by the emotional intensity of the scene. From young Gilbert to stern and serious Antony, salty liquid spilled from their eyes. Before long, it was as if a tsunami of tears had flooded the Great Hall. Sniffles and sobs echoed throughout the vast chamber and there was much scrambling through purses, pockets and backpacks for tissues and handkerchiefs. The reporters and photographers recovered first, wiping their eyes on their sleeves and scrambling to record this moment for posterity.

Tom's thoughts drifted far away. Still in Castle Rohan, but decades in the past, those happy days of his childhood in the golden years before Europe was torn asunder by two terrible wars. He had studied with the best private tutors on the Continent, but the most lasting lessons came from his parents: that great wealth and power carries great responsibility, and the importance of justice, mercy, wisdom and love. Above all, love. It was if the years had drifted away in the mist, and he was once again a boy, the castle quiet and serene, just his mother and father and a few trusted servants and advisors.

He could have remained enveloped in those pleasant memories for hours, but he realized that all 200 eyes were staring at him, wondering what he would say next. So he decided to give them a story he was sure they would remember. "My mother was much more demanding than Papa," he began.

"Mama arranged for the messenger to deliver small flowering plants in pots to me on a regular basis. She knew that when the plants actually began to bloom, the messenger would bring the cut flowers and blooming plants in pots back to the local market in the village and that some of these flowers would eventually make their way up to the castle."

Tom's face broke into a smile. "You see, Mama was very clever. She was checking up on me, making sure I was doing due diligence."

Brigitte's eyes once again filled with tears. "Your parents filled the solarium with all the flowers that kept arriving from this unknown source. They spent their final days and hours in the sun room, surrounded with all that beauty."

Once again, Tom felt himself being drawn into the past and from his heart he sent an unspoken message to his mother and father: *I have always been with you.* Aloud he said, "I must have gotten most of my genes from Mama. She was always happiest in the garden, and I seem to have inherited her green thumb. I studied botany extensively at university and it was one of my favorite subjects."

Tom continued, "Of course, I don't mean to slight the contribution that dear Papa made in my life. It was he who gave me freedom and encouragement to pursue an ordinary career and to live an ordinary life. He always told me that living a contented and productive life is far more important than all the trappings of royalty."

He allowed himself to float in this nostalgic reverie for one more moment, then forced himself back into the present. In a loud, firm voice, he said, "André? Are you here?"

Brigitte scurried off to search through the crowd, while the assembled persons in the Great Hall whispered to each other with a new question on their lips: who was this André that Tom Rohan was asking for?

Before they had a chance to wear themselves out with speculation, Brigitte returned to the altar, trailed by a sixty-year-old man who walked with a slight limp. He knelt before Tom and said with great awe, "Lord Maximal!"

Tom helped the man back to his feet and embraced him warmly. Then he turned to the audience and said, "André's father, and then André himself served the Rohan family for two generations. They were the messengers! All of us owe you our highest gratitude for the service you and your father gave us."

André's face broke into a smile that Tom knew very well, and he said, "The king and queen loved nothing more than to sit in the solarium with all of the flowers you sent. I don't know how you did it, but you managed to send flowers all year round. Even in the coldest months of winter, your parents were surrounded by beautiful blooms."

Before Tom could respond, Brigitte said with excitement. "Did you know your mother also had a secret photograph that she cherished above all others?"

The historian scrambled with the laptop, obviously not expecting this turn in the presentation. Another color photograph appeared on the projector screen, newer, the colors brighter and more vibrant. The same woman from the earlier photograph, but slightly older, surrounded by five small children. A caption read, "Antoinette in a beautiful garden with her five children."

"Your garden at your home in Dijon, I assume?" Brigitte asked.

"Yes, of course," Tom said.

Understanding descended upon all the 200 souls assembled in the Great Hall. These were not ordinary people, royal blood or no. Here was a father who had created exact plans down to the millimeter of the traditional family dining room, with the dragon symbolizing the blessing of the generations of ancestors. Here was a mother demanding flowers, sending them in small starter pots to her son and receiving armloads of gorgeous, fragrant blooms in return. One could say that this was all they could do to stay in communication once Tom had determined to disappear from the public eye. But something more—something powerful and mysterious and awe-inspiring—was at work. This mother, father and son had forged a bond through love that nothing could put asunder, not distance, and not the passage of time.

Tom sensed that André wished to say more and nodded at the loyal messenger to continue. "Your father always told me that one day, Maximal will come back. He will return as the full King. It will be as if Maximal Oto Thomas Rohan had never left!"

Once again, Tom could not halt the tears that spilled from his eyes and ran down his cheeks.

André waited for his king to compose himself, then placed his hand in Tom's, tugging at the royal cloak so that both hands were covered and no one could observe the movements being made. Then, using the ancient secret coded hand-signals, he sent a message. "Your father always had two elite squadrons guarding you, Lord Maximal. I am a member of one of them. There are six of us in and around Castle Rohan."

Tom signaled his approval. "God bless you. I will come back to you."

He then turned his attention back to the audience and, with a light smile, said, "Now I will tell you the story of Maximal Oto Thomas Rohan from the very beginning. I was born 101 years ago on March fifth. My birth certificate shows a date of March 25. That's because I was born two weeks earlier than expected and weighed only slightly more than two kilos. Two medical doctors were in attendance when my mother gave birth and both doubted I would survive. When I made it through the first week, and the second and the third, they decided I was going to live after all and my birth was officially recorded."

Tom paused in his tale, secretly amused at the pandemonium that was erupting in the Great Hall over his latest revelation. The reporters couldn't feed updates into their cell phones and computers fast enough, while the photographers fired away with their cameras at a rapid pace. He felt a wave of pity for the royal historian, frantically tapping away on his laptop while simultaneously flipping pages in the old record books and ledgers in a desperate search for proof of what Tom had just said. Some five minutes went by before the historian gave a sigh of relief and projected onto the screen an image of a handwritten birth record. "The proof is here," he announced, holding aloft a small leather-bound notebook. "The daily journal of one of the attending physicians."

"Baby Maximal was a most cherished child," Tom said. "My crib was placed right between the thrones of the king and queen. When I was but a toddler, my father insisted that I be seated to the right of him, as that is traditionally where the heir to the kingdom of Rohan is seated."

Tom waited for this latest information to sink in, then said, "When I was four, Papa brought in tutors for me. I well remember Monsieur Beaumont, and Monsieur LeGrand, and Mademoiselle Dubois who came in to give me piano lessons. Then there was a proper English nanny, Louise. When I was little, I couldn't pronounce her name correctly, so I just called her Weezie."

Once again, he paused to allow the historian time to search through his records and catch up with the story. After several minutes of page-turning and entering search data into the laptop, he placed an image on the projection screen of a list of Castle Rohan staff from the years when Tom would have been a child. Four names stood out: Beaumont, LeGrand, Dubois, and a Louise Entfield.

By now, excitement had reached a fever pitch in the Great Hall as even the most doubtful and cynical of the journalists and financial leaders were beginning to realize that this unassuming man standing before them might really be who he claimed to be—the legitimate heir to the Rohan dynasty. Tom, meanwhile, continued to project confidence and quiet dignity as he observed members of the Rohan board of directors crowding behind the historian, double-checking his records. *They're only doing their jobs,* he told himself. *I would be doing the same thing, making absolutely certain of the proof of my claim, if I were in their shoes.*

The Great Hall buzzed as if an invisible electrical current were crackling from one person to the next. This was the moment of truth as Tom continued to prove without a doubt the veracity of his claim.

"As I grew older," Tom told them, "I was allowed to attend classes at the little school in the village as well as continuing with studies with my tutors. Mama and Papa knew it was important for me to come in contact with ordinary people, to understand that not every child enjoyed the luxuries that I took for granted, and to have other children to play with and thus learning to get along with others. It was through my interactions with the simple and lovely people of the village that I came to realize that was the sort of life I wanted, not the power and privilege that came with the accident of royal birth."

Many in the audience nodded their approval, and some even responded with light applause. Encouraged by this response, Tom said, "I continued my studies both at the village school and with my private tutors until I was seventeen and went away to university. This is when I decided to start calling myself Tom—Maximal Oto Thomas, but backwards—and to tell no one about my royal heritage. I just wanted to blend in, to be an ordinary student like everyone else."

As Tom spoke, the historian placed more images up on the screen: report cards, diplomas, class photos.

Tom finished, "And then, sixty-five years ago, at age thirty-six, I decided to go into hiding permanently. This was strictly for personal reasons, you understand. I had studied chemistry and biology at university and opened a small chain of drug stores and a pharmaceutical research lab. But most important of all, I met and married the love of my life, my dear Antoinette—" Here he paused to embrace his wife—"and had the privilege of raising seven wonderful children."

Tom knew he was leaving something very important out of the narrative—his early marriage to Duchess Marie de Courcillon when he was forty-seven and she just sixteen. But he told himself it was a union in name only, simply to satisfy old traditions of both families, meaning nothing. He knew the duchess had already appeared on France's all-news TV channel to tell her story and to verify that he truly was Maximal Oto Thomas Rohan, so he saw no point in repeating this story from so many years ago.

Instead, he turned once again to the 200 persons assembled in the Great Hall—students, chaperones, teachers, castle staff, guards, journalists, Rohan board members, Lombardi men—and said with confidence, "I'm sure you all have many questions. So… who wants to go first?"

CHAPTER ELEVEN

What followed were a series of intense questions that made Tom feel as if he was once again facing the oral defense of his PhD dissertation. He handled each with his usual dignity and self-assurance.

What role had the Rohan family played during World War II, and was it true they were prominent if secret members of the resistance? Yes, and proud of it.

Where was he during the student riots and demonstrations in Paris in May of 1968, and what did he think of them? Immersed in biological research, and only saw it on the news. Too focused with his research to form an opinion on events outside the laboratory.

What was the name of family that ran the village bakery prior to the German invasion of 1940? Guardard. The pastry chef, Cedric Guardard, made the most wonderful éclairs.

Could he name each and every of the 37 French Prime Ministers since the end of World War II? Yes, he could and did.

Then, from a reporter from the tabloid magazine *J'Accuse!* came the most ridiculous question of all: Was it true he had been the inspiration for Colette's novel *Chéri*, about an older woman having a love affair with a much younger man? To that, Tom could only throw back his head in laughter, placing an arm around his wife's shoulders and saying, "Colette is a national treasure, but she had a very active imagination. The only love of my life stands next to me."

While Tom busied himself in concocting answers to these and numerous other questions, answers that he hoped were both factual and witty, the historian and his assistants bustled about to verify the accuracy of each and every statement he was making. The historian's head bobbed up from his laptop and the piles of dusty old books to signal his approval. "All of his majesty's answers line up perfectly with the historical record," he said. "It is difficult to imagine that someone could have all of these memories without having actually lived through these events." With a wry smile and classic Frenchman's shrug of the shoulders, he added, "As to the rumor that he was the inspiration for Collete's *Cheri*, that is impossible to say. *C'est la vie.*"

The historian's voice grew stronger and more confident. "As incredible as it may seem, I am convinced the man standing before you is, indeed, the King of Rohan. Duke Maximal Oto Thomas Rohan." He ended with a deep bow in Tom's direction.

Just as Tom thought the questioning would come to an end, one of the students raised her hand. "With all due respect, your majesty, but, well…" Her voice trailed off in uncertainty.

"Yes, *le petite fille?*" Tom spoke in a gentle voice.

"Well, that is…" the girl continued to stammer.

"It's all right," Tom said kindly. "You have as much right to ask a question as anyone else in this room. Don't be shy, and do speak up."

The young student's voice grew stronger and more confident with Tom's encouragement. "King Rohan, if you're really one-hundred and one years old, how did you do it? What is your secret?"

The girl's innocent question opened a floodgate. Tom was peppered with questions from every corner of the Great Hall. "Yes, how did you do it?" "It's impossible. How do you explain it?" "Do you actually expect us to believe you're over one hundred years old?"

Tom simply beamed down at the audience and with great modesty said, "Ah, I wondered when one of you would get around to asking that." Looking directly at the girl, who had her face buried in her hands in embarrassment, he said, "Congratulations for being so bold to ask the obvious. You are a very brave young lady. But the fact is, this must remain my secret for now."

He waited for the groans of disappointment to subside, then said, "I will give you two clues. One, I have a doctorate in the pharmaceutical sciences and own a research lab. Two, I disappeared and traveled to every corner of the globe for many years."

Tom let these two nuggets of information sink in and listened to the whispered comments. "He searched around the world for the fountain of youth and found it—that explains it," and "His secret could be worth far more than all of the Rohan assets!"

Another hand shot up, this one from a reporter from the weekly news magazine *Paris Match*. "If you cannot tell us the secret of youth at this time, at least let our readers know why you and your mother and father kept this veil of secrecy in place for so long. Why were you in hiding for so long and why did your parents go along with it?"

"Excellent question," Tom responded, "and the one I was most anticipating. You see, my dear Mama and Papa gave me the greatest gift a son could ask for—they allowed me to choose the life I wanted for myself instead of insisting that I follow the path that they would have preferred. They knew my greatest dream was to live quietly, out of the spotlight, and to run a biological and pharmaceutical research facility. They supported me one hundred percent."

Tom paused to allow a sudden catch in his throat to clear. "I cannot help but think," he continued, his voice halting as if coming from the depths of his emotion, "that at times they wished I had fulfilled my destiny as the King of Rohan. I think it was their greatest regret, that they did not convince me—or force me—to stay on and carry out my royal duties."

He took a deep breath and let the waves of nostalgia and emotion subside. "Perhaps if I had been a better son, I would have realized this was their wish for me, that I ascend to the throne as soon as I reached the age of majority, and I would have done so. But they gave me the gift of freedom, and that was the most precious of all."

Brigitte waited a respectful moment, approached Tom, and spoke to the assembled audience. "Regretfully, the time for questions must come to an end. It is now ten forty-five, and a grand feast is scheduled for one this afternoon. Of course, you are all invited. In the meantime, his excellency will be meeting with the officers and staff of the Rohan corporation."

Victor Monet took charge, leading Tom and Antony into a windowless chamber in back of the Great Hall. By any other standards, this room would have seemed spacious, but in comparison to the oversized scale of Castle Rohan, it appeared small, almost cozy. Through the centuries, it had served as a safe haven for women and children when the castle was under siege, a private sanctuary for prayer and study, storage space for the many props and costumes needed for the elaborate pageantry of the Great Hall, and a hiding place for the local Resistance during the Second World War

Today, it had been outfitted as a conference room befitting a billion dollar corporate board of directors, with a long table of burnished mahogany, cushy leather executive chairs, and the latest technological devices needed to conduct a business meeting. Each table setting included a notepad bearing the Rohan family crest and a Mont Blanc pen. A sideboard held coffee and tea service, as well as an array of flavored and sparkling waters.

Even in the best of times, Tom was unimpressed with luxury and grandeur, so focused was he on the twin passions of his life: his family and scientific research, and certainly no more than today. Antony, meanwhile, swept the room for hidden listening devices, declared it to be secure, and said, "I suppose this is a place the Americans would call the situation room."

"Indeed," Tom said as father and son seated themselves. Tom expected Antony to immediately launch into a discussion of tactics and strategy for keeping the family safe. Instead, he surprised Tom by saying, "You sure were keeping a lot of secrets from us, Papa. What's this about being descended from Charlemagne?"

Tom smile at his firstborn. "History was never your favorite subject in school, was it?"

"Only if it had to do with military history. Napoleon, Phillipe Pétain, Marquis de Lafayette..." For a moment, he seemed lost in a reverie, picturing heroic campaigns from centuries past. Just as quickly, he snapped back to the present, 100 percent focused on the mission before him. "If I am to be of any assistance to you and our family, I must have complete information. Background. A full understanding of the events leading up to our current crisis."

"Very wise," Tom said to his firstborn.

"It's true, then? All this time, we were descended from royalty, a direct line all the way back to Charlemagne?" Antony mused.

"So it would seem," Tom agreed.

"And you kept it a secret from all of us. That little farmhouse in the Dijon countryside, you and Mama struggling so long and hard to keep your business going. And all along, we could have been living…"

"Like kings, yes," Tom finished the thought with a wistful smile. "But you see, Antony, I didn't want all this." Tom spread his arms to indicate the grandeur and luxury of Castle Rohan. "All I wanted was to be part of a loving family and to contribute to the good of humankind through my research. By that standard, one might say I am far richer than any king in the world." He paused, then asked gently, "Are you angry with me, Antony?"

"Anger serves no useful purpose at a time such as this," Antony responded firmly. "We must remain focused if the family is to survive this ordeal. Anyway—" and here the general flashed one of his rare smiles—"no one can stay angry with you for long, Papa."

"Nor I with any of my children," Tom said, warmth and relief welling up inside as he realized his relationship with his eldest son was as strong as ever. "Now, as to our family history, it is true: we trace our lineage back to the Carolingian empire. In other words, to Charlemagne. During the early Middle Ages—basically, the ninth century—the Carolingians ruled western and central Europe. They had ruled over the Franks since 751 and the Lombards of Italy since 774."

"And then along came Charlemagne," Antony said.

"Correct. Pope Leo III crowned him emperor with the plan of reviving the Roman Empire in the west. This worked out reasonably well until civil war broke out in 840."

"Civil wars rarely end well," Antony observed.

"In this case, the empire was divided into autonomous kingdoms. Yes, there still was one king—Lothair Rohan, our ancestor—who was recognizes as the overall ruler, but in reality, he had little power. However—and this is the important part—the unity of the empire and the hereditary rights of the Carolingians continued to be acknowledged. All of this is part of the historical record."

Antony nodded thoughtfully. "What we didn't know up until now is that there are two secret societies, and their identities must be closely guarded. Only the two of us must know the full truth."

"So it would seem," Tom said.

Antony, now taking the lead when it came to dispensing information, said, "The Carolingian Sacred Heart has been protecting the family for more than 1200 years, along with the Lombardi Society of Italy. It was the Lombardis who saved your life in Paris and brought you back to us. They are guarding us even now. The French government promises to send in storm troopers, and the Carolingian Sacred Heart is involved in our protection, but until the security troops arrive, the Lombardis are our best line of defense."

"Go on," Tom said, his brow furrowed in concentration.

"One of the top managers of the Rohan organization is a member of the Carolingian Sacred Heart, but his identity cannot yet be disclosed. Brigitte is one of his recruits, but she does not yet know the existence of the Sacred Heart."

"And you received this information from General Miliot?"

Antony glanced around and lowered his voice, as if not trusting the room truly was secure from eavesdroppers. "Yes, General Miliot is my source of information. But you must never disclose this fact to anyone."

Tom digested this information, then said, "Some of your brothers and sisters may need to go home. The castle may no longer be a place safe for them. We don't really know who we can trust, besides each other." He sighed deeply. "We need to be doing more to build a circle of trust, not only for the Rohan corporation, but among all the factions who have a financial interest in how this is going to play out.

"Agreed," Antony said. "We can trust the Lombardi and the agents with DGSI. I hope we can rely upon Brigitte and André, but we don't know for sure. I just wish General Miliot's storm troopers would arrive. What can be keeping them?"

Tom tapped the expensive pen against the notepad. "First and most important, we must convey the danger and seriousness of the situation to all of your brothers and sisters. Secondly, we need to know what safety nets we can count on, and how to execute them prudently." He let the writing instrument drop to the table and gave it a little slap with his hand, his mind made up. "You, of course, shall stay. And Antoinette. We'll probably require legal advice, so Julia shall remain here. Also Philip, with his expertise in finance and banking. Everyone else must be sent home."

"Always helps to have a good lawyer on the team," Antony said with a tense chuckle. "And a competent money man."

"So true," Tom said. With a pang of regret, he added, "Poor Gilbert! He set all this in motion by winning the invitation to tour the castle. A reward for his achievements at *lycée*. And now he's to be sent home like a naughty child. It hardly seems fair."

"It's for his own safety," Antony said, his voice offering no room for argument.

A discreet knock came on the door. Antony tensed, ready to spring into action to repel any intruder. He opened the door a crack and found only the familiar face of Victor Monet. "Begging your pardon, majesty," Monet said. "It is time for the coronation to begin."

Tom consulted his wristwatch. Exactly 11:00 a.m. "Yes, best to get this over and done with," he said to Monet.

As the two Rohans re-entered the Great Hall, Victor Monet placed identical sheets of paper, heavy and creamy and embossed with the seal of the House of Rohan, into their hands. In elaborate calligraphy, they found the agenda for the coronation process. It was to be chaired by Brigitte and begin with a formal introduction of the various directors and department heads of the Rohan corporation, plus a description of their fields of responsibility. This would be followed by a presentation on the current state of affairs when it came to the corporate finances and legal issues. Finally, at the very end, came the moment they'd been anticipating—the coronation.

Father and son exchanged amused glances. "Are you thinking what I'm thinking?" Tom whispered.

Antony nodded. "Very glad I helped myself to those refreshments you provided for the students. I don't think I could sit through all these reports and presentations on an empty stomach."

Tom made it a point to project calm confidence as he took his place in the chair in front of the altar and faced the imposing assembly of Rohan corporate department heads, the five directors, representatives of the six groups having a major financial interest in the Rohan empire, and crews from four television networks. Just a formality, he told himself. It will be over soon enough, and then everything will be back to normal.

Just as he was finishing that reassuring thought, a woman rose and introduced herself as Alexis Montague, the chief legal counsel for the Rohan corporation. Unfortunate circumstances had given her a body that was both short and stout, and the boxy business suit she wore did little to camouflage her figure faults. Her blonde hair was styled in a short, severe cut. Lips that seemed to bear a perpetual frown bore lipstick in a harsh, deep red shade. Tom had heard that Madame Montague's close associates referred to her as Sandy, but he could not imagine addressing this formidable woman by such a nickname. Though Tom did not like to think ill of any human being, he decided the Lombardi men were paragons of warmth and innocence compared to Madame Montague.

"There shall be a change in the agenda," Madame Montague announced. "Victor Mont will chair the proceedings. You are excused, Brigitte."

The older woman was far too elegant and poised to show any upset or to raise any objection. She merely nodded, uttered a cool, "As you wish, counselor," and yielded her spot to Victor Monet.

Tom looked at Antony to see if he felt any apprehension over this development, but like Brigitte, he wore a mask of polite indifference. So be it, Tom thought, reminding himself that it really didn't matter who chaired this exercise in formality.

"Furthermore," Madame Montague continued, "A new agenda item will be inserted right after item two, which was to be the roll call and introduction of the staff."

She gave a dramatic pause, presumably to let Tom sink into tension and worry over this new agenda item.

Madame Montague glanced at a legal pad, then intoned, "This agenda requires Monsieur Rohan to provide proof of his claim to be the King of Rohan. He must show the actual birth certificate and legal identification, not just photographs." She made a dismissive wave of her hand toward the screen where the castle historian had been projecting images of the Rohan family's legal documents. "Plus the land certificates bearing the Carolingian seals and the Duke's royal seal, and—"

Another dramatic pause as nervous silence filled the Great Hall. "He must produce fifty Rohan coins."

CHAPTER TWELVE

Tom felt his stomach drop at this dramatic turn in the proceedings. Too much to hope for, he thought, that this coronation process would take place quietly, without drama or controversy. He knew he was up to the challenge, but all-in-all, he wished he could avoid unpleasantness and get back to the things he held dear: his family and his research.

"Motion!" A familiar voice rang out from the middle of the hall. Tom felt his spirits rise. "I have a motion."

"Identify yourself and proceed," Madame Montague said in an icy tone.

The owner of the voice rose and said with strength and confidence, "I am Julia Rohan, the Paris Seventh District Circuit Court Deputy Judge. I also happen to be the second child of the gentleman before you, Maximal Oto Thomas Rohan."

The assembled corporate directors, department heads, guests and news media buzzed with shock. Tom's heart filled with pride at the bravado and brilliance of his eldest daughter, as well as the boldness of this stroke, finding and piercing its target right from the beginning. *Well played, Julia!*

Julia continued, "Let the official record reflect that the original agenda was changed at the last possible moment. I demand proof that the appropriate process was followed to amend the agenda in this unusual manner, and an explanation as to why it was done."

Madame Montague looked at her fellow directors for direction, but found none. Sounding unprepared and nervous, she said, "As you wish. The explanation is a simple one, really. Victor Monet is already the Director General of the Rohan organization, so the board decided he is the logical person to chair the proceedings, and not Brigitte."

"What about this trumped-up requirement for proof of identity?" Julia persisted.

"The board of directors has decided this issue is too crucial to be handled lightly."

"Even after the castle historian verified all of my father's statements?" Julia folded her arms and stared down Madame Montague. "Not one discrepancy was found. Your delaying tactics are without foundation."

"Nonetheless, it is prudent that we pursue a diligent authentication process."

"Objection!" This time, the interruption came from Brigitte in her role as Director of Operations, in charge of the administration and daily operation of the castle. "The only reason you are bringing in these last-minute so-called requirements is because of that interview on France 24 by Duchess Marie de Coucillon."

"Duly noted," Madame Montague said sullenly.

"Duly noted?" Julia put in. "Let the record state that even the Duchess Marie de Coucillon has confirmed my father's story. She married him when she was sixteen and he was forty-seven. This man seated before you is without question who he says he is, Maximal Oto Thomas Rohan."

Madame Montague's bearing brought to Tom's mind someone with her back was pressed against the wall, no escape. "Yes, well," she said defiantly, "if a television news program is making such an extravagant assertation, then all the more reason that we should scrutinize Monsieur Rohan's claim to the letter. Furthermore—" those red-painted lips took on a sneer—"even his own wife and children were not aware of his claim. Why would he keep such a secret from his own family?"

Victor Monet chose this moment to throw himself into the verbal fray. "The updated agenda presented to us by our learned counsel is sound and prudent. Let us proceed."

*　　　*　　　*

At the exact moment Tom and Antony had been discussing the need for a circle of trust in the situation room, a black Citroen C6 had pulled up to Castle Rohan and Victor Monet's twin brother had raced across the drawbridge. Now Gabriel Monet sat in one of the upper balconies and observed the drama being played out between the Rohan family and the corporate attorney in the hall below.

He caught the eye of his twin brother and sent a silent signal. *You didn't think you could get away with this so easily, did you? Thwart all my plans to take over the Rohan fortune? Not without a fight!*

While Gabriel Monet's signal and bearing exuded power and menace, inside he squirmed with discomfort. For sitting right behind him were two men whom he recognized from the Lombardi crime syndicate—Big Bobby and Alex. He had no idea what he had done to offend the Lombardi, but he knew all-to-well that the gang was ten times more powerful than all of the muscle he could put together, and at least ten times more brutal.

For some reason, the Lombardi had taken an interest in Gabriel Monet. And one thing he knew for certain—they could be a deadly foe.

*   *   *

Back on the floor of the Great Hall, Victor Monet announced that the proceedings would move to the first agenda item: the formal roll call of the directors and key staff members, and a description of their responsibilities.

Brigitte, as the Director of Finance and the operation of Castle Rohan, was the first named.

Then came Victor Monet as Director of Human Resources and Public Relations, as well as the current Director General. Tom knew that Victor and his twin brother, Gabriel, were the illegitimate sons of Pierre Rohan by his mistress, who had the last name of Monet. But beyond the fact of his birth and his official job titles, Tom was unclear on where Victor's loyalties were positioned. General Miliot vouched for Victor Monet, but Tom wondered if the man really could be trusted. On the one hand, he came across as antagonistic, critically challenging the authenticity of Tom's claims. And yet, Tom had a good feeling about Victor Monet, his instincts telling him that deep inside, Victor Monet had his best interests at heart.

Alexis "Sandy" Montague was the next to be introduced and to describe her duties as Chief Legal Counsel. She was followed by a young woman named Chloe Durand, who enthusiastically outlined her duties as Director and Curator of Rohan History and Art, and then by a cheerful middle-aged woman who identified and described herself as Sophie Laurent, Director of Special Projects. What felt like an endless string of introductions of department heads and key staff members continued until Tom wondered if this item on the agenda would ever come to a conclusion.

End it did, giving Tom the opportunity to issue a heartfelt thank-you to all of these professionals who had dedicated their time and expertise to keep the Rohan corporation running smoothly.

"And now," Victor Monet said with gravity, "we come to the second item on the agenda, the authentication of Monsieur Rohan's identity. As our attorney has informed us, we shall require actual birth certificates and identification documents, not photocopies, ten or more land deeds with the Carolingian seal and the Duke's seal, and fifty Rohan coins."

Brigitte rose and said, "Before this item moves further along, I make a motion for clarification as to this so-called requirement for proof of identity. On what legal basis is it being made?"

"Now, now," Tom said, calmly and mildly. "Let us all be respectful of each other's opinions and viewpoints. I feel confident the Rohan family can provide the proof the attorney requires."

This peace offering brought murmurs of approval from the assembled dignitaries, while Victor said, somewhat slyly, "Very well. We shall respectfully proceed."

Tom made eye contact with his wife, who was seated in the front row and had been quietly watching the drama unfold with nervous anticipation. With a little wink in her direction, he said, "Antoinette, I assume you packed my briefcase, yes?"

"I most certainly did not," she said, immediately picking up on the game. "This is supposed to be a relaxing and restful family holiday, not a business trip. Or have you forgotten that?" She finished with a defiant toss of her long black hair.

"Quite right, *ma cherie*." Tom turned to Victor Monet. "I had my briefcase hidden under my overcoat when I arrived at Castle Rohan this morning. As you have just heard, I had to keep it a secret from Madame Rohan or I would have had to face her disappointment in ruining our family holiday. I believe you will find it where I stashed it, inside the sideboard in the Duke's private dining room. Please, if you would be so kind, send someone to fetch it."

Victor nodded to one of the docents, still in her medieval costume, and she scurried off to fulfill the request.

Tom knew that later, he would owe his loyal wife an explanation. She'd been absolutely right—he hadn't packed the briefcase on their original journey to the village four days previous. At the time, he'd agreed with her—this was to be a relaxing and fun-filled family reunion, nothing more.

But after the assassination attempt in Paris, the situation became all-too-clear. Much more was at stake: the safety of his family for one, and the stability of the world's financial markets for another. So, in the Lombardi limousine on the drive from the farmhouse-hideout to Castle Rohan this morning, he'd instructed Alex and Big Bobby to make a quick stop at his home to retrieve certain documents from his safe and place them carefully in the briefcase.

When this was all over, he promised himself to give Antoinette something extra-special for behaving so admirably throughout this ordeal. Perhaps he could arrange for a *real* family reunion to make up for the one that had gone so terribly awry. A small, peaceful island in the Aegean where no one could find them sounded very inviting to Tom at the moment.

If they managed to survive this one.

The docent returned several minutes later toting a vintage Louis Vuitton briefcase. It had been a gift to Tom from his parents when he had earned his PhD. Though Tom would have chosen something far less ostentatious for himself, he cherished the piece as a reminder of the loving generosity of the givers. He took meticulous care of the briefcase and, as Antoinette well knew, was rarely seen without it.

Now he undid the monogrammed silver clasp and withdrew a parcel. With great care he opened first a waterproof pouch, then an oversized, fire retardant envelope. Finally came an archival-quality linen wrapping. As Tom slowly undid the bindings, those clustered nearby noticed a faint musty aroma signifying items of great age that had been in storage for a very long time.

"Is this the proof you seek?" Tom asked as the wrappings fell away, revealing a small pile of documents, some in protective sleeves, some simply loose. Tom gingerly picked up the item at the top, careful to hold it by the edges.

"Behold," he said, secretly amused at how kingly he sounded. "The original certificate, signed and sealed, testifying to the birth on the twenty-fifth of March of Maximal Oto Thomas Rohan, the fifty-fourth descendent of King Rohan, the elder son of Charlemagne. The father is Raymond, Duke of Rohan, the fifty-third descendant of King Rohan. The mother is Elizabeth, the elder daughter of King Orschwill.

The corporate officials led by the ever-suspicious Madame Montague, gathered in closer to look. Some stuck out their hands, demanding that Tom hand over the documents for their closer inspection.

"Objection!" Julia said resolutely. "These are priceless, irreplaceable historic artifacts. Most are in delicate and fragile condition. This must be done in an orderly fashion under museum protocols. Each original document must be photographed and certified, and the chain of custody must be strictly enforced."

"Quite right," put in Chloe Durand, the young Director and Curator of Rohan History and Art. "You cannot just pass these things around."

She and the castle historian leapt into action, donning white cotton clean room gloves, motioning for three more experts from the History and Art Department to assist, and assembling all the components of an archeological field lab: microscope, laptop, infrared reflectography gear, and a chemical kit. Tom recognized much of the same equipment that he used daily in his pharmaceutical lab and wished he could do something to help.

After much bustling about, peering through the microscope, rapping the computer keyboard, filling pipettes with chemicals and snapping photographs, Mlle. Durand addressed the assembly in a clear, confident voice:

"The paper is genuine for the period in history. The ink is likewise authentic and shows no signs of forgery. The seals check out. All of these documents—" she waved an arm to indicate the birth and baptism certificates, the school diplomas, the identification cards, and the PhD certification arranged on the table before her—"have passed the most rigorous of tests under the circumstances. They are indeed authentic."

So poised and knowledgeable for someone so young, Tom thought as the curator continued, "In our expert opinion—and, I might add, this is unanimous—these documents provide sufficient evidence that Tom Rohan is indeed Maximal Oto Thomas Rohan. Further verification may not be necessary." The rest of the five-member team bobbed their heads in agreement as Mlle. Durand made this announcement.

The Rohan corporate directors and managers, the representatives of the financial interests, and the news media didn't even bother to keep their voices down. Speculation rose and fell like waves throughout the Great Hall. Similar tumult swirled around the hotel in Strasbourg where the world's wealthiest and most powerful financial wizards kept their eyes glued on the television monitors. What will this mean for the corporation? For the Rohan land holdings? For the world's money markets?

And for the bankers, brokers and billionaires gathered in Strasbourg, adding to their nervous questioning: What will this mean for my portfolio? My shareholders? My job? And in more than one case ... my alimony payments?

When the hubbub had subsided, Victor Monet said, "Very good. The documents have been properly authenticated. Now, onward to the other required proofs."

Julia rose and spoke. "Motion! Let the record reflect the findings of the team of experts. 'These documents provide sufficient evidence that Tom Rohan is indeed Maximal Oto Thomas Rohan. Further verification may not be necessary.'"

Tom once again felt his heart swell with pride as he observed his eldest daughter. As a child, Julia had been quiet and shy, just like her mother. Like Antoinette, she had long, glossy black hair that cascaded down her back and around her shoulders. Now his little girl had transformed into a tower of strength, a beacon of justice.

With a look of gratitude to Julia, Tom carried on with his usual serene dignity. "As you wish," he said to Victor. Tom's hand made another trip into the briefcase, this time pulling out a box of microfilm. "My apologies for last century's technology, Is there any chance you might have a microfiche reader on the premises?"

Victor nodded once again to two of the docents. After several long moments passed, they returned, trundling a large, heavy machine on a cart. "Sorry for the delay," one of them said, panting. "Had to go all the way to the basement storerooms to find one of these."

The elderly castle historian threaded Tom's film into the machine, while the younger members of the authentication team watched in curiosity, obviously never having seen such a device before. They huddled around the screen as the historian slowly turned the crank.

"I keep meaning to digitalize this material," Tom said with a rueful chuckle as the experts continued with their meticulous work. "But you know what they say, out of sight, out of mind."

At last the historian raised his head from the bulky machine and spoke in an awe-struck voice. "These are twelve genuine Rohan land deeds with the proper Carolingian seals and Duke Raymond's certifications."

The hall hummed with excitement at that pronouncement. Most expressed approval and satisfaction with this finding, though a few disgruntled comments could be heard.

"This proves nothing," Madame Montague grumbled. "These are just microfilm copies of the deeds, easily faked. Where are the originals and why are they not here?"

"As to where—in a safe deposit box in my bank back home in Dijon," Tom answered smoothly. "As to why—I would have made a detour to the bank to pick them up, but my driver and security detail—" here he paused and dipped his head in acknowledgment toward Big Bobby and Alex in the second balcony—"convinced me that we needed to arrive at Castle Rohan in all due haste. Given the present circumstances, it seems they gave wise advice."

Several in the hall smothered laughter with their hands at Tom's sensible and reasonable explanation, while Madame Montague seated herself with a little "harrumph" of dissatisfaction.

"I believe we have seen more than enough evidence," Victor said, clearly humbled. "I move that we call a halt to the verification process and declare the present evidence to be sufficient. After all, fifty gold coins are very heavy and of course very, very valuable. It simply isn't practical to travel with them."

Madame Montague was on her feet again, the blazing color on her cheeks a match for the dark red lipstick. "Objection! Verification of fifty gold coins is on the agenda and is part of the legal verification process. We must not deviate from protocol. Due diligence demands that we see proof that Monsieur Rohan is in possession of the fifty Rohan coins."

Victor, obviously annoyed at having his authority questioned, declared, "With all due respect, we are fundamentally in a verification process. When Monsieur Rohan gave his prayer, the castle historian determined that he is, indeed, Maximal Oto Thomas Rohan. If that is not enough to satisfy you, Duchess Marie de Courcillon stated unequivocally on national television that this man is Maximal Oto Thomas Rohan. If you require still more proof, our team of experts confirm the authenticity of his two rare pieces of identification. Likewise, the experts have determined that the Carolingian deeds are authentic."

As Victor continued to speak, Tom reminded himself to keep breathing evenly and sent a silent message to Victor. "Stay calm and in control. Do not let them rattle you. As the Americans would say, keep your cool."

Victor finished with a dramatic sweep of his arm. "Enough! We will make ourselves look foolish if we ask Monsieur Rohan to produce fifty gold coins."

One of the board members who had thus far remained silent rose to speak. He was a relatively young man, late 30s, and came across as far too serious and hidebound for his years. "Objection!" he said. "The verification of fifty gold coins is on the agenda. A true king would not have sold his coin to an antique shop—it is a disgrace! As a matter of fact, two members of the board hold Rohan coins, and there is a possibility of a third. Therefore, it is impossible that this man would be able to produce fifty gold coins."

The harangue was interrupted as a French government security squad in full tactical gear marched into the Great Hall with a loud clattering of boots and chattering of two-way radios. Their leader was a tall young man whose muscles strained against his camo jacket. He must be Major Dumas, Tom thought. Antony had told him back in the Situation Room that Major Dumas would be in charge of all local police and security.

Major Dumas ignored the formal courtroom-like atmosphere and strode straight up to Victor. "A word in private with you and Monsieur Rohan."

Victor called a brief recess and the three, plus Antoinette and Antony, retreated to the Situation Room.

"We regret to inform you, Monsieur Rohan, that your home in Dijon has just been burglarized," Major Dumas said. He spoke bluntly without softening the blow.

Tom groaned and dared not look at Antoinette, knowing how distressed she would be at this violation of the sanctity of the home she loved so much.

Major Dumas spoke directly to Tom. "The thieves were very thorough and methodical. A very professional job. They obviously knew exactly what they were looking for."

"Fifty gold coins," Tom said.

"It would seem so, sir. Regretfully, they found what they wanted and escaped with the loot before the local police could apprehend them."

Tom barely had time to digest this latest development in a morning of one amazing event after another as Victor was ushering them back into the Great Hall. "The vultures are starting to close in," Antony muttered to his father.

Victor called for attention and said, "The security team has just informed us that King Maximal Oto Thomas Rohan's home was burglarized this morning. The culprits got away with all the gold coins."

Gasps of shock met this unexpected announcement as Victor continued, "As the chair of the corporation, I have determined that we have more than sufficient evidence and authentications that Monsieur Rohan is who he claims to be, King Maximal Oto Thomas Rohan. I move that this meeting be adjourned. The financial reports and any comments by financial interests in attendance will be tabled until tomorrow. Any objections? Motions?"

Tom normally shrank from the spotlight, much preferring to work in quiet anonymity in his lab and spending precious free moments with his family. But now, he found himself secretly enjoying himself as he observed the consternation that he—the unassuming pharmacist—was creating among these assembled dignitaries.

In a cheerful tone, Tom spoke. "Chair, might we have another two or three minutes to produce the Rohan coins?"

Once again, the hall broke into controlled chaos with much whispering among the directors, managers and news media. Then they settled themselves as Tom confidently strode to the stone wall. He ran his hands along the rough surface as if testing for cracks or weaknesses. Satisfied that he'd found the correct one, he used both hands to wriggle the stone loose.

Exclamations of wonder followed as Tom placed the stone onto the floor. He then removed a second stone that had been hidden behind the first, revealing a small cavity roughly the size of a modern wall safe that one would hide behind a painting. Tom thrust in both hands and with great care, retrieved a box with a curved lid. With its cracked wood and tarnished brass fittings, it resembled nothing so much as an ancient pirate's treasure chest.

Tom smiled as he placed the box on a table and said. "You forget, I grew up in this very castle. I know every hidden passageway and secret hiding place."

Then he made a little bow toward Antoinette and said, "*Ma cheri,* would you give me the great pleasure of doing the honors?"

"With pleasure," she replied, clearly enjoying her husband's moment of triumph.

With great delicacy to preserve the integrity of the relic, Antoinette undid the clasp and pushed back the curved lid. Following Tom's lead to maintain the suspense, she ever so slowly tilted the box forward so that everyone in the hall could see the glittering contents.

The atmosphere was positively electric as the collected dignitaries began to fully understand what they were seeing. Gold coins! Safely hidden away in Castle Rohan all along!

Tom spoke to Victor. "You will, of course, have escrow verify the certification of each coin. I fully trust there will be no difficulty. But first, my dear wife and I must count them as the assembly bears witness."

Those closest to the front of the room could clearly sense the sparks that flew between the couple as Antoinette removed coin after coin from the box, held it aloft and handed it to Tom, who announced, *"Un... deux..."* It was if they were newlyweds once again, loving each other's company as they playfully worked on a joint project.

A hush fell over the vast chamber as Tom solemnly intoned, *"Quarante-neuf."* Forty-nine.

The crowd waited in breathless expectation for Antoinette to triumphantly withdraw the fiftieth Rohan gold coin from the chest and hold it high, and for Tom to voice the magic word—*Cinquante!* Fifty!

Instead, Antoinette lifted the box with both hands and turned it upside down. She gave it a little shake for dramatic emphasis. Nothing fell out except a few puffs of dust.

In the stunned silence that followed, the director who'd earlier raised objections and two other directors leapt to their feet, their voices competing to be heard. "We can help you ..." "My people have access to the fiftieth coin..." "...of course, there will be certain expectations if we assist you..."

Through all these attempts at reasonable compromise at best and outright extortion at worst, Tom remained cheerful and serene,

Antoinette matching his regal demeanor. In a calm, thoughtful voice, he said, "Only forty-nine coins. How disappointing. Ah, well ..." he gave a little shoulder shrug "...I never came here with the intent to reclaim the throne. I only wanted to provide a memorable reunion for my family. I had no idea I'd be upsetting the world money markets, nor that I would be creating so much consternation for you fine people who have gathered here today."

The young director who had raised the original objections asked to be recognized. "I represent a consortium that now owns the coin that you sold to the dealer in Paris. We paid two million Euros. I understand you received two hundred thousand Euros for it. It would seem," he said with a little chuckle, "that you made a very poor bargain. And now you no longer have the fiftieth coin. But we do."

A second director rose to speak. He was tall and angular, seemingly all arms and legs, and spoke with slight German accent. "We are also in possession of a Rohan gold coin. We have information that indicates the Duchess Marie de Courcillon stole one from you. That is why she was so reluctant all those years to disclose whether you were still alive or where you were living."

Next a white-haired director who stood slowly and leaned on a cane had this to say: "My group also has a gold coin, one that you gave Brigette when you left the castle to live on your own."

Brigette could be heard weeping in the background. "I am so sorry, my lord. I sold it for a handsome sum to raise the money to purchase a home and to feed my family."

Another shock rocked the Great Hall. Three factions, each claiming to hold the fiftieth Rohan gold coin? Plus the coins stolen from Tom's home in Dijon—how could that be?

Tom's equanimity remained unruffled throughout the tumult. "Now, now," he teased. "No one ever said there were *only* fifty Rohan gold coins, did they?"

He turned serious as he realized he now faced at least three powerful entities that did not want the King of Rohan to exercise his power of attorney over the vast real estate holdings. He kept the smile on his face as he said, "One gold coin from each of you will enable me to exercise my power of attorney over the Rohan land holdings."

He paused to let each of the three directors ponder the significance of this, then said, "We shall begin the negotiations in private, one-on-one, tomorrow morning."

Before anyone could react to Tom's pronouncement, Victor addressed the assembly.

"Excellent plan. The financial interests and those with related issues will meet tomorrow morning at ten. Brigitte shall be the chair. Now, thanks to all of you, we have the great pleasure to confirm Doctor Tom Rohan is our King Maximal Oto Thomas Rohan. He is our lord!"

This was greeted with a mixture of applause and grumbling. The director who represented the investment group that had purchased the gold coin from the shop in Paris said, "With all due respect, Doctor Rohan presented only forty-nine Rohan coins. That is one coin short of the required number. We, as the board of directors, reserve the right to challenge the validity of his qualification."

Victor waited for this motion to be recorded in the meeting minutes, then pounded the gavel and declared, "I, Victor Monet, as chair of the Rohan corporation and having performed all due diligence, confirm Doctor Tom Rohan is King Maximal Oto Rohan. He is our lord. Meeting adjourned!"

A collective sigh of relief arose from the hall as everyone, regardless of the factions they represented or opinions they held, let the tension of the morning dissipate. No matter what surprises lay in store for the afternoon or later, at least for now they could move about, consult with each other in private, and catch up with their emails and text messages. The scene was not so tranquil at the hotel in Strasbourg, where the world's financial leaders shouted and gesticulated, behavior better suited for the commodities trading pit than a luxurious French hotel. News broadcasts from around the world broke in with breathless bulletins with updates on the developments at Castle Rohan.

Just as the directors, corporate managers and news media were about to begin exiting the Great Hall, they paused, realizing something of great import was about to happen. They returned their attention to the ornate altar at the front and saw Victor Monet leave his chair, walk to the right of Tom, fall to his knees, and declare, "My lord, King Maximal Oto Thomas Rohan."

Tom touched Victor on the head and shoulders and said, "My god and the Rohan ancestors bless you. Please stand."

Just as he had earlier that morning, Victor pulled Tom's hand under his suit jacket so no one could observe and the pair exchanged the secret signals that Tom had learned from his father as a boy. Victor repeated his message that he was a protector from the Carolingian Sacred Heart, and that five others were available to provide protection. Tom responded with thanks and requested to meet the protectors, while Victor said the time was not right for them to reveal themselves.

Tom immediately grasped the situation. Five of these protectors must be connected with the French government and thus could not disclose their affiliation with a secret society, as it would cause a serious conflict of interest when it came to their loyalties. They would be torn between their duties to the government of France and their oaths to the Carolingian Sacred Heart.

Aloud, Tom said to the occupants of the Great Hall, "May god and the Rohan ancestors bless all of you!"

Tom seized the moment to reflect on the knowledge he had on the Carolingian Sacred Heart. This much he knew: The order consisted of sixty elite members with five elected councils chaired by General François Miliot, the chief of staff of the French Armed Forces. He also knew that Victor Monet was a member of the order and could be trusted, even though he outwardly appeared align with his gangster brother, Gabriel.

The latter was quite possibly the most significant of all—Gabriel Monet and his vow to bring down the House of Rohan. How ruthless was he and how much power did he really wield? Tom had a feeling he'd be learning the answers to that question all too soon.

Victor made a motion as if to withdraw his hand, but Tom grasped it firmly. Still using the secret code, he sent a message to his half-brother. "Lord bless the Carolingian Sacred Heart. Lord bless the Carolingian knight who stands before us."

The dignitaries watched in astonishment and confusion as tears streamed down Victor's face. The new king had just given him the highest of honors—a knighthood. As for Tom, he felt a huge wave of relief knowing that he had the top manager of the corporation, and the ever faithful André, firmly in his camp.

While the corporate directors and department heads were unaware of what had passed between Victor and Tom, they sensed that something momentous had occurred. Regardless of loyalties, they all lined up behind Victor and bowed their heads to the new king as Tom said a loud voice, "Thank you each and every one! May god and the Rohan ancestors bless all of you."

So that settles it, Tom said to himself. *I really and truly am the King of Rohan.*

He had assumed he would have to endure a long, elaborate coronation pageant and was glad to have escaped such a fate. As a quiet and private individual, Tom never enjoyed being in the spotlight for too long.

The hall slowly emptied and Tom made his way back to the Situation Room with the unsettling thought that a public coronation ceremony, with all the attendant pomp and drama, would be the least of the dangers he and his family were about to face.

CHAPTER THIRTEEN

Gilbert Rohan remained rooted to his chair in the family section of the Great Hall, unable to move. In all of his eighteen years, he had never experienced such a roller-coaster of emotions. If he didn't know better, he would assume he'd just woken up from a long and disturbing dream. What had started in the morning as a much-anticipated exclusive, behind-the-scenes tour of Castle Rohan had ended at the noon hour with the revelation that his father was the long-lost King of Rohan, that he'd inherited vast riches, that the family home in Dijon had been burglarized, and that the Rohans must be facing great danger. Why else was the family section surrounded by all these soldiers in camouflage uniforms and tactical gear? Not to mention those large, swarthy men who reminded Gilbert of the thugs in gangster movies.

If my father is a king, Gilbert mused, *then what am I? A prince? Just wait until everyone at school hears about this!*

He was roused from his thoughts by his older brother Antony tapping his shoulder and giving a gruff order. "Move it, *petit frère.*"

Gilbert obeyed, following a line of family members entering a room at the back of the chamber. He'd watched plenty of scenes of corporate board rooms in movies and on the news, and that's what he thought of as he stepped through the door. This particular chamber, however, seemed much more luxurious and contained far more sophisticated electronic devices. Though a relatively large space, it soon took on a cozy atmosphere when all of the seven Rohan offspring, their spouses and children, managed to squeeze inside. Some of the smaller children ended up sharing a chair, and most of the men leaned against the walls. Gilbert joined them, offering his seat to two of his young nieces.

Gilbert didn't even have a chance to wonder what surprises awaited him next. As soon as Antony had finished sweeping the room for listening devices and declared the place secure, Gilbert's father began speaking from the head of the conference table.

"As some of you already know, I was kidnapped in Paris and an attempt was made on my life. That's why I was missing for those two days while all of you were enjoying your family fun time." Papa paused, a wistful look on his face. Then his expression turned grave. "I was the victim of a carefully-laid trap, lured to Paris under false pretenses. We believe it was connected to the Rohan gold coin I sold to finance our trip. Unfortunately, when a Rohan coin resurfaced in the marketplace after all those years, it tipped off certain parties who do not, shall we say, have our family's best interests at heart."

Papa's concerned expression eased somewhat. "Fortunately for me, and for all of us, a second faction became aware of the plans of this first group. They rescued me and gave me shelter in a safe house until the time was right to put in an appearance here at Castle Rohan."

Gilbert observed the worried looks and whispered conversations among his brothers and sisters. "What does this mean for us?" they were asking. "For our children, for the safety of our families?

Antony stepped in to answer their concerns. "No question, the situation is dangerous. We must take these threats seriously. But we are surrounded by the local police, the General Directorate for Internal Security, and by the elite tactical squad of the French Armed Forces. Plus, we have the protection of two secret guards that our grandfather kept on permanent assignment to our family."

Gilbert looked around, wondering who these secret protectors might be. *This day is becoming stranger by the minute. Will my friends back at school ever believe any of this?*

"Castle Rohan is probably the safest place for us," Antony continued. "Nonetheless, we must plan to vacate this sanctuary at five this afternoon. Everyone except Papa and Mama, Julia, Philip and me will be going home."

Gilbert slumped against the wall in disappointment. *They're going to make me go home? They wouldn't even be here if it hadn't been for me winning that prize at school. It isn't fair!*

He was about to blurt out these very words, but his brother Ronald, the university professor, spoke first. "I shall escort Adele and Louise and their families to their homes and make certain they arrive safely. As for Gilbert, I shall take custody of him as his temporary guardian. He is welcome to stay in our home until all of this is sorted out."

Once again, Gilbert came close to raising his voice in protest. He liked Ronald well enough, but the professor was almost twice his age, more like an uncle than a brother. *I'm eighteen and you're treating me like a baby*, he wanted to say. *I don't need a guardian. I can take care of myself!*

"You look like you want to say something, Gilbert," Papa said.

Gilbert picked up on the loving concern in his father's voice, as well as the atmosphere of tension in the room, and something vital shifted inside his young soul. "I think I should be allowed to stay," he said boldly. "After all, this trip was supposed to be an early graduation present. But—" He raised his hand, palm forward, to stave off any attempts at interruption—"I also understand how grave this situation is. The biggest contribution I can make to the safety of our family is to stay out of harm's way. I shall respect your wishes and gratefully accept Ronald's invitation."

The new King of Rohan wiped tears from his eyes as he rose to embrace his youngest son. "Nothing that has happened on this day could make me prouder," he said. "You are wise beyond your years, *mon fils.*"

Next Papa made his way around the room, solemnly handing each of his children a white envelope made of fine linen paper and bearing the Rohan royal seal. He explained that each contained a letter and a Rohan gold coin. "All I request is that you not open the envelope until one year has gone by, or until I expressly ask you to do so," he said after he'd finished handing out all seven packets.

"I shall add to those instructions," Antony put in. "Stay safe, and never let your guard down. And if you see men from the Lombardi syndicate near your homes, give them a warm welcome. They are friends of the family and can be trusted."

Once again, Gilbert's head swam with yet another astonishing revelation. *The infamous Lombardi gang? They've been guarding our family all this time? Unbelievable!*

Papa returned to his place at the head of the table and addressed his family. "The great wealth that we have inherited can be a wonderful thing. But it also makes us very vulnerable. So many different factions and interest groups want a piece of it. Some of them could turn to violence to achieve their aims. There could be other groups out there that we don't even know about. We're only just now figuring out all the different alliances and affiliations. Who knows what the future will bring?"

He took a sip of water and continued, his voice growing louder for emphasis. "Danger is lurking around every corner. Just consider the assassination attempt in Paris—what a narrow escape that was! As Antony says, we must never let down our guard. He is a brilliant military strategist, and I have asked him to be the key person in handling our family's security."

Papa seemed to relax, his mood brighter. "We must never forget why we are together in the first place—a Rohan family reunion! For the second time in four days, we are gathered in one place. So let us enjoy every one of these precious moments that we have."

Then he did the most astonishing thing of all. He began to laugh, his head thrown back, his eyes sparkling and his mouth turned up in an expression of pure joy. The seven offspring looked at each other, puzzled and concerned. Had the stress and excitement of the day finally unhinged the head of the family?

Papa turned to Mama, winked, and said in a mischievous voice, "I saw your mama do something naughty during the escrow process with the gold coins."

Now it was Mama's turn to laugh, a pleasant, musical sound. "I was only demonstrating my expertise with the tricks you taught me," she said to her husband.

"You always were my most brilliant student," Tom said, still in the light, teasing tone.

"What is going on?—What?" demanded Gilbert and his six brothers and sisters.

Instead of answering directly, Antoinette stuck out her left arm and loosened the cuff of her silk blouse. Out slid one of the gold Rohan coins!

The seven Rohan siblings looked at each, dumbstruck, while several of the younger cousins squealed in delight as if watching a magic show.

"You mean there really were fifty gold coins in the box all along?" Philip, the banker, demanded. "Why did you play such a trick on us?"

"It was much more than a mere parlor trick," Papa responded. "The fact is, the family is in a vulnerable position and those who claim they are holding the fiftieth coin will undoubtedly use that knowledge to their advantage. It is the secret cards they hold to gain power over us. This was my way of bringing them out into the open, discovering who is friend and who is foe. Luckily my lovely and clever wife has a few tricks up her sleeve."

"And my handsome and clever husband was the only person in that entire Great Hall to notice," Antoinette said, still giggling.

Just as quickly as it had arrived, Papa's playful mood vanished. "We do not know for certain which side key people are taking, and what their interests are. So many unknown factors that must be explored! We need to establish a trust network, and the sooner the better."

"We don't know who we can trust, nor who is on our side," Antoinette said. "They have already tried to assassinate my husband and they have robbed our home. Meanwhile, we are in the dark. It feels like we are building our core trust group from zero."

Gilbert watched as his father leaned toward Antony and said something in a low voice. He couldn't catch everything, but heard the names Victor Monet and André, and the words "core members of the Carolingian." He knew Victor was the head of the Rohan corporation, and he'd gathered from everything he'd observed in the Great Hall that the old man named André had played a key role in Rohan security over the years. He'd read in his history books about an ancient order known as the Carolingian Sacred Heart. He wasn't sure if he understood the connection, but judging from his father's tone of voice and Antony's serious look, it must be important.

While this exchange was taking place, Mama continued to speak. "We need to sow the seeds of trust and nurture them until the plants are strong and tall."

"Don't forget, we do have the police and army on our side, as well as several private groups," Antony said. "We are fortunate to have such a strong safety net surrounding us. They will be providing escorts for those in the family who will be leaving Rohan Castle and returning to their homes."

Mama turned businesslike now, issuing instructions for every castle staff member to be interviewed and their résumés reviewed, as well as inspections of the account books for discrepancies. "I suggest Julia, with her brilliant legal mind, and Philip, with his strong financial background, take the lead in this," she said.

Then she excused herself to notify Brigitte to begin checking the backgrounds and loyalties of the castle staff.

Papa turned to Antony, his eldest son and first in line to the Rohan dynasty, a questioning look on his face.

"The Chief of Staff of *Armee de Terre* has given me a two week extension of my leave," Antony said, anticipating his father's concern. "They consider this a matter of national security. Thus I am at your service, Papa."

Antoinette returned to the conference room. "Well, there is no going back," she said cheerfully. "The reality is, we are Rohans, so let us accept our fate. And for today, I propose we enjoy our time together."

She continued, "At the banquet, we should mingle with the staff and the corporate directors. Sit with them, get to know them better, establish a rapport."

Gilbert would have preferred to sit with Adele or Louise, who were closest to him in age, but he saw the rationale behind his mother's plan. In a social setting like a banquet, people let down their guard. It might prove easy to determine who was siding with the Rohans, and who to watch out for. Plus, grown-ups don't pay that much attention to teenagers and usually fail to see them as a threat.

Gilbert grinned to himself as pictured his new role as an undercover spy for the family.

As if reading his thoughts, Mama spoke again. "I know you'd all rather sit together as a family, but it's important that we get to know more about these people as soon as possible, determining who is likely to be a friend, and who a foe. After the banquet, we'll gather at the small hotel in the village where we spent our first two days and have our family reunion. Whether we're blessed with three hours together or only two, let's make the most of it and enjoy our time together."

Many smiles and nods of approval greeted this remark.

"At five o'clock," Mama said, "we will regretfully have to say goodbye to Ronald, Adele and Louise and their families, and of course our dear Gilbert. But, they will be accompanied by plenty of bodyguards supplied by our friends the Lombardis, so we know they will be in good hands."

Gilbert pictured himself arriving back in Dijon with his own personal bodyguard, just like a rock star—a bodyguard from the notorious Lombardi crime syndicate, no less—and despite the disappointment of being sent home, he couldn't prevent a big smile from spreading across his boyish face.

At 12:20, Brigitte arrived in the Situation Room to update the family on the details of the upcoming banquet. As King and Queen, Tom and Antoinette would, of course, sit at the head table. She recommended that Julia and Philip join the tables with the legal and financial departments to get better acquainted with their counterparts in the Rohan corporation and begin the process of accessing pertinent documents. Antony was instructed to sit with the Rohan security team and with André, now known as a trusted member of the Carolingian inner circle. As to the rest of the Rohan family, Brigitte urged them to seat themselves with the castle and corporate staff.

When she began discussing the financial meeting scheduled for the days to come, Philip said, "Please schedule meetings with as many of the special interest groups as possible. I will need to spend at least thirty minutes with each of them and may be asking them to come back for a second round of discussions. Make sure they understand they are to provide information as to their affiliation and relationship with the Rohan corporation. I shall also require a commercial analysis of their company, as well as details of their general and specific interests. Please ask them to bring six hard copies of their presentation and to provide an electronic copy as well."

Tom and Antoinette smiled at each other as they heard Philip speak with so much command and confidence. Once again, they had a living example as to how well they had raised their children, as well as proof of the wise choice they had made in appointing Philip as the financial expert on their team.

Brigitte then escorted the Rohans out of the Situation Room, always under the watchful eyes of the security team, and into a large banquet hall. The seven Rohan offspring and their families entered first and followed the uniformed wait staff to the tables to which they'd been assigned. As Tom and Antoinette set foot into the dining hall, each and every occupant rose to attention and applauded as the new king and queen took their places at the head table.

The room held thirty round tables, each seating eight, for a total of two-hundred forty attending the formal banquet. Each table was outfitted with the finest china, crystal and linens, and was topped with a beautiful centerpiece composed of blooms and greenery from the castle greenhouse. Tom was certain the entire seven-course meal, from *l'apertif* to dessert and *demitasse* would be of the highest quality, but he and Antoinette barely had time to savor a single delicious bite. Instead, they spent their time traveling from one table to the next as they greeted their guests. They exchanged handshakes or the traditional French kisses on both cheeks, offered words of gratitude and encouragement, answered questions as best they could, and left everyone they met—students, chaperons, corporate directors and Castle Rohan staff—feeling as if they truly had just been in the presence of royalty.

When the couple reached the table where the Lombardi dined, Big Bobby pulled Tom aside. "I just received word from my operatives,"

Big Bobby said. "They've captured the two guys who burglarized your home in Dijon."

"Excellent news," Tom said. "Who were they?"

"We think they were connected with Gabriel Monet, part of his mob, but not acting under direct orders from him."

"Interesting developments," Tom said. "Were your men able to recover the gold coins?"

"The two burglars had forty-one coins on them when my people caught them."

"Yes, that's the correct number." Tom smiled up at the large Lombardi kingpin. "You and your associates have come through for me again."

"Glad to be of service." Big Bobby made a deep bow. In a low voice, he added, "What do you want us to do with the coins, your majesty? Bring them here this evening?"

Tom thought this over and said, "Keep them at the police station for now." He uttered more words of gratitude to Big Bobby and his loyal Lombardi team, then excused himself as he realized Victor Monet was heading in his direction.

"May I re-introduce you to André?" Victor said, indicating the older man at his side. "André has agreed to assume his post as security chief of Castle Rohan, if you so desire."

"Absolutely. Accept my gratitude for your long and faithful service to my family," Tom said to André.

Victor next beckoned to a red-faced man wearing a soft, brimmed cap and tweed jacket, and introduced him as Louis, the head groundskeeper and the person in charge of all the fresh produce grown in the castle gardens. When Louis shook Tom's hand, he felt the other man making the finger signals to offer a special, private greeting. *So, he, too is Carolingian, just like André,* Tom thought. Tom smiled at both men and gave them a look to convey the message that difficult times may lie ahead, but that he had full confidence in their loyalty.

As the waiters cleared the cheese course and were preparing to serve the dessert of *Pears Belle Helene,* Tom gathered Antoinette,

Antony, Julia and Philip around him to announce that André would be resuming his traditional role as head of castle security. "I have full confidence in his abilities and his loyalty," Tom told them.

"Is it time to go back to the hotel in the village?" Antoinette asked. "So we can enjoy at least a few hours of our family reunion, like we talked about?"

Tom was about to voice his assent and to suggest that Antoinette begin to gather together the brothers and sisters and their families. Then he took one more look at the huge banquet hall, the happy buzz of conversation, the delicious aromas that lingered even after the dishes had been cleared, and the men and women who scurried about so tirelessly to make it all happen.

"Soon," he said. "But first, I propose we visit the kitchen and thank all who were responsible for preparing this memorable feast."

*   *   *

At long last, the Rohans were alone as a family unit, inside the lobby of the small hotel in the village where they'd first gathered four days earlier. Had it really only been four days? To Tom, it felt as if a lifetime and more had passed by since the family had first dined together in this unpretentious small inn.

"How shall we spend the little time we have left together?" Antoinette asked.

"I know just the thing," Tom said with a teasing smile. "And as luck would have it, it's only a short walk from the hotel."

He instructed his children and their families to change into comfortable clothing suitable for outdoor activities and sturdy walking shoes. A short ramble through the quaint village and along a tree-lined country lane brought them to a wrought-iron gate bearing a sign that read *Jardin Botanique*, followed by an admonition that this was a private botanical garden, open by appointment only.

"I made a few phone calls while you were getting into your play clothes," Tom said, thinking once again that in moments such as this, it was fun to be the king. On the downside was the constant reminder of the danger his family faced, evidenced by the soldiers and security guards who constantly followed the Rohans at a respectful distance, even in this serene setting of natural beauty.

Tom felt all of the cares and tensions of the morning melt away as he led his wife and offspring through the floral-lined paths, reveling in this world of beauty and botany, eagerly pointing out examples of the rare orchids and ferns for which the garden was famed. The younger children delighted in exploring the maze of hornbeam hedges, while Gilbert and the younger teen cousins took each other's pictures in front of topiaries shaped like dragons and other mythical beasts. Tom took in the laughter, joy and love as if it were a life-giving elixir, and would have gladly given a king's ransom to make these magic hours last forever.

All too soon, however, it was time to depart the botanical garden and return to the hotel. Tom's heart ached at the thought of saying goodbye to four of his children. *It's not right for the family to be torn apart. Is it too late to change my decision?* Then he thought about the words Gilbert had spoken that morning, about how the greatest contribution was to keep himself out of harm's way, and he realized his youngest child had been the wisest.

Now five o'clock, the moment of departure, had arrived. Ronald, Adele, Louise and their families, plus Gilbert gathered with their luggage in front of the three armored Lombardi limousines that would return them to their homes. Tom and Antoinette embraced their two sons and two daughters, holding them tightly and whispering words of love and encouragement while the drivers discreetly stowed the bags into the large trunks of the vehicles. One by one, the spouses and children climbed into the limousines, followed at the very last by Ronald, Adele, Louise and Gilbert. The doors slammed shut and the drivers started their engines.

Tom held the hand of his weeping wife and turned his back from the road, unable to bear the sight of the three long, black cars as they headed down the country lane toward the highway, finally disappearing from view, seemingly forever.

When—if ever—will we all be together again?

CHAPTER FOURTEEN

The five remaining members of the Rohan family—Tom, Antoinette, Antony, Julia and Philip—gathered in a small dining room for a light supper prepared by the hotel staff. After being able to enjoy only a few bites of the grand banquet earlier that day, the newly-crowned king and his royal wife dove into the onion soup and salad with grateful gusto.

"So wonderful to be able to relax at last," Antoinette murmured between bites.

"Agreed," Tom said. "And to be honest, I much prefer this simple, honest food with just family instead of that fancy seven-course meal in front of all those people."

"It's been quite a roller-coaster of a day for you, Papa," Julia observed. "You must be exhausted."

"I think I'm too overwhelmed by it all to notice that I'm tired," Tom said. Then he chuckled. "I can't help remembering how surprised you all were when Brigitte came forward with my sword and belt."

"It wasn't very nice, keeping that secret from us for so many years," Antoinette said, gently teasing.

"And then when you removed that stone out from the wall and withdrew the box with the gold coins—that was absolutely epic," Philip said. "Like King Arthur pulling the sword out of the stone."

And so they continued between bites of supper and sips of wine, reviewing high points of the last four days. Antoinette said, "It's just too bad, Tom, that you won't be spending the night in the king's quarters in the castle. This humble little hotel seems hardly fit for a king."

"The king's quarters are very luxurious, or so they were from my memories as a boy," Tom said. "But as long as I have my dear wife at my side, I feel as if I'm living like royalty." At this statement, Antoinette sent him an adoring look and the three grown children rewarded Tom's sentimental statement with a round of applause.

At seven that evening, just as the staff was clearing away the supper service, the concierge entered the dining room to announce that Doctor Rohan had visitors. Tom rose and greeted Victor Monet and five others. Tom recognized André, the head of security, and Louis, the combination groundskeeper and gardener. As previously, Louis wore a tweed jacket and a soft woolen cap pulled low over his forehead. The three greeted Tom with hand signals identifying them as members of the Carolingian Sacred Heart.

Victor introduced the three new faces in his entourage: Frank, a senior accountant with the Rohan corporation; Jacques, a former police chief and Brigitte's husband, and Roland, a local *gendarme*. Tom invited all six into the dining room and rearranged the seating around the long, oval dining table so that Victor, Antony, André, Jacques, and Roland occupied the chairs to his left, and Antoinette, Julia, Frank and Philip were seated to his right. Tom positioned himself at the head of the oval and placed Louis at the foot.

Tom surveyed the assembled family and advisors with satisfaction. "Thank you for joining us," he said to the new arrivals. "You have no idea how meaningful it is to me and my family to know that we can welcome you into our circle of trust. You are like family to us."

"I'm sure I speak for all of us," Victor said, "when I say the pleasure is all ours. For more years than I could ever count, we have waited for the return of the rightful heir to the House of Rohan. And now here he is, among us." He gestured toward Tom and bowed his head in reverence.

"As all of you know, I never wanted any of this," Tom said. "But now that the moment has arrived, let us enjoy each other's company and work together. This situation that I find myself in offers great opportunity as well as great danger. I propose we dedicate ourselves to making the most of the former, and to neutralizing the latter."

With that, Tom directed the wait staff to offer a celebratory round of cognac and divided the team into study groups: Antony with André, Jacques and Louis to discuss security and management issues, while Philip and Julia teamed up with Frank for an update on financial matters, including accessing documentation online, and preparing for the meetings with the various financial interest groups.

Tom and Antoinette had their own meeting with Victor, as Tom was very curious about the evolution and development in and around the castle since he had left sixty-five years ago.

"Farming of wheat and barley has done very well over the years," Victor said. "As for cattle and pork, we can hold our own with Bavaria. Many of our local farmers are branching out into organics, especially when it comes to fruit and salad vegetables."

Tom nodded his enthusiastic approval at the mention of organic farming. Victor continued, "Like much of Europe, this region experienced a huge demand for new housing after the end of World War II. For a while, it was difficult for the construction industry to keep up. Brigitte and Jacques were very lucky to find a large, two-story home in an upscale neighborhood only six to eight minutes driving time from the castle."

Using one of the Rohan gold coins to finance the purchase, Tom thought to himself. Still, he easily forgave Brigitte. It was only money, after all, and she had put it to prudent use.

"In recent years, tourism has given a tremendous boost to the local economy," Victor said. "It seems that your castle is a popular tourist destination and, as you saw this morning, the docents in their costumes are excellent tour guides."

"They are indeed," Tom said. "I just wish I'd had more time to enjoy the tour. How I would love to see my parents' flower garden, and to visit the rooms where they lived and where I grew up just one more time in my life." He felt his eyes misting as he thought about the happy times he had spent inside those castle walls so many years ago.

"Begging your pardon, majesty," Louis said. He doffed the cap out of respect, revealing a bald crown surrounded by tufts of rust-colored hair. "But I could not help overhearing. You will be happy to know that your mother's greenhouse and gardens are always well-maintained and open for visitation."

Tom beamed his approval and Louis continued, "As for your parents' living quarters, they have been sealed for the past twenty-five years, but we can do a quick cleaning and open them up for you. Will ten-thirty tomorrow morning be convenient for your majesty?"

"Only if it does not present undue pressure for you or your staff," Tom said, still not quite used to being addressed by the royal honorific, nor with his wishes being fulfilled so quickly.

Victor rose and glanced frequently at a legal pad as he announced the schedule for the next four days. "Breakfast will be served at eight tomorrow in the Rohan family dining room. Tomorrow will be devoted to preparation for the business review, which has been scheduled for the following day. After that, another day of preparation followed by a second day of business review. Brigitte shall chair all of the business reviews, and she will present a detailed plan at breakfast tomorrow."

Antoinette settled back in her chair and sipped the cognac, only half-listening to all of the planning and strategizing flying about the room. She was just happy that for the past four days, she'd had the entire family, children and grandchildren, gathered around her and that they had enjoyed many warm, loving moments, making memories that would be cherished for years to come.

If she were being honest with herself, she had to admit it was fun to actually experience the fantasy and glamour of royal life with the vast wealth and power that went along with it. But she knew her husband all too well. Sooner rather than later, he would be ready to leave all this behind and return to Dijon, to pick up his life as an obscure pharmacist of modest means. This, she knew, was what his heart and soul craved. His parents had understood this and released any hold they might have had on him. Antoinette had realized it too when she married him—it was what had made her fall in love with him all those years ago, his certainty as to who he was and how he wanted to live his life.

The only question, she mused, *is when. How soon before Tom gives all of this up and we return to Dijon?*

She also knew that Tom would refuse to accept the ancient land deeds and all those gold coins, and would return them to Rohan Castle. Likewise all of the royal titles that went along with the position of king—a man such as Tom had no use for honors that he had not earned through his own diligence and intellect. With that thought, a fresh worry crossed her mind. They would be returning to Dijon as ordinary citizens, not royalty, and after paying for this expensive trip, their finances would be in even worse shape than when they'd started out. *One step away from the poorhouse!*

Antoinette took a large swallow of the fruity alcoholic beverage in an attempt to banish the unsettling thought. She told herself that at least they'd gained not only their own family, but a large circle of trusted friends and advisors, as if the size of their family had more than doubled. *At this stage in our lives, friends and family are probably the most valuable assets we have.*

With that, she relaxed and smiled, ready to enjoy the next few days as an extended vacation, as well as to fully accept that the good times would not last forever. Tom would inform her that they would be returning to Dijon—and that moment would come very soon.

Tom observed Antoinette's satisfied smile and saw a certain look in her eyes that he knew very well. Just as Antoinette could read his every mood, Tom had grown quite adept over the years at interpreting his wife's voice, expressions and body language to the point where he could almost read her mind. Now he could tell that she was preparing herself for a talk, and when she got started—watch out! For someone normally so reserved and retiring, when Antoinette felt strongly about a subject and comfortable with the people surrounding her, she could—and did—dominate a conversation that could last three or four hours.

Knowing what was about to happen, Tom nodded and smiled at Antoinette. His three children, likewise sensitive to their mother's mood, also beamed their approval and waited in anticipation to discover what, exactly, was on her mind. Victor and his five associates could tell that Antoinette wanted to have the floor and they, too, became silent.

"You know," she began, "I had the most interesting conversation with Gilbert before he returned home this afternoon. You'll never guess what he asked me."

Ten pairs of eyes stared at Antoinette in anticipation. Tom could tell his wife was thoroughly enjoying this moment, drawing out the suspense as long as she could.

"At first, all he wanted to talk about how much fun he'd had, and of course the unbelievable surprise of discovering that his father is the head of a royal family, and how sad he felt about having to leave, even though he understood the reason why. But then…"

She paused, drinking in the eager, questioning looks on the faces of family and the inner circle of associates. Even Tom appeared puzzled.

"He asked me about the rumors of Rohan treasure hidden deep within the castle. 'Mama,' he said, 'I've heard there's an archive dating back a thousand years and more, all the way to back Emperor Lothair, a complete record up to Papa's own parents. Is it true?' That's what he asked me."

No one spoke, so Antoinette continued in a teasing voice, "These historical artifacts could be even more valuable than the Rohan gold coins. Do you suppose these rumors are true?"

If Antoinette had expected a reaction, she was not disappointed. The temperature actually seemed to drop in the room. Victor excused himself, checked the room's windows and door to guard against eavesdroppers, and positioned himself next to the entrance to make sure no one, not even the hotel staff, could come in.

"Well, I believe you just got your answer," Tom observed dryly to Antoinette. He, too, had heard rumors of hidden treasure while growing up in the castle, but had never seen any firm evidence that it existed. Still, he was enjoying Antoinette's playful conversation and didn't want to spoil her fun. "I remember Papa taking me down to a dungeon when I was seven or eight," he said. "I don't remember how I got there, but I do remember an old desk, like some sort of sign-in or registration desk." He laughed and added, "Oh, there may have been a few big bookcases. That's about all I can remember. Oh, wait—one more thing. I'm certain that's as far as Papa took me. If we'd ventured further under the castle, I would have memories of that. And I certainly would have remembered treasure if there'd been any down there."

Antoinette let her gaze fall on one Rohan staff member after another, inviting the next speaker. She stared at Victor, who moved his eyes away from Antoinette and passed the challenge on to Louis. Before long, all of the Carolingians had focused their attention on Louis, causing Tom to conclude that the groundskeeper must have a special identity or role among these six Carolingians.

Louis rose and began to walk toward Tom, moving with the energy and erect posture of a man at least ten years younger than his sixty-five years. He stopped when he stood behind Tom. The new king could feel Louis's fingers on his back, tapping out a coded message. *Do not talk about that desk or those bookshelves in public!*

While Tom digested the warning Louis had just sent him, Antoinette continued with her playful monologue. "Wouldn't it be amazing if there really was a huge treasure deep inside the castle? As for me, I'm not interested in gold or jewels. But how exciting it would be for all humanity if we discovered new historical artifacts. We Rohans could end up changing the understanding of human history—how fascinating that would be!"

Antoinette kept her gaze fixed on Louis as he returned to his seat. She said, "Wouldn't you agree, Louis, that this would be a significant find for historians and archeologists if there really is a vast archive hidden in the castle?"

Louis chuckled nervously and said, "Well, ma'am, I have heard some of those same tall tales. I suppose there might be a few shallow dungeons in the castle, and one or two might have an old desk lying around ..."

Tom couldn't help but feel amused at this exchange, knowing that Louis couldn't reveal the entire truth, but also knowing that few men could withstand Antoinette's questioning for long.

"Rumor has it that the Rohan treasure has been in existence for a thousand years," she said. "With so many people believing these stories, there must be some truth to them. Wouldn't you say so, Louis?"

Louis twisted the cap in his hands, looked left and right, and realized there was no escape from this gentle but determined inquisitor. Picking out his words slowly and carefully, he said, "Historians generally agree that Emperor Lothair lived from 795 to 855 and was sixty years old when he died. He was the eldest son of the Carolingian emperor known as Louis the Pious. He wanted to make Lothair's half-brother, Charles the Bald, a co-heir to the land the family owned and controlled in what is now France. On more than one occasion, Lothair led his full brothers, Pippin the First of Aquitaine and Louis the German, in revolt against their father."

The ticking of a grandfather clock was the only sound in the small dining room as everyone sat in admiration at Louis's vast knowledge and his ability to recite these facts from memory.

"When Louis the Pious died, the two brothers turned against Lothair," Louis went on. "This caused a civil war that lasted for three years and ended with the breakup of the empire of their grandfather, Charlemagne. This laid the foundation for the formation of the countries we know today as France and Germany."

Throughout this recitation, Antoinette's eyes never left Louis. Now she said, "That's all well and good, Louis, and easily verified by checking any good history textbook. But what does it have to do with the Rohan treasure?"

Tom was about to step in and rescue Louis from further interrogation by his wife. But then he told himself that this is France, where intellectual challenge is an art and lively discourse part of the social norm. So he sat back and enjoyed the drama being played out before him, and observed that the others in the room seemed fascinated with this obviously intelligent man being humbled by the brilliant, petite lady who happened to be married to the king.

"What does this have to do with the Rohan treasure?" Louis repeated the question. "Two things."

The Rohans and the Carolingians looked at Louis with new respect, their expressions begging him to continue. He seemed to take encouragement from his audience, breathed deeply, and said, "First of all would be the Viking invasion of France."

"Bad enough that the brothers were fighting among themselves,"

Antoinette said in amusement. "Then they had to deal with a Viking invasion. That's never a good thing."

"You are most correct, my lady" Louis said. "The Vikings were a ruthless and murderous foe. Their leader was a chieftain named Ragnar Lodbrok. He commanded a fleet of 120 ships carrying thousands of men that sailed up the Seine in 845. Perhaps you've heard of the Sack of Paris."

He paused and Tom's imagination held a vivid picture of the terror that must have been created among the Parisians when the Viking ships with their carved dragon figureheads and their armies of plunderers and marauders invaded the City of Light.

Louis went on, "Charles the Bald was king of the Franks at this point, but his army was no match for the Vikings. After plundering Paris, the Vikings withdrew only when Charles the Bald paid a ransom of seven thousand pounds of silver and gold."

"Very true, Antoinette said with a smile. "An enormous amount of wealth from the war chest of Charles the Bald. But many people believed that Lothair had a similar amount of wealth at his disposal, his own war chest if you will."

At Antoinette's bold statement, murmurs of amazement swept through the room. *Could this be real, a war chest holding that many pounds of gold and silver?*

Louis, not to be outdone by Antoinette's knowledge, went on with his tale. "When Louis the Pious lay dying in 840, he sent the imperial insignia to Lothair, who was forty-five years old at the time. Lothair took this as a sign he could claim the entire empire for himself with no regard for his brothers or half-brother. As you can imagine, the brothers did not take kindly to this and turned against Lothair."

A few expressions of agreement could be heard from the ten listeners. Louis continued, "Lothair and his nephew, Pepin II of Aquitaine, fought gallantly in the Battle of Fontenay-en-Puisaye in 841, but they were defeated. Lothair fled to Aachen. He tried again to defend his claim, but once again, the forces of the brothers were too strong. But here's where it gets interesting: Lothair had collected quite a cache of treasure and in the end, he had to surrender it to the brothers."

Louis paused to let his audience ponder the implications of this, then concluded, "This is my second reason for believing the Rohan treasure exists. Or, at least it did at one time. No one knows how long it remained intact."

Antoinette gave another one of her wise smiles and said, "You have given us two reasons to believe that Lothair did, indeed, have a war chest. History tells us that Lothair died miserably after suffering defeat after defeat in his wars against his brothers. And just like his half-brother Charles, he had to fend off Viking raids."

She looked around the room as if daring anyone to challenge her, then said, "Let us assume that Lothair's war chest does exist. Why would anyone think that the treasure is right here in Rohan Castle?"

This time, Tom broke the ice and spoke hesitantly. "For centuries, my ancestors have lived in that castle and no one has ever found anything remotely resembling a medieval war chest consisting of thousands of pounds of gold and silver. Or if they did, they never left a written record."

"Exactly my point," Antoinette said with a merry laugh. "For centuries, the people of Alsace have scoured the countryside looking for the fabled Rohan treasure. They've found nothing. Why? Because it's been hidden in the castle all along. Think about it—Castle Rohan is a huge garrison, one fortress built on top of one another on a foundation of solid bedrock. If the Rohan treasure truly does exist, what better place to hide it? It is likely right there!"

No sooner had Antoinette made her astonishing conclusion than a loud knocking sound caused everyone in the room to startle. Then they broke into nervous giggles as they realized that it was only a tree branch banging against the outer wall of the hotel in the wind—proof of the tension all were laboring under, and the power of the fascinating intellectual discussion they'd just witnessed.

"The hour is growing late," Tom said, "and I don't know about you, but this has been a busy day for me. In fact, I cannot recall any day in my life that had more amazing events packed into one twenty-four hour period—except, of course, for the day I met dear Antoinette."

He waited for the laughter and smiles to subside and said, "I propose we all do our best to get a good night's rest. We shall regroup tomorrow at eight for a working breakfast in the family dining room in the castle."

With that final royal decree, Tom took Antoinette's arm and led her out of the room they'd occupied for the past several hours and toward the stairs to the bedchambers. He stifled a yawn and told himself the following day could never match this one for sheer drama—and yet, he couldn't shake the unsettling feeling that it would do exactly that.

CHAPTER FIFTEEN

"Papa, I feel as if I'm right back home in our old dining room in Dijon," Julia marveled the next morning. Tom had just finished praying and giving a short welcome speech as breakfast was being served in the family dining room at Rohan Castle.

"Indeed," Philip said. "You did an amazing job in re-creating this room here in the castle down to the last detail. I think even the scratches on the dining table are exactly the same."

"I just wish you could have been there to see the looks on their faces when they first saw this room on the tour yesterday morning," Antony said to his father. "They were so shocked I thought I might have to call the EMTs to revive some of them."

"Speak for yourself," Philip joked. "As I recall, your jaw just about dropped to the floor when you first realized that 'our' dragon was hanging from the ceiling of the castle."

Tom wished this warm, happy time could last the entire day, but of course he knew that wasn't possible. Before he'd even had a chance to spread jam on a *tartine* and enjoy a cup of *café au lait*, Victor rose to introduce Brigitte and announce that she would be chairing the review of the Rohan finances and operation, as well as an evaluation of the affiliates and special interest groups.

Brigitte then went over the upcoming schedule. This day would be spent on individual and team preparation for the financial and operational review the following day starting at ten in the morning. On the day following that, the sixth day of the Rohan family saga, she had scheduled a review of the affiliated businesses, with emphasis on pharmaceuticals, and also international investments. The seventh day would be once again devoted to preparation, climaxing on the eighth day with an evaluation in the morning of commercial property, security, and the charity fund, and in the afternoon with an inspection of the books of the financial alliances—possibly the most important one of all.

Tom felt his head start to ache just to think of sitting through all these meetings and making myriad important decisions that affected so many people's lives, but he realized that it must be done. He vowed to handle the job with the same scrupulous attention to detail that he gave his scientific research.

When Brigitte finished, Louis excused himself to finish preparing the private family quarters for Tom's visit. Antoinette turned to André and asked, "What are the chances of visiting the queen's garden and the floral conservatory? It would mean so much to my husband."

"Absolutely, my lady," André replied. "Antony and I just finished going over the security measures and I shall be happy to escort you personally to the gardens."

Tom felt his mood lighten just anticipating the chance to visit the lovely grounds he remembered from his childhood, the place that had meant so much to his beloved mother. He observed his two offspring, Julia and Philip, conferring with Brigitte, Victor and Frank on how to best access the Rohan financial and legal documents, both electronic and hard copy, and experienced another surge of gratitude at having such a competent team at his side.

"*Ma cherie*, what have I done with my briefcase?" Tom asked Antoinette.

"Inside the sideboard, just like where you put it back in Dijon when you arrive home from work every day," Antoinette replied, gently teasing.

"I am nothing if not a creature of habit, am I not?" Tom returned the affectionate mocking tone, opening the door of the lower cupboard and retrieving the well-worn Louis Vuitton case. He undid the clasp and peered inside just enough to satisfy himself that three items were still present: a roll of microfilm containing four of his father's drawings, a portable, foldable, compact microscope, and an ancient key. He felt his excitement quicken just gazing at these items, with their silent invitation of discovery, the tools for unearthing the truth behind ancient myths and historical mysteries.

Like Antoinette, Tom shared a fascination with stories of ancient treasure. And like his wife, he wasn't interested in wealth for its own sake, but rather the thrill of discovery, the chance to shine the light of truth on heretofore hidden aspects of the distant past.

The more he thought things over, Tom realized he wasn't sure who the legal owner would be should any treasure actually be found. Lothair had been born in Aachen, now part of Germany but near the border with France. The Alsace region had been fought over for centuries, tossed like a ball between Germany and France depending on the details and concessions hammered out in the latest treaty.

Would France have the rightful claim to the treasure? Germany?

Or his very own Rohan family?

Tom told himself that Antoinette had advanced very convincing arguments the previous evening as to the possibility that a great treasure actually existed deep inside Castle Rohan, certainly worth pursuing.

At the thought of his wife, Tom felt his insides tighten with dread. He never wanted to be king and had rejected his claim to the family heritage many years ago when he left home to pursue a life as a scientist and as a humble family man. Though outwardly calm, he had cringed inwardly the previous day when his personal life had been exposed for all the world to see to prove his right to call himself the king of Rohan. Sure, it had been fun when he had pulled the stone from the wall to reveal the chest full of coins, but all-in-all, he was ready to give it all up and return to his life of quiet obscurity when the next four days had concluded. He'd known with rock-hard surety that he didn't want any of this the instant Victor had announced that Doctor Rohan had passed all the tests and examinations and was, indeed, the King of Rohan.

But... what about Antoinette? He'd lived his entire life knowing he was of royal blood, and that he could reclaim the throne anytime he wished. Antoinette had only found out less than twenty-four hours ago that she was married to a king and had rightful cause to call herself a queen. How did she feel about that? She'd lived all her adult life in a small country house with him, producing seven children, barely getting by financially some years, making sacrifices and doing without—and always without complaint. And now they had the opportunity to live out their years in comfort and luxury beyond their wildest imaginations.

What right did he have to ask her to give all that up?

Tom had been so deep in thought he hadn't noticed that everyone else had cleared out of the dining room. Everyone, that is, except Antoinette.

"You have that look," she said from the entryway, her voice soft and kind. "That look you get when you're worried about something."

No time like the present, Tom said to himself. He beckoned Antoinette to seat herself in the chair next to him and took both of her hands in his. "I was just wondering how you feel about all this," he said hesitantly. "You know, being part of a royal family, living in a castle, having access to all this wealth…"

"I have to admit, I was excited at first," Antoinette said. "What woman wouldn't want to wear designer clothes and live in a castle and ride in a chauffeured limousine and have invitations to all the best parties?"

Tom's heart sank at these words, though he did find one glimmer of hope. "At first?" he ventured to ask.

"I thought about it some more. A lot, actually, last night while you were plotting and planning with Victor and André and all the rest."

"And…?"

Antoinette ran the back of her soft hand along Tom's cheek and jawline. "*Mon cheri*, I know you all too well. I know you detest being in the spotlight and would be miserable trying to run a major corporation. You cannot wait until the moment you can give all this up and go back home to Dijon. To pick up our lives where we left off, like this never happened."

"And you're comfortable with that decision? You'll support me when I announce my abdication?" Tom asked in wonder.

"Of course," she replied as if there never could have been any doubt. "Your happiness means more to me than all the wealth and power in the world."

Tom was too overcome to speak.

Antoinette continued, "All I ask is that for the next four days we enjoy all the fun and privilege of living the royal life. We'll live like a king and queen, but only for four days. Call it an extended vacation, the best adventure of our lives."

"You're on!" Tom gently removed her hands from his and stood. "Let's go out and start hunting for treasure!"

Tom and Antoinette hurried to catch up with Antony and André as they walked along the corridor opposite the family dining room. With André in the lead, they turned right and took three steps down. Tom's heart began to beat faster when he realized the faithful old guardian was leading them along the long hallway that led to the rooms that he had grown up in. Tom's father had passed away thirty eight years ago, at age eighty-eight, his mother outlasting him by six years, dying at age ninety-three. These rooms had been sealed ever since his mother's death. As for Tom, he'd not set foot in the family quarters for over thirty years.

Tom was swept with overwhelming nostalgia, so much so that he had to grasp Antoinette's arm on one side and Antony's on the other for support. Though three long decades and more had passed since Tom had breathed this air and trod this carpeted walkway, he instantly recalled every inch of it. Every step brought another fresh wave of longing and grief over the people he had lost.

The family living quarters were located in an upstairs corner of the castle, surrounded by a balcony and overlooking a sunny courtyard. As they drew closer, André asked, "My lord, would you prefer to enter through the inner aisle or to visit the balcony first?"

Tom knew the inner aisle would lead to a pair of seldom-used guest rooms, a recreation room and bathroom, and then the nursery, playroom, and schoolroom and where Tom had spent his childhood. Finally would come King Raymond's own chambers.

"Thank you," Tom replied. "I would like to see the queen's gardens first."

"Very well, my lord," André said, guiding the party through the door to the right. From the balcony, the four could peer through windows and see the private living quarters of the Rohan royal family. Flowering potted plants had been placed on stands at regular intervals along the balcony, so that anyone living in those rooms could look out and see a gorgeous floral display. Even though no one had occupied this part of the castle for more than a quarter-century, Tom was pleased to see that the tradition had been preserved.

Tom lingered at the window that gave him a glimpse of his childhood chambers—the cradle that had been kept in the nursery and the narrow bed that had served him during his boyhood and teen years, the desk and walls lined with books in the schoolroom, where he had spent many happy hours with his tutor, and the shelves of playthings. To Antoinette he pointed out his much-loved teddy bear, armies of toy soldiers, model airplanes crafted of balsa wood, and perhaps the most precious of all—a microscope and junior chemistry set.

"What a wonderful childhood you had," Antoinette said, for whom all of this was new. "Parents who loved you, private tutors, all the toys you could ever desire."

"I was a very lucky child," Tom agreed. "But in the end, all that mattered was the love."

"But what of your younger brother?" Antoinette asked. "The docent mentioned a younger, brother, Pierre, when we toured the Portrait Gallery yesterday."

"Ah, yes, *petit frére* Pierre," Tom said. "You see, I came along when my parents were quite young, while Pierre was a late-in-life baby. I was already away from home and out in the world by the time he came alone. I never actually met him."

Antoinette shook her head and wonder. "For the past year, the world has assumed the Rohan line had ended with the death of Pierre's grandson, Duke Michael. And then you came along."

"And then I came along," Tom agreed with a smile.

At last, the couple tore themselves away from this glimpse of Tom's early years and followed André into the courtyard. Immediately they were embraced by the radiant sunshine and the intoxicating perfume of the flowering plants. Tom was pleased to see the same shrubbery and flowers that he had remembered from his growing-up years, and that he had replicated at their home in Dijon. Though the species were common to France, they represented the rarest of breeds, with brilliant color, a longer blooming season, and more resistance to bad weather.

With great excitement, he pointed out the Café au Lait Dinnerplate Dahlia, breathtakingly beautiful with ten-inch blooms in creamy white blushed with shades of pink, peach and mocha. "No two blossoms are exactly alike," Tom said. "They make a stunning bouquet."

With the glee of a child, he strode around pots and beds, pausing to exclaim over a particularly stunning example of a Bougainvillea that climbed about the castle walls, trailing vibrant blossoms of red, purple and pink. At the rose garden, he sighed, "If only I had time to keep up with the dead-heading, I think I could have roses in bloom all year round."

Encountering a bed of impatiens, he asked André, "Are the gardeners cutting them back so they can grow and bloom from year to year?"

"Absolutely, my lord," came the reply.

"Good to hear," Tom said. To Antoinette and Antony he said, "Most gardeners consider impatiens to be annuals and only expect them to provide color during the summer months. But the fact is, with a little cutting back, they can bloom for more than one year. They do well in window boxes and hanging baskets."

"Don't forget ground cover," Antoinette said. Her knowledge of botany was almost as extensive as that of her husband. "At our home in Dijon, we use impatiens for ground cover and borders."

"So many of these plants originally came from the greenhouse at our home in Dijon," Tom said. "They almost feel like family to me."

He lingered over two cast-iron pots that held colorful impatiens and that were positioned on the ground against the castle wall. "So glad that these are still here, and in their same places, after all these years," he said.

Then Tom surprised everyone by stooping, placing both hands on either side of one of the pots, and making a zig-zagging motion, slowly moving the heavy pot away from the wall. Antony attempted to assist, but Tom waved him off.

"What the…?" he muttered to Antoinette.

She shrugged and said, "Nothing he does would surprise me anymore."

Tom maneuvered the kettle-shaped flower pot a few inches away from the wall, far enough so that all four could see that a small chamber had been exposed, guarded for many decades only by innocent little flowers. Tom rolled up his sleeve, placed his hand into the hole and retrieved a cylindrical metal tube.

Antoinette, Antony and André clustered closely and saw that instead of the smooth metal that they'd expected, the tube was covered with small bumps.

"It's known as a cryptex," Tom said, anticipating their questions. "A medieval device for hiding messages, money and jewelry." He let them study the rings of raised symbols, which they could now see were alphabetical letters and numbers. "It operates on the same principle as a bicycle lock. Line up the letters or numbers to the proper code and presto! The cylinder opens."

Tom grinned as he saw their astonished expressions. "According to legend, some of these devices even contained poison. If someone entered the wrong code, the tube would release poison gas, causing immediate death."

"Would you like me to give it a try?" he teased, knowing full well that no Rohan would ever indulge in such deadly trickery.

Tom seated himself on one of the garden benches, peered through his glasses at the letters and numbers and slowly lined up the correct Carolingian code, amused to observe his wife, son and André slowly backing away, just in case. His fingers put the final letter into position. With a soft click, one end of the cylinder popped open.

He gently upended the device and eased out a rolled piece of parchment. With great care, Tom unrolled the sheet and studied the words printed upon it in elegant calligraphy. He knew both parchment and ink had been carefully chosen to last many years, centuries if needed.

When he'd finished reading, he removed his glasses, wiped his eyes, and handed the parchment to Antoinette. "You read it," he said, his voice choked with emotion.

"Dear Maximal," she began aloud. "This message is written with great joy, because you are the only one who possesses the code to open the cryptex. Thus, it must mean that you have returned to Castle Rohan at last. Blessings to Antoinette and all of your children. You must have a large family by now, maybe even blessed with grandchildren by the time you read this. It has been many years since the photograph was taken that your father and I treasure on our nightstand. Your father had a grand, sacred mission for you to complete for the Rohan dynasty. Details may be found in the lower right corner of the second engineering drawing that your father sent you."

Antoinette cleared her throat, then continued, "Your father always wanted you to be king and knew you had the talent and temperament to be a wise and strong ruler. Yet you chose a different destiny. You were born a king, and yet not a king. He allowed you to choose the way you wished to live your life. He regretted and rejoiced at the same time. Blessings and graces to each and every one of you!"

Antoinette finished, "It is signed 'Elizabeth, the daughter of King Orschwil.' That is your mother, am I not right?" she said to Tom.

He simply nodded, still too overcome to speak.

"What does it mean?" Antony whispered to his mother.

Antoinette studied her first-born. "You're the military expert. You know as well as I do."

"A campaign of immense proportions is about to get underway."

"Very good," Antoinette said. "We've just received more proof that the rumors of Rohan treasure are not just tall tales. We're on the right track—discovery is imminent—I just know it."

CHAPTER SIXTEEN

Antoinette watched as her husband seemed to recover from the emotional cascade that had been created by the letter from his mother. He approached the second cast-iron flower pot and repeated the same zig-zag motion, pulling it away from the wall. Once again, a small chamber was revealed, containing a cylinder that appeared to be an exact duplicate of the first. Tom entered the code, the end popped open, and a piece of parchment slid out.

"Here, you read it," he said, handing it to Antoinette without bothering to glance at the words. "I don't think I can."

Antoinette adjusted her reading glasses and scanned the elegant calligraphy, obviously penned by the same hand as the previous letter. "It's very similar," she said. "It's addressed to Maximal and talks about how your father has a grand sacred mission for you to complete, and how you can find details in the lower right corner of the second engineering drawing he sent you. Then there are all the blessings, and your mother's signature."

She gave the letter a second glance. "Oh, wait. Here's something new. She says you will find a letter with additional instructions in your father's nightstand."

"Excellent!" Tom exclaimed. His face turned pink and Antoinette knew it was not from the sunshine that beamed down into the courtyard, but the sheer excitement of the discovery. "These are very promising leads as to the existence and location of the Rohan treasure. Who knows how many missing historical artifacts we will find?"

Antoinette realized that the idea of unearthing heretofore unknown historical artifacts was just as exciting to Tom as discovering a cache of gold and silver. More, even. Great wealth would just mean additional responsibility, not to mention exposing the family to danger. And in any event, Tom would not be king for long, so any discovery of treasure would be meaningless.

This last thought caused her to reflect back on the conversation she'd had with Tom earlier that morning in the dining room, how concerned he'd been, how considerate of her feelings and desires. *How could he have ever thought for even a minute that I might actually want to be a queen?* She shook her head ruefully. *Men! The Americans have a word for it—clueless.*

She found herself eagerly anticipating the next step in this amazing journey of discovery. Like Tom, she was more excited by the process than the reward, and the idea that they might unravel one of the great mysteries of history thrilled her like no prize of gold or silver ever could. *It's just like being in one of those Indiana Jones movies,* she said to herself.

"What are we waiting for?" Tom said with great enthusiasm, interrupting Antoinette's thoughts. "Time to take our first step on the path of discovery."

With that, the party left the warm sunshine and lush beauty of the garden and re-entered the castle and into the section that held the private family living quarters. With great reverence, they tiptoed slowly into the King and Queen's bedchamber. Even though this room had not been occupied for a quarter-century and more, a hushed silence fell over them, as if King Raymond and his queen might be napping, and the slightest noise might awaken their ghosts.

Antoinette marveled over the luxury of the bedchamber, which reflected both tasteful simplicity and royal opulence. A massive four-poster bed, carved in dark oak and draped in the finest linens, dominated the room. Plush Persian carpets were scattered throughout, and Antoinette was pretty sure she recognized an original Monet hanging on one wall. From a partially opened armoire, she could see gowns from the finest houses in Frances: Dior, Chanel, St. Laurent and Madame Grès, costly in their day and worth a small fortune now on the vintage clothing market. For a moment, Antoinette experienced a pang of regret over giving up all of this. She gave herself a mental shake. *This is not the life for you, and certainly not for your husband.*

Aloud she said, "These pieces belong in a museum. Think of all the history this room has seen over the centuries. It's just breathtaking."

She could see that Tom was paying only slight attention to her words, his focus solely on the clues supplied by the letters in the cryptex and the instructions to be followed. Once he had overcome his awe at entering his parents' private chamber after so many years, he headed straight for the nightstand at his father's side of the bed. Quickly he opened the three drawers that stood one atop the other, and after taking a quick glance, he just as quickly shut them.

Antoinette, Antony and André uttered sighs of disappointment when the third drawer slide shut. All three had been empty.

Tom, however, remained cheerful and undisturbed. He returned to the second, middle drawer and pulled it completely out of the nightstand. Then he rooted around with his hand and found a small, secret fourth drawer. This he opened and removed a white envelope in thick, creamy stationery bearing the Rohan family wax seal.

Antoinette crowded close, Antony and André at her side, as Tom broke the seal, and removed a single sheet of paper topped with the Rohan crest. He cleared his throat and began to read:

"Dear son Maximal:

"The happy fact that you are reading this message means that you have returned at long last to your ancestral home. Blessings and mercies on you and your family as you begin this quest to discover your Rohan heritage. This room will lead you to five locations deep underneath the castle that contain the roots of all Rohan generations since Emperor Lothair."

The four gazed downward in wonder, feeling the tremendous forces of history quite literally under their feet. Antoinette nodded, urging Tom to continue reading.

"The information you need is included on the second sheet of the architectural and engineering design drawings I sent you for the Rohan family dining room. Look near the title block on the lower right corner. I know you will not delay, nor will you shirk this sacred duty. I bequeath to you the responsibility to discover and steward the Rohan family heritage."

Tom gave the envelope another shake, and a key, obviously old and curiously carved, landed in the palm of his hand.

"He gave you the key, but where is the lock?" Antoinette wondered.

"I'm not sure," Tom answered. "But the key must be important, or why else would Papa have hidden it with this letter?" He carefully placed the key back into the envelope and slipped it into his satchel.

Tom, apparently taking to heart his father's trust that he would neither delay nor shirk, immediately reached into his satchel and withdrew the microfilm images of the original blueprints for the dining room and a 30X folding compact magnifier. "The first marker is right here in this room, just like Father said it would be," he reported with great excitement. "It's right behind his armoire."

He beckoned Antoinette to his side and placed the magnifier into her hands. "Here, you give it a look," he said. "Your memory is even better than mine when it comes to facts and figures."

"With pleasure, *mon cherie*," Antoinette responded as she accepted the device and peered through the lens. One of the major factors that had first attracted her to Tom, and that had cemented their relationship over the years, was his acceptance of her academic brilliance and his willingness to admit that in some areas, her intellect surpassed his own. While he cherished her beauty and her tender disposition, he never failed to treat her as an equal partner in all aspects of their life together.

Now she joined Tom in his conclusion that the first marker on the drawing directed them to look right behind the armoire that held King Raymond's Savile Row suits and bespoke shirts.

Just one problem—the antique piece of furniture was heavy beyond belief. Even with all four tugging and pushing, they could not force it to budge one inch, almost as if the clothing chest had been permanently affixed to the castle wall and floor.

After several moments of fruitless exertion, André said, "Louis may be the only person who can help us. He knows this castle and its secrets better than any living person on the planet." He reached into the armoire, pulled out a silk shirt, and wrapped it around his hand. Then, using the secret Carolingian hand signals, he sent a coded message to Tom. In it, he explained that Victor is only the local Carolingian leader. Louis is one of two Carolingian grand masters, the highest authority next to the King, charged with guarding the most sacred of the Rohan empire legacy.

To everyone, André said, "I shall fetch Louis at once. In the meantime, make sure no one else knows about any of this."

With that, André scurried off, leaving Antoinette to amuse herself by poking through the armoire to see if she could detect any secret doors or hidden compartments. Tom, meanwhile, re-read the letter from his father found in the nightstand. "Father must have been referring to the prior castle and the dungeon under the entrance," he said. "This is where the historical archive and objects dating back to Lothair Rohan must be stored. He's telling me it is our mission and responsibility to bring all this sacred history to the world, and to be the stewards."

Antoinette saw the look of wonder on her husband's face and the awe in his voice as he said "I never actually believed any of these legends were real. And even if they were, no one has ever told the full story after all these many years. How could anyone keep a secret like that for so long?"

He made another long study of his father's letter. "Father is clearly telling us there are five vital areas right under this very castle and that we must find them. What could these objects be and why are they so important?"

Tom then looked at Antoinette, and in a serious tone, said, "You realize this could go beyond merely interesting and curious. What we are about to undertake could be spooky, even dangerous."

"Didn't I tell you so?" Antoinette replied with a playful smirk. "This is going to be interesting and challenging. This is your chance to explore and make important discoveries. And have fun!"

André returned, followed by Louis. Antoinette was immediately struck by the dramatic change in the latter man's demeanor. Gone was the humble castle caretaker, utterly vanished. Now Louis projected an aura of firm resolve and respectful dignity. Like a medieval knight, she thought, sent here to guard us and guide us.

Louis had arrived with a duffle bag. Now he unpacked it, revealing fifteen battery-operated flashlights, a headlamp, two long ropes and five sets of industrial hand gloves. But it was the final item that caused Antoinette's pulse to beat faster.

Five facial masks, the kind used to protect the respiratory system against smoke and ash. Or deadly gasses.

Well, I wanted adventure, Antoinette ruefully reminded herself. *But I never expected anything quite like this.*

Chapter Seventeen

Tom watched approvingly as Louis emptied the duffle bag and inventoried the contents. He would have expected nothing less from a Carolingian Sacred Heart grand master, holder of the authority to guard the Lothair Rohan heritage. *My parents make a wise choice in Louis,* he thought.

Louis sent a coded signal to André, a message Tom immediately decoded. *Clear the royal living quarters. Everyone but Tom, Antoinette and Antony. Even the gardeners and housekeepers must leave. No one must see us entering the most sacred of historical passageways.*

With André standing guard at the entrance to the king's quarters, Louis positioned himself before the open doors of the armoire. He pushed the suits and shirts to both sides, then pressed his fingers against a back panel. It swung forward like a door, effortlessly and with as much ease as if it had been opened and closed many times every day instead of sealed shut for decades.

Tom felt his heart begin to race. This was the first location marked on his father's engineering drawings! Could they really be about to enter Lothair's ancient treasure chambers? The possibilities were tantalizing, the suspense almost unbearable.

With great courtesy and deference, Louis assisted Tom, Antoinette and Antony into the dresser and through the narrow back entrance.

As his eyes adjusted to the dim light, Tom became aware of a set of spiral stairs leading steeply downward, like a corkscrew drilling into the very heart of the earth. Louis donned a headlamp, giving him the appearance of a noble coal miner. He next distributed flashlights and gloves to Tom, Antoinette and Antony, choosing a larger flashlight for himself as he would be leading the procession.

"Keep your hands on the metal rail," Louis instructed. "If you lose your footing, the results could be most unpleasant."

Tom needed no further warning. He gripped the handrail as if his life depended on it, keeping an eye on his petite, delicate wife to make sure she was doing the same. Antony positioned himself in front of his parents. "Don't worry, if either of you take a tumble, I'm here to catch you," he said. Tom could tell his son was trying to reassure them, but he caught a note of worry in Antony's usual confident tone.

And so they began the descent into the mysterious depths under the castle, Tom carefully placing one foot in front of the other on the steep, narrow steps, always careful to make sure Antoinette was safe. At times, he felt more as if he were climbing down a ladder instead of descending a spiral staircase. "Maybe Louis should have given us mountaineer's ropes and harnesses," he muttered to Antoinette.

The light from Louis's headlamp momentarily disappeared. Tom was about to call out in alarm, then realized their leader had reached the bottom of the stairs and entered a new chamber.

"The air smells fresh and cool," Louis called back to the others. "That means there must be a source of good ventilation. Very unusual."

Tom, Antoinette and Antony ducked single-file under a low entryway and found themselves in a subterranean chamber carved out of the bedrock that lay under the castle.

A large wooden desk was the only furniture in the cave-like chamber. It was crafted of dark wood, large and heavy, and riddled with cubby-holes and tiny drawers. Tom wondered how on earth anyone managed to wrangle such an unwieldy item down that spiral staircase. Could it be, he thought, that it was a relic from the days when this was the first floor of the original castle? Could the desk really be that old?

A leather log book, appearing as old as the desk itself, stood on the writing surface, and Tom realized that this was the second spot that his father had noted on the engineering drawings.

Louis placed his large flashlight on the desk and said, "This log book has kept a record of the visitors to this chamber for more than six hundred years." He reverently dusted off the cover and opened it to reveal parchment pages covered with signatures and notations. "Every five years or so, the reigning King of Rohan would enter this chamber and sign the log book. He would also make a brief notation as to where he had been in these underground rooms and passages, and what he did."

Tom, Antoinette and Antony clustered around the log book, while Louis aimed the light so they could get a better look at the writing on the pages. Tom felt as if he were staring down the very timeline of history—six hundred years of Rohan royalty all captured in this one volume!

He made note that his father, King Raymond, had signed the book eleven times over his lifetime. His first visit was with his own father, and for the final two, he had been accompanied by Louis. Then King Raymond's signatures ended, and for the past twenty-five years only Louis had made the dark, dangerous journey and added his signature.

Tom took a second look at his father's notations in the book and experienced a jolt of pure shock. For there in black-and-white, his father had written, "with my son Maximal."

"But-but," Tom stammered, "I've never been this far under the castle before. Papa never took me below the first level with the desk and the log book." Moments earlier, he had been holding Antoinette's arm to make sure she didn't stumble on the spiral staircase. Now he clutched her small, delicate hand to steady himself, depending on her for strength.

"Ah, but you *have* visited this chamber before," Louis said. "Consider the date. You were but two years old, little more than a babe in arms, when King Raymond brought his son Maximal to this very spot. Of course, you would have no memory that visit."

Tom was still too amazed to say anything, rooted in place in stunned silence. He only stirred with Antoinette patted his arm and said, "I know you were a brilliant little boy, but let's face it, *mon cherie,* even you would have too young to sign your name when you were only two."

Her gently mocking tone brought Tom back to reality. His sharp scientific mind now went to work cataloging his father's many observations over the decades. For instance, he had detected a rotten egg smell upon entering ZB2, indicating the possibility of poison gas, and had turned back. On another visit, King Raymond had checked QL1 to make sure it had been properly locked.

"We know about ZB2 and QL1," Tom said to Antoinette. "Father clearly marked them on the second drawing in the set of blueprints."

"Your father, King Raymond, told me he believed there might be archives in those two locations," Louis said. "However, we never entered either of those spots together. Neither have I done so when I have explored on my own."

From his jacket pocket, Louis removed a Mont Blanc pen and handed it to Tom. "You must sign the log book as the reigning King of Rohan."

As Tom placed the point of the pen on the ancient parchment and began to inscribe his name, he felt another shiver of excitement and awe as he added a record of his existence to the distinguished pantheon of royalty through the ages.

While Louis assisted Antoinette and Antony in penning their signatures into the log book, Tom cast the beam of his flashlight across the desk and into the numerous cubby-holes. He discovered many contained documents and objects: paperweights, letter-openers, embossing devices for wax seals, a stereopticon from the Victorian era, a sextant, and other antique devices that Tom could not identify.

"Think of the historical significance of these documents and objects!" he exclaimed. "We must make a careful catalogue of all of them."

"Indeed," Louis replied calmly. "But that is another mission for another time. Today, our quest lies onward. Come."

Louis bowed when passing through the Carolingian arched gateway, then led the three visitors into the next room. An inside window covered with a metal grill gave Tom a first impression of a cell, possibly for monks, possibly for prisoners. He peered around the bars of the window and discovered a room below, roughly twenty-five by thirty-five meters in size. He perceived a shaft of sunlight and breathed in fresh air coming from the room.

Next, Tom's attention was drawn to five bookcases and the dozens of rolled documents encased in leather. This must be the royal archive!

"You are looking at the very place where the inner circle of the Carolingian Sacred Heart has met for centuries," Louis said. "Nowadays, they meet here only on rare occasions, to carry out vital business. But in medieval times, this room was frequently used as a gathering place for the knights of the Sacred Heart brotherhood."

Louis went on to demonstrate how the King could look through the window and see all of his knights and their attendants gathered in the room. "This room is accessible from the outside yard of the castle," he added. "But the path to go down directly from this cell has never been found."

"This is another spot marked by my father," Tom said. The air quality continued to be quite healthy, pleasant even, especially give how far underground they now found themselves.

Louis positioned his large flashlight so that it illuminated the bookcases. Tom could now see that the scrolls contained dates, some as far back as the eighth and ninth centuries.

"These represent an extensive library from the Carolingian Renaissance," Louis said. "The scrolls contain not just scriptural studies, but also books of art, architecture, medicine, the humanities... you will even find songbooks and stories in this collection."

"The Carolingian Renaissance? Never heard of it," Antony said.

"That's because you slept through most of your history classes. Unless the day's lesson had to do with battles or military strategy, you had no interest." That was Tom's initial thought. Aloud, he said gently, "If it had not been for the Carolingian Renaissance, western civilization as we know it might not have survived."

"Really?" Antony said. "Now you've got my interest."

"Really," Antoinette responded with a smile. "During the reign of Charlemagne, this area of what is now France saw a resurgence in study of the arts and sciences, knowledge and advances thought lost after the fall of the Roman Empire."

Antony still had questions. "Then why did it take until the

fifteenth century for the 'real' Renaissance to begin?" To his father he added, "See, Papa, I did pay attention in at least some of my history classes."

"Very good," Tom replied. "The fatal flaw with the Carolingian Renaissance is that the learning was confined almost solely to the clergy. Also, the Carolingians were looking backward, trying to revive the glories of the Roman Empire. Whereas the Italian Renaissance of the fifteenth and sixteenth centuries was much more widespread, and was truly forward-looking, taking western civilization from medieval times to the dawn of the modern era."

"And yet," Antoinette said, "we must give credit and honor to those early scholars of the Carolingian era for creating a common language and writing style. This allowed the various tribes and feudal states scattered throughout Europe to communicate with each other. And as we know, communication is the keystone for any civilized society."

Louis waited for the importance of what Antoinette had just shared to sink in, then said, "This could very well be the richest and most complete archive of the Carolingian Renaissance. Many of the scrolls were rescued from the village when it was buried by an earthquake in October of 1356."

"The earthquake." Antoinette said. "I'd almost forgotten about that."

"Indeed, it decimated all of the Alsace. And what Mother Nature didn't destroy, the Armagnacs took care of during the civil war with the Burgundians."

Tom could stand it no longer; the temptation to examine one of these ancient scrolls that had survived so much devastation was simply too great. He began to pull one of the leather-bound scrolls from the shelf, sending up a cloud of dust.

Louis's arm immediately shot out, placing a firm, restraining hand around Tom's own. "Stop, your majesty, I beg of you," he implored. "These scrolls have not been stored in climate-controlled archive conditions. The slightest touch and they could disintegrate. Then all would be lost."

Tom reluctantly removed his hand from the scroll and allowed

Louis to ease the relic back onto the shelf with great care. "I suppose you're right," Tom said with a sigh. "Let the experts come in and handle them. If only..." He could almost feel his fingers itching with desire to unroll and read just one of those recordings of a much earlier time, discover the secrets it had been hoarding for so many centuries.

Only by promising himself that he would return with a team of experts could Tom reluctantly tear himself away from the bookshelves and their tempting treasures. Louis led the trio to a huge engraved Carolingian shield that hung on the wall next to the bookcases. Tom recognized yet another landmark from the details on his father's blueprint and knew they would find another secret entryway behind the shield.

As the beams from their flashlights crossed the shield, the cross seemed to sparkle and shimmer. "Is that gold?" Antoinette whispered in awe.

"Absolutely," Louis replied. "Only the finest materials are used by the Carolingian Sacred Heart."

Louis then placed his hands on three stones and made a turning motion, almost as if he were working the dial to open a safe. "Locking stones," Tom whispered to Antoinette.

"I've heard of such things, but never actually seen them in action," she said, just the stones clicked into place and the huge shield swung forward, revealing another passageway. Much like the doorway hidden in the armoire in the royal bedchamber, the shield moved effortlessly, with no creaking or groaning, as if as light as a feather—a feat of medieval mechanical engineering that Tom could only marvel over.

Antoinette took Tom and Antony's hands in each of her own, and all three inhaled deep breaths of anticipation as they ventured through the passageway in back of the shield. Did the fabled Rohan fortune lie behind this door? Would their next sight be of a pile of gold bars and coins?

Instead, what lay before them was yet another spiral staircase, leading downward. Louis must have picked up on their unspoken disappointment, because he said, "Patience, my lord and lady.

Remember, Castle Rohan was built twice. The one that you visited yesterday was built later, on top of the prior castle. We are now entering the heart of the earlier castle."

Once again, the party made a cautious descent down the spiral staircase. In the rocky chamber at the bottom, Louis aimed his light at a sturdy table holding a wooden structure that reminded Tom of the scale models one might see in a museum. "This is a re-creation of the first Castle Rohan, built by Lothair in 844," Louis said. He then aimed the light on a series of tiered stone structures running horizontally along the floor of the chamber. "What you see now is the original footing of the 844 castle," Louis said. "Four years of hard labor was required to build the castle that you see in the scale model. Even so, it was much smaller than Lothair's half-brother's fortress in Paris. As you may recall, by 844 Lothair had given up his other bases in the north."

"This is amazing," Antoinette said as she ran her hand along the rough stone. "Just think of the base of this structure lasting for over one thousand years, supporting the castle all that time."

"And so well preserved," Antony added. "Truly remarkable."

Tom, meanwhile, was lost in a memory, fuzzy around the edges, but still flickering in his consciousness. "I've been here before," he said in an awestruck whisper. "I remember seeing this with my father."

"I'm afraid that is impossible, my lord," Louis said. "The log book clearly states that you entered these chambers only once, with your father when you were three years old. You couldn't possibly remember."

"But I do remember," Tom said with a wistful smile. "Father carried me in his arms down the spiral staircase and when we reached this chamber, he set me down and let me explore. I remember climbing up on the first level of the footing and jumping off. At first, Papa was afraid I might hurt myself, but when he saw how much fun I was having, he let me do it over and over again."

His story was rewarded with skeptical nods from Louis, Antoinette and Antony. "I know it seems impossible," Tom told them, "and to be honest, I only recall bits and pieces. But I do remember climbing on the footing of the original castle very clearly. 'Just like a Rohan,' my father said."

Tom gazed at the solid stone base of the castle, wishing that for just one moment he could be a child once again, enjoying innocent pleasures like climbing and jumping, always with the secure knowledge that his dear papa was there to keep him safe and secure. Then he pushed the desire to the back of his mind, telling himself to shoulder his adult responsibilities. He followed Louis to a passageway to the right. "According to my father's directions, this must lead to the QL room," Tom observed.

"Quite right," Louis said as the party halted in front of a large wooden door with a metal frame. The three Rohans stood, stunned, each uttering oaths and exclamations of sheer surprise and astonishment.

For the door contained not just one lock, but dozens, one hundred perhaps—from top to bottom and side to side, keyhole after keyhole.

"Got to be something pretty damn valuable behind that door," Antony finally said, scratching his head in puzzlement.

"Indeed," Louis said. "Tom, you have the key, I assume."

"Of course," Tom said, taking his father's envelope from the satchel and removing the antique key. "But where do I begin? Talk about a needle in a haystack!" He tried the key in several locks at random, but nothing happened.

Antoinette peered closely at several of the keyholes and said, "Each one of these locks has a small insignia with three leaves, but the leaves are not all identical. Some have three lobes, others two, and some a combination."

"What is the significance of that?" Tom asked with a mixture of curiosity and impatience.

"By process of elimination, only the locks that have insignia with the three leaf lobes will turn," Antoinette said.

Not for the first time, Tom felt a wave of admiration for his clever wife. "Brilliant! You've just reduced the field down to ten locks." With fingers shaking with eager anticipation, he inserted the key into the ten holes with the three leaf lobe design.

The massive door moved slightly. Once again, Tom was awed by the precise craftsmanship of those long-ago laborers who designed and built the castle. The counter-balanced suspension was of such excellent quality it could have done duty on the most advanced space station.

"Something very special must be behind this door," Tom said. "Why else would my ancestors have constructed a door of such high quality and sealed it behind such intricate safeguards?"

"Built so well it has lasted for over one thousand years,' Antoinette marveled.

Antony let out an impatient sigh. "All this history is well and good, but the door is open is only open a few millimeters and isn't moving any further. Now what do we do?"

"All good keyholes are distributed like the key handle, like a cross, except for one" Antoinette observed. "Try that one and see what happens."

Tom located the lock that Antoinette described, turned the key, and the door eased open a few more millimeters—encouraging, and yet frustrating, for they could still not catch even the slightest glimpse as to what lay beyond.

"Papa, I think your ancestors were deliberately trying to drive us crazy," Antony grumbled.

"Just being prudent," Tom replied calmly. "And remember, the more difficult the journey, the more precious the prize."

Tom and Antoinette huddled with Louis, trading theories as to what to try next to coax the door to fully open. They were interrupted by Antony. "Take a look at this!" The three followed the direction of Antony's pointed finger—four additional keyholes at the bottom of the door, unmarked and finished to blend in with the wood, easy to overlook.

"Very good, son," Tom said with a smile of approval. "Now we've got it down to only sixteen combinations, so let's try each one."

Tom knelt on the stone floor and began inserting his key into various combinations of the four plain locks at the bottom of the door. At last, the door swung smoothly open, once again demonstrating remarkable craftsmanship for such a huge weight. Another dark cavern greeted them.

"May I?" Antony asked his father, indicating his desire to enter first.

"Of course," Tom replied. "After all, we never would have opened this door all the way if you hadn't been so observant."

The normally stern and stoic army general glowed under his father's praise as he strode through the opening, his right arm outstretched with the flashlight.

At first, the beam only bounced off of stone walls, the same rough, reddish-gray surface the four explorers had been seeing ever since they ventured through the armoire in the king's bedchamber.

Then Antony trained the light toward the floor and chamber suddenly burst into a shimmering, radiant light, so bright it hurt the eyes to stare at it for long, so pristine it was as if no time at all had passed instead of some twelve centuries.

Gold. Pure, precious gold. Gold, gold and more gold.

CHAPTER EIGHTEEN

At first the four could only stand there, frozen in shock. Antony was the first to recover, striding boldly into the cavern and sticking out a hand toward the glittering pile. The other three rushed forward, voicing urgent pleas not to disturb the treasure until it could be properly inspected and assessed by experts.

"This could very well be King Lothair's war chest," Antoinette said. "Or that of one of his contemporaries."

"His contemporaries?" Antony said, sounding skeptical. "I thought all of this belonged to our ancestor, King Lothair."

"Likely it does," Antoinette agreed. "But recall that in the year 845, the Vikings, mostly Danes, sacked Paris and refused to leave until Lothair's half-brother, Charles the Bald, paid them 5,670 pounds of silver and gold. This pretty much emptied his war chest."

"So this might be Viking plunder?" Antony asked.

Tom interrupted the discussion. "That is for the experts to decide. Meanwhile, though, no harm in us taking a closer look, as long as we touch nothing." He edged closer to the mounds of shimmering gold coins, feeling as if he were being drawn by a powerful magnet, so great was the lure of this vast hoard.

After shining a beam from his flashlight over as much of the treasure as he could without disturbing even one piece, he said, "Most of these coins appear to be Roman in origin."

"Meaning?" Antony queried.

"Meaning they must have been struck prior to the fall of Rome in 476."

He deferred to his wife to supply the details. "The Roman *Solidus Nomismata* was the primary trade currency of the Mediterranean up until the tenth century," Antoinette said. "So these coins certainly would have been in circulation during Lothair's time in the eight-hundreds and could easily have made their way this far north."

"Especially during times of battle and turmoil," Antony mused.

Tom bent down and examined one of the coins closely. "Some of them bear Lothair's insignia," he declared.

"That seals it, then," Antoinette said, clapping her hands in excitement. "This most certainly is King Lothair's war chest."

Then she turned serious and stared at her husband in awe. "Then all those stories are true," she whispered.

"So it seems," Tom said, trying to sound nonchalant and failing miserably. In truth, he felt as stunned as his wife. Even more so, because he had been hearing vague hints all his life, family tales of untold wealth from ancient times waiting for them right under their feet—if only someone knew how to find it. Whereas Antoinette had only learned the day before that her husband had descended from royalty. To her, this was all brand-new.

More to himself than to anyone else, Tom said softly, "Ever since I was a child, I've heard stories about King Lothair and his treasure. I always assumed they were legends and fables, no more real than the tales of King Arthur and the Round Table. But now …" he gestured toward the heaping piles of pure gold, unable to continue.

Just as quickly, Tom remembered his responsibilities and turned back to business. To Louis and Antony he said, "Day after tomorrow, we must return with cameras and better lights. It is imperative that we make a record of what we've discovered, not only here, but in all other major areas under the castle."

Antoinette had been training her flashlight around the cavern. Now she said, "You realize, there are several other, smaller chambers leading off this one."

Tom's eyes followed the beam of Antoinette's flashlight. He observed the same dark recesses that she had found and said, "Absolutely, at some point we will need to explore these places as well and see what treasures they might be hiding."

Suddenly, he was overwhelmed at the immensity of the undertaking, and his initial excitement over the discovery began to fade. "This is a huge mission that faces us, introducing these historical artifacts back into the world after a millennium and more. Not to mention, the responsibility of handling such a vast windfall."

"Remember what I said last night?" Antoinette said, laughing lightly. "We don't even know for sure who is entitled to all this money. The Rohan family? The French government? The Germans? Don't forget, both nations have laid claim to this region over the years."

"Yes, but last night, it was only a theoretical discussion, a philosophical game of "what if"" Tom said, joining his wife's rueful chuckle. "Now it's all too real."

After a moment's thought, he turned to Antoinette and said, "I suppose our first step is to create a brief summary of what we've done today, where we've been and what we've found. Is that something you'd be willing to undertake?"

She readily agreed with an exclamation of "Excellent idea," while Tom produced a notebook and pen from his satchel. Soon she and Antony were walking off distances and making estimates of the height and weight of the mounds and stacks of gold.

They spent nearly twenty-five minutes in the chamber of gold, unwilling to tear themselves away. Once again, Tom felt that strange magnetic pull, almost a physical force, created by close proximity to such unimaginable wealth. Finally Louis managed to break the spell by reminding them that there were several other rooms at this level, all locked. "We don't know what's in any of them except the jail cell," he said, adding, "We've been underground for over three hours. A bit too long—best we begin to retrace our steps and return the day after tomorrow."

He led Tom, Antoinette and Antony out of the QL room with its extraordinary treasure hoard. Tom carefully locked the door, giving it an extra shake for good measure before turning his back to it.

The Rohan trio followed Louis. When they reached the old jail cell, Louis shone his flashlight through a window so that they could see two single beds, joined side-by-side.

"This is another major entry point from Papa's engineering drawings," Tom said excitedly. "If his calculations and my interpretation are both correct, underneath the second bed there could be a passageway to Emperor Lothair's original chamber."

For Tom, the possibilities were even more tantalizing than the heaps of gold coins. "Just think of the historical artifacts and documents that could be stored there. This could really change our understanding of human history. Such a find would truly be monumental, worth more than all the gold in the world."

Louis appeared in lost in thought, as if peering back through the very timeline of history. In a calm, dream-like voice, he said, "The old lord always told me that below the second bed was an entry into Emperor Lothair's inner court, and all his other rooms. The old lord would only stay in the room a few minutes because of the foul odor, like rotten eggs."

He began to lead the party back up the spiral staircase, each lost in thought and in their exertions in climbing the steep, ladder-like passageway. When they arrived at the first chamber with the desk and the logbook, Antoinette only noted that they had traveled as far as the QL room—not one word about the treasure.

"Quite right," Louis said in approval after reviewing Antoinette's notation in the log book. He then called for attention, his face and tone serious. "Can you imagine what will happen when word gets out that the new King of Rohan has found piles of gold under his castle?"

Tom groaned. "Every fortune-hunter from around with world is going to show up with a pick and shovel, thinking they're going to find more treasure."

"Exactly," Louis said. "What happened to you on the tour today, what we've discovered, must remain absolutely confidential," Louis said. "Tell no one—not even your other children." To Antony, he added, "Not your wife, not even your commanding officer."

The three Rohans nodded in understanding, while Louis continued, "There are two exceptions. Tom, as the current King of Rohan, you have the discretion to share this information with your heir. And I, as Carolingian guardian, may reveal the details to my successor if I chose to do so."

Louis waited for his charges to absorb this information, then added, "In case you are wondering, I have never told André nor Victor anything about what lies beneath the King's bedchamber."

He raised a finger and with a little smile said, "One more thing." He pressed a panel on the ancient desk and a tiny drawer revealed itself. Tom, Antony and Antoinette huddled closely in curiosity. "Two more keys," Louis said to Tom. "Just in case you or your heir gets careless and loses the first key."

"I shall guard the key and these secrets with my life," Tom said with a nervous laugh. "But what shall we tell the others as to how we spent our day?"

"Easy," Antoinette replied with a smile. "We had a lovely time admiring the royal garden and touring the private family chambers. After all, what could be more relaxing than sunning oneself in the garden, relaxing with a good book?" At this, everyone broke into laughter.

When the amusement subsided, Louis said, "The old lord told me more than once that the Rohan treasure is much larger than what one would see upon first entering the QL chamber, and the historical archive is even more impressive and extensive than anyone could expect."

"What are you trying to say?" Tom said, a knot of fear growing inside.

"You must prepare yourself, mentally and emotionally, and, yes, physically," Louis said. "It is my belief the value of the treasure in the dungeon could be far greater than all the assets the Rohan dynasty has on paper above-ground."

"More than the land holdings, and the business assets and the deposits in banks all over the world?" Tom asked, his unease growing.

"Indeed," Louis said. "The Rohan fortune may be even greater than that of all the royal houses of Europe combined, greater than the wealth of the Vatican, the Arab oil sheiks, the tech billionaires…"

Tom raised the palm of his hand for silence. "No need to go on. We all understand what you're telling us. We understand all too well."

Antoinette was clinging to his arm, her eyes wide with the enormity of the challenge facing them. One week ago, she had been an obscure scientific researcher and housewife. Now she was looking at sharing the responsibility—and dangers—of controlling a vast fortune. Even Antony, the stern and controlled army general, looked ill-at-ease, unsure how to tackle this latest challenge.

Tom squared his shoulders and injected as much confidence in his voice as he was capable of. "We are Rohans! Never forget, we are descended from Charlemagne, one of the greatest rulers Europe— and the world—has ever known. His blood flows through our veins. So let us follow his example and prove that we Rohans are still capable of greatness."

The bedside clock read three in the afternoon when the party finally emerged from the armoire and back into the king's bedchamber. Though exhausted from the final climb up the steep spiral staircase, the four were also exhilarated, fairly bubbling with excitement, over their adventures and the astounding discovery.

"If only you weren't trapped in business meetings all day tomorrow," Antoinette said to her husband with a small sigh of disappointment. "I don't know if I can stand to wait through another whole day before we get to continue our exploration."

"I feel much the same," Tom said. "But, I suppose I must not shirk my royal duties. And as they say, patience is a virtue."

"Quite right," Louis said. "We will have plenty of time for another trip into the dungeon and beyond the day after tomorrow."

Tom's expression turned serious as he said, "Our most important task now is to safeguard the treasure. We must impose the strictest of security measures. Louis, is this something you an Antony can arrange while I am trapped, as Antoinette would say, in my business meetings tomorrow?"

Both men nodded their assent, with Louis adding, "Very wise, my lord."

The discussion was briefly interrupted as André arrived, bearing a tray with the makings of *le goûter*, the French answer to the British afternoon tea. The four eagerly helped themselves to bread, cheese, fruit and *pain au chocolat*, not realizing how famished they were until food suddenly became available.

After several moments during which nothing more important than chewing and swallowing took place, they drew chairs into a tight circle. Tom said, "I've been thinking about the equipment we shall require for our next journey underground. Ropes, for certain, and better lighting. Everyone needs to have a head lamp."

"Understood, my lord," Louis said, removing a notepad and pen from his pocket and starting a list.

"Goggles and clean-room gloves, suitable for handling ancient relics," Tom continued.

"Don't forget two-way radios," Antony contributed. "Our cell phones aren't going to work so far underground."

"You'll need a good camera," Antoinette said to Tom.

"Absolutely, put a camera on the list," Tom said to Louis. "The best you can find on short notice. Capable of creating sharp, clear images in very low light conditions. No flash—a flash could seriously damage historic artifacts."

"Quite right," Louis said. "And while I'm at it, I might as well make sure it's waterproof. You never know what we might run into."

"You never know," they all said, laughing nervously.

When the momentary hilarity subsided, Tom said, "I want to explore that old jail cell, but the foul odor is not a good sign. We should all have respirators of some kind."

Antony swallowed his last bit of bread and cheese and said, "Military grade oxygen masks are often available at chemical supply stores. I can help locate them tomorrow."

"Excellent," Louis said. "And while you're there, also pick up a toxic gas detector."

"Since we're on the subject," Tom said, happy to share his expertise as a bio-chemist, "at the chemical supply store, you should also pick up approximately thirty gas sampling bags, so we can check out the air at all the various locations we visit. Later on, we can send them to a lab for analysis of outgassing composition, information that will be extremely insightful."

Antony nodded and said to Louis, "Are you getting all this on your list?"

Louis, intent on scribbling down the various requests, barely looked up and uttered only a brief, "Will that be all, my lord?"

"Well, there is one more thing," Tom said. "Lay in a supply of common bags for taking surface samples—dirt, bricks, stone, whatever we might find. We'll want to have all of it analyzed for composition and age."

And then with a gentle smile to the faithful Louis, Tom said, "I believe that is the end of the list."

André reappeared and announced that he would be escorting the Rohans to the rooms that would provide a home to them for the next several days. Tom and Antoinette were assigned to Tom's boyhood chamber, the bedroom and study they had glimpsed through the window earlier that day. It was just as Tom remembered, with one change—while they were exploring the underground caverns, André had arranged for Tom's narrow boyhood bed to be temporarily removed and replaced with a comfortable double bed for him and Antoinette.

Tom beckoned Antoinette to the east-facing window. "See that?" he said, pointing. "That's the town of Saint Meyer there on the foothill."

"Is that the Rhine out there in the distance?" Antoinette asked.

"It is," Tom said. "Some 20 kilometers away. I used to stare out this window for what seemed like hours when I was a boy, wondering what it would be like to be floating down that river, seeing what lay past the bend and beyond."

"As wonderful as this castle is, it must have felt like a prison at times, especially when you were a boy," Antoinette observed.

"Indeed," Tom said. "No matter how luxurious the surroundings or how loving the caregivers, in the end a cage is still a cage. I was just lucky my parents were willing to grant me my freedom when I was ready to leave."

He tore himself away from the window and began to slowly reacquaint himself with the fixtures in the room: his old desk, where he had studied his schoolbooks and prepared his lessons, a dresser, cases bursting with books, and a shelf holding a collection of cast-iron, enameled toys. He picked up a miniature automobile and said,

"This was one of my favorite things in the whole world, besides my books, of course."

"I'm guessing a vintage toy like that would fetch a fine figure on eBay," Antoinette joked. "Something to think about if it turns out we cannot lay claim to that treasure down below and we're hard up for cash."

"Never!" Tom replied in the same laughing tone, clutching the beloved trinket close to his chest.

André interrupted this moment of gentle teasing between husband and wife to show them the two guest rooms that he had been prepared for the other members of the Rohan family. Each had a window with the same view as Tom's room, a double bed, a nightstand, a small desk and a closet.

"We always kept the doors of these rooms open when I was a child," Tom recalled. "We rarely had guests and when we did, they were almost always close family relatives."

"I've arranged to have your luggage moved from the hotel in the village to here," André said. "Your rooms and your possessions will be available no later than five-thirty."

Tom nodded his thanks, then in a low voice, said to Louis and Antony, "What about the king's bedchamber? We can't have anyone wandering in there, no matter how innocent their purpose."

"Understood," Louis said. "Antony and I have been working with André to impose strict security measures. New locks have been installed and the door will be guarded by a member of the Carolingian order at all times."

Once again, Tom was overcome with gratitude toward these many loyal people, unknown to him until now, who were risking their lives to ensure the safety of him and his family. When he attempted to give voice to his sincere thanks, Louis politely cut him off. "It is not only our sacred duty to serve, but also a distinct pleasure to be in the service to someone as gracious and kind as your majesty."

With that, Louis suggested that Tom and Antoinette freshen themselves and proceed to the family dining room for an early supper. "After all, you have another challenging day ahead of you tomorrow," he reminded them.

In the family dining room under the familiar watchful eye of the dragon, Julia and Philip joined Tom, Antoinette and Antony. Julia immediately inquired of her parents as to how they'd spent their day.

Tom and Antoinette exchanged cautious glances, then Antoinette said breezily, "We had a joyful and informative day exploring the castle. We entered Tom's mother's secret garden, admired all the original plants and flowers from your papa that lasted and regenerated for decades. We entered the King's and Queen's rooms, examined them in detail and even encountered much beyond that— but all that needs further verification. We will not say anything before our discoveries are fully verified and understood"

Julia took a sip of wine, nodded slowly and gave her father a knowing look. Tom understood the silent message behind that look: his eldest daughter completely understood the implications: much more had occurred, but it was too soon to reveal the details. Whenever her mama was in the process of discovering a new drug, she never disclosed any information until the final verification stage had been completed to her satisfaction. For Julia, much the same was true for legal issues. When a case is in process, it is always tightly sealed, the details never revealed to an outsider.

"So while we were puttering around in castle and the garden, Julia and Philip, I trust your work went well?" Tom inquired.

"Let's just say it was intense," Philip said. "Very, very intense."

Tom waited for the server to dole out portions of a flavorful cassoulet and leave the room, then said, "I am lucky to have a son and daughter who are so smart and so conscientious." He finished by raising his wine glass in appreciation.

Julia nodded in acceptance of the compliment and said, "If you really want to show your appreciation, you won't ask any more questions. Let us enjoy this short break before we must go back to work."

For the next half hour, the Rohans did just that, savoring the excellent meal and exchanging talk of nothing more substantial than the plants and birds observed in the castle gardens. As the dessert plates were being cleared away, three men entered the dining room: Jacques, Roland and Major Dumas.

Julia and Philip excused themselves to return to work, while Antony immediately left the room with Major Dumas to discuss security strategy. André and Louis expressed the need to attend to other matters and disappeared, leaving just Tom and Antoinette with the two other newcomers: Jacques, the retired police chief and husband of Brigitte, and Roland, the local policeman. Tom recognized both as members of the Carolingian Sacred Heart, but otherwise knew little about either man. He wondered how he and his wife might entertain them until inspiration struck.

"What do you say about a little evening stroll around the castle grounds?" he suggested.

"A wonderful idea!" Antoinette chimed in. "We haven't gotten nearly enough exercise today, have we, *mon cherie?*"

The pair exchanged amused glances, as Jacques and Roland both shrugged and allowed as how a postprandial walk might do them a world of good. With that, the four left the dining room and emerged into the evening air of the castle grounds. At this late spring date, the sun hung low on the horizon, still providing enough light to make a garden stroll a delight instead of a danger. As a botanist, Tom reveled in the delicious aroma of freshly mowed lawn and the perfume of the many flowering plants, just as he admired the interesting shapes made by the lengthening shadows against the trees and bushes.

"I understand both of you have been members of the Carolingian inner core for many years," he said to Jacques and Roland as the party walked along a garden path. "How is it that you became involved in the order?"

Both men answered with blank looks, as if Tom had asked a question that had no easy response. "The order has always been a part of my family," Jacques finally said. "My father, his father, and so on as far back as any of us can remember. The Carolingian Sacred Heart has always been a part of our lives, as essential as the air we breathe and the water we drink."

"That was the way it was for me also," Roland said. "My father, my grandfather, my uncles, my brothers… it is a sacred mission, the core around which our lives are structured."

Tom shook his head in wonder. "I had no idea," he whispered.

Beyond the castle walls, he could see the looming peaks of the Vosges mountain range. Though he could not see it from beyond the stone walls of the garden, he knew somewhere out there lay the Rhine, making its silent way from its headwaters in Switzerland to Germany, The Netherlands and finally emptying into the North Sea. The Rhine had formed a natural border between Germany and France for centuries, but Tom was well aware of the many dangers that had breached its banks through the decades, from the armies of Bismarck in the Franco-Prussian War to the Kaiser's troops during World War II to the twin threat of the Nazis and the Russians in the second World War.

During all those conflicts, the members of the Carolingian Sacred Heart had never shirked their duties, keeping Castle Rohan and its hidden treasure protected from all invaders and plunderers. More importantly, they had protected the Rohan family, keeping the bloodline intact for all these many decades.

For that last especially, Tom vowed that no matter in whose hands the cache of gold might end up, he would make sure the Carolingians would be repaid for their loyal service to his family.

It would be, he decided, his own sacred mission, one which he would fulfill or die trying.

CHAPTER NINETEEN

"**R**eady to face the lions, *mon cherie?*" Antoinette gently teased as she took her husband's hand into her own.

"All-in-all, I'd rather be in the dungeon," Tom responded in the same quietly mocking tone that the couple had used in communicating with each other for so many years.

It was just a few minutes before ten in the morning. Antoinette and Tom stood outside the room that had given the family shelter two days earlier, during those tense moments during which the Rohan board pored over Tom's *bona fides* to determine whether he had the right to bear the title of King of Rohan. Today, that same chamber would serve as the corporate board room.

"Duty calls," Tom finished as he opened the door and ushered his wife inside. Just like two days ago, he found himself in a conference room worthy of a billion dollar corporate board of directors, with the expected massive table, comfortable leather chairs, electronic gadgets and. a sideboard stocked with coffee and tea service, flavored and sparkling waters, and pastries. The other participants in this meeting had already arrived and were busy booting up their laptops, shuffling through papers, and pouring coffee.

Tom spotted Antony in the room and pulled his son aside. "The security measures are all in order?" Tom asked in a low voice.

"Absolutely," Antony replied. "Major Dumas is commanding the Special Forces to ensure that no intruders come anywhere near the castle."

"Major Dumas is reporting to you, then?" Tom asked.

"Technically, yes, but I am not giving him any direct commands. He is quite capable of making his own decisions." Antony continued,

"The French secret police are on high alert, and the *gendarmes* from the village are patrolling the grounds. Members of the Carolingian Sacred Heart, including Jacques and Roland, are also at your service."

"Excellent," Tom said. "And the Lombardi?"

"Ah, yes, the Lombardi," Antony said with a small chuckle. "They have interacted well with the Special Forces. But let us just say they would rather not come in close contact with law enforcement."

"I can well imagine," Tom said, returning the laughter. "Still, I will always be in their debt. They may be gangsters, but if they hadn't rescued me from the streets of Paris, you might be planning my funeral this morning instead of security for this meeting."

As the ten o'clock hour chimed, Brigitte seated herself at the head of the table and called the meeting to order. As Director of Operations, including finance and the day-to-day running of the castle, she would be chairing the meeting. Tom took a seat next to Victor Monet, both men's faces grave as they contemplated the serious nature of the proceedings. Tom took comfort in the close proximity of his family at the table: Philip and Julia, and of course his dear wife Antoinette.

Tom was pleased to note that Philip and Julia both projected confidence. Brother and sister seemed almost relaxed and were definitely in good spirits. *All of their hard work yesterday, studying all those documents, was time well spent,* Tom told himself.

Antony, meanwhile, stationed himself at the door, where he could provide yet one more level of security, and could easily slip outside to update himself on the movements and activities of the various guards. Of all the people in the room, Antony most fully understood the continued threats of kidnapping and other acts of violence against the Rohan family.

Tom exchanged a brief nod of greeting with Alexis "Sandy" Montague, the Rohan corporation's Chief Legal Counsel. She had been the source of much of the contention during the coronation process two days earlier, but Tom now recognized a conscientious and intelligent legal mind who had simply been carrying out her responsibilities.

Rounding out the participants in the meeting were Chloe Durand, the young Director and Curator of Rohan History and Art, and Sophie Laurent, the middle-aged woman who seemed to always wear a smile and had the title of Director of Special Projects.

Brigitte began by stating that a financial review would occupy the first hour-and-a-quarter of the meeting. Then she laid down the ground rules. "This meeting is strictly confidential and off-the-record. All materials, either printed or electronic, and all verbal communications must not leave this room, and absolutely may not be divulged to any outside financial interests."

The elegant older woman surveyed the members of the chamber, locking eyes with each, then said, "There is simply no easy way to put this. The Rohan organization has had a negative cash flow for the past ten years under the direction of Duke Michael. The situation has only gotten worse, not better, since his death some twelve months ago."

Brigitte paused, took a deep breath, and said, "In a word, our financial situation is nothing short of disastrous."

The shock was so profound, nobody moved. No one uttered a sound.

But how could this be? Tom asked himself. *Only yesterday, I was faced with the challenge of managing immense wealth. Now we're going broke?*

Brigitte, sensing the question on everyone's minds, continued in a calm voice, "The fact is, Duke Michael in essence halted all new business development, nor did he update any contracts for the past five years. One could speculate as to his mental state or his greedy nature, but it would be only speculation at this point."

At the mention of Duke Michael, Tom had a memory of his grand-nephew, grandson of his younger brother Pierre, the serious-looking man with black curls.in the Portrait Gallery who had died at the age of forty.

Brigitte allowed her listeners to absorb this information, then went on, "Instead of attending to business, he used every opportunity to support his so-called charities. In my view, nearly all of the organizations that he funneled money into were dubious at best, downright fraudulent at worst."

At this statement, the cheerful smile that Sophie perpetually wore quickly vanished, turning into an expression of panic.

Brigitte concluded, "The Rohan general operating budget represents twenty percent of our income, but the money going to these quote-unquote charitable organizations, plus the donation of art, amounts to one hundred ten percent of our income. Thus are the Rohan cash and reserves being drained every year, to the point that they stand at only thirty percent of the level of fifteen years ago."

Philip was the first person to speak. "Thank you, Madame Chair," he said in a calm, pleasant voice. Now, if we may ask, an itemized list of the major accounts that need attention and action."

Antony had just slipped back into the room and gave his father a quick nod, indicating all was well with the security forces outside. Julia, meanwhile, was listening attentively, and Tom could almost see her keen legal mind busy at work. Once again, he marveled at his luck to have produced three such loyal and capable offspring.

"Of course," Brigitte said to Philip. "We anticipated just such a request and have prepared that information." With that, she signaled to an aid to distribute a two-page outline to each person in the room.

After each had had a chance to make a quick review of the contents, Brigitte spoke in a voice sober and serious. "This list represents only the top twenty-five of bad business deals and failed operations year after year. We actually know of at least seventy-five, maybe more. We shall require additional time and effort to put all into a computerized enterprise system and actually track them."

Philip responded in his calm, upbeat manner. "Thank you, and do not concern yourself. We shall sort everything out and resolve these issues to everyone's satisfaction in all due haste."

Then he smiled and said, "We should not dwell on the negative, but rather look at the positive side of this situation. This gives us an opportunity for new business development, improvements in our operating procedures, and revitalization of projects new and old. All of these have the potential of bringing in new revenue."

Victor had become increasingly agitated during this discussion and could contain himself no longer. "Twenty percent operating budget and one-hundred ten percent going to charity? That is completely out of proportion and just plain idiotic!" He issued an apology for his outburst, and continued, "Duke Michael was personally involved in all sorts of charity groups, throwing money around right and left, far outpacing our income. And he never paid the slightest attention to the bottom line."

Sophie put the phony smile back on her face and spoke up. "As Director of Special Projects, I feel I must remind you of the great impact to humanity the Rohan corporation has made. You people seem to have forgotten that. We have donated to over one hundred fifty wonderful and just causes: war refugees, teenage single parents, arts programs, schools, the deserving poor among us…"

"Yes, and you were once the president of one of those so-called charitable organizations," Victor said, his face stern and cold. "And then Duke Michael brought you in as Director of Special Projects, isn't that right?"

Sophie did not deny the allegation.

Victor continued, "As of this moment, eighty percent of our expenditures are charitable donations. You seem to be ignoring a very basic fact of life, that one must live within one's budget and to keep a balance between income and expenditures. Everyone knows that, from the wealthiest nation in the world to the smallest family unit."

He concluded his tirade. "Special Projects should not just be finding new ways to spend our money. Special Projects should also be looking at ways to bring in additional revenue in a positive and legal manner."

Victor turned to Chloe Durand, the Director and Curator of Rohan History and Art. "You've been keeping quiet during these proceedings. What do you have to say about all this?"

"My department has not had a budget increase in the past decade," the young woman said. "Ten years ago, we had eleven staff members. Now, we can afford to retain only four full-time employees and three part-timers. All of the Rohan history and art programs are in jeopardy."

At this last statement, Tom felt a pang of regret. History and the preservation of historic artifacts was dear to his heart, even more so than the piles of gold that lay under the castle. Now this sincere and conscientious young woman was telling him the Rohan history preservation projects were in jeopardy.

Sophie spoke again. "The contributions of the Rohan organization have been recognized by chiefs of state and key members of society throughout Europe. Just look at the number of times Duke Michael has been invited to be a keynote speaker at their fundraising events. Fifteen times this past year alone! This is an outstanding achievement, a real feather in the Rohan's cap. Our efforts should be highly respected instead of called into question."

Brigitte, clearly unpleased, clapped her hands for silence. "We must sort out every expense and take immediate action. Time is running out. The Rohan corporation is on the brink of bankruptcy. Meanwhile, this session must end soon as we have the outside financial group waiting to meet with us."

Sophie, however, was not to be shut down. "Before this session ends, may I remind you that the corporation has committed to an additional forty endowments to fulfill?"

That phony, mocking smile was back on her face as she clearly enjoyed the shocked expressions throughout the room, especially on the faces of Victor, Brigitte and Chloe.

Once again, Philip remained calm and cheerful. "Yes, we are aware of twenty-five of them as we worked with the finance team yesterday. These twenty-five endowments were in review because, in total, they represent three-hundred percent of the Rohan organization's income. In addition, when we looked deeper into these organizations, we discovered most of them do not have good track records when it comes to fiscal responsibility and sound business practices."

"Those twenty-five endowments were among the duke's favorites,' Sophie burst out.

"I'm sure they were," Philip said smoothly. "And what of the other fifteen endowments? We could find no record of them at all."

"These were... well... verbal commitments," Sophie said, her bravado fading. "Made by Duke Michael and myself."

Brigitte shook her head. "Have you forgotten about our standard endowment procedure? The charitable organization wishing for a Rohan donation must turn in paperwork stating the amount requested, the purpose for which it will be used, and the impact our donation will make. All documentation is to be reviewed by our financial and legal teams."

"You people simply have no idea how great the Rohan reputation is in the public eye," Sophie sputtered. "When an organization comes to us for help, we check our reserves and make a spontaneous verbal commitment right on the spot. That's enough to move the money over to them. This is how the nonprofit world works. The Rohan corporation is highly respected and trusted by all, thanks to the work done by Duke Michael and myself." With that she settled herself in her chair in a huff.

"Madame Laurent, with all due respect," Philip said, "if you had been checking the reserves as you said you were, you would have known we were in the red in terms of liabilities for the past two years."

He consulted his notes and continued, "Looking at the short-term, mid-term and long-term debts and liabilities, we've been operating under a major negative cash flow for years, and our reserves would also be in the red if we were to include outstanding debts."

Brigitte sighed. "Duke Michael never was one to pay much attention to debts and liabilities."

"But what about the Rohan land holdings?" Sophie jeered. "Strasbourg, Stuttgart, Milan... even a fraction of just one of these would be ten times or even fifty times the puny amount of Duke Michael's endowments."

For the first time, Philip dropped all pretense of cheerfulness. "For everyone's information, the Rohan corporation is already bankrupt. The lenders could—and just might—take entire control of everything. Our land holdings, our assets, even this very castle.

Everything. They could sell us lock, stock and barrel for pennies on the dollar to recoup some of their losses. We have six months of time left to rescue the Rohan corporation—six months if we're lucky."

Now Sophie was furious, her arms gesturing wildly to make her point. "This is not how Duke Michael would have run the operation. You people are all too small-minded! You don't see the big picture and you have no concept of philanthropy."

"This session is ended," Brigitte said firmly. "Let me remind everyone, I do think it likely the Rohan corporation will be dissolved and taken over by outside forces within six months if we do not take immediate and drastic recovery actions."

With that, Sophie bolted upright and stormed out of the room, tossing out one more verbal barb before making her flounce through the doorway. "Duke Michael would be so ashamed of you people!"

Julia rose, signaling with her hand that all others should remain in the room. Once she had assured herself that Sophie really had disappeared and was not within hearing distance, she firmly shut the door and returned to her seat next to Sandy Montague, the Chief Legal Counsel. The two lawyers whispered briefly between themselves.

Julia lifted her head from her notes and faced the room, her expression a mask of grave concern. Tom could not recall a time when his daughter had looked more sober and serious.

"We must face reality," Julia said. "The Rohan corporation doesn't have six months. We are lucky if we have two months left."

Once again, the occupants of the board room reacted with stunned and silent surprise, utterly disbelieving.

Tom felt as if his world were crumbling around him. But he told himself he must remain strong. He found Antoinette's hand under the table and gave it a reassuring squeeze, as if to say, "We have Julia and Philip on our team. They'll figure out how to get us out of this situation."

Julia began to speak. "Just one example. We are facing huge underground water pollution fines due to land we lease to three plants in Stuttgart. The management of these three plants has been asking for permission for four years to construct a massive on-site water treatment facility. All they lacked was Duke Michael's signature on a document. Due to his inaction, the city has levied a fine of one-point-two billion Euros. Even with all of our reserves, our cash, and the possibility of liquidating all of our assets, we are unable to pay a fine that large."

She concluded, "This is most likely our worst case. But there are four other cases out there of similar size, and all have reached the critical level."

"But what about our land holdings?" Tom asked. "Surely they are worth that, and more."

Sandy Montague studied notes on her legal paid, and said, "Here's the situation with the land holdings. At least forty percent—maybe as high as seventy percent—of the leases have long expired. This means that whoever is using the land, whoever is sitting on it, can claim we have abandoned it and they have the legal right of ownership." She sighed, and for a moment this strong, capable woman looked helpless. "I have done my best to stay on top of these cases, but the Rohan legal department has been severely cut back in recent years. It's down to just me and a part-time paralegal."

Julia rose and distributed a thick sheaf of documents to each person in the room. "This is a summary of twenty legal issues facing us: liens, ongoing litigation, and pending lawsuits."

With one glance at the names of the powerful corporations and prominent individuals who had filed legal actions against the Rohan organization, Tom felt his hopes wither away. He looked at Antoinette and Antony and saw the same expression of despair etched on their faces.

"We are on a collision course in every aspect," Brigitte said. "Only fast action can save us. And even then, that may not be enough."

"Well, at least we now know the full extent of our financial and legal status," Philip said cheerfully. "Now that we have a better understanding of our situation, we can better formulate a plan of action. It is my belief we have a good chance of negotiating with the financial institutions to whom we owe money to give us time to reorganize and reposition ourselves. After all, if we fail, they will never get their money back. And as for the city of Stuttgart, they may be willing to reduce the penalties if they see we are committed to meeting their codes and standards."

Tom could tell his son was trying to raise everyone's spirits by shining the best possible light on a dire situation, and felt a wave of gratitude.

"So," Philip concluded, "I propose we all take a break and enjoy our lunch together."

Brigitte cleared her throat and with courage and determination said, "As chair of the financial review, before we adjourn for lunch it is imperative that we put a monetary figure onto each of these major items. Only then can we gauge the situation precisely and determine our best course of action."

She pressed a remote control and a screen lowered from the ceiling. From her laptop, Brigitte projected financial data from the previous year:

- Rohan expenses totaled sixty million Euros, twenty-five million for operational expenses and thirty-five million for castle repair and maintenance.
- Rohan farm and tourist income balanced out at sixty million Euros.
- Rohan real estate asset income showed two-hundred forty million Euros, but the charity endowments took away three-hundred thirty million.

"So you're saying we outspent our real estate income by nearly ninety million Euros," Tom observed.

"Correct,' Brigitte answered. "That is why we have a reserve of only three hundred million. Meanwhile, according to Madame Laurent, we have commitments of some six-hundred million in charity endowments. There is simply no way we can meet that."

"Keep in mind, Papa, we also have fines totaling over a billion Euros due to the situation in Stuttgart," Julia said. "And some eight-hundred million in litigation and ongoing liens."

Brigitte gestured toward the figures on the screen. "When you look at our income against the expenses—liability, litigation, fines and charitable endowments—the situation is obvious. Rohan is in deep crisis. In two months, maybe less, all of our property could be in the hands of the lenders."

A smile flickered across her features. "There is some good news to report. My staff has completed the scanning of all of the Rohan documents and has securely stored them on the cloud."

"Excellent," Tom said. "So if anything is stolen or destroyed from our archive, at least we have an image back-up."

Encouraged by this support from the king, Brigitte went on to explain how her staff was in the process of digitalizing all of the financial and legal data, making it easier to create crucial analyses of the situation. She said, 'Eventually, we want all of the Rohan systems and documentation to be part of an enterprise management system so we can easily extract the status of our liabilities and payments."

She looked at Julia and Philip for confirmation, and summed up her presentation. "On the negative side, our debt and liability is around eight times our ability to pay. On the positive side, much of that liability is in the charitable endowments, which we might be able to terminate. Julia and the legal team may be able to negotiate lower penalties for the fines and other litigation, but they will need to act fast. The real estate forfeitures may be the toughest battle."

Tom knew that everyone was waiting for him to say something, and that this was a moment when he needed to act in a stately manner befitting his royal status. In an optimistic tone, he said, "Yes, the Rohan organization is in deep financial crisis. But, this could also be a great opportunity to move forward. We can wring our hands over the fact that we only have two months left. Or, we can use those two months to produce a great turnover package."

He saw nods of understanding and approval from around the table, so he continued, "We can be satisfied knowing that all of our documents have been digitalized. Or, we can congratulate ourselves that we have created the perfect starting point. Now, we'll be able to call up any document or spreadsheet in an instant and know exactly where we stand." Looking at Brigitte, Antoinette, and the others in the room, he concluded, "It would appear to me that our priority is to strengthen our I.T. department. And, of course, the legal team."

"Exactly!" Brigitte said with enthusiasm. "We need two teams, each with twelve to fifteen staffers, for I.T., accounting and analysis."

"My department could really use about six more lawyers and ten paralegals," Sandy said sincerely. "A common practice is to hire a legal consulting firm. They are quick and effective, but expensive, three times the cost of us having our own staff."

"I am prepared to approve these expenditures immediately, assuming I have the authority," Tom said resolutely. To Brigitte he added, "Please enlighten me as to exactly what authority the King holds when it comes to the day-to-day running of the Rohan corporation."

"A more than reasonable request, your majesty," Brigitte said. "The King has a budget for his own family. Likewise, all departments have their own budgets. I, for example, have the authority to spend up to two-hundred fifty thousand Euros. Anything up to five-hundred thousand requires authorization from the legal department, and beyond that, it requires approval of the finance and legal departments, and the King himself."

She concluded, "For the emergency recovery effort, I estimate fifteen million Euros per year in discretional funding."

"You certainly have my approval," Tom said.

"And mine," Sandy chimed in.

"Excellent," Tom said. "Brigitte, please begin staffing up the I.T., accounting and legal departments immediately."

"Of course, your majesty." Then Brigitte's expression grew serious. "This afternoon, we will be meeting with our most difficult land tenant, Foremost Pharmaceutics of Stuttgart. They are the source of our one-point-two billion Euro fine, as well as numerous legal and business entanglements."

She returned to the presentation on the screen. "These are the five crucial Rohan business partners that we will be meeting with this afternoon and the day after tomorrow:"

- Foremost Pharmaceutics of Stuttgart, Germany. Holder of one Rohan coin, is proposing a major update of their facilities.
- International Investment AG of Basel, Switzerland. Holder of one Rohan coin, a real estate property management firm, will propose improvements to cooperation and processes.

- Resource Commercial Property, holder of one Rohan coin, manager of two-hundred sixty Rohan properties in Strasbourg and likely embezzled from ninety of them.
- Security Investment Bank, one of major lenders.
- Trust Charity Funds, the biggest recipient of Duke Michael's endowments.

Brigitte switched off the projector and adjourned the meeting for lunch. Antony opened the door and two members of the castle culinary staff entered, along with a rolling cart holding boxed lunches. Little was said as the meeting participants glumly gathered up their belongings, picked up their lunches, and began to leave the room. Julia and Philip departed together to find a quiet place where they could dine and prepare for the afternoon's meetings, while Victor, Antony, Sandy and Chloe left together and headed in another direction.

Tom picked up two lunches, one for himself and one for Antoinette. Then he noticed Brigitte walking away by herself, one of the white boxes tucked under one arm and a sheaf of notes in the other. On an impulse, he strode forward and extended his hand to the elderly woman who had borne so much responsibility these past two hours. "Perhaps you will be so kind as to join Antoinette and myself for lunch?" Tom said gallantly. "I thought we might enjoy some quiet time in my mother's garden."

Brigitte smiled and the cares seemed to melt away from her face. "I would like that very much, my lord."

For the next hour, Tom, Antoinette and Brigitte did not talk business, but instead simply savored the delicious lunch prepared in the castle kitchen and basked in the sunshine, the sheer beauty, and the pleasant aromas of the Queen's flower garden.

All too soon, however, the appointed hour for the afternoon meetings drew close. Antoinette gave a little sigh and said, "How sad to think that in two months, all this may belong to someone else, someone with no connection to the Rohan family. What will happen to this lovely garden? Will the new owners even know how to care for such rare and special specimens?"

Similar unsettling thoughts had been crossing Tom's mind, but he knew better than to dwell on them for too long. To Antoinette he said, "Who can tell what lies in our future? As for me, as long as I have a small plot of land and a few seeds, sunshine and water… why, that's all I need to be happy. And you, of course."

CHAPTER TWENTY

For most of his adult life, Philip had recognized that he possessed a rare combination: not only did he have a razor-sharp mind for numbers and finance, but he also had an uncanny sense when it came to dealing with people. Still, he knew that the challenge that lay before him this afternoon would test his skills to the maximum, forcing him to rise to the occasion when it came to quick thinking and leadership. Adding to the pressure: his family's corporate business was at stake, and his father and mother would be watching.

Before the official start of the afternoon meeting, Philip drew together the family members, plus Brigitte, Sandy and Victor, for a quick strategy session. "This first group we are about to meet with, Resource Commercial Property, has a long history of questionable deals," Brigitte warned. "They hold one Rohan coin, as do the next two companies we will be meeting with."

Philip said, "Julia and I have been extensively researching this company the past twenty-four hours. We've discovered they have recently spent a million Euros and more. To spend that much money so quickly, they must have a hidden agenda."

Antony opened the door and beckoned for two men to enter. They were obviously government agents, strong and confident, armed with pistols and wired with communications devices. "We believe this first group may be involved with the attempt on Papa's life in Paris," Antony explained. "And remember, Strasbourg is the home of Gabriel Monet, and is where we believe the kidnapping gang is active. So I have arranged to have two members of law enforcement stand guard over this meeting."

"Very good," Philip said to his older brother. "Brigitte, Julia, Sandy and I should sit together. Our best strategy is to say little, give away nothing, and record everything."

With the hour now reaching 1:30, Brigitte signaled one of the guards to open the door and allow the five representatives of Resource Commercial Property to enter.

Two women and three men walked into the conference room. Philip watched his potential opponents. They didn't so much walk as swagger, exuding bravado.

He studied the team without any outward emotion, but inwardly he shook his head in disapproval. The man who introduced himself as the CEO wore khaki slacks and a polo shirt, more like he was preparing for a round of golf than a serious business meeting. The other two men at least had bothered to put on business suits, but their shirts were rumpled and their ties knotted loosely. As for the two women, one of them looked like she was on her way to a casual lunch with her girlfriends, while the other wore a dress more appropriate for a cocktail party, low-cut and softly flowing. Both females sported far too much jewelry, large and flashy.

No respect, Philip thought. *They obviously want us to think this meeting is no big deal, like they're in control.* He exchanged a glance with Julia and she returned a similar look. *These people are in for a big surprise!*

However, Philip never let his annoyance at their arrogance show in either his voice or his manner. Introductions were exchanged, and the CEO said, "We are one of the top property management companies in Strasbourg. We manage over six-hundred properties, two-hundred sixty that are or were Rohan properties. We were honored when King Raymond entrusted us with the management of his real estate holdings thirty-five years ago. We have provided a positive cash flow and cordial relations with the Rohans for all of those thirty-five years,"

Making eye contact with each member of the Rohan family, he continued in a friendly voice, "May I remind you, Strasbourg is the seventh largest city in France and is capital city of the Grand Est region, formerly Alsace. Our fair city is also the formal seat of the European Parliament, and with our position on the border with

Germany, we blend the best of both cultures. We are proud of our thirty-five years of service to the Rohan corporation and, of course, the royal family."

The chief legal counsel for Resource Commercial Property spoke next. Unlike the CEO, his tone was anything but friendly. "In case you have forgotten, our company holds one Rohan gold coin. We continue to maintain and uphold the rule that the failure of Mister Rohan to produce all fifty gold coins undermines the integrity of his claim to the throne. But of course, as Resource Commercial Property holds the fiftieth coin, we could easily resolve that situation... if this so-called King is prepared to meet our demands, of course."

Philip had expected something along these lines from RCP, but was somewhat taken aback by the boldness of the move. As chair of the meeting, Brigitte gave a slight nod to Sandy and Julia, and finally Philip. He returned the tiny nod, silently acknowledging the fact that another forty-one coins had been found, and that Tom could easily prove he owned fifty and more Rohan gold coins if he chose to do so.

Instead, Brigitte responded to the demand by saying quietly, "Thank you. We are very interested; your gold coin could be of high value to us."

The head of the real estate management company appeared encouraged by this apparent show of weakness on the part of the Rohans. *Good,* Philip thought. *Let them dig their own grave,* as the CEO began to speak. "We are planning an ambitious program of development for the Rohan commercial land in Strasbourg. High density dwelling units ..."

Philip raised a hand and said, "Before you continue, if I may..." Without waiting for the CEO to respond, he continued, "According to our brief review, ownership rights to ninety of the two-hundred sixty properties in Strasbourg owned by the Rohan corporation and managed by you have been transferred to other entities. This was done without the approval of the Rohan corporation or even giving us notice. How do you explain that?"

"I am not aware of any such transactions," the CEO said after several stuttering starts. "Nothing on such a large scale would have been carried out without my knowledge and approval."

Sandy directed the real estate management team's attention to the computer projector screen, where numerous legal documents bearing official seals scrolled by. "These are property transaction records from the City of Strasbourg," she said. "Rohan lost ninety properties in the past eight years, all without our consent."

This brought an arrogant response from RCP's legal counsel. "I don't have all the details with me, but I can assure you that Duke Michael was fully informed of all of the property transfers. End of discussion."

"Not quite," Julia said. "As you already know, I am Julia Rohan, the second child and eldest daughter of Tom Rohan. What you do not know about me is that I am the Paris Seventh District Circuit Court Deputy Judge."

Philip couldn't help smiling at the reaction among the five members of the RCP team. Their faces blanched; they whispered urgently to each other, and they began scrambling through laptops and briefcases. Philip nodded at his sister to continue.

"What Duke Michael received from the City of Strasbourg are ninety obscure liens on the properties. He was not of competent mind to understand the implications and the causes behind the liens, so he took no action. If you had been doing your jobs properly, you would have arranged with the city to send the liens to RCP, not to Duke Michael."

More muttering and sifting through documents from the RCP delegation, but nothing was said aloud.

Julia's voice went stern and she stared directly at the real estate company's CEO. "Our investigation shows the tenants purposely made complaints and triggered the liens. Then, they paid off the lien and transferred the address for city correspondence to themselves. With the property tax bills now going directly to them, they paid them for the next three years."

"And your point is?" the CEO said with a sneer.

"After paying the property taxes for three years," Julia declared, "they went back to the city and claimed Rohan had abandoned the properties and transferred the property rights to themselves."

She held a sheet of paper aloft and finished, "These tenants never existed! They were fictitious names all created by Resource Commercial Property. In our modern world we have a name for this type of activity. It is a scam!"

Before anyone on the RCP team could say a word, Sandy said, "As legal representative of the Rohan corporation, I demand immediate access to your company's property deed transaction database, system and files."

The RCP attorney stood and pointed a finger first at Sandy and then at Julia. "Your demand is unacceptable and absurd. And your allegations have no basis in fact." By now, he was all but sputtering with anger. "Your preposterous stories and demands do a disservice to the prestigious royal house of Rohan."

Sandy, unruffled and unperturbed, said, "Ladies and gentlemen, I would call your attention to two special guests." She gestured toward the two men standing in the back of the room, whom all had assumed were simply security guards.

The older of the two agents spoke. "My partner and I are fraud and crime investigators for the Strasbourg Police Department. We have been following this scam for years. You will come in for questioning at police headquarters immediately following this meeting."

The CEO's face went from pink to red to purple. "You have no right!" he shouted.

"Oh, but we do," the investigator said smoothly. "This is not an invitation; it is a command."

The RCP team continued to raise their voices in protest and wave their arms in frustration. One of the women even looked like she was about to bolt from the room.

The investigator and his partner moved in closer, surrounding the five dishonest businesspeople. "You can cooperate and come in peacefully," he said. "Or we can start putting on handcuffs. Now, which will it be?"

Brigitte adjourned the meeting as the five shuffled out of the conference room, their heads hanging low and shoulders hunched in defeat. Philip observed the sharp contrast to their arrogant arrival and almost felt sorry for them.

The Rohans plus Sandy, Victor and Brigitte began to gather up their possessions. The meeting had lasted only fifteen minutes and the next presentation wasn't scheduled until 3:00 p.m.

Tom approached Philip and Julia and said, "I am proud of you, my dear son and daughter. You both handled what could have been a very ugly situation with intelligence, tact and diplomacy."

"If anyone had doubts about our royal blood, you really demonstrated what you are made of," Antoinette added.

Philip basked in the glow of approval from his mother and father and said, "At least we Rohans have experienced some vindication. Slowly the world will begin to see how we were the victims of scams and cheating. And yet..."

"It's disturbing to know the world includes people who are capable of fraud on such a grand scale, yes?" his father suggested.

"Precisely," Philip said. "I'm glad we were able to expose them, and that justice will be served. But I wish we never had to deal with such people in the first place."

"Your mother and I feel much the same," Tom said. "Happy to see our son and daughter perform so well, pleased that wrong-doers have been exposed and will be dealt with appropriately... but sad just the same."

Too soon the three o'clock hour arrived, the appointed time to meet with potentially the most difficult situation of them all— Foremost Pharmaceuticals, and the huge fine levied by the City of Stuttgart over water pollution.

Five men in dark business suits entered the conference room and took their seats at the table. Philip knew by reputation that these executives would be no easy opponents, but at least they had understood the gravity of the meeting and demonstrated proper respect in their dress and demeanor. Still, Philip knew that he and his sister would have to be as sharp and focused around them as they had been with the real estate scam artists from Strasbourg.

Brigitte opened the session by welcoming the delegation from Foremost Pharmaceuticals to Castle Rohan. "We have had a long-term relationship with Foremost for the past half-century, perhaps even the past seventy or eighty years," she said. "We hope that cordial relationship can continue for many decades to come."

Herr Hans Mann, Chief Financial Officer for Foremost, returned the greeting and gave a brief outline of the company's pharmaceutical business and portfolio.

No sooner had he finished than Sandy took the floor. "The Rohan corporation has five major land holdings in Stuttgart. Foremost and two other medical device companies hold long-term leases on prime land. We want to maintain good relations with you, but the fact is, your company has filed complaint after complaint with city officials. The fines have escalated, and now we face a penalty of one-point-two billion Euros."

Brigitte nodded to Philip. To Herr Mann, he said, "We know you hold one gold Rohan coin. That could certainly be of help to us in solidifying our position as the rightful heirs to the Rohan throne. Meanwhile, our study of your leases shows that other similar properties are going for ten to thirty times what you are paying." He paused to let this information sink in, then said, "How do you propose we move into a win-win situation?"

"I'll take that question, if I may," said the attorney for Foremost, Herr Bernard Schmidt. "We have tried without success to negotiate with Duke Michael to build an underground water treatment plant to meet the city's requirements. We never received anywhere close to a positive response. Just more questions and postponements of crucial decisions."

While the Foremost executives and the Rohan team exchanged words, one man had been sitting quietly with the Foremost delegation. He couldn't have been more than forty, and like his colleagues, he was impeccably groomed in conservative business attire. His look and manner exuded a calm confidence that never bordered on superiority or arrogance. It was, Philip realized, the very same image he did his best to project in all of his business meetings.

Speaking perfect French with only a slight German accent, he said, "It is my pleasure to pay my deepest respects to the Rohan family."

All eyes in the room were on him as he continued, "I am Fritz Gerhardt, the new CEO of Foremost Pharmaceuticals."

"On behalf of the Rohans, it is our pleasure to make your acquaintance, Herr Gerhardt," Brigitte said.

"Please, call me Fritz," he said with a friendly smile. Turning serious, he continued, "What you say is true; our company purchased a Rohan coin for one-point-three million Euros because we thought it would give us an edge when it came to leveraging. I deeply regret that purchase and personally apologize to the Rohan family."

Philip looked at Julia and in her eyes saw the same astonishment that he was now feeling.

"I hereby direct Herr Schmidt to return the coin to the Rohan family immediately and without any strings attached," Fritz said.

Scarcely believing what he was seeing, Philip watched as Herr Schmidt removed an archive-quality glassine envelope from his briefcase. Through the transparent paper, he could easily see that the envelope did, indeed, contain a gold coin. Herr Schmidt held the envelope open so all could see and verify the contents, and passed it over to Sandy while Fritz continued to voice apologies.

Sandy looked at Brigitte and Tom and, receiving nods of approval from both, said, "We are grateful to accept this coin, and appreciate the return of a valued family relic," she said.

On his legal pad, Philip scratched out a note to Julia: "A good sign, yes?" Julia took the pad and pen from her brother and answered, "An excellent sign!" She handed the pen back to Philip, who added two more words: "Win-win!"

While Philip and Julia were exchanging notes, Fritz continued to expound as to how grateful he was that key policy-makers at Foremost were finally able to meet with their counterparts with the Rohan corporation. "I believe that within ninety minutes, or even sixty, we can have all of our issues resolved."

Philip was beginning to understand how such a young man—appearing only slightly older than him—could have risen to the top position of a major business entity. He was obvious intelligent and competent, but beyond that, he had a special quality difficult to describe, an aura of calm, quiet, positive energy. It was as if he had the ability to smooth over the emotions of everyone in the room just by his mere presence. Philip had encountered only one other person who demonstrated that quality in an even greater degree—his father, Tom Rohan.

All eyes were now riveted on Fritz, who returned the even gaze from his blue-gray eyes, finally stopping at Philip. "I have a confession to make," Fritz said. If there was anyone in the room who had not been paying close attention, this statement jolted their awareness. "That huge fine was at least in part a strategic move by Foremost. We were hoping that Rohan would allow us to move forward in modernizing our plant, including the underground water treatment facility. Instead, the penalties kept piling up, which is why they now stand at a staggering one-point-two billion Euros."

"We're well aware of the amount of the fine," Sandy said, sounding testy.

"Of course you are," Fritz said smoothly. "I recommend we join forces and work with the city in a positive manner. Show them how sincere we are about cleaning up the pollution problem and meeting their requirements. Once they realize we are acting in good faith and are actually installing the water treatment facility, it's my belief they will forgive the fine, all one-point-two billion Euros of it."

At that statement, several members of the Foremost team exchanged surprised looks. The Rohan family members and Brigitte, Sandy and Victor could not help breaking into grins and huge sighs of relief. *Could it really be that easy?* Philip wondered. *A huge fine just disappearing like that?*

With this positive turn of events, Philip said, "My sister and I have had the opportunity to review fifteen land leases that we have with Foremost. All of the terms are greatly under market value."

"We are more than willing to pay fair market value," Fritz said. "In Stuttgart's prime business area, most businesses are bringing in ten times in annual revenues compared to what they are paying to lease the land where their manufacturing plants sit. Unfortunately, some of the Rohan real estate holdings in Stuttgart are in depressed areas without proper water treatment facilities. This is another example of how we need to work together to solve the problem. We made many overtures to Duke Michael over the years, but he would never respond."

"Well, the Rohans are more than prepared to respond now," Philip said with a smile.

"Foremost wants to build a new plant," Fritz said. "And I happen to know that two of our neighbors are also looking to renovate their manufacturing facilities. I'm fairly certain I can convince them to join us—another win-win situation."

Though encouraged by all Fritz had to offer, Philip could feel his elation sag. *Where on earth will the Rohan corporation find the money to pay for a water treatment facility?*

As if reading the expression of doubt on Phillip's face, Fritz said, "I am proposing that Foremost allocate funds to cover all capital expenses. In exchange, we ask Rohan to give us land use rights for forty-five years. Furthermore, we will increase our lease payments by twelve times the base level, which is in the mid-range of what it is actually worth, subject to annual adjustment based on market fluctuations. I truly hope and believe this is a win-win situation that will allow Foremost to build a world-class pharmaceutical production facility and lift the burden of the fines from the Rohan corporation."

Brigitte had been busily entering data onto her computer as Fritz outlined his offer. Now she dimmed the lights and projected her findings onto the screen. Necks craned to see as everyone in the conference room studied the summary.

- Fines totaling one-point-two billion Euros to be removed.
- Lease terms increased by a factor of twelve. In two years, that would bring in thirty million Euros, up from the current twenty-five.
- The details will require diligent work from the finance and legal departments.
- A win-win situation.

Brigitte raised the lighting and pressed a button on her remote control, causing the screen to retract into the ceiling. Now everyone had their attention focused on the newly crowned King of Rohan for his reaction.

"I will have to admit, all of us in Rohan management expected a long, bitter and turbulent bargaining session with Foremost," Tom said in a pleasant tone. "The last thing we expected was this win-win situation. It feels as if difficulties and entanglements that have lasted five years and longer have been resolved in forty-five minutes."

With smiles to the members of the Rohan and Foremost delegations, Tom said, "Of course, it is only prudent that Rohan dedicate a contingency team that will work with Foremost in vetting all finance and legal issues in the next thirty days. However, since we have all the decision-makers in one place this afternoon, let us sign a provisional agreement. Once our vetting team gives us the green light, our agreement will be effective as of today's date."

Brigitte hastily printed out an agreement based on the information in her PowerPoint presentation, and the principals from both sides gathered around the conference table to affix their signatures. With that, the meeting adjourned with handshakes, warm wishes, and even exchanges of *la bise,* the traditional French air kiss on both cheeks.

As Fritz was about to exit the conference room, Philip pulled him aside. "I cannot thank you enough," he began in a low voice.

"No, it is I who should be thanking you," Fritz said. "For years, our expansion plans have been put on hold due to the difficulties in dealing with Duke Michael. Now we can move forward and build the new plant. With that, comes the potential for far greater profits."

"But still, you did not have to be quite so generous in your offer to us."

"Be that as it may, it is a pleasure to sit across the table with competent professionals like you and your sister after so many years of dealing with an individual who... well, let us say no more on that matter. As long as we can continue to deal with you and Julia, I predict a cordial and profitable relationship between Foremost and the Rohans for five, ten, maybe even twenty years down the line."

"We would like that very much," Philip said, feeling as if the weight of the world had just lifted from his shoulders. "And thank you for returning my father's gold coin." To himself, he added, *A strong and friendly alliance with Fritz Gerhardt is worth far more than one gold coin.*

CHAPTER TWENTY-ONE

Tom suddenly found himself alone in the conference room except for one remaining security guard, everyone else having departed in a chorus of applause and cordial bonding. He almost didn't know how he was supposed to feel: relieved, happy, sad, worried... he'd ridden an emotional roller-coaster for the past six hours.

Realizing that the best cure would be another visit to his mother's garden, he made his way to that very destination. He assumed Antoinette had also retreated to the park-like castle grounds and was surprised when she was nowhere to be found among the meandering paths, shady trees, and formal beds of flowering annuals and perennials. Then he looked up and spotted a tiny lone figure on the narrow walkway at the top of the castle wall, leaning over the parapet.

What on earth is she doing?

Tom raced up the ancient stone steps leading to the top of the wall and carefully picked his way along the ancient walkway. Over the parapet was a sheer drop of several hundred meters, ending at the bedrock that formed the castle foundation.

"Antoinette! What do you think you are doing?" he demanded between gasps for air.

She turned to Tom with a faraway look in her eyes, her long brown hair swirling gently in the late afternoon breeze. "Just hoping I could see Dijon and our home." She pointed in a southwest direction, across miles of forest far below.

"Ah," Tom said, his voice calming as he understood. "Too far away to pick out with the naked eye, I'm afraid."

"Still, I can pretend I can see it, can't it?"

"If it will make you feel better, *petite femme*."

"We've been gone six days," she mused. "A lot can happen back home in six days. Look at everything that has happened to us!"

"We haven't done too badly for ourselves, have we?" Tom said, slipping an arm around her waist and joining her gaze over the castle wall.

"I was just thinking of how it all started, with Gilbert winning a prize at school. And now you're the King of Rohan and we've sent Gilbert home. Poor *bébé!*" she sighed. "I can't help worrying about how he's getting on, staying with Ronald's family and going to school surrounded by bodyguards."

"He's doing fine," Tom reassured. "Those Lombardi guards are probably teaching him their favorite self-defense moves, or how to win at poker, even as we speak."

"But what of Ronald?" she continued to fret. "Adele and Louise? Have you forgotten about your other children?"

Tom knew all too well that she would worry herself into a dither if he allowed her to continue. "It is getting a bit chilly up here, wouldn't you say?" he said soothingly. "Come back to our rooms where it's warm and cozy, and you can call Gilbert on the mobile. He should be getting home from school right about now."

Moments later, Tom chuckled to himself as he observed Antoinette happily lounging in an easy chair, the phone clamped to one ear, chatting merrily with *mon doux bébé*. He knew she'd be occupied for at least ninety minutes, first with Gilbert, and then Ronald, Adele and Louise and quite possibly the grandchildren as well.

"I'll see about arranging for dinner," he said to her in a low voice, knowing she was far too preoccupied to hear or care.

Tom made his way through the cold, silent halls of the castle in search of the kitchen and the chance of dinner. Even though he knew there must be a bodyguard unobtrusively following his every move, he was suddenly overwhelmed with loneliness. Through the tense financial meetings today, he'd scarcely had a chance to interact with Julia, Philip or anyone else on the Rohan team. Though grateful for their loyalty and expertise, he couldn't help feeling tiny and insignificant as his footsteps echoed through the vast, empty halls. Just like Antoinette, he needed to reach out and talk to another trusted human being.

When he reached an alcove just outside the kitchen with an antique rotary-dial phone, he could stand it no longer. Picking up the receiver, he was relieved to hear a dial tone, and even more elated when Louis picked up on the first ring. "My lord, I was just about to call you," Louis said. The sound of his voice immediately lifted Tom's spirits.

"I was hoping to see you sometime this evening so we can do a final check on our equipment before embarking on our discovery tour tomorrow," Louis continued. "Where are you?"

"Just outside the castle kitchen. I was about to go in and make arrangements for a spot of dinner for Antoinette and myself."

This was greeted by a roar of laughter from Louis.

"Did I say something funny?" Tom asked.

When his guffaws finally stopped, Louis said, "There are two local secrets that you should know about."

"Secrets? What kind of secrets?"

"The first secret—the kitchen in Castle Rohan is not very good," Louis said, still amused. "In fact, it's downright lousy."

"But that can't be," Tom said, still mystified. "We've had excellent meals since arriving here. The coronation banquet, last night's supper, even the box lunches today… everything was superb, like a five-star restaurant."

"Ah, that's where the second secret comes into play. You see, the chef at the hospital in Saint Meyer is excellent, one of the best in the nation. He is the top chef in all of Grand Est."

"Hospital food?" Tom asked doubtfully.

"Indeed, hospital food. The coronation banquet? All the meals you have had here at the castle, right down to those box lunches? They were all catered by Chef Jean, not the castle kitchen."

"I had no idea," Tom said, impressed.

"The fact is, the only meals the castle kitchen prepares are lunches for the full-time staff, the gardeners and housekeepers and the like.

And even some of them head down to the village for their lunch break," Louis said with another chuckle.

"I have but one question," Tom said, momentarily forgetting all about the gear for tomorrow's adventure. "How can Antoinette and I get a reservation for dinner tonight at the hospital restaurant?"

"No need for that, my lord. André has already ordered dinner for six and is already on his way back from picking it up."

"That André, he thinks of everything," Tom said, once again thinking to himself that sometimes, it was fun to be the king.

Retracing his steps to the suite he shared with Antoinette, Tom suddenly realized how hungry he was. *Funny what sitting all day in a tense financial meeting can do to a man's appetite,* he thought to himself.

He found Antoinette just finishing her final phone call. With a deep sigh, she said, "Such a torturous day. I feel as if I could eat my way through *La Grande Epicerie.* What is the plan for dinner tonight?"

"Tell you what," Tom said playfully, "let us pray that a gourmet meal will magically appear in, oh, say, five minutes."

As if truly by magic, a knock came on the door. Louis entered, holding a bottle of the finest champagne to be found in Alsace in each hand. André and Antony followed, carrying four large baskets wrapped tightly in table linens. The homey warmth and tempting aromas wafting from the baskets immediately filled the room.

"We heard you might be wanting a bit of dinner," Louis said with a twinkle in his eye. "What we have here is not just an entrée, but also salads, soup and of course, dessert.'

With a cry of delight, Antoinette grabbed one of the baskets and hurried to the suite's dining table. She spread a table cloth and began to lay out place settings, humming a little tune to herself. Tom was overjoyed to see her so happy with the food, the wine, and the present company, in contrast to her worried state of the late afternoon.

"How wonderful and considerate," Tom said to Louis. "You have really made us feel right at home."

Louis beckoned Tom closer and in a low voice said, "Chef Jean can be considered one of us. He is descended from one of the original knights of Rohan, and is about to become a member of the

Carolingian Sacred Heart."

Life could not be better, Tom decided after enjoying a meal of truffle filet mignon, basil salmon, butter vegetables, and dessert, accompanied by an excellent local red wine. *Good food, good people.*

Just as the dessert dishes had been scraped clean, the phone rang. Louis answered, and after a moment's conversation, motioned to Antoinette. "Would you like to speak with Chef Jean?"

"I'd be happy to," Antoinette replied, patting her lips with her napkin and rising. After voicing gratitude for the wonderful meal, she ended the call and reported to the party around the dining table, "He's ecstatic that we liked his food and happy to be of service to us. He even invited me to visit his restaurant in in the Saint Meyer hospital."

After the final drop in the second bottle of red wine had been consumed, Tom finally remembered the original purpose of the meeting with Louis: to go over the equipment needed for the explorations planned for the next day—especially the protection against the poison gas that they were pretty sure lurked deeper in the dungeon.

Tom did a thorough inventory of the equipment that Louis had procured. Each person would be given a backpack containing goggles, a head lamp, an oxygen bottle and mask, and each team would be equipped with a camera specially designed for low-light conditions, a toxic gas detector, gas and material sample bags, a first aid kit, two-way radios and several long ropes.

The dinner party began to break up shortly before nine o'clock, leaving the royal couple once again alone.

"You know, you haven't really experienced Castle Rohan until you've seen a sunset from the turret," Tom said to Antoinette with a smile of invitation.

"Let me guess," Antoinette said, returning the affectionate look. "This time of year, late spring, sunset is about fifteen minutes away."

"You must admit, we have perfect timing." Tom took Antoinette's hand and guided her through the labyrinthine hallways and up a long spiral staircase to the top of the look-out tower, the tallest point in the castle.

Clouds had rolled in like ocean waves covering the valley below, but leaving Castle Rohan open to the sky. Far to the west, the sun was just beginning its final descent behind a range of hills barely peeking above the clouds. "How magical," Antoinette said, her voice carrying the wonder of a child. "It's almost like being in an airplane, but even better."

"Indeed," Tom said. "When I was a child, I always felt free as an eagle up here in the turret at sunset, like I was in my own secret world."

For the next ten minutes or so, the pair was silent, entranced by the spectacular show of light and color being put on by the sun, the clouds and the rotation of the planet.

Though reluctant to break the spell, Tom gently pointed out that the light was dimming and they'd best return to their suite before the turret became dangerously dark. "We have a big day ahead of us tomorrow," he reminded her. "Not just the treasure room, but also those other doors that we haven't yet looked in, and the jail cell that might give us access to the original Rohan court chamber. We have no idea what we're going to find, or the dangers we may encounter."

"Admit it," Antoinette teased. "You'd rather face a dragon than sit through another day of financial review meetings."

"You know me too well, *ma cherie*." And with that, the royal couple ended the day with a passionate embrace and kiss.

CHAPTER TWENTY-TWO

Excitement and anticipation crackled in the atmosphere as if electrically charged as Tom, Antoinette, Antony and Louis gathered in the king's suite the following morning. Today they would see what new treasures might be hidden behind the doors in the chamber with the gold coins. The jail cell provided access to the original Rohan royal court—who knew what priceless relics might be found there? But the persistent rotten-egg smell, surely an indicator of poison gas, reminded them that dangers also lurked in their path.

Tom addressed the trio: "Today's objective is to create the best record we can as to what lies beneath Castle Rohan. We will do that by surveying with rough measurements, sketching out a diagram of the layout, and taking quality, detailed photographs. Antoinette and I will both be equipped with waterproof cameras designed for low-light conditions."

He split the group into two teams: Antoinette and Antony would take the cavern with the gold coins and the hidden rooms beyond it, while he and Louis would enter the Rohan chamber by way of the jail cell. "Above all, do not disturb any artifacts," he said. "Try not to even touch anything. And don't forget to take air and surface samples to be sent to the lab for analysis."

Next, the group tested the two-way radios, making sure all knew how to operate them properly. "Just in case anything happens to us, we can signal Antony on the walkie-talkies," Tom said. "Antony will then go outside for help."

"Do not expect much in the way of help so deep inside the

castle," Antony warned. "Best to use caution so we do not have to depend on outside help."

With that, the four shouldered their backpacks and retraced their steps from the previous day: through the armoire and down the spiral staircase, stopping to make a notation in the logbook, and then onward and ever downward. After leaving Antoinette and Antony in the chamber with the gold coins, Louis and Tom arrived at the jail cell. The pair eagerly removed the boards from the second bed, revealing another layer of planks beneath it, and a small door. Tom used his father's key to unlock the door and found yet another spiral staircase.

"Here we go!" Tom said, feeling more like a twelve-year-old boy than a one-hundred year-old father and grandfather. Each man strapped on a headlamp and goggles, and donned an oxygen mask. Louis tied a rope to help guide them down, and held the toxic gas detector at arm's length.

If Tom had though the spiral staircase in the turret was steep, this latest passageway was truly more like a ladder—a narrow, rickety ladder—than a staircase. He was very glad that Louis had thought to bring a rope, because without it as a guide, he surely would have lost his footing. To occupy his mind and distract himself from the very real danger, Tom counted the steps and recorded the height, approximately five meters.

At the foot of the stairway, Tom and Louis found themselves in a small room with a door at the far side. They looked at each other with smiles of relief. "At least the poison gas detector hasn't gone off yet," Louis said.

Once again, King Raymond's key worked in the lock. The door swung open to reveal three steps. Though they did not breathe the ambient air, they could tell from the cool flow on their skin that the air was moving and it seemed fresh.

"How could it be, such good ventilation in a sealed environment?" Louis asked.

"If my ancestors figured out how to bring in fresh air to this underground chamber for so many centuries, that would be quite a puzzle," Tom agreed.

The two explorers descended the three steps into a large chamber of approximately one-hundred fifty square meters. "This must be it!" Louis crowed. "Your father used to tell me that Lothair's chamber was directly below the old jail cell."

Tom was speechless with wonder, imagining himself standing in the very spot where over one thousand years ago, his direct ancestor, Emperor Lothair, had ruled what was left of his empire. He recalled the historical details that Antoinette had imparted that night in the hotel following his coronation, how Lothair had hidden his war chest, did his best to fend off Viking invasions, and finally made peace with his warring brothers and half-brothers, in this very room at Castle Rohan from 845 until his death ten years later.

A shelf covered with parchment rolls immediately commanded their attention. Though neither man dared touch any of the artifacts, they drew close enough to see the inked lettering in Latin on the surface of one of the centuries-old parchments. Tom snapped photographs and by increasing the magnification of the lens, could clearly make out the writing. "It appears to be a log book of some sort," Tom told Louis. "The date of 845 appears several times."

"More proof that we really have found the seat of Lothair's government," Louis said with awe. "After all these years, I scarcely dare believe it."

Louis dislodged his oxygen mask slightly and took a tentative sniff of air. "Not bad, only a slight hint of that rotten egg smell." He raised a hand to remove the mask, but Tom warned him not to do so, that other toxic gasses might still be lurking in the area.

Tom keyed his walkie-talkie to speak to Antony. "We are safe and we are almost certain we have discovered Emperor Lothair's court chamber," he reported with excitement.

They continued to sweep the beams of their headlamps around the chamber, next discovering two large chairs trimmed with gold on a raised stone slab. "This must be Lothair's throne," Tom said with great reverence. "And a chair for his queen."

He took numerous pictures of both thrones from various angles, and then turned his attention to the rows of desks and benches facing the two large, ornate chairs. "I'm guessing this must be where his staff and trusted advisors did their work," Tom said.

Louis meanwhile, pointed out another set of shelves holding clay and bronze vases, bowls, and drinking vessels. "They seem to be very well provisioned, and very well organized," Louis observed.

Tom was becoming annoyed at the gas mask, as it created an obstacle in positioning the camera. As the toxic gas detector had not sounded an alarm, he took a chance, removed the gas mask, and took a breath of air. Though he did detect a slight odor of rotten eggs, the air felt quite fresh and cool.

As a trained chemist and biologist, Tom knew that the rotten egg smell was caused by hydrogen sulfide, a product of decay. In residential areas, it is usually due to decomposition in septic or sewer systems. While he understood the gas could be deadly in high concentrations, he also knew that the human olfactory system could detect hydrogen sulfide at levels one four-hundredth lower than the threshold for harmful health effects.

Tom held a brief update with Antoinette on the two-way radio, and then busied himself with Louis is making rough sketches and diagrams, taking plenty of pictures and gathering lab samples.

At last, they tore themselves away from the many intriguing aspects of the royal chamber and followed a hallway. A hand-painted wooden sign hung above the door to a small room to the right. Though the lettering had faded through the centuries, the dire message of the hastily scrawled letters could still be made out: DANGER! BLACK DEATH REMAINS!

"Do you see what I see?" Louis asked in a shaky voice.

Tom nodded, causing the beam from his headlamp to bob over the contents of the room: three stone coffins fronted by small wooden tables for holding memorial objects, one still containing the stub of a candle. He stepped tentatively into the space, quickly took photographs, measurements and samples, all the while feeling as if he couldn't get out of that space fast enough.

"Spooky stuff," he said with a shudder.

"A fact of life in Europe in the fourteenth century," Louis said. "One of the reasons I feel fortunate to live in modern times."

The next room along the hallway could only be reached by descending a wooden stairway. As usual, Louis led the way. Suddenly there came a loud crack, following by a groan of pain, as one of the steps, rotten with age, gave way, tripping Louis. He grabbed for the handrail, but instead of helping him steady himself, it tore away from the stone wall and clattered down the steps. With no handrail to assist him, Louis tumbled down the stairs along with the ruined handrail.

Tom took in the dire situation in an instant. Nails protruded from the section of handrail, rusty with age but still dangerously sharp— and aimed directly at Louis's head. Tom immediately sprang into action, leaping across several steps and using his elbow to fling the chunk of wood with its piercing nails in the opposite direction. With a couple of rolls worthy of a martial arts expert, he landed at the bottom of the stairway and rose to his feet.

Tom helped Louis into a sitting position. "I'm fine, I'm fine," Louis protested, clutching his lower left leg. "Just a minor cut."

"Nonsense," Tom said, calling on his medical background to take charge of the situation. He whipped off his oxygen mask, pushed up Louis' pant leg, and examined the wound. "There appear to be no broken bones or tendons," Tom reported. "But you do have bruising and a cut of some four or five centimeters."

Digging into his backpack, Tom located the first aid kit and began to clean the wound with hydrogen peroxide. Next he applied antiseptic ointment and wrapped the gash with surgical gauze.

Louis rose, put his weight on his left leg and took a cautious step. Tom could tell his companion still suffered some pain, but Louis insisted, "Don't stop because of me. I may limp a bit, but I'm fine."

Tom knew better than to suggest they curtail their adventure, so he and Louis continued their way into the second room.

The chamber with the coffins had been unsettling enough, but nothing had prepared either man for what they saw in this second, larger space. Skulls and bones, pile after pile. Bars and rails, like a prison. Another, larger sign with the same warning: DANGER! BLACK DEATH REMAINS!

Instantly Tom and Louis went into full protection mode, donning gloves and oxygen masks. Slowly they crept in, Tom snapping photographs and Louis collecting samples. With great trepidation, Tom reached out a gloved hand to pick up one of the skulls. He almost dropped it in sheer surprise. Thanks to his training in the pharmaceutical industry, he knew what a human skull should feel like, and how much it should weigh. He returned the cranium to the crumbling pile where he'd found it, and carefully studied other remnants of bones and skulls.

Then he burst out laughing.

"What? What?" Louis demanded, shocked at the sound of merriment in this chamber of horrors.

"They're fakes!" Tom said when he was able to talk. "Someone's trying to fool us with wooden carvings. Very clever, but still fakes."

"Are you sure?"

"A few are real, those right at the front," Tom said. "But the rest? Pure *tromp l'oeil.*"

"But why?"

"To scare away people like us, of course."

Tom spotted a small box partially hidden behind the heap of bones. Eagerly he dug it out and lifted the lid. "Aha!" he said with a triumphant grin, tilting the box toward Louis so he could see the yellow block inside. "Someone has placed hydrogen sulfide in solid form in here to emit that rotten egg smell. There is no decay or decomposition going on. Just more trickery."

"Whoever they are, they are going to great lengths to convince explorers such as ourselves to turn around and go back," Louis observed. "There must be more treasure lying ahead."

"Or a secret too powerful or dangerous ever to be revealed." Tom removed his oxygen mask and used his five senses to test the air: cool, clear, tasteless, and just the slightest odor of rotten eggs, and again he wondered at the source of fresh air. "The air is perfectly safe to breathe," he told Louis. "But you know what happens when people are already frightened and on edge. They latch onto their worst fears instead of considering the empirical evidence."

Tom was about to continue that thought, but stopped. "Do you hear something?" he asked Louis.

Louis cocked his head. "Indeed, my lord."

Both men were silent as they considered the very faint rumbling noise, almost mechanical in nature. Finally Louis spoke. "Do you suppose it is some sort of engine for ventilation, forcing fresh air into these chambers and tunnels?"

"If so, these medieval people had engineering skills far beyond anything known in history."

"It seems to be coming from there." Louis pointed to a wood panel behind the bone heap and removed it. Before them stood a wooden door with a metal frame, similar to the door that guarded the entrance to the room with the gold coins.

Tom pressed his ear to the heavy, old wood. "The noise is definitely coming from the other side of the door," he reported. "And I can feel fresh air flowing in around the gaps in the door frame."

Louis joined Tom in leaning his head against the door. "So powerful," he said. "Hard to believe a sound like that could be coming so far below the surface of the earth. What could it be?"

"Only one way to find out," Tom said with a grin. Once again, he protected himself with the oxygen mask and strapped on the head lamp. Using his father's key and the complicated series of combinations, he undid the locks and let the door wing open.

Immediately they were overwhelmed by a rush of cool, clean air, and the source of the rumbling sound became all too obvious. Almost at their feet flowed a rushing stream of water. While the scene had the appearance of an ancient sewer tunnel, the roaring rapids were obviously clean and pure. The liquid even sparkled from an unknown source of sunlight!

With no obvious danger, Tom and Louis removed their respiratory protection, and Tom made a grab for a two-way radio. "You would not believe what we have found," he exclaimed breathlessly to Antoinette as soon as she answered. "Water! A veritable river, flowing right under the castle."

Antoinette responded by briefly describing the exciting finds she and Antony had made in the treasure room and the chambers beyond. "What are you going to do next?" she asked.

"Find the source of light, of course," Tom said. "Louis sustained a minor injury, but there's no reason why I cannot forge ahead."

"A minor injury? Let me speak to him," Antoinette said. Tom knew she was reverting to her protective mother role, and that there was no stopping her, so he handed the walkie-talkie to Louis. After clucking over Louis's injury and ordering him to watch his step, he heard her say, "Whatever you do, do not let my husband do something foolish. I can hear that water on my end of the two-way, and it sounds like it is moving swiftly. There may be rapids or even a waterfall up ahead."

"Yes, Madame," Louis replied dutifully.

"Make sure Tom is securely attached to the rope. Tie the other end onto something firm, like a rock or a post. If he slips, make sure he does not get washed away or slide into a waterfall."

"As you wish, Madame."

Though both men rolled their eyes at Antoinette's caution and concern, Tom learned almost at once the wisdom of her instructions. No sooner had he taken a few steps on the slippery rock on one side of the rushing water than he lost his footing. Before he quite knew what was happening, he was knee-deep in water and feeling himself caught by the flowing liquid, hurtling downstream. A tug on the rope around his waist from Louis stopped his progress and brought him back to the rock pathway.

A slow, careful walk of around fifteen meters brought him to the end of the tunnel. He stopped to make a photographic record of all he saw, and to draw sketches and make calculations as to size and distance. By leaning far to the right, he could see the water flowing into a huge cave. Echoes of powerful surges of water, roaring and raging, warned him that a waterfall surely dropped precipitously not too far away.

From far back at the doorway came a shout from Louis. "Lord, you should not venture any further. We can always come back another day with more people and better equipment."

"But I can see it," Tom protested. "A huge cave, water rushing into it, and it looks like man-made structures."

"That's exciting," Louis said. "But do not go any further. Come back now, I beg of you."

Tom took a look back and saw Louis tying a second rope to the end of the rope that tethered Tom to a post by the doorway, basically doubling the distance that Tom could safely travel. *He tells me to come back, but he knows I won't,* Tom said to himself with a small chuckle.

Knowing Louis had securely tied him to the post, Tom leaned forward as far as he dared. What he saw almost took his breath away. He'd been right about man-made structures. What he found was a well-preserved city with what appeared to be a chapel or a guild-house. Many of the structures were in ruins, but others still had roofs, doors and windows intact.

What was this place? Why was it buried beneath the earth, and how had it remained hidden for unknown numbers of centuries? The thought of bringing the news of such an incredible find back to the scholars and researchers of today filled Tom with an elation that he had seldom felt before.

While these thoughts and emotions continued to swirl through Tom's mind and heart, his body kept its steady forward motion, the fingers constantly tapping the shutter of the camera. He adjusted the lens to twenty-five times the normal resolution in an attempt to record as much detail as possible, especially with the temple.

So engrossed and enthralled was Tom that he simply lost focus on whatever warning signals his body might have issued. One moment he was perched on the slick stone path, leaning forward, eagerly recording all the wonders that his eyes were taking in, and the next moment his feet were slipping out from under him.

He tumbled into the chilly water, chest deep. Frantically, he tried to regain his footing, but it was simply no use: the current was too swift, the stones at his feet too slippery. The powerful current had Tom in its grip and was carrying him with relentless force to only one destination: the waterfall. He flailed his arms and legs, desperately trying to regain some sense of balance, but he was no match for the current, and soon only his head managed to stay above the waterline.

At first, Tom heard shouts from Louis, but as he was swept farther away, those human sounds were drowned out by the roar and rumble of the waterfall, drawing inevitably closer. He tipped his head back to allow his mouth and nose to stay above the water and gasped desperately for life-giving oxygen.

Still he struggled, doing everything he could to stay alive, knowing all the while that if he did hurtle over the torrent, it was highly unlikely he would survive. And yet despite his desperate efforts, the churning waters refused to yield, and the turbulence of thousands of cubic meters of water crashing over a sheer, rocky drop grew all the more loud.

A new image entered Tom's mind: the previous evening, watching the sunset with Antoinette from the castle turret and the loving tenderness that followed. *If this is to be the end for me,* he thought, *at least Antoinette will have that moment to remember, and I will have it to carry with me to the next world.*

And with that, he felt a measure of peace as the current carried him closer and closer to the edge.

CHAPTER TWENTY-THREE

Atug on the rope. Almost imperceptible. Or did Tom imagine it? He was too exhausted to know whether the tiny motion represented reality, or just the hallucinations of a man about to die.

Another firm jerk, and this time there was no mistake—Louis was slowly but surely reeling Tom back from the watery precipice.

Clinging to the rope like the lifeline that it was, Tom let Louis pull him back toward the rocky shelf that served as a path. Using every ounce of strength in his upper body, for the rocks remained far too slippery to offer firm footing, Tom heaved himself out of the water and onto the ledge.

At first, he could only lie there like a fish out of water, sputtering and shaking water out of his hair and clothes. Louis's panicked shouts soon brought him back to full consciousness. He rose and looked back, only to see Louis's hands wrapped around the post that held the rope, leaning backwards with all his might. As quickly as Tom dared, he picked his way back along the slippery walkway until he arrived, panting and dripping, in the doorway with Louis.

"Sure glad we put a waterproof camera on the shopping list," Tom said gleefully, hoisting the camera, still on its strap around his neck, above his head. "And sure glad I managed to hang onto it. I seem to have lost my glasses, though."

"We can always replace your glasses. My lord, I thought for sure we had lost you," Louis exclaimed, finally removing his hands from the post and embracing Tom in a hug.

The instant Louis's firm grip left the post, it popped out of its foundation like a champagne cork being released from the bottle.

Post and rope flew into the water. Tom hastily untied the other end from his waist. Another few additional seconds and his end of the rope would have dragged him back into the river, and he would have found him right back where he'd almost met his doom.

"That was a close one," Tom said.

"In more ways than one," Louis agreed. "You have cheated death at least twice this afternoon."

Louis examined Tom for injuries, but found only bruises and scrapes from the rocks that he'd tumbled against in his battle against the raging waters. "The King of Rohan seems to have more lives than a cat," Louis murmured as he applied ointment to the scrapes.

"You have no idea what I've discovered," Tom said, indicating the camera. "I must take more measurements and samples."

Louis shook his head firmly. "We're going back. Now."

"But there's so much more to explore..."

"No buts. If nothing else, we've got to get you into some dry clothes."

Tom had to admit, the idea of dry clothes did sound appealing, and without his glasses, his effectiveness as a researcher had been severely hampered. He allowed Louis to lead him back to Emperor Lothair's court chamber, and up the spiral staircase.

"You realize the most dangerous part of our journey lies ahead of us, don't you?" Louis asked as they made the climb.

"How so?"

"Facing Antoinette when she finds out I let you do something foolish and almost turned her into a widow."

"*Mon dieu*," Tom agreed with a knowing chuckle. "I think I'd rather take my chances with the waterfall."

Antoinette reacted just as Tom and Louis knew she would when both men limped into the uppermost chamber with the desk and logbook. She gave Louis a dagger-like look, and insisted on examining the injuries on both, ignoring their insistence that they were fine and needed no treatment.

"You're going to the emergency room, both of you," she declared. To Antony she said, "Arrange for a town car. Nothing conspicuous. No ambulance. Call ahead to the nearest hospital and let them know two VIP patients are about to arrive and they are to be treated with the strictest privacy."

Tom and Louis could only sit by helplessly as Antoinette bustled about, issuing orders. When they emerged in the king's chambers, she sent for André and directed him to pack extra clothing for all four of them and to be ready to place it in the town car when it arrived.

"Don't forget my briefcase," Tom told Antoinette. "I'm going to want my laptop and the camera."

"What you want is medical treatment and rest," Antoinette retorted, but she did as he asked.

Before he could quite take in what was happening, Tom found himself being hustled into a comfortable black car and whisked down the twisty road, away from the castle. He noticed matching unmarked SUVs leading and following, and remarked on the coincidence to Antony.

"That's no coincidence, Papa," Antony replied. "They're part of the security detail lead by Major Dumas. Perhaps you were unaware of their presence, but you have been under their protection ever since your coronation."

They arrived at the nearest town, Saint-Meyer, located at the foot of the mountain that featured Castle Rohan at its peak. Though the city appeared small and little changed since at least the 1800s, it boasted a comprehensive and up-to-date medical facility. Bypassing the usual hospital check-in system, Tom and Louis were immediately taken to a secluded examination room. Antoinette continued her take-charge role, informing the chief medical officer that as far as his staff was concerned, Tom and Louis needed only routine medical check-ups. "All records, test results and x-rays are to be turned over to us," she said. "No record of our having ever been here is to remain in your system. Is that understood?"

"As you wish, Madame," the chief medical officer said with a slight bow.

Despite her best efforts, word quickly spread throughout the small hospital that new King and Queen of Rohan were present in their facility. Timidly and then more boldly, the staff gathered at the door of the examination room to peek inside. Tom even overheard one nurse say to the other, "Can you believe he's one-hundred one years old? He has the face and body of a man in his early sixties."

"No respect for our privacy," Antony muttered. "Shall I shut the door, Papa?"

Tom shook his head. "They're not causing any harm," he said. "Remember, this region has a long tradition with the Rohan family and the legends of Emperor Lothair for a millennium and longer. Of course, they're excited. Some of these doctors and nurses could very well be our distant cousins."

More medical personnel arrived, and Tom and Louis were helped out of their damp, dirty and bloody clothing and placed in hospital gowns. Next followed various routine medical tests, plus a thorough examination of their injuries.

"You are very lucky," the physician told Tom. "No broken bones. Just a lot of nasty bruises and scrapes." He arranged for a temporary pair of glasses for Tom, with lenses that matched his own well enough. As for Louis, the gash on his leg proved to be deeper than he'd first thought, and required several stiches to close. The doctor wrote a prescription for mild painkillers for both men, and informed them that they would need to remain in the hospital for several more hours until the test results came back, and until it was certain no infections would develop or that they were suffering from delayed effects of exposure to potentially poisonous gas.

Tom and Louis were offered separate private rooms, but they both insisted they'd prefer to share quarters while they waited for the return of the test results. They were transferred to a large room with two beds, a sofa for visiting family members, a desk, and a screen between the beds in case privacy was required. An orderly brought in a tray of light bread, cheese, apple juice and milk.

Louis helped himself to the snack, then curled up on the bed and immediately fell into a deep sleep. Tom, still too keyed up from the day's adventures to even think of resting, sat at the desk, grabbed his briefcase and removed the laptop. Between bites of bread and cheese, he uploaded some four-hundred photos from the waterproof camera onto the cloud, where he knew they would be safe. Only then did he allow himself to relax slightly.

Antoinette, seated at his side, gasped in amazement as she viewed the coffins, the plague warning signs, the heap of fake bones, and the box of hydrogen sulfide.

"That's nothing," Tom said. "Wait until you see this." He advanced the images on the computer screen to the tunnel and running water, the cave and the sun shining at the far end.

"Do you suppose that river flows to Saint-Meyer?" Antoinette asked.

"Perhaps," Tom said. He then clicked forward to the prize of the collection, the photos of the ruined city and the chapel.

"But-but... that's impossible!" Antoinette said. "How could there be an entire city so far underground?"

"I know," Tom said. "This is a discovery of great importance. It may change our understanding of the history of this region."

For several moments, the couple scrolled through the photographs silently, lost in wonder. Finally Tom said, "But I've been ignoring you. I'm sure you and Antony have exciting discoveries of your own to share."

"We were only able to enter one of the three rooms," she said. "Inside, we found jewelry and artwork, as if it were a vault for Emperor Lothair's most valuable possessions. Antony and I were searching for a key to open the other two rooms when we found what may be the most important prize of all."

"And that would be?" Tom asked his wife.

"A long parchment roll with an inventory of all the materials, documents and other possessions in the treasure rooms."

"That is indeed significant."

"And it's safely recorded right here," Antoinette said with a grin as she lifted her camera by the strap. Then her expression grew serious. "I've got to get these stored on the cloud."

While she worked on the computer, she provided details of her find to Tom. "The scrolls and parchments come from the original sacred site of Villa Meyer, a typical manorial villa established after the fall of West Rome in 476. It's believed that Saint Meyer was born there."

"Ah yes, the namesake of the town, and this hospital," Tom said.

Antoinette clicked to one of her photographs of the scrolls. "This particular document tells of an earthquake in 1356. Villa Meyer was buried under the landslide."

"We know Villa Meyer was the center of the first Carolingian renaissance," Tom said. "Perhaps the city and chapel that I discovered is the original Saint-Meyer that was buried in the earthquake. But we won't know until I can go back there and make further explorations."

"You're not doing any more exploring until you've recovered from this one," Antoinette warned. "And speaking of that, it's time for you to take a nap."

Tom knew it was best to humor her and offered no resistance as she helped him up from the desk and toward the bed. "What will you do while I'm snoozing?" he asked as she tucked him in.

"I'm going to check out this famous gourmet hospital cafeteria I've heard so much about. After all," she said with a sly smile, "we've already sampled Chef Jean's cuisine and we know he's one of the best in all of France."

*   *   *

Antoinette followed the signs to *cafétéria*, leading her to a large room, brightly lit and spotlessly clean, with tables and chairs in light woods that presented an image that spoke of both simplicity and elegance. Three walls were decorated with modern pastel artwork, while the fourth wall consisted of a floor-to-ceiling window offering a breathtaking view of the Vosges Mountains and Castle Rohan. With three security guards following at a discreet distance, she purchased a coffee and an individual fruit tart and found a small table in a deserted corner. She was aware of people watching her, pointing out the new Queen of Rohan to each other, and gave them gracious smiles in return.

Two men in white coats approached the security guards, showed their identification, and were ushered to Antoinette's table. As they drew closer, she could see one wore a hospital lab coat, while the other was attired in a chef's jacket. The man in the lab coat introduced himself as Pierre Leblanc, the assistant chief of staff at the hospital. "And this," he said, indicating a small man with a bright smile, "is the famous Chef Jean."

Antoinette greeted both men warmly and invited them to share her table. Docteur Leblanc said, "Chef Jean and his staff would be honored to prepare and present their best desserts and beverages for *le goûter* this afternoon and a four-course dinner for the King and his family this evening."

"You are too kind," Antoinette said. To Chef Jean, she added, "We so enjoyed the baskets you prepared for us last night. You must tell me about your career and credentials."

Chef Jean did just that, describing to Antoinette the various government officials and celebrities that he had cooked for over the years. He signaled one of the waitresses to bring a menu. When the young woman returned, she had two of her co-workers in tow, all curious to see this charming new Queen. Soon they were joined by the entire kitchen staff, and then by the medical personnel. Soon Antoinette found herself surrounded by dozens of cooks, busboys, orderlies, surgeons and nurses. Her security team hovered close by but did not interfere, recognizing that these people were professionals who only wished to pay their respects.

Antoinette felt her natural shyness melt away in the face of this warmth and affection. She moved to a large table in the center of the dining hall, invited all to follow her, and for the next half hour she cheerfully chatted, answered questions, and even signed autographs. This would be a moment both she and the hospital staff would remember with great fondness.

Carrying a tray loaded with coffees, hot chocolate, biscuits and desserts, Antoinette returned to the room occupied by Tom and Louis, with Antony standing guard at the door. She was followed by Docteur Leblanc and Chef Jean.

Antoinette discovered Tom sitting up in bed, still tapping away at his laptop, and she doubted he'd obeyed her orders to take a nap. Too filled with happiness to be annoyed, she introduced the assistant chief of staff and the hospital's culinary genius. "Chef Jean would like all of us to dine in the hospital cafeteria this evening," she said, winking a signal to Tom that he should accept the invitation.

An hour or so later, Tom and Louis donned the clean, dry clothes that André had thoughtfully packed for them, with Antoinette urging to Tom to include a tie and jacket with his ensemble. She, meanwhile, had changed out of the pants and blouse she had worn while exploring the castle dungeons, and into a black cocktail dress and simple strand of pearls, with her hair pulled up in a classic chignon. It was, she knew, one of Tom's favorite looks.

Antoinette could hardly contain her excitement as Tom took her arm and the pair made the short walk to the cafeteria, Louis and Antony following. She could tell Tom was still in some pain, as he moved stiffly, and Louis continued to limp.

As they entered the dining hall, Antoinette eagerly watched as a look of pure astonishment appeared on her husband's face. Instead of the unassuming, quiet cafeteria that he expected, he found a festive atmosphere, the room packed with hospital staff and their families, all applauding their new King. *Just like a surprise party,* Antoinette thought.

Tom was speechless for several moments, then asked Antoinette, "Did you have anything to do with this?" She was relieved that he sounded only curious and surprised, not annoyed or angry.

"A little bit," she admitted, sharing her experience when she made a trip to the cafeteria that afternoon for a simple coffee and dessert. "But I didn't expect quite so many people to show up on such short notice."

The couple was shown to a large table with a beautiful floral centerpiece. Already seated were Julia and Philip, along with Victor Monet.

"I'm simply overwhelmed," Tom said as he helped Antoinette to her seat. "I just don't know what to say."

"It's obvious these people have waited for the return of their King for a very long time," Antoinette said. It was apparent to her and everyone at the table how truly humble and grateful Tom felt. "They have a long Carolingian heritage," Antoinette said. "After all, this is their land—the land of Lothair!"

Halfway through the main entrée, a security guard with his face creased with concern appeared at their table, bent down, and whispered something into Antony's ear. "It seems a crowd of some one hundred townspeople has gathered outside the hospital hoping for a glimpse of the King and Queen," Antony said to Tom. "Shall I have Major Dumas's people send them away?"

Antoinette waited for Tom's response, her fork poised halfway between plate and mouth. She knew her husband disliked the spotlight and much preferred the simple life of an obscure scientific researcher to one of a royal leader. But these people had been nothing but gracious and kind to them. She nodded slowly to Tom, sending a silent wish that he make the polite and gracious decision.

"Send them away? Absolutely not—the people of Saint-Meyer are our friends and family," Turning to Docteur Leblanc, Tom said, "Does the hospital have a balcony or a terrace?"

"A terrace, my lord," the physician responded.

"Excellent," Tom said. "Please arrange for a podium and a public address system."

To his son, Tom said, "I know you're concerned about my security, and you're doing an excellent job. I have total confidence you and your people will keep me safe out there."

The crowd size had swelled to two hundred and more by the time Tom and Antoinette finished their dinner and made their way to the terrace. The evening was comfortably warm in late spring, and with sunset still two hours in the future, there was plenty of natural illumination. A shaft of brilliant sunlight shone on Tom as he stood at the podium and accepted the applause of the assembled townspeople.

Tom began by thanking them for their show of support and introduced the members of his family. He gave a brief summary of the history of Castle Rohan and its occupants, sprinkled with anecdotes both humorous and poignant of growing up within its walls. He described the difficult decision to forsake the royal life and how he finally returned when he youngest son won a trip to Castle Rohan at school. He paused to accept handshakes from the chair and members of the town's municipal council, and even answered a few questions shouted from the audience.

Antoinette stood at his side throughout the presentation and could sense how deeply Tom was touched by this show of loyalty and affection from the citizens of Saint-Meyer. But the sunlight was starting to dim, and she could tell he was beginning to tire— understandable for a man of his age at the end of a long and arduous day. From under the podium, she squeezed his hand, silently urging him to wind things up.

"I shall never forget this night and the warm welcome given to me and my family by the people of Saint-Meyer," Tom said into the microphone. "The land we stand on has been the prize fought for in many battles and wars over the centuries. We are not solely French. We are not solely German. We are the children of Emperor Lothair. Tonight, we are all Rohans!"

Antoinette knew she would remember the thunderous applause that followed for the rest of her days.

CHAPTER TWENTY-FOUR

With Tom and Louis being issued clean bills of health, both were discharged from the hospital after the town meeting, each with a bottle of mild painkillers, a tube of antibiotic ointment, and instructions to keep their wounds clean and to refrain from strenuous physical activity for the next few days. The same town car that had delivered them to the Saint-Meyer clinic that afternoon navigated the steep, serpentine road back to Castle Rohan.

Louis checked his phone for messages and followed Tom and Antoinette, both yawning and eager for nothing but sleep, as they stumbled back into their private suite. "General Miliot is calling a special meeting of the Carolingian Sacred Heart for tomorrow morning at six-thirty," Louis said.

"Six-thirty?" Tom asked, certain he had heard wrong.

"I'm afraid six-thirty it is, my lord."

"What on earth could be so important that he needs to roust us from a good night's sleep at such an hour?"

"A number of pressing issues," Louis said, studying the phone screen. "Membership recruitment, for one. Historically, the numbers had been dwindling, as membership was open only to direct family members. The past ten years, they've opened up membership to Saint-Meyer's guilds."

"The trade unions? Interesting idea," Tom said.

"Many of the guild members are connected by blood to Carolingian families or have a long history in the area," Louis pointed out.

Another glance at the phone screen, and he continued, "The current guild chair is a retired historian and professor, Doctor Bruna

Lombardi. As her surname would imply, she is a Lombardy descendant and has studied extensively on Carolingian history. She has great insights on the histories of the Lombardy family, the Carolingians and the Rohans, and could provide some missing links."

He finished with a smile. "Don't forget, Chef Jean is a descendant of a Carolingian knight. I don't think it would take much convincing to get him to cater a gourmet breakfast for our meeting."

Tom returned the smile and said, "That early wake-up call doesn't sound so bad after all."

*   *   *

True to his reputation, Chef Jean prepared a sumptuous breakfast buffet of pastries, fruit, omelets, waffles, juices and coffee in the Rohan family dining room, under the eye of the ever-present dragon. The participants in the meeting—Tom, Antoinette, Antony, Louis, Victor, André, Chef Jean, plus Roland and Frank from the local Carolingian lodge—heaped their plates and gathered in Louis's office just down the hall.

At precisely six forty-five, Tom's cell phone pinged and he found General Miliot on the other end. Tom immediately put the phone in speaker mode and placed it in the center of Louis's desk so all could hear.

General Miliot announced to the group: "My lord, Louis and I, Grand Masters of the Sacred Heart, the highest authorities next to the King, call this meeting to order. It is my pleasure to note that this is the first meeting to be graced by the presence of a King of Rohan in thirty-eight years."

All leaned forward toward the phone to hear the Grand Master's next words. "Sadly, membership in our ancient and sacred order has declined by half and more during that same time period. We must determine a path to recruit new patrons or face extinction. Perhaps changing our organization to a public interest group would be just the thing to bring us into the twenty-first century."

Several in the room murmured thoughts to themselves or each other, but no one spoke aloud. General Miliot went on, "Professor

224

Bruna Lombardi is one of us in blood. She has deep knowledge of our past and has insights into the missing links, which could prove crucial to our lord's mission."

General Miliot then turned the meeting over to his fellow Grand Master, Louis. He began by passing around copies of two local newspapers. Each featured a close-up of Chef Jean in his hospital kitchen, plus shots of the crowd in front of the Saint-Meyer clinic.

"Fortunately for the royal family's desire for privacy, the media did not get wind of what was taking place until later in the evening," Louis said. "However, the jubilation and celebrations continued well into the night both inside and outside the hospital."

Tom immediately grabbed both newspapers and scanned the articles about his visit to the hospital. Only when he reached the end of the second did he breathe a sigh of relief. "Chef Jean and Docteur LeBlanc were both very discreet," he said. "They only reported to the press that Louis and I had undergone a routine physical check-up and nothing out of the ordinary was found."

Antoinette, who'd be reading over his shoulder, added, "Mostly they wrote about how the hospital staff and the townspeople were pleased at the return of the King of Rohan, and how excited they were to meet us. Thank you," she beamed a smile in Chef Jean's direction.

"It was our pleasure," Chef Jean said, returning the smile. "As soon as we saw that the Queen of Rohan was sitting all by herself, drinking her coffee and eating her little fruit tart—well, what could we do? We couldn't help ourselves for wanting to show her and her family the very finest in our local hospitality."

His face took on a troubled expression. "The hospital staff took many pictures, and a few ended up in the local press. I hope we did not act in error and that you are not displeased, your majesty."

"Not at all," Antoinette said with sincerity. "My husband and I will never forget the warmth and respect that you and your town have shown us. If a few innocent photographs end up in the local newspapers, it is of little concern to us."

Chef Jean relaxed, and Louis took this opportunity to note, "The

Saint-Meyer guild is meeting tonight at five-thirty. Is there any chance the two of you might grace us with your presence?"

"Of course," Tom and Antoinette both said. "We'd be delighted."

*   *   *

At precisely nine, the Rohan family and their advisors gathered in the luxurious conference room to undergo another day of negotiations with the various financial factions in which the Rohan corporation was entangled. Philip made sure everyone was present and issued a pleasant good morning and added, "I have two announcements that may be of interest or importance to all of you."

Philip spoke with confidence, but Tom knew his son was speaking with some trepidation. They'd discussed the announcement after the breakfast meeting with General Miliot, and Philip's decision had Tom's total support. Still, there was no knowing how the rest of the family and the Rohan corporate officials would react.

Everyone looked up from their laptops and paper note pads, wondering what was about to come.

Philip did not keep them waiting. "First, I have resigned my position from the bank so that I may devote myself fulltime to my family's business interests." He waited to take in the beams of approval from around the room. "Second, it is my duty to inform you that Madame Sophie Laurent is no longer in the employ of the Rohan corporation. She has been terminated and our attorneys plan to prosecute her for fraud and reckless endangerment of the company's resources. Until all of this settles down, the Legal Department shall oversee the Department of Special Projects."

More nods and murmurs of approval, and Tom felt himself relax, knowing that Philip had matters well under control.

Brigitte took charge of the meeting. She nodded to Antony to open the door and announced, "Lord and all Rohan colleagues, please welcome the delegation from International Investment Aktiengesellschaft."

Tom glanced at his notes. International Investment AG was also known as Swiss Basel Group, associated with the Rohan dynasty for centuries—as long as seven hundred years. The group represented twenty-five percent of Rohan's land lease income, and handled over ninety percent of all Rohan accounts, most of them small.

Perhaps most significantly, they were the holders of one Rohan coin.

Tom looked up from the legal pad and his eyes widened. He glanced at Antoinette, Philip and Julia, and saw that they, too, appeared as stunned as he was.

Shuffling into the room were four old men, obviously brothers, with thinning gray hair and beards. Each of them could easily have been cast as the grandfather in a remake of *Heidi*. They wore business suits in a style fashionable some fifty or sixty years ago, when they would have been young men.

The four slowly and cautiously lowered themselves into chairs around the table. Three of them took laptops from their satchels and slowly began the process of booting up and connecting to WiFi. The laptops were at least ten years old and Tom marveled that they even still functioned. The brothers conferred among themselves and the one without a laptop announced, "I shall speak for the four of us, as I am the only one without an electronic tether." He waited for the ripple of amusement that followed this remark to die down, then said, "Allow me to introduce myself. I am Vance Gessner, representing the four principals of International Investments Aktiengesellschaft, based in Basel, Switzerland."

Philip returned the welcome, saying, "We know you hold one Rohan coin. It could certainly help us in positioning ourselves." The brothers leaned forward, obviously having difficulty hearing Philip's soft voice. He raised his volume as he continued, "Just so you know, today's meeting is being recorded, both electronically and on paper. Please, begin," he said, gesturing toward Vance Gessner.

The old man launched into a history of Basel, a city on the Rhine River in northwest Switzerland, close to the border with France and Germany. "Basel traces its roots to medieval times," he said, "and due to the industriousness of its early settlers, the region became quite prosperous. Unfortunately, this wealth drew bands of raiders and pillagers known as Armagnacs, due to their allegiance to the king of France. Our firm has served the Rohan royal family since 1445, when the Armagnacs were looting the entire Alsace region. We have held land leases and transaction records in an archive that dates back to that year—1445."

Tom felt his heart swell with wonder and gratitude. An alliance that went back five hundred years! He immediately rose and bowed. The rest of the Rohan team—Antoinette, Antony, Philip, Julia, Victor, Brigitte and Sandy—followed his lead in this sign of respect. Tom walked over to the side of the table where the four brothers were seated, shaking hands and embracing each. As his hand touched theirs, he realized that each of them knew the Carolingian Sacred Heart signal, though their aged and arthritic hands fumbled a bit. Tom took hope from this sign of support and seated himself with the Basel delegation. "This feels more like a family reunion than a business meeting," he told the others in the room.

Vance whispered a request to one of the brothers, who clicked on a remote control device to lower the projector screen. He tapped on the laptop and an image of an elegant Swiss country estate with an attached barn appeared.

"This is our land deed archive in the Basel countryside, along the beautiful Rhine River," Vance said. "We believe we have at least four times the archive as Castle Rohan. We have kept careful records of all transactions since 1445."

The Rohans craned their necks, some standing, to take a closer inspection of the large, imposing structure. Brigitte traded looks with Antoinette and Victor, as if saying, "It took us nearly two years to scan all of our paper documents and archive them properly. Now we face a task four times in enormity."

Tom, however, could only smile, thinking of the tremendous historical value of such a cache of records.

Vance continued to plow through his presentation, saying to his brother, "Peter, could you show us an example of just one of our scanned documents?"

When Tom realized that Peter was having difficulty in navigating through the PC, Tom kindly jumped in to help. As the next image materialized on the screen, everyone in the room squinted their eyes and tilted their heads in an attempt to make sense of it.

"My apologies," Vance said. "This shows only one-eighth of the original document. When we tried to scan it, we ended up with eight separate images due to its size. So, you'll need to glue the eight pictures together in your mind to get an idea of what it actually looks like."

"No need to apologize," Tom said with empathy. "You're doing the best you can." He was glad to see that everyone else on the Rohan team showed similar sympathy and support and even admiration for these four old men who were trying so hard to make a good first impression.

Vance offered thanks and added, "Rest assured, these priceless documents, some of them nearly six hundred years old, are being stored under the strictest museum, climate-controlled conditions. We have a state-of-the-art security system, and the location of the archive is a closely guarded secret."

With a voice filled with nothing but respect, Philip inquired as to the brothers' accounting and record-keeping systems. "Do you use a computer at all?"

"Well, not really," Vance admitted, a blush of embarrassment creeping into his cheeks. "We have computers, as you can see, but we rarely use them. We keep all of the property management records by hand, just as our fathers and their fathers have done over the centuries."

With Tom's assistance, Peter made another click of the computer's track pad and a new image appeared on the projector screen. This showed a vast room very much like a fine university library or a study in an exclusive club or private estate, with polished wood tables and chairs, a large globe, a parquet floor and a high ceiling. The walls were lined with shelves crafted of the same brightly polished wood as the furniture.

Tom took a second look and realized that the shelves were filled with books, hundreds of them, ledger books, in perfect order from the present year going back five centuries and more.

He could not help uttering a gasp of surprise and wonder. Tom looked at Antoinette and at the other members of his family and staff. Their faces all bore the same expressions of jaw-dropping awe. This was a great treasure, not just for the Rohan family, but for world history, a continuous record going back at least six hundred years. When Tom recovered himself, he realized that above all, he felt gratitude—profound gratitude that this Swiss family had kept this archive in such meticulous order for so many generations.

"We cannot help but be curious," Philip said, still speaking with respect, "why did you buy one of the Rohan coins?"

"Ah the coin," Vance said with a chuckle. "At our age, we decided to play detective. We felt it might be prudent to find out how the coins are getting back on the market, and thought we might be able to trace it back to its source."

Vance then waved his hand in the air. Tom quickly realized that Vance was attempting to send a secret Carolingian message and signaled Victor to intervene. Victor did so, rising and covering Vance's hand with his own.

"There is no need to explain or defend yourselves," Tom said kindly. "We trust you, and believe you must have had a good reason for obtaining and keeping a Rohan coin."

"There's something else you should know," Vance muttered. "In many cases, the properties have been rented for far under market value. For instance, in the central district of Milan, rents could be in the millions, and we are still charging only thousands."

Once again, eyes grew large on the Rohan side of the table, and Julia whispered "Holy cow!" to Philip.

"We were always honest about conveying this information to your predecessor, Duke Michael," Vance said to Tom. "But he never seen terribly interested."

Tom continued to utter pleasantries while his mind was spinning. *This is going to be an arduous undertaking, creating a computerized, up-to-date accounting system. This will require a tremendous outpouring of Rohan resources to support them.* Then he reminded himself of the many positive aspects of this meeting. *This old guard has kept our business afloat for centuries and never abandoned us. This will make our legal issues much easier to resolve. Best of all, they are loyal to the Carolingian Sacred Heart.*

Feeling on the whole that the positive far outweighed the negative,

Tom, accompanied by Victor, personally escorted the four elderly brothers across the castle drawbridge to the limousine that would take them back to Basel. Tom embraced each and once again, they exchanged the traditional Carolingian hand signals of friendship and fidelity.

CHAPTER TWENTY-FIVE

As the Rohan family and support staff regrouped in the conference room, Philip knew the upcoming meeting would not be nearly so pleasant. The next session would be devoted to the three charity groups that benefitted the most from the Rohan's largesse. A trio of executive directors, each impeccably groomed and expensively attired and flanked by their attorneys and fiscal advisors, filed into the room and seated themselves. A fourth man, gray haired and wearing a plain business suit, slipped in and seated himself in a corner, apart from either side.

Doing his best to start the meeting on a positive tone, Philip said, "We are very impressed with your portfolios and with the keynote addresses that Duke Michael was able to present at your functions."

Philip paused for a moment, then continued. "Now, if the Rohan corporation were to reduce its contribution to your organizations by fifty percent, would you still be able to carry out your good work effectively and efficiently?"

The atmosphere immediately turned hostile. "That is impossible!" Monsieur Delotte, the executive director of United Charitable Foundation, all but exploded. "At half the level we were expecting, this will jeopardize our recipients and our mission to support the arts, and services to the poor, students, refugees… just for starters."

The executive directors of the Paris Light Foundation and the Brotherhood Association chimed in with similar protests.

Philip acted as if nothing unpleasant had just occurred and said mildly, "What if we were to reduce our contributions to twenty-five percent. Which aspects of your donation portfolios would you like us to consider?"

The three executive directors raised their voices. "Unthinkable!" "Impossible!" Monsieur Delotte added, "Duke Michael would never have agreed with this!"

"Unfortunately, Duke Michael is no longer with us," Philip said. Turning to Madame Montague, he asked, "Do we have any sort of binding legal agreements with these three charitable organizations?"

"We make an annual pledge to each organization," Sandy said. "Any fund can be rescinded given one month's notice."

"That is what my research shows as well," Philip said. He produced three sheets of paper and slid them across the table to the executive directors, passing out copies to Brigitte, Sandy, Victor and Tom. "These are the funds that I consider to be critical to the good of society and humanity, causes that benefit children and special health projects. We will continue to support those programs financially. The other causes are more properly the function of government. Those funds will be frozen immediately."

The faces of the three executive directors turned red and their shouts of protest could be heard throughout Castle Rohan. The Rohan team remained calm and dignified. Brigitte said, "The steering committee will accept Philip's proposal. Eighty percent of the Rohan charitable contributions will be halted within thirty days. We have also accepted Philip's request to eliminate the position of Special Projects Director and place that function under my supervision."

While the shouts of "Unacceptable!" and "Despicable!" went on, the fourth man who had been observing quietly from the back of the room stood up. "Respectable Chair Brigitte, Chief Legal Counsel Montague, Prosecutor Julia and of course, our esteemed King Tom Rohan and Queen Antoinette, I am public prosecutor François Lévesque."

The room became deadly quiet, waiting to see what Monsieur Lévesque would have to say next. "We have already arrested Madame Laurent for transferring Rohan funds into her personal account," he said. "We have conducted a lengthy and thorough investigation of fraudulent dealings between Madame Laurent and United Charitable Foundation." He went on to explain how Sophie Laurent conspired with Monsieur Delotte to set up false business identities and diverted large sums of the Rohan charitable donations into their own personal accounts.

"Monsieur Delotte, you are under arrest for fraud, forgery and misrepresentation. As for you and you—" he nodded at the heads of Paris Light Foundation and the Brotherhood Association—"Your presence is required at the local police station immediately following this meeting. We have many questions."

Philip felt a burden lift from his shoulders as the three charity executive directors and their retinues slunk out of the meeting room. He and the rest of the Rohan team barely had time to recover and regroup from that unpleasantness when the next guests were ushered in. Two somber and official-looking men represented Security Investment Bank, which Philip knew to be ethical, proactive, creative and progressive.

The elder of the two, Monsieur Penald, began by stating that the bank had analyzed nearly eighty-five percent of the Rohan corporation's large holdings and found that the Vatican managements' findings were incorrect. "The majority of investment funds were managed by old funding corporations," he explained. "At least ten percent, perhaps as many as twenty-five percent, ceased to exist after the two world wars."

With that blunt statement, Philip almost dropped his pen. He stared, eyes wide, at his sister and father and saw the same expressions of astonishment reflected back at him.

He paid close attention as Monsieur Penald said, "We believe long-term the Rohan's worth can be increased twenty-fold. But in the short term, the next two to four years, you can expect your organization to experience great pain as you make your way back to fiscal health. These are the pains of transition."

The Rohan team silently digested this news, while Philip ventured to say, "Are you sure about this?"

"The problem is your large land deeds and facilities on that land," Monsieur Penald explained. "Under Duke Michael's leadership, or lack thereof, the facilities were allowed to become deteriorated and outdated. In short, they are municipal eyesores. We have proofs and analyses to validate our conclusions. Without making difficult decisions about these and other issues, the Rohan organization will collapse."

Philip was about to respond, but then noticed that his father was rising from his chair after remaining silent for so long. Curious, Philip yielded the floor to Tom Rohan.

"We are thankful and grateful for your insightful analyses and sound prediction as to the looming financial fiasco facing the Rohan corporation" Tom said. "It is not a tall tale, nor is it mere speculation. It is a highly likely near-term reality! The Rohan organization could very likely collapse in the near future, and this is very shocking and sobering news to us."

Philip and Julia looked at each other and nodded. As always, their father was setting just the right tone—polite, dignified, forthright— when it came to representing the family's interest.

"The abuse of our charitable giving is just the tip of the iceberg," Tom said. "The deeper Philip, Julia and Brigitte probe into our financial situation, and the more they tell me, the greater concern I have about our future. The next three to five years will be difficult and challenging for us."

Everyone in the room leaned forward in rapt attention, not wanting to miss a word of the sovereign's message. "I have total confidence that we have the resources to meet these challenges as long as we act with wisdom, employing prudent business measures, and with concern for our ethical and social responsibilities. I believe Philip and many of us in this room would support me in my motion to retain Security Investment Bank on our advisory board, and even to invite them to be our core partner as we restructure and redevelop."

Brigitte waited for a nod of approval from Philip, and said, "We are impressed and encouraged by the careful analysis and potential plans proposed by Security Investment Bank, and we look forward to further cooperation leading to a long-term relationship. I would propose that we continue this discussion in the afternoon."

"Madame Chair and Monsieur Penald, if I may." All eyes were now riveted on Antoinette, speaking up for the first time. "When you do your corporate development and financial analyses, I would encourage you to use scientific models and analytical tools. As you know, my husband and I are both scientists and we know this is the system that produces unbiased, empirical results. Of course, we are vitally concerned about the future of our family's business, and trust you will include us in all future meetings."

Philip wanted to lead a round of applause to honor Antoinette, but he knew it would not be appropriate in this setting. Growing up in the Rohan household, he knew very well how motivated and intelligent his mother was. Not satisfied with a mere PhD in pharmacology, during her children's growing-up years she never gave up on furthering her education through self-study and night classes. She was an expert on artificial intelligence, data mining and data modeling. He knew she would be a valuable member of the Rohan-Security Investment alliance when it came to strategic business decisions.

Monsieur Penald and his associate, obviously taken by surprise, held a brief, whispered consultation. Monsieur Penald said, "Your recommendation is most reasonable. We will all benefit from scrutinizing and vetting our analytical processes, our prediction formulation and our data analysis models."

Philip smiled to himself. Not only had this meeting achieved the assistance of a group as prestigious as Security Investment Bank, but they'd also been issued a wake-up call from the King and Queen. They now were well aware that their studies and planning needed to be bullet-proof, based on observable, scientific principles.

Tom gave his wife a grateful nod and once again took the floor. "I direct you to use the massive resources that the Rohan corporation can put at your disposal and put us back on the path to financial stability. Always keep in mind our values: honest and ethical business dealings that benefit humankind, not just by funneling money into charities, but to projects that will positively impact science, technology, and education."

With that declaration from the King of Rohan, the morning session finally came to its conclusion.

CHAPTER TWENTY-SIX

Tom entered the Guild House just across the street from the hospital in Saint-Meyer and felt the tension from the past eight hours of financial meetings lift from his shoulders. Antoinette was at his side, and he was followed by Antony, Louis, André and Victor.

"I don't think I could have made it through all those meetings without having this evening to look forward to," Tom said to Antoinette.

"Especially the part about another wonderful dinner prepared by Chef Jean to look forward to," Antoinette agreed.

A mood of brotherhood and reverence permeated the centuries-old hall as some sixty guild members applauded their sovereign. Tom immediately sensed the pride and honor brought about by five hundred to twelve hundred years of shared history. Many of the guild members had ancestors who had practiced the same trade for many hundreds of years.

Tom and Antoinette were seated at places of honor at the head table. Each guild master approached to make a formal introduction. Chef Jean represented the cooks, bakers and millers. He was followed by Hugo Béringer, master of the guild of merchants, textiles and banking. Next came cattle and butchers, carpenters and masons, blacksmiths, goldsmiths and physicians. The guild of farmers and vintners was represented by Simon Dufour, also the town's mayor. Finally came the guild of teachers and historians, led by the one female guild master, Dr. Bruna Lombardi.

"Dr. Lombardi is also the head of all of the guilds," Louis told Tom. "She is held in very high esteem. One of her ancestors was a

Carolingian knight. She earned her doctorate from the University of Bologna and taught at the University of Paris until her retirement ten years ago."

"It is my pleasure, lord," Bruna Lombardi said, making a curtsey to Tom and Antoinette. She was a petite woman of perhaps sixty years, wearing a simple white cotton shirt and a blue skirt. Her dark hair was neatly styled in a knot at the nape of her neck.

"No, the pleasure is mine, to meet such a distinguished historian," Tom said. He introduced the members of his entourage and said, "We are all very much looking forward to your keynote address, as we have many questions about our history, and want to learn more about the issues facing Saint-Meyer today."

"I hope I shall not disappoint, my lord," she said, offering another curtsey.

After a half-hour of socializing, Chef Jean and his staff served a dinner that proved to be every bit as delicious and sumptuous as the meals he had previously prepared for the Rohans. "After this is all over, you are going to have to send me to a spa to shed all the weight I must be gaining," Antoinette said to Tom after tucking away the very last bite of opera cake.

"You and me both," Tom said with a satisfied smile.

All small talk ended as Mayor Dufour rose to make the formal introduction of Dr. Bruna Lombardi and the start of the much-anticipated keynote address

* * *

Just as Tom and Antoinette were finishing their dinner in the guild hall in Saint-Meyer, in an upper middle-class neighborhood in the village next to Castle Rohan, Brigitte and her husband were likewise setting down their forks and patting their lips with their napkins. Jacques, a retired police captain, and Brigitte had been married for forty-five years. Even though he was Brigitte's second husband, the couple had been together for so long that Brigitte could barely imagine a time that he had not been a vital part of her life.

Sharp knocks at the front door almost caused Brigitte to topple her wine glass. *Who would be disturbing the peace of an elderly retired couple during the dinner hour?* Worried, Brigitte timidly opened the door and saw two younger men, one tall, bald and burly, the other shorter with brown hair. Both had arm and chest muscles straining the seams of their cheap suits.

Before Brigitte could utter a word of greeting, the two men hustled her into a small entry room, hardly larger than a coat closet, just off the foyer.

"You are the cause of the failure of our mission in Paris," the larger man spat out. "Our big boss is very unhappy!"

Despite her best efforts at self-control, Brigitte felt her eyes tearing up. Her voice trembled as she said, "Kidnapping is a serious offense and I do not take orders from your so-called big boss."

The shorter, brown-haired man said, "Kidnapping? Who said anything about kidnapping? We just wanted to ask him a few questions, find out who he was, that's all. We knew he possessed the Rohan gold coins and those are of vital importance not just to the Rohan family but to financial markets world-wide."

The larger man added, "We had photos of the target. We knew we were looking for a man in his fifties, sixties at most. The King of Rohan, if he still lived, would be a very old man, one-hundred one years old. So why would we think our target in Paris was actually the king?"

Through her tears, Brigitte still exhibited defiance. "I hear you and your people tried to force him into a car, right there in broad daylight in the street in front of his bank in Paris. Other people witnessed this and came to his rescue."

"Exactly," the larger man said, pointing a finger in Brigitte's face. "You are the one who introduced the Lombardi gang to us. Instead, they turned on us. We would all be dead if Tom Rohan had not intervened. Now, why would you do something like that, put a mole right in the middle of our group?" Not waiting for a response, he finished, "You did it because you had an affair with Tom many years ago!"

Brigitte felt her fear turning to anger as she said, "Tom Rohan is one of the kindest and most decent persons in the entire world. No young woman would fail to fall in love with him. I have never had an affair with him, and even if I had, it is none of your business."

The shorter man said, "We're wasting time. Our boss is very angry and doesn't like to be kept waiting. You will come with us tonight and explain yourself to him."

Brigitte shrank back as the larger man tried to grab her arm. Just then, Jacques burst in, holding a handgun, followed by a younger man with a rifle. She recognized him as Roland, one of the police officers Jacques had trained as a young recruit and an excellent sharp-shooter. "Hands up!" Jacques ordered.

Instead of obeying, the two thugs exchanged smirks. "Did you really think we came here by ourselves?" the larger man sneered. "We have your house surrounded. If you dispose of one of us, two more will take our place."

Jacques responded by raising the handgun and aiming.

"Fine. Hold your fire and we will leave." The larger man nodded to his partner and the two slowly raised their hands and began to back away out of the small room and toward the entrance

They opened the door and took a step outside, Jacques following just behind, still aiming the handgun. Brigitte felt her terror lessen to a degree as the immediate danger appeared to be over.

A shot rang out—from where, Brigitte could not tell. The next thing she knew, she was hearing a groan from Jacques. He clutched his upper right arm, dropped the gun, and slowly sank to the floor.

Brigitte screamed in horror while Roland dragged her husband back inside and slammed the door shut. Roland barked out orders: "Turn out all the lights! Call the police for backup and an ambulance. Stay close to the floor and hide behind something solid if you can."

Roland slowly opened the door one inch, just enough space to fit the rifle barrel. He fired just one shot, hitting the shorter man in the head. The larger man turned to check on his partner, but when he saw him on the sidewalk, bleeding from a bullet in the back of his skull, he began to run in the opposite direction.

One of the gang members who had been surrounding the house began to creep across the lawn toward the front door. Roland pulled the trigger just once and the man fell to the ground, blood spraying from his chest.

Brigitte sat on the floor of the front parlor, where she applied bandages to her husband's wound and took quick peeks through the darkened window to the action outside. She watched in grim satisfaction as the large man who had terrorized her earlier in the evening didn't even stop to check on the second gang member—he just kept running.

Good riddance to bad rubbish, she thought. *That will teach them to threaten us.*

*   *   *

Tom leaned forward and listened in rapt fascination as Dr. Bruna Lombardi began her keynote address. She first discussed the common belief that the church with their monks and nuns was the only source of higher education during the medieval era. "Actually, there was a tradition for centuries among the wealthy to hire tutors for their children, as well as opportunities for a very select few to travel and study with learned scholars. This is, for example, how the Socratic Method was preserved and passed down through the generations."

She praised the guild system as a major source of higher education, responsible for founding both the University of Bologna and Oxford University, among others. "As the guilds encouraged men to gather and to share the secrets of their trades, they began to explore other disciplines—civil and canon law, for instance, as well as medicine and the humanities."

She then shared much of the insights that Antoinette and Louis had discussed at the inn the evening of Tom's coronation, how the Carolingian Renaissance had resulted in great strides forward when it came to communication among the many tribes and feudal societies in medieval Europe. "Not only a great military leader, Charlemagne founded schools and attracted the most learned men in Europe to his court," she said.

Dr. Lombardi continued, "Anecdotal evidence points to a huge archive of the Carolingian Renaissance right here in Saint-Meyer and at Villa Meyer. Sadly, almost nothing exists today."

She paused to let her audience ponder the obvious question—what happened to this trove of historic treasures from the Carolingian Renaissance? "During the 1300s, this region was hit with a series of misfortunes," Dr. Lombardi said. "First came the plague, which decimated the population. Then in October of 1356, an earthquake struck and the Villa Meyer commune and village were buried in a landslide. Next, you had the 100 Years War, during which the Armagnacs looted and burned everything in their path throughout the Alsace. The result is that today, only about twenty artifacts from the Carolingian Renaissance exist, original writings and artworks that have been preserved in museums and private collections."

Tom and Antoinette looked each other in the eyes, knowing full well what the other was thinking: all those scrolls, parchments, books, artworks that were found in the dungeons under Castle Rohan. They must represent the lost artifacts of the Carolingian Renaissance!

Unable to contain himself no longer, Tom sent a secret hand signal to Dr. Lombardi: "Do not despair—at least ten times that number of artifacts still exists."

His excitement grew as he recalled the village he'd discovered, remarkably intact, in the cave. It must be Villa Meyer! That meant even more priceless scrolls, books and artworks may still be preserved.

Tom grew reflective as he made a profound realization. If it had not been for the earthquake, burying the villa and its surrounding community, surely it would have been burned to the ground by the Armagnacs when they came through the region on their vicious quest to loot, terrorize and destroy. Of course, the earthquake must have been a horrifying event when it happened, but in the long vista of history, it may have served a positive purpose.

With that comforting thought, Tom turned his attention back to Dr. Lombardi's fascinating lecture, careful not to miss one word.

*   *   *

Major Dumas, followed by at least a dozen French army storm troopers, raced up the hill to Brigitte's home and surrounded the building. The radio call from the local police dispatcher had been urgent. One elderly man inside the house had been wounded and required immediate medical attention. Shots were still being fired, seemingly at random, at the house.

"This is the French National Security Force and the local police," Major Dumas said into a bullhorn. "Surrender now, or we will use deadly force."

There was no response, other than the sound of a car speeding away. And yet, the bullets continued to fly at rapid and regular intervals without appearing to be aimed at any particular target. It was as if the unseen gunman simply wanted to create chaos and confusion.

One of Dumas's soldiers let out a yell and waved his arms just as the sound of gunfire stopped. When the troops arrived at his position, they discovered an automatic rifle had been attached to a tripod with a rotating mechanism, much like a lawn sprinkler system, and rigged up so that the trigger would continue firing without any human intervention.

"I disabled it as soon as I found it, sir," the soldier reported.

"Good job," Dumas said. With no more danger of being shot, he dispatched two of his men to attend to Jacques until the EMTs could arrive, and sent the rest of the troops to search the grounds. They soon reported back that they had found no living being, just two bodies, each exhibiting just one gunshot wound indicating they had been felled by an expert sharpshooter.

"We also found a trial of blood leading to the street," one of the soldiers reported.

"That explains the car we heard speeding away just as we arrived," Dumas said.

He folded his arms, surveyed the landscape, and added up everything he'd observed about the situation and heard over the police radio. "You know what this means, correct?" he said to his troops.

In the dim light of a late summer evening, he saw the questioning looks on their faces. "They lured us here on purpose, created a diversion, just so we'd be away from Saint-Meyer and preoccupied with this supposed crime scene."

The men nodded, waiting for their next command.

"We must return to Saint-Meyer immediately!" Major Dumas declared. "Tom Rohan is in great danger!"

CHAPTER TWENTY-SEVEN

Julia shifted her weight in a hopeless attempt to find a more comfortable spot in the hard, straight-back chair in the Castle Rohan Archive Room. "I sure hope Mama and Papa are having a better time at that dinner at the Guild Hall," she grumbled.

"A medieval torture chamber would be more comfortable than this," Philip said, chuckling in agreement. "Still, our mother and father have earned a night off after all they've been through."

"Very true," Julia replied. "I just hope we can straighten this mess out for them."

Brother and sister hunched over a small table in a cramped, dusty room illuminated only with three old-fashioned desk lamps. They were surrounded on all sides with shelves of ledger books and banker boxes stuffed with documents stretching back for decades and even centuries. They'd be at their work for at least an hour, ever since the last meeting broke up at five. As far as they knew, they were the only two people still in the castle, other than the seven government troopers who guarded the huge stone edifice.

"Found anything yet?" Philip asked his sister.

She responded with a shake of her head and a sigh as she opened the lid of yet another banker box.

The siblings were searching for the original contracts mentioned by Security Investment Bank, the most promising of all the financial groups they had met with. That morning, Monsieur Penald had stated that the Vatican management's findings concerning the Rohan's large land deed profile were incorrect, and that as many as one-quarter of the old funding corporations had ceased to exist after the two World

Wars. Julia and Philip had made it their mission to find those original contracts, now over seventy years old.

One of the uniformed troopers entered the chamber to announce that Chef Jean had sent up several hampers with dinner for Julia, Philip and the guards, and that the spread was waiting for them in the staff break room.

"You know what I'm thinking…" Philip began.

"Same thing I'm thinking," Julia replied with a wide smile.

With that, brother and sister packed up three cartloads worth of material to transport to the staff break room, which they knew to be large, well lit, with comfortable chairs and tables, and boasting amenities like coffee, tea and snacks.

"Hard to believe, all the excitement our family has been through the past four days," Julia said after she and Philip had consumed another excellent meal from Chef Jean. "What a huge mess!"

Philip put down his fork, wiped his lips with his napkin, and said, "The problem is, the people running the Rohan corporation the past twenty or thirty years had no awareness of modern digital technology, nor how to use that capability to benefit the corporation. Then you had Duke Michael at the head, and all he seemed to care about was fashionable charity causes, where he could hobnob with the rich and famous and get his picture in the newspapers."

His meal finished, Philip excused himself to make one more sweep of the Archive Room to see if there might be a box or ledger book that they had overlooked.

Left to her own devices, Julia began to take an interest in the young troopers who were still devouring their dinner in the break room. Though happily married, Julia was also a healthy young woman with a natural attraction to the opposite sex. And these troopers were excellent specimens: young and fit, trained and poised for action. She stared at their weapons, the automatic handguns and the assault rifles, and wondered what it must feel like to have such awesome power of life and death at one's disposal.

She was just starting to engage several of the troopers in conversation, asking them where they were from and what their families were like, when their two-way radios squawked. She couldn't make out the message, but she definitely picked up on the urgency.

"An emergency at Brigette's home," their commander said. He pointed at two of his men and said, "You two stay behind and guard the castle. The rest of you—follow me!" With a clatter of boots, the five special forces troops raced out of the castle.

Julia felt pinpricks of uncertainty—what was happening at Brigitte's house?—but she decided there was nothing she could do, that the troopers surely had the situation well in hand. Her best course of action was to continue the work she had started to untangle her family's financial difficulties. She turned on all the lights and emptied the contents of one of the banker boxes across the table. As a lawyer and judge, she always felt more comfortable when she had the pertinent documents concerning a case spread out in front of her.

Just as she was beginning to relax in her familiar task, gunfire rang out.

*   *   *

With Dr. Lombardi's keynote address finished, the next order of business in the Guild Hall was a town hall meeting led by Tom Rohan and Mayor Simon Dufour. After warmly greeting the guild members and the citizens of Saint-Meyer who showed up for the meeting, Tom said, "In the past four days, my family and I have met with key members of the Rohan corporation, as well as the financial institutions that my family has done business with over the decades and centuries. While we have numerous urgent problems to attend to, we also want to acknowledge the deep ties we have with the people of this region. Many of you share hundreds, if not over a thousand, years of kinship with us. If you would be so kind and open as to share your issues and challenges, I would be very interested in hearing them."

Tom listened with genuine concern as the representatives of the various guilds spoke up. A pattern soon became all-too clear. Most of the traditional trades and crafts were no longer profitable, and with no other options, the region had become dependent on tourism and vineyards for its economic survival. The population was aging, as most of the town's young people were leaving for greater economic opportunities in the cities, not only Paris but also Lyon, Marseilles, Toulouse and Bordeaux. The mood in the Guild Hall took on a melancholy atmosphere as Mayor Dufour summed up the situation: "I have been mayor for six years and have attended numerous conventions and sought expert opinions on this subject. And yet, the population continues to decline and along with it, our fortunes."

With great sympathy, Tom said, "Yes, I understand this is a problem facing many small towns and villages, not just in France but throughout Europe."

Encouraged at this support from the sovereign, Mayor Dufour continued, "I have heard experts talk about the concept of 'smart shrinking' when it comes to towns like Saint-Meyer. Towns with 'smart shrinking' have populations that are engaged, civic-minded, and with strong social networks. They have learned how to bridge social capital—in other words, help people connect across society."

"Go on," Tom said. "This is fascinating."

"Populations in towns like Saint-Meyer will continue to decline because of factors outside our control," Mayor Dufour said. "It's not about population loss, but rather working within that context to stabilize and improve the quality of life."

Tom and Antoinette positively beamed in agreement, while the guild leaders nodded their approval. Mayor Dufour had obviously struck a chord.

*   *   *

Julia's cell phone pinged and she saw Philip's name on the caller ID. "What's happening?" she demanded. "Are you all right?"

"For the moment, yes. As to what is happening, I couldn't say, other than we appear to be under attack."

"What shall we do?" she cried as more gunshots were fired.

"There's a house phone in the break room, correct?"

"Yes, but..." Julia had no idea why her brother would be asking about such a mundane thing in this time of danger.

"Listen to me. Put it on speaker, and on record mode."

Julia immediately understood. She still had two soldiers here in the break room, but Philip was alone and unarmed in the archives. His only hope would be that someone would hear his plight and come to his rescue.

She became aware of two things happening simultaneously. One of the troopers clutched his abdomen and fell to the floor. The other trooper grabbed her by the waist and forced her behind the couch while also returning fire.

"No, no," Julia insisted, gesturing toward the wounded trooper. Just minutes ago, he'd been telling her about his girlfriend back home in Lyon and their plans to marry that summer. Now his blood was spilling out onto the stone floor of the castle. "We can't just leave him there."

Julia emerged from her hiding place just long enough to crawl to the trooper and drag him back to relative safety behind the sofa. Like all other courthouse personnel, she'd undergone first-aid training. Now she desperately hoped she remembered the proper procedures. One more hurried foray into the open fire and she was able to snatch a clean, white tablecloth. This she applied to the soldier's wound. "It's going to be all right," she repeated over and over, hoping to soothe him—and herself.

The soldier who had not been injured popped out from behind the sofa to return fire, but he was hopelessly outnumbered. He retreated, cursing in frustration, and joined Julia and the wounded soldier in their relatively safe refuge.

Another rapid volley of gunshots and a glass cabinet directly in back of the couch shattered. Shards of glass cascaded onto Julia and she began to bleed from numerous cuts on her arms and scalp. With one hand, she continued to apply pressure to the soldier's wound while she desperately pressed 1-1-2 on her cell phone. "Send an ambulance to Castle Rohan, now!" she shouted. "And back-up security."

Within a few seconds, the emergency dispatcher had patched her through to Major Dumas. "We've been ambushed," she said breathlessly. "We're outnumbered. I believe there are at least seven of them. Only two of your men are left, and one has been wounded."

Major Dumas cursed under his breath and said, "Another diversion. These people are very clever." Julia could hear him shouting orders to his men, ordering four of them to continue on to Saint-Meyer to guard the Guild Hall, and sending the rest up to Castle Rohan. "No sirens, no flashing lights," he said. "We want to hit them by surprise."

Julia cowered behind the couch in utter panic with the two soldiers and watched helplessly as the seven thugs moved swiftly through the breakroom, loading the ledger books and banker boxes onto handcarts and departing. *It's not me they want—it's the archives!* While the realization made her slightly less fearful for her physical safety, it filled her with anger. *They have no right—these records have been in Papa's family for centuries!*

With the thugs obviously in possession of everything they wanted from the break room, six of them departed, leaving just one to stand guard, making sure Julia or the two soldiers did not leave, nor that anyone else could come in.

After the most agonizing ten minutes of her life, Julia sensed another presence in the break room. One of Dumas's men crept silently behind the man with the gun and with one swift martial arts move, kicked his legs out from under him and snatched the gun. Things happened very quickly after that: the gunman was placed in handcuffs and led away, paramedics rushed in to tend to the wounded soldier, and Major Dumas helped a dazed and shaking Julia from her hiding place.

At first, she could say nothing, just gasp and sob and point to the house phone, still sitting on one of the dining tables, hoping Major Dumas would understand.

Instead, he pointed out the cuts on Julia's arms, still oozing blood, and the glass shards in her long brown hair. "Forget the phone," he said gently. "We need to get you to the emergency room."

"No, no," she cried helplessly. "Listen, please!"

On the other end of the line came the sounds of orders being barked out, men grunting and straining as they seemed to be lifting heavy objects, and carts being wheeled over stones.

"My brother!" Julia pleaded.

*   *   *

At the Guild Hall, Mayor Dufour turned his attention away from "smart shrinkage" to the topic of "smart growth."

"Economic development is a slow and steady process," he told the guild members and citizens who packed the hall. "These days, most people want instant success. Short term growth may feel good, especially for a small town like Saint-Meyer, but economic development has more long-lasting results. That is how we are refocusing the economy of our community."

Many heads nodded in agreement, including Tom's. Mayor Dufour concluded, "Our overall mission is to demonstrate the power of local economic and community development efforts, especially for rural areas such as ours. We understand that every community is unique, with its own set of challenges. Yet, we intend to lead by example and demonstrate the tremendous potential that even the smallest town can have."

Mayor Dufour now looked directly at Tom. "We are counting on the splendor and prestige of Castle Rohan to partner with us in bringing in the right kind of tourists to our region—those who are sincerely interested in our history and culture, as well as serious researchers from the academic and scientific worlds."

All eyes were now on Tom, the first king to attend a Guild Hall meeting in forty years. Tom graciously thanked Mayor Dufour, the guild masters, and the citizens for their insights and for sharing their concerns so frankly and thoughtfully.

"Castle Rohan will be honored to dedicate resources to ensure that Saint-Meyer remains a vital and viable town for many years to come," Tom said. "After all, we have been together for hundreds and hundreds of years. I have every intention of maintaining that relationship for many more years. Everything you said about 'smart shrinking' and 'smart growth' will stay in our minds and hearts. We will certainly keep all of this in mind as we continue our planning process."

After many handshakes from the local citizens, Tom and

Antoinette were finally able to exit the hall and make their way toward the limousine that would take them back to the ancestral home. In the darkening twilight, the spires and battlements of Castle Rohan were barely visible high atop the mountain.

"Looks so peaceful at night, doesn't it?" Tom remarked to Antoinette.

* * *

Philip knew his situation was dire—trapped in the Archive Room, no way out except the one door, not even a window. He just prayed that someone would pick up on the sounds they were hearing over the house phone in the break room. Listen, understand—and act.

Heavy footsteps pounded on the hard flooring of the castle. The door to the Archive Room burst open and six men rushed in, their guns trained on Philip.

Philip raised his hands, just like he'd seen captives do in the movies, and tried to sound as meek and unassuming as he could. "I'm just a clerk, cleaning up the filing."

A tall, balding, burly man appeared to be in charge. He reached into Philip's pocket and removed his wallet. After a quick glance at Philip's ID, he made a disgusted sound and said, "Just a clerk? Yeah, right. You are Philip Rohan, this so-called king's fourth child." He took a swing, connecting with Philip's jaw. "That's for lying," he growled.

Philip told himself to stay calm as he said, "That may be, but I am merely the family's accountant. I am here only to audit some of the recent transactions."

The big man responded by shoving Philip into a chair, instructing him to stay out of the way. He and his five cohorts began rudely pulling ledgers and boxes from the shelves, loading them onto carts and wheeling them out of the room. With no way to see what might be going on elsewhere, Philip could only assume they had a truck parked somewhere close by.

"Hey, boss, there's a lot more stuff here than we thought," one of them said when he returned with an empty cart.

"Yeah," his partner said, wiping sweat from his forehead. "We're running out of room in the truck. And out of time."

The large man pounded a fist into his opposite hand and turned to Philip. "We're looking for land deeds and transactions in the Strasbourg area. Where are they?"

"Certainly, I can help you with that." Hoping to appease the thugs with a show of cooperation, Philip began to rise from his chair.

The big man immediately shoved him back down. "Don't move. Just show us where they are."

Fine. If you want to play rough... Philip deliberately pointed to a shelf that he knew had nothing to do with land issues in Strasbourg.

The boss man pulled a banker box off the shelf and began riffling through the contents, throwing a fistful of paper onto the floor. "Nothing about Strasbourg in here." He loomed over Philip. "You lied to us again!" Another punch, this time to the opposite side of the jaw.

"Hey, boss," one of the thugs said. "Look at this." He pointed to a shelf with a small label reading "Strasbourg." The shelf was empty.

"How can that shelf by empty?" the big man roared, his face purple with anger. "Someone must be working with you. Who took them? Who has them now?"

Philip knew very well that these were the very boxes and ledgers that Julia had taken with her for a working dinner in the staff break room, but he wasn't about to let these crooks know that. So he said, "I must have accidentally filed them in a different box. Here, let me find them for you."

Now all six men were in the Archive Room with Philip and the air was thick with curses and with suggestions as to what to do next. "Lied to us again!" "Burn the place down." "Get rid of him!" "We don't need liars." "Burn the place *and* get rid of him."

"Now, now," Philip said, still trying to project calmness. "No need to burn anything or kill anyone. I will help you find the documents you need."

Once again, he attempted to rise, and once again he was shoved back into the chair.

The big man punched a number on his cell phone while keeping his other huge hand firmly on Philip's shoulder, pinning him to the chair. When the person on the other end picked up, he said, "You'll never guess who we found in the Archive Room."

Philip couldn't quite pick up on what was being said on the other end. The big man said, "Yeah, none other than Rohan's son. Claims he's just an accountant, but we know better, right?"

Now Philip could pick up laughter on the other end—rude, crude laughter—and he wasn't liking the direction this conversation was going one bit.

"Acts like he's better than us. Refuses to help and keeps lying. I'm thinking we should just get rid of him?"

Get rid of him? Does that mean …?

Through the speaker, Philip could hear a man shouting in the background. "No killing!"

"He's seen our faces—he can identify us—and he knows what we're looking for," the big man said.

Now Philip could clearly hear the first man on the other end of the phone line. "Kill him. Kill him and burn the place."

The second voice continued urgently. "No! No killing! Burn everything up if you have to, but no killing!"

Who are these men, and why is one of them trying to save my life?

The big man acted as if he couldn't hear the voice in the background. "I'll get rid of that lying son of Tom Rohan and all of the evidence," he said into the phone. "Consider it handled."

Philip squirmed and writhed helplessly in the chair, but it was no use. The big man held him securely, now with both hands pressed on his shoulders. One of his henchmen began making a pile in one corner out of the loose documents that had already been tossed onto the floor. He held the flame of his cigarette lighter to the stack of paper. It began to flicker and smoke.

The big man raised his gun, cocked the trigger, and aimed it at Philip's head. With certain death staring him in his face, Philip felt a riot of emotions cascading through him: regret that he would never see his children grow up, sorrow that he never had the chance to tell his wife he loved her one last time, and yet resigned to his fate. *If I must die, then at least it is for a just cause, in service to my family.*

CHAPTER TWENTY-EIGHT

One shot—but instead of the impact that Philip had braced himself for, the boss man pitched forward, narrowly missing Philip, and crashed to the floor. Blood gushed from a gaping wound in the back of his head.

Major Dumas and his troops, including Roland the sharp-shooter, stormed into the archive room. Three of the thugs immediately surrendered, while two others took off on a run and managed to escape in their truck. One of the soldiers put the fire out with a can of dry extinguisher before it had a chance to burn more than a dozen or so pages. Major Dumas immediately radioed for additional security to be sent to the Guild Hall.

"Are you hurt?" Dumas asked Philip.

"I don't think so," he said, rubbing his jaw. "Nothing that a few aspirin won't cure. What about my sister?"

"She'll be fine," Dumas reassured him. "She sustained some cuts from flying glass, but nothing permanent. She is being treated at the hospital at Saint-Meyer."

*   *   *

Antony considered himself above all to be a man of action. Only rarely did he allow himself to indulge in doubt or indecision. Now, though, a worm of worry had managed to work its way deep inside his soul. He'd been sure that his father and mother and the townspeople at the Guild Hall would be safe that evening. After all, more than fifteen of the nation's top security people had a presence, highly trained in close combat, armed with powerful weapons and equipped with the latest technology in night-vision goggles. Confident that he had the situation well under control, Antony had made the decision to allow the meeting at the Guild Hall to go on as scheduled, and not to distract his father with any concerns about security.

And yet, the gang had managed to penetrate both Brigitte's home and Castle Rohan. Brigitte's husband and Antony's dear sister Julia were both at the Saint-Meyer hospital receiving treatment for their wounds. As for Philip, if Roland the sharpshooter had arrived on the scene one second later, or if his aim had been less than accurate … Antony did not even want to think about it.

Giving himself a stern warning that doubt and indecision are how battles are lost, he shook off his worries. It was time to swing into action and take charge of the situation.

In a small conference room at the hospital, he found Julia and Philip, plus Victor. Antony breathed a sigh of relief when he saw that Julia had not been seriously wounded, and that the cuts from the shattered glass would heal without scarring.

Also in the room were Major Dumas, the local police chief and a detective from *Police Nationale*. All three were busily taking notes as Julia and Philip, their voices still shaking, described what had happened to them that evening at the castle.

The detective took out his mobile phone and explained that he had made a copy of the sounds that had been picked up and recorded by the house phone in the staff break room. "Brilliant idea, to put the phone on speaker and record," the detective said to Philip. "The evidence will be invaluable in building our case."

He then proceeded to play back the recording. Antony's blood ran cold as he listened to the ruthless voices arguing as to whether Philip should be gotten rid of—permanently.

Victor was the first to speak when the recording ended. "The man shouting in the background that there should be no killing is Gabriel Monet."

"Are you certain about that?" the detective asked.

"I would know his voice anywhere. After all, he is my twin brother."

"What about the other man, the one who wanted Philip eliminated so he could not identify them as a witness?"

Victor shuddered in disgust. "That man is my brother's partner, Chris Giroux."

"He's one of the gang members who got away," Major Dumas said. He began to bark orders into his two-way radio.

*   *   *

Tom and Antoinette were about to climb into the limousine that would take them back to Castle Rohan at the conclusion of the Guild Hall meeting when a steady stream of police vehicles, sirens blaring and lights flashing, broke the peaceful atmosphere of an evening in late spring in the small town. Tom barely had time to wonder what might be happening when two uniformed officers politely but firmly hustled him and Antoinette into an armored vehicle.

Moments later, they were being helped to exit and found themselves in the bright lights and antiseptic smell of the ambulance bay at the Saint-Meyer hospital.

"I don't understand," Tom said. "Neither I nor my wife require medical care."

Neither officer responded. Instead, Antony strode forward and embraced his mother and father. "Just glad to see that you are safe," he said gruffly.

"Will someone please tell us what is going on?" Antoinette said, her voice rising in anxiety. "Why wouldn't we be safe?"

As briefly as he could, Antony laid out the facts as to what had transpired at Brigitte's house and Castle Rohan that evening as the three of them strode down a hospital corridor toward the conference room. Though he kept his voice calm and his emotions in check, there was simply no way Antony could disguise or minimize the great danger that his brother and sister had faced. When he reached the part when one of the thugs was preparing to shoot Philip, Antoinette uttered an anguished cry, flung open the conference room door and threw herself, sobbing, in Philip's direction.

Tom followed almost as quickly, wincing when he saw his pretty daughter swathed in bandages. He seethed with anger toward the men who had put her and Philip at such risk. *This is my fight. Why did they have to bring my innocent children into this?*

"Don't worry, Papa," Julia said when she saw Tom's stricken face. "It looks much worse than it actually is. The doctors assure me there won't be any permanent scars."

Tom could only blink back tears as he drew both son and daughter close to him. "If anything had happened to either of you…" he began, and then could say no more.

Composing himself and turning to Antony, he said, "They will catch all of the criminals who did this, won't they?"

"Absolutely," Antony said. "Major Dumas has called in all his forces and commenced a thorough search. They won't get far."

Tom nodded his approval. "I know I can always count on you to handle our family's safety and security."

"Speaking of that," Antony said. "I think it's best if you and Mama spend the night here in the hospital. And Julia and Philip, of course. Major Dumas and his forces can provide a much higher level of security here than at the castle."

"If you think it is for the best," Tom said with a little smile. "This place is almost starting to feel like home."

"I'll send one of the men up to the castle to pack your personal items and a change of clothing for all of you," Antony said.

Antoinette, now recovered from her agitated state over Philip's brush with death, joined the conversation. "With Chef Jean running the hospital kitchen, at least we know we'll have excellent meals. And with Antony providing the security, what more could we ask for?"

*   *   *

Though the hospital staff did their best to provide pleasant accommodations for their royal guests, neither the elder nor younger Rohans slept well. They were aware of sirens disturbing the peace throughout the night, of guards prowling the halls and two-way radios crackling, and were far too emotionally overwrought to make sleep come easily.

The next morning, they regrouped in a corner of the hospital dining room. "I hope I don't look as tired as I feel," Julia said, sipping coffee.

"I don't think I slept more than an hour or two," Philip agreed. "Everything just finally caught up with me."

Antony strode into the dining room, looking polished and confident as always in his general's uniform. He pulled up a chair and began to slather jam onto a croissant.

"You look like you have good news to share with us," Tom said.

"Absolutely," Antony said. "For starters, Gabriel Monet turned himself in early this morning."

"That is good news," Tom said, while Antoinette, Philip and Julia nodded agreement, already looking less frazzled and exhausted.

"He confessed fully to his role in the events last night, and in the attempt to kidnap our father in Paris," Antony said.

"But why?" Antoinette asked. "Why would a man with Rohan blood, distant though it may be, turn on his family like that?"

"It seems Gabriel Monet had been involved in a land embezzlement scheme," Antony said. "When the king resurfaced after all these years, and when Julia and Philip started to conduct their investigations, it was only a matter of time before his misdeeds would be uncovered."

Antoinette stirred milk into her coffee and said, "I hope they keep that horrible man locked up for a long, long time."

"Well ..." Antony began slowly. "A judge allowed him to post two million Euros bail and the prosecution agreed to release him."

"What?" Antoinette cried, almost upsetting her coffee. "That creature is back out on the streets?"

"He's agreed to cooperate fully, to provide all information needed by the police and the prosecution," Antony said. "Not only that, but Major Dumas's men have rounded up the other gang members and they've recovered the truck with the Rohan documents intact."

"Good work," Tom said. "But what about the man who ordered Philip to be killed? Chris Giroux?"

Antony pressed his lips together, knowing he would not be delivering good news. "He managed to escape. We think he may be on his way to Poland. But we will find him and bring him in, no matter what." Antony pounded his fist on the table for emphasis.

"I know you will," Tom said reassuringly. To Antoinette, Julia and Philip he said, "Now we know that the Rohan land holdings in Strasbourg were the cause of all of this death and destruction. All but one of the gang members has been captured, and Gabriel is cooperating with the authorities, I think we can put this unpleasantness behind us and move on."

"What are your plans, *mon cheri?*" Antoinette asked.

"Such a beautiful morning," Tom said, his gaze taking in the lovely surroundings in the dining room, the sunshine pouring in through the windows, and the view of the Vosges Mountains beyond the village. "A perfect day to begin planning a Rohan heritage tour."

He was pleased to see Antoinette, Julia and Philip begin to relax and chatter excitedly about the possibility of a holiday exploring their Rohan heritage.

"As for my immediate plans," Tom added, "I intend to enjoy this delicious breakfast that Chef Jean and his staff has prepared for us, and I recommend you do the same."

*   *   *

Thirty minutes later, Tom had made good on his promise of consuming his breakfast with gusto and strolled out onto the hospital terrace where two night's previous he had given his triumphant speech in front of the Saint-Meyer townspeople. Now the terrace stood empty, except for the birds and butterflies that fluttered about in the warm sunshine and crisp mountain air. Soon he was joined by Louis and André and eagerly shared his plans to organize a Rohan heritage tour.

"We've got the ideal person to help you with that, right here in Saint-Meyer, don't we, André," Louis said with a conspiratorial look at his companion.

"Indeed," André chimed in. "The perfect person."

Tom was puzzled for a moment, then broke out in a smile. "Of course. Bruna Lombardi! I was so impressed with the talk she gave last night. Chair of the combined guilds, descendant of a Carolingian chieftain—who could be better?"

"And the first woman accepted into the Carolingian Sacred Heart," André reminded Tom. "As well as the first new member recruited from outside the ranks of current family members."

Louis said, "I have already taken the liberty of discussing such a possibility with Docteur Lombardi and she is eager to help organize a Rohan Heritage Fellowship. Chef Jean is also on board with this exciting new project."

"Excellent," Tom said. "Not only will we be preserving the Rohan heritage, but we know we will have superb food."

The three men laughed and Louis said, "Speaking of food, I will organize a lunch meeting with Bruna for this very day. I would suggest inviting Antony to join us and, of course, your lovely wife."

"Another fabulous meal prepared by Chef Jean? She'd never forgive me if I didn't take her with me," Tom said, prompting another round of chuckles.

Louis waited for the laughter to die down and spoke to Tom in a low voice, as if fearing the hospital staff might overhear. "Be sure to bring the photographs and notes from your explorations of the dungeons. She can be trusted, and if anyone can help you identify and confirm the sites you have discovered, it's Docteur Lombardi."

CHAPTER TWENTY-NINE

The Rohan family and their advisors found themselves back in the hospital conference room where the previous evening, Philip and Julia had told their stories of terror to law enforcement. Today, the chamber presented a much more pleasant atmosphere, thanks both to the company and the delicious lunch catered by Chef Jean.

Tom, Antoinette, Antony, Louis and Dr. Lombardi were grouped around the conference table, while from a monitor mounted on the wall, General Miliot participated in the meeting via Skype.

Louis noted that the local chapter of the Carolingian Sacred Heart had given provisional approval to Dr. Lombardi joining the historic organization as both the first female and the first not to have a family connection—pending the approval of Tom, King of Rohan.

"With full pleasure and deep respect, I will grant my approval," Tom said. To General Miliot he said, "Still, I would be interested in hearing your reasoning and justification."

General Miliot spoke with confidence and enthusiasm, explaining how Dr. Lombardi was much more than just a distinguished scholar and professor. Her ancestor was a Carolingian chieftain, and she was a direct descendant of the Kingdom of the Lombards, which dated almost three-hundred years earlier than the Lothair Empire. Her aunt, Maria Lombardi, was the High Duchess of the Lombardy region of northern Italy.

Tom felt a shiver up and down his spine just thinking about the ties to a kingdom even older than his own Lothair empire, and the fact that the scholarly woman seated at this table was the niece of Maria Lombardi. He stood and bowed in Bruna Lombardi's direction. Antoinette and Antony followed suit and Tom said, "At this moment, we Rohans are humbled by the extraordinary heritage and history you bring to the Carolingians."

Dr. Lombardi, appearing slightly embarrassed, motioned for the three Rohans to seat themselves. As they did, Tom said, "As the fifty-fourth King of Rohan, I fully approve the exception recommended by General Miliot and Louis. Dr. Bruna Lombardi is now conferred full membership in the Carolingian Sacred Heart."

A round of applause followed, including from General Miliot from the Skype monitor. Tom said, "According to Louis, Dr. Lombardi will lead an open association—the Rohan Heritage Fellowship—with the assistance of key figures like Chef Jean."

More sounds of approval filled the conference room, and then Louis took the floor. "Lord Tom and I have talked about setting up a Rohan Heritage Tour. Duchess Maria Lombardi has invited King Tom and his family to visit the Lombard Chateau—now called Convent Lombard—on Lake Lugano. You may have heard of this site, very difficult for outsiders to visit as it is technically in Italy but accessible only from the Swiss side of the lake."

"Indeed," Tom said. "And I would like to visit the barn-chateau in Basel and take a look at this archive with its six-hundred years' worth of historic materials."

General Miliot added from the Skype monitor, "Excellent! May I propose adding a visit to Zünft House Carolingian on the north side of Lake Lugano. It is the seat of the Carolingian Sacred Heart."

With that, the group broke into an excited discussion of travel plans. Antony, always alert to his family's safety, added, "Be sure to keep our itinerary secret, and to use only Sacred Heart and Lombardi security services."

One of Chef Jean's trusted assistants arrived to clear away the lunch dishes. The Skype monitor went dark and Louis, Antony and Antoinette drifted away. Soon Tom and Bruna Lombardi were the only two individuals left in the conference room.

Tom pulled out his laptop. "Stay for a moment, if you would be so kind," he said to Dr. Lombardi. With a sly smile, he added, "I have a few images you may find interesting." With that, he began scrolling through the album of photographs from his explorations of the dungeons and caverns under Castle Rohan.

For several moments after the last photograph flickered on the screen, Dr. Lombardi simply sat in stunned silence. At last she said in wonder, "This could be a find as important as the Villa of the Papyri in Rome."

"Ah, yes, the only ancient library with a collection surviving to the present day," Tom said.

"Some eighteen-hundred scrolls have been found in the Roman city of Herculaneum in a villa that historians believe was built by Julius Caesar's father-in-law," Dr. Lombardi said. "When Mount Vesuvius erupted in 79 A.D., the library was buried and fortunately for us, preserved under a ninety-foot layer of volcanic ash."

With Tom's assent, Dr. Lombardi took control of the laptop's touch pad and scrolled through the photographs once again, pausing at those she found particularly interesting, lingering on the room full of art behind the vault with its pile of coins. "It appears there are at least two thousand scrolls on those shelves," she said. "If these are what we think they are—the lost records of the Carolingian Renaissance—just think of what an incredible discovery this will be."

"Historians have known relatively little about the Carolingian Renaissance," Tom said. "Only that it saw an upsurge of learning in the arts, medicine, theology and general literacy."

"But now it appears we may have details," Dr. Lombardi said. "The worth of these scrolls could be far greater than that of the gold coins. The value to historians could equal or even be greater that the Villa of the Papryi."

The professor took a long look at the photographs of the buildings Tom had glimpsed in the cave, enlarging them and peering at the detail. "I would have to see these in person to know for sure, but I feel confident these buildings are the Villa Meyer and the school. Do you realize there could very well be another huge archive inside the school?"

Tom had not considered that possibility and felt almost dizzy with the implications and possibilities. "You realize," he said, "if it had not been for the earthquake of October 1356, Villa Meyer and the school would surely have been destroyed by the Armagnacs when they came through here pillaging and looting."

"Instead, the village and school were buried when the earth shifted," Dr. Lombardi said. "Tragic for the loss of life at the time, but very fortunate for researchers centuries later. We will need to assemble a team of archeologists to excavate the site."

"I've been thinking the same thing," Tom said. "The structures are surely fragile and hazardous. It will be a tremendous undertaking."

"But just think of it," Dr. Lombardi said, turning to Tom with a smile as large and eager as a child on Christmas morning. "All this history, art, literature, not to mention the monetary value. This could easily turn out to be the most important medieval site in the world. And we haven't even started to review those Roman coins, the Lothair war chest, and all of the other rooms with their art and jewelry."

"It's almost overwhelming," Tom agreed.

"My recommendation would be to keep this under wraps for the time being, until we can plan how to best authenticate and preserve this incredible find."

"Indeed," Tom said, thinking of the deadly and desperate activities of Gabriel Monet and his co-conspirators the previous evening. "It seems there are still gangs of modern-day Armagnacs who would like nothing better than to pillage these treasures for their own profit instead of preserving them for the good of all humanity."

*   *   *

Forty-eight hours later, Tom sat in the passenger compartment of an armored limousine and watched from a window as the mountains of France gave way to the jagged peaks of Switzerland. Antony drove, while also in the passenger seats were Dr. Lombardi and Louis. A similar armored vehicle containing three Lombardi security guards followed.

The Rohan Heritage Tour had just begun!

The first leg of the journey would last around seventy minutes and take Tom and his party to Basel, where they would meet with the principals of International Investment AG. Tom was eager to spend time with the four elderly Gessner brothers who had proved to be so helpful to his family, and he looked forward with great anticipation to visiting the Carolingian Zünft House and Convent Lombard.

Only one detail marred his happiness. Antoinette was not at his side.

"I'm needed back home," she had declared to Tom when he first proposed the Rohan Heritage Tour to her after meeting with Dr. Lombardi and showing her the photographs of the dungeons. "It's not that I wouldn't love to visit Switzerland with you," she'd said. "But Gilbert needs me. A mother can always tell."

Tom had learned from long experience never to interfere with Antoinette when she was concerned about her children, especially her *bébé*, Gilbert.

"But it won't be half as much fun without you with me," Tom had protested weakly.

"Perhaps I can join you later, when I know everything is in good hands at the home front. But I've got to get off this emotional roller-coaster. For now, this must be *au revoir*."

The two loyal Lombardi bodyguards, Big Bobby and Alex, whom Tom and Antoinette had grown to love and trust implicitly despite their gangster-like appearance, escorted Antony and Antoinette to Ronald's home, where Gilbert had been staying. They returned Antony to Castle Rohan later that day. Tom had been briefed on the plan: the following day, a Lombardi would drive Antoinette and Gilbert back to Dijon—back to the family home where it had all started.

Had it been only twelve days since Gilbert first came home from school with the exciting news that he'd been chosen for a trip to Castle Rohan? Tom shook his head. It felt like a lifetime had passed. Twelve days ago, he had been a simple, obscure pharmacist. Now he was the crowned head of one of Europe's oldest and most powerful dynasties, facing hundreds of responsibilities—and with danger lurking around every corner.

As the limousine motored along the Rhine and drew near Basel,

Tom brought Dr. Lombardi up-to-date on the Rohan's dealings with International Investment AG, concluding with, "They handle one-quarter of our land lease income, and over ninety percent of all the Rohan accounts, mostly small ones. They have kept an archive of our land leases and transactions since 1445. Basel was able to resist the incursions of the Armagnacs, and thus the archive was preserved for all those years."

"Amazing," Dr. Lombardi said. "Six hundred years of continuous record-keeping is an achievement worthy of a world-class museum."

The vehicle entered a dark forest. Dr. Lombardi said, "Your story about the Gessner brothers reminds me of something I just heard on the news. Did you know that the City of London is still paying rent to the Queen of England on land it leased back in 1211?"

"You must be joking," Tom said, instantly intrigued. "Really?"

"It's true," she said, clearly enjoying the moment. "Every October, there's a ceremony where the city pays rent to the queen—a knife, an axe, six horseshoes and sixty-one nails."

"Rent for what?" Tom wanted to know.

"A forge and a piece of moorland."

"Only in England," Tom said and they both laughed.

Their car made a turn onto a narrow country lane. A herd of goats grazed in a grassy, green field, while ahead stood a castle-like structure, almost as large as Castle Rohan, though not as remote or well-fortified. Next to it was a huge, barn-like structure made of stone and brick and appearing to be centuries old.

"That's it?" Dr. Lombardi said. "That's the archive?"

"So it would seem," Tom said. "They showed me a photograph of the barn where they are storing our records and documents. I had no idea it would be anything this big or this impressive."

The four elderly Gessner brothers stood in a row in front of the barn, waiting to present themselves to the king and his entourage. As Tom emerged from the limousine, his first impression was that he had arrived in a place of peace, beauty and security. Vance Gessner warmly welcomed Tom, Dr. Lombardi and Louis on behalf of the Gessner family. Though Vance's eyes sparkled and his voice conveyed genuine hospitality, Tom noticed that the faces of the other three brothers bore serious, almost grim, expressions. What could possibly be amiss under these brilliant blue skies, amid these verdant fields, and in this lovely chateau and barn?

Dr. Lombardi must have likewise sensed some unease among the brothers, because she turned to Louis and whispered, "Something's not right. What's going on?"

Big Bobby and Alex burst out of their car and immediately approached Antony. "The king and his party must stay where they are," Big Bobby said in a low voice. "We must thoroughly inspect the premises before he may be permitted to enter."

Antony conveyed this message to Vance, who gave a little bow and said, "Of course. Your request is more than reasonable and quite prudent."

Big Bobby and Alex wasted no time in entering the barn, Antony and Vance following. Tom, Dr. Lombardi and Louis spent the next ten minutes or so making small talk with the other three brothers— or at least attempting to do so. It seemed that no matter what topic they raised—the breathtaking scenery, the fairy-tale castle, the frolicking goats—the brothers responded politely, but with few words and with the same stoic expressions.

The two Lombardi, Antony and Vance returned, reporting that all was in order and that no dangers or security risks were found in the barn. Tom had assumed that the brothers would relax at this news, but they remained stiff and serious.

What is going on? If there are no hazards, then why do they seem so sad and worried?

As Bruna Lombardi had just said, something's not right.

CHAPTER THIRTY

Vance and the brothers led Tom and his party into the barn-like structure. Tom still picked up on the tension among the Gessners, but almost forgot about it as he was swept away by the beauty and grandeur of the first room they entered. This chamber was more like a ballroom in a baroque-style manor than an archive in a museum. From the polished wood floor to the lofty ceilings, everything was meticulously organized and reflected luxury, taste, and refinement.

Tom gave a sigh of pure pleasure and said to Bruna and Vance, "This room makes me feel like I want to sit by the window with a coffee and just surround myself with history from the past six hundred years."

Instead of the smiles and expressions of thanks that he was expecting from the brothers, he only received the same grim, nervous faces.

The eldest brother, Peter, finally spoke. "Lord and all dignitaries—we are truly sorry."

Tom stared back in surprise. What could these kind and helpful brothers possibly have to apologize for? He gave a friendly nod, urging Peter to continue.

"What you see here," Peter said, his voice shaking, "is the archive representing the first three hundred to four hundred years. Since the early 1800s, the number of documents has grown by at least ten-fold. They are being stored in three rooms, much smaller than this one. We are running out of resources to expand. We have tried to do our best..."

Tom exchanged looks with Bruna, Louis and Antony and could

tell all were thinking the same thing: Is that all? This is the reason for so much concern among the Basel group?

In a gentle voice, Tom said, "Please, please, do not worry yourselves any further about this. Think about it—this is a good problem to have. You have kept our records save and secure for six hundred years. That is an incredible achievement for which I am eternally grateful."

"That is very kind of you, majesty," Vance said, still looking nervous. "But you must understand how embarrassing this is for us. We are Swiss. We are supposed to be efficient and well-organized."

"We understand," Antony said. "Perhaps you would be so kind to show us the room with the most recent records."

Tom gave Antony a nod of approval, immediately understanding that the room with the most recent documents would likely be the one most crowded, the most needing of attention.

Big Bobby led the way, Alex at the rear, as the party left the beautiful, well-organized historic archive and made their way to the room with the newest material. As the brothers had warned, it was indeed a sharp contrast to the clean and orderly archive they had just seen. In this much smaller room, ledger books and boxes were crammed onto shelves from floor to ceiling. Other material was simply piled on the floor, the available shelf space obviously having run out decades ago. There seemed to be little in the way of order. Some of the boxes didn't even have lids, and the contents spilled over the tops. The room smelled musty and a film of dust coated every object.

Tom attempted to thread his way through the chaos, with Big Bobby moving some of the boxes and stacks of books to clear a path. Rather than commenting on the messy jumble, Tom simply asked if he might take a look at a typical recent account transaction book.

Peter responded by picking a ledger book off of one of the stacks on the floor, brushing off the dust and handing it to Tom. He opened the cover and discovered two years' worth of accounts for a rental house: income received versus taxes, utility bills and repairs. Tom realized that if all of the books and boxes in this room contained similar material, they could be reduced to one or two small hard drives with a computerized accounting system.

He next requested a quick tour of the other two rooms containing recent material, and suggested they all re-group in the original historic archive room to determine their next course of action.

Once that had been accomplished and the group had returned to the pleasant surroundings of the grand archive, Tom said to the brothers, "I very much appreciate your being so open and honest with me. And, of course, your diligence in storing my family's records for six hundred years."

He was pleased to see the demeanor of the four Gessners visibly relax, and only regretted that they had obviously been suffering such inner turmoil, worrying themselves sick over the potential of their king's displeasure over the disorganized state of the recent documents. Even the Lombardi security force, Big Bobby and Alex, seemed to have let down their guard somewhat as they realized there were no dangers facing their lord for the moment.

Tom continued, "Your current situation is caused not by lack of good will or positive intentions, but simply a lack of resources. Perhaps you are hampered by ancient restrictions requiring you to keep every scrap of paper. Perhaps you are hamstrung by rent control laws that limit your income."

Peter limped over to a bookcase and fetched a glass box inlaid with gold. Tom could see that the box held a leather scroll. Peter donned a pair of cotton clean-room gloves and handed a second pair to Tom, while Vance covered a table with clean, white paper. Slowly and with great care, Peter removed the scroll from the box and unrolled it on the table.

Bruna, Louis and Antony crowded around along with Tom and stared with wonder at the one-foot by four-foot scroll and the words written upon it in Latin. Peter said, "This is the original agreement between your ancestors and mine some six-hundred years ago. It requires the Gessner family to keep records of all of the Rohan land transactions until such time as the Rohans request that the records be returned to them. It allows the Swiss Basel group to keep six percent of the income as salary, and sets limits on the amount of rent we may collect and the amount we may spend on utilities."

Peter waited until Tom and his advisors had a chance to discuss the implications of this, and then said. "Under Swiss record retention laws, we are required to keep records for only ten years, or twenty at the very most." His voice ranging from apologetic to downright horrified, he added, "One of our staff members has suggested we simply burn all of the records more than ten years old. Or, perhaps we could sell them to a recycler for ten Euros per kilo."

At this, Bruna leapt out of her chair. "Absolutely not! Think of the history that would be lost."

"My colleague is correct," Tom said. "We would never permit one single record to be destroyed. Instead, the Rohan family will take possession of the archive and will digitalize them to make sure they are preserved for posterity. I am appointing Docteur Lombardi to take charge of that project. I have full faith that she will ensure that these documents are treated well."

Tom lowered his voice and asked the brothers to share the details as to their actual compensation. He was shocked to learn that the rental income was only twenty-five percent of market value, and that the brothers were keeping only six percent of that per the terms of the original agreement from six-hundred years ago.

Tom turned to Antony and said, "Make a note. The salary for the Gessner brothers shall be increased by four times, retroactive to ten years ago."

When the four elderly brothers realized the generosity of Tom's offer, their faces finally lost the last traces of the tension they'd been carrying for so long, and they appeared genuinely happy.

In that convivial mood, the group made the short walk up to the main, castle-like house where a luncheon had been prepared for them. With the weather of late spring being so pleasant, Peter directed the food to be served on a terrace overlooking the brilliant green pastureland.

They enjoyed a typical Swiss meal: a salad of fresh, local vegetables, a savory meat pie, and for dessert, a local specialty known as *Basler leckerli,* or Basel cookie, sweet with honey. Several bottles of prosecco were opened and toasts made to the continued happy and profitable relations between the Swiss Basel group and the Rohan family. Even Big Bobby and Alex appeared at ease, as if they were among their own, trusted people.

Peter drained his glass of sparkling wine and declared, "My goodness. I keep forgetting—we have a gold coin to return to the King of Rohan."

Vance excused himself from the table, saying he would fetch the coin forthwith, but Tom put up his hand, indicating he should return to his seat. "Please don't concern yourself about the coin," he said. "It is for the Basel group to keep as a symbol of friendship and trust between our two families. This is the least we can do to reward you for six hundred years of service, fellowship and brotherhood."

Antony then asked for the floor and proceeded to outline seven action items having to do with the preservation of the archives. These involved moving the more recent materials to the custody of the Rohan family for preservation and digitalizing, from the newest to the oldest, while keeping the historic items in the grand archive in place for now. He also recommended that Dr. Lombardi be given full, unfettered access to the historic material with an eye toward cataloguing the most valuable pieces and determining how they should best be preserved for future generations.

Tom took a sip of the bubbly, sat back in his chair and once again marveled at his incredible luck in having produced children who were smart, resourceful, insightful and loyal to the family. Antony's recommendations were just the latest example. Tom immediately saw the logic in digitalizing the most recent documents first, as this would free up storage space for newer material as it came in.

With minor refinements, Antony's recommendations were accepted by all, and the meeting ended with handshakes and air kisses, and the knowledge that the bonds between the two families were firmly in place.

*   *   *

For the next leg of the Rohan Heritage Tour, a three hour journey from Basel to Lugano, Big Bobby switched places with Louis. No sooner had the limousine left the country lanes surrounding the Swiss Basel archive and entered the motorway than Big Bobby sprang into action. From his mobile phone, he issued instructions to the Lombardi in the Lugano area: search the Carolingian Zünft residence, check the credentials of the household staff, and don't forget to investigate any person attempting to deliver a package. And keep an eye on the surrounding streets.

Tom knew Big Bobby must be feeling a sense of guilt at the tardiness of his initial response at the Swiss Basel archive. Tom and his party would have blithely waltzed into the barn without a second thought. Only at the last minute had Big Bobby and Alex intervened, insisting on a security check. What if the remnants of Gabriel Monet's gang had been waiting inside?

Bruna gave Tom a look of impressed amazement as she listened to Big Bobby's phone calls. Tom guessed Antony must be having the same thoughts up in the driver's seat. Big Bobby was speaking to his various contacts in fluent Italian, Swiss German, German and French. This swarthy brute who looked as if he belonged in a gang on the gritty streets of a big city was conversant in four languages— who knew how many more?

They listened, fascinated, as Big Bobby broadcast a message to all of his contacts to report in, as the vehicle was about to enter the Gotthard Tunnel and would be incommunicado for the thirteen or so minutes it would take to travel from one end to the other.

Major Dumas was the first to respond. His people had spotted one member of the Gabriel Monet gang and two troublesome media people. "There's little we can do as we have no authority to take action in Switzerland."

Speaking in French to Major Dumas, Big Bobby said, "I am a Swiss national, and so are several members of my team. They can stay close to the three subjects you have identified."

The large man burst into laughter when he took in the astonished looks on Tom and Bruna's faces. "Who knew, right? Born to Italian nationals just over the border in Switzerland, so that gave me dual citizenship. Then I served in the French Foreign Legion for five years, saw action around the world. That gave me the right to French citizenship."

Tom could only shake his head in wonder. He knew members of the French Foreign Legion were highly trained in all areas of military operations. Add to that his ease with languages and his meticulous management style, and Big Bobby transformed in Tom's mind from a gangster to a real life James Bond. He searched for something to say to this multi-talented man who had done so much for his family, but could only exclaim, "Incredible!"

Big Bobby stared at his hands with a humble demeanor. "Nah, it's nothing, really. See, being from a Lombardi family, we're often treated, shall we say, special. On law enforcement's watch list, know what I mean? So we had to develop street-smarts when we were still practically in diapers. When people think the worst of you, you develop a thick shell. As to the languages—no big deal. Growing up just a short dirt path away from Italy, of course we kids learned both Italian and Swiss German. And then we had French in school."

"And your military service?" Tom asked.

"All Swiss males have to serve in the military. In addition, I decided to do it the hard way and joined the French Foreign Legion," he said with a grin. "By the time my five years were up, I was an officer, a Special Forces platoon commander."

Tom could only repeat, "Incredible," as he told himself how lucky he was to have two such highly trained military men—his son Antony and Big Bobby—right here in the car with him.

The limousine zoomed into the Gotthard Tunnel, a 10-mile long engineering marvel that sliced through the Swiss Alps.

"I used to do the drive over the pass before they built the tunnel," Tom said to Bruna and Big Bobby. "Very winding, very treacherous, and often impassable due to snow in winter. The trip took at least two hours."

"Lucky for us they built the tunnel," Bruna remarked.

"Yes, I suppose," Tom said. "Yet on a good day, the old road could be beautiful with breathtaking look-out spots. I remember stopping once at a monastery where they raise St. Bernards. The puppies were so cute. Smart and friendly, too."

Just as the long, dark tunnel was about to press in on them, the limousine cruised back out into the sunshine and all in the car seemed to visibly relax.

Lake Lugano came into view, as well as the namesake town, an Italian-speaking metropolis of some sixty-three thousand, dating to the Middle Ages and earlier. Though Tom was glad a three-hour road trip was about to come to an end, he sensed growing tension from Big Bobby. The large bodyguard stayed on his mobile phone constantly, checking in with his various agents and operatives, as well as Alex in the vehicle immediately behind their own. Major Dumas reported in that the two troublesome media people had been tagged by the Lombardi.

Antony maneuvered the limousine through the narrow streets until they reached the Carolingian Zünft House, the Guild Hall. In contrast to the multi-story, half-timbered Guild Hall in Saint-Meyer, this building was a Mediterranean-style villa situated on the northeast shore of Lake Lugano. One of fourteen major Zünfte Houses in Switzerland, it was also the headquarters of the Carolingian Sacred Heart.

Big Bobby ordered Antony to park in the back, avoiding the main entrance, and for Tom and Bruna to stay put until he personally had the opportunity to thoroughly check the building for security risks. After a wait of least thirty minutes, he returned and reported that it appeared safe for Tom to enter through a back hall.

Tom climbed out of the limousine, stretched, and took a big gulp of fresh air. It felt so good to be outdoors and in motion after being cooped up for three hours. But he had little time to admire his surroundings as Big Bobby and Alex were hustling him into the Guild Hall and down a long, back hallway.

The entourage rounded a corner. Tom could see the passageway open up into a larger room. Then he became aware of a commotion, urgent voices and hurried footsteps. Suddenly bright lights flashed in front of his face, almost blinding him.

Paparazzi!

After all the security precautions, Big Bobby's careful management of every aspect of their journey, how could they have known exactly where to find him?

Unless... someone on the inside tipped them off.

CHAPTER THIRTY-ONE

"**I** recognize those photographers," Tom said to Big Bobby and Antony. "I've seen them lurking around the castle and Saint-Meyer the past few days. They must be getting information from a Rohan insider as to my whereabouts."

Antony nodded. "Only a few people know about our travel itinerary. We know we can trust the Carolingians. Perhaps it's someone involved with the limousine dispatch team?"

"Makes sense," Big Bobby said. "They would have known that Lugano was our final destination for today. Which would explain why those media vultures didn't bother us in Basel—they didn't know we were making a stop there."

"Then let's beat them at their own game," Antony said with a grin. "We'll tell the car service that our next destination is Zurich. We'll even send out two decoy cars, let the paparazzi waste their time and resources following the wrong vehicles. Then we'll procure two different limos for our trip to Lombardy."

"Excellent plan," Big Bobby said. Turning to Tom, he advised, "Don't talk to the paparazzi; don't even look at them. They'll do everything they can to get you to respond—begging, threats, rude comments. Ignore them. Just keep walking."

With Antony on one side and Big Bobby at the other, Tom did as he was told, striding purposefully and with eyes focused straight ahead as the trio made their way past the flashing cameras. They entered another doorway and Tom found himself in a well-appointed club room with comfortable chairs and a breathtaking view of beautiful Lake Lugano.

The trio seated themselves and allowed a butler to serve them cold, refreshing beverages. Once he was certain they were alone, Big Bobby said. "We swept both cars this morning before leaving Saint-Meyer and didn't find any tracking sensors or listening devices."

Antony looked shocked and sober. "Horrifying to think of my own father being tracked and spied upon. Makes me think we need to bring in an intelligence team to Castle Rohan to do background checks on all the staff. We know there are one or more moles within the organization. Better to weed them out sooner than later."

"Gabriel Monet promised the authorities that he would cooperate," Big Bobby mused. "Then you've got those bogus charities. Some of their officials might be willing to provide insight in return for leniency. Of course, you've got access to French intelligence."

Anthony responded to that suggestion by pulling out his phone and calling Major Dumas to update him on the situation.

Tom, Antony and Big Bobby moved in closer to hear the major's response. "Give me fifteen minutes, then call Castle Rohan to advise them of your supposed new itinerary."

The minutes ticked by. Antony called Louis to ask him to inform the car pool team that Tom and his entourage had decided to travel to Zurich the following morning to visit the Zûnfte House.

Another quarter hour passed before Antony's phone pinged with a call from Major Dumas. "Louis's call was picked up by the main receptionist at the castle. She passed along your message to the head of the motor pool. He informed one of the mechanics of your supposed travel plans. That individual made two calls. One we know for certain was to the paparazzi that stalked you to Lugano. The other was to a European mobile number. My people are still tracking that one."

Major Dumas called back after another fifteen minute wait. "We talked to Gabriel Monet. He believes there are two small groups inside Castle Rohan working for outside factions. The mechanic is one, trading information for money. Then there's a housekeeper named Liesl who has ties with an Eastern European syndicate." He finished by recommending that Tom and his party wait until further intelligence work had been completed, and named four suspects that warranted further investigation.

With nothing further to accomplish in the way of security, Antony and Big Bobby escorted Tom to an assembly hall where Louis was presiding over a gathering of the Carolingian brotherhood. The baronial room could have comfortably seated two hundred or more, but Tom saw less than twenty seated in a semi-circle of chairs in one corner.

Louis welcomed the royal visitor and his team. With a voice tinged with apology, he went on, "The last time we gathered in this place, the sacred brotherhood numbered forty-five. Today, due to attrition and the passage of time, we are down to thirty-one." With a bow in the direction of Bruna Lombardi, he said, "The addition of the distinguished professor brings our number up to thirty-two."

He must have noticed a look of puzzlement on Tom's face, because he said, "What you see is true. Only eighteen of sacred brotherhood are with us today. The sad fact is, most of our members are elderly and some are too frail to make the journey."

"Perfectly understandable," Tom said with his usual graciousness.

Louis continued, "If we are to continue, we must evolve into an open association. No more secrecy, no more recruiting solely from the old families. We must draw our membership from a broader base."

Tom told Louis he understood the situation and asked to be introduced to each member of the brotherhood who had taken the time and trouble to attend the meeting. With great enthusiasm, he warmly greeted each member, asking about careers and background. He was genuinely interested in the men who had served his family so loyally for so many centuries—plus, he knew that gathering a bit of unique information about each would help him remember their names.

A sumptuous dinner with generous amounts of excellent wines followed. When the dessert course was being cleared away, Louis approached Tom and said it was time for him to meet some distinguished visitors who, for reasons of security, could not dine in the main banquet hall.

With that, Louis and Big Bobby escorted Tom and Antony to a heavy, locked door. Big Bobby nodded to two large, stone-faced men who stood guard on either side of the door, and Tom guessed they must be part of the Lombardi security force. One of the guards undid a lock and the door swung open just far enough for Louis, Big Bobby, Tom and Antony to enter.

Inside, Tom found a smaller version of the elegant banquet hall he'd just left, with General Miliot, Bruna Lombardi and a tough-looking man in a wheelchair seated around the dining table. Tom judged the latter person to be in his sixties and Italian.

Tom greeted General Miliot with friendship and shook hands, while Antony executed a snappy military salute. The general returned the gestures of respect and said, "As a leader in the French military, it would not be appropriate for me to also be involved in a secret society such as the Carolingian Sacred Heart. However, I have never experienced a conflict of interest between my military role and my membership in the brotherhood."

A look of pleasure crossed his stern features. "You'll be seeing me take a much more active role in the coming months and years. You see, my retirement has been approved. In two months, I will be a civilian and will be able to carry out my role fully in the Carolingian Sacred Heart."

A round of enthusiastic applause followed. When it died down, General Miliot continued, "We have a hero in our midst. Docteur Lombardi, if you would be so kind as to introduce us to your cousin."

"It would be my pleasure," Bruna replied. Gesturing to the man in the wheelchair, she said, "My cousin, Carmine Lombardi, is not only a hero to my family, but is the ultimate Lombardi commander. He and four others defended the Lombardi family and the U.S. Special Envoy against a foreign professional special force operating on Swiss and Italian soil. They had ten times the firepower, and yet my cousin and his men prevailed."

A flicker of a smile appeared on Carmine's tough, weather-beaten face. "I took five bullets and lost a leg. But the family was saved, as well as the delegation from the United States."

The old man went on, "But the real hero is the man who rescued us just as we were about to die. He and his team sent twenty of our attackers to hell, sank them right to the bottom of Lake Lugano. He took three bullets in the process." A bark of a laugh issued from Carmine's lips. "That hero, too, is right here in this room."

The small gathering looked at each other in wonder. Who or what was Carmine talking about? Their gaze finally settled on the most likely candidate—Big Bobby.

"Correct," Carmine said. "Roberto—Big Bobby to you—saved all of us. He and a handful of Swiss soldiers from the village against three times the firepower: assault rifles, grenade launchers, bullet-proof armor. Thanks to his training in the French Foreign Legion, Big Bobby was able to repel the attack with merciless force."

Big Bobby listened to the accolades silently, his hands clasped at his waist and his eyes appearing to study his shoes. Once again, Tom felt a wave of respect and awe toward this young man. Beneath that surface of a common street thug lurked not only keen intelligence, but the ability to apply lethal force if necessary.

Eventually, the conversation ebbed and those gathered in the private room returned to the main banquet hall. Before adjourning the meeting of the Carolingian Sacred Heart, Tom strode to the head of the room and said he had several announcements to make. The chamber hushed as Tom said, "Invoking the power vested in me as the King of Rohan, I am awarding first level knighthood to General Miliot and Louis."

Both men expressed profuse thanks, and Tom continued, "I am likewise bestowing third and fourth level knighthoods to the core members of the Sacred Heart and the Lombardi family. As to my nephews, Victor and Gabriel Monet, I am making small land grants to each as they are both sons of my late brother, Pierre, and of royal blood. Victor has a record of long, loyal service to our family. As for Gabriel, he undoubtedly saved my son's and daughter's lives by insisting that no killing take place during a crucial moment. He has earned this reward."

He concluded by announcing that he was awarding houses to Brigitte and other Rohan directors, and generous bonuses to all long-time Rohan staff.

As the long day drew to a close and the members of the

brotherhood began to drift away to their bedchambers, Tom pulled Antony aside into a private corner. "It's high time you learned the secret Carolingian hand signals, yes?" father said to son.

"Absolutely," Antony said, adding with a chuckle, "I always wondered what you were doing with your hands hidden under a napkin at the dinner table."

"Just keeping in practice," Tom said, returning the laugh. "My father first taught me the secret code when I was eight years old, right here at this very Carolingian Zûnfte House. It is an ancient tradition, and as next in line to the throne, it's appropriate and necessary that you learn."

Tom then proceeded to introduce Antony to the basics—light pressure on various knuckles, taps to the palm, fingers entwined—to signal such concepts as "I am on your side" or warnings about pending danger. "Always remember to keep your hand covered," Tom concluded. "In public, a pullover or jacket draped over your arm will work. Or a large handkerchief. Or—as you discovered—a dinner napkin comes in handy."

Some ninety years ago, King Raymond had introduced his young boy to the hand signals. Now, Tom was passing on the tradition to his eldest son in the very same room. Before King Raymond, dozens of other Rohan patriarchs had shared the secret knowledge with their offspring. Presumably, many more would do the same in the future. Tom felt a shiver of awe at the twists of fate that were allowing him to play a part in this grand arc of history.

*　　　　*　　　　*

The journey from Zûnfte Carolingian to the Lombard convent is only three kilometers via boat, from the northeast beach of Lake Lugano to the southeast. But by overland vehicle, it's an entirely different story.

The following morning, Tom and his entourage—Bruna, Big Bobby, Antony, General Miliot, Louis—seated themselves in an armored limousine. Two heavily fortified SUVs accompanied them, one in front and one in the back. From the Swiss town of Lugano they entered Italy for a drive through the forested mountains, finally through Swiss soil, then in Italy once again as they arrived at the convent.

"Lugano is surrounded on three sides by the Lombardy section of Italy," Tom remarked as the large, heavy vehicle maneuvered around another sharp turn in the road. "Not to mention all these forests and mountains. No wonder it's easier to make the trip by boat."

"Easier, perhaps," Big Bobby said, "but far more dangerous. We simply could not guarantee your safety in a vessel on open water."

"Understood," Tom said with his usual good cheer. "Did you know the name Lombard comes from the German word *langbärte*, meaning 'long beard'?"

"He's right," Bruna said. "This region has a fascinating history. Originally inhabited by the Celts, then occupied by the Gauls, and finally conquered by Rome in the third century. After the fall of the empire, the region was taken over by the Goths, then the Lombards, and then finally the Carolingians. It was from the latter that the feudal system developed here."

The armored vehicles arrived at a rambling compound of stone buildings with tile roofs. A tower held a single bell, while a fountain gurgled pleasantly at the front. A large number of armed men poured from the courtyard. Big Bobby signaled for all passengers to stay put until he and his men had a chance to thoroughly inspect the buildings.

Finally satisfied that he could ensure the security of the royal visitors, Big Bobby and his fellow Lombardi bodyguards escorted Tom and the other passengers into the cool, quiet convent and into a conference room. They seated themselves around an oval table and a nun materialized to offer tea and light refreshments.

Bruna rose and with a glance of acknowledgment at the Lombardi brothers, Tom and General Miliot, she said, "Welcome to Convent Lombardi. Our ancestors have inhabited this sacred spot for nearly fourteen centuries, since the fall of Rome."

She went on to explain that the monks' quarters were located to the right, behind the main section of the compound, while the nuns lived in a wing to the left. "Princess Maria, my aunt, lives in the nuns' quarters," she said. "She is eighty-one years old and rarely, if ever, leaves. Usually men are not permitted to enter her section of the convent. Today, we are making an exception. Maria, Princess of Lombardi, has invited King Rohan and his eldest son, Antony, as well as General Miliot, to pay her a call. Please follow me."

Before anyone had a chance to leave their chairs and answer Bruna's invitation, Big Bobby called for attention. "Princess Maria is coming our way. All rise for Maria, Princess of Lombardi!"

The Lombardi men snapped to attention and all others in the room stood.

A small, slender woman wearing a simple gray dress entered. She stood erect and exhibited none of the infirmities of age. Only the soft wrinkles in her face and the gray in the soft curls that drifted to her neck gave away her advanced years. She was accompanied by an old woman in a classic black-and-white nun's habit, and a much younger woman whose lithe, muscular body gave evidence of many hours spent in a gym. Must be a female Lombardi bodyguard, Tom thought.

Princess Maria greeted all Lombardi by name and invited Bruna to sit at her right, and one of the top Lombardi leaders next to Bruna.

Her blue-gray eyes fell on Tom, issuing a message of peace and respect. "Lord Rohan, if you would be so kind as to take the seat next to me on the left. Next to you, General Miliot and then the young General Antony Rohan."

All did as they were instructed. With immense grace and charm, the princess welcomed her guests. "This convent is the very heart of the Lombards," she said. "Our family ruled nearly all of what is today's Italy from 568 to 774, nearly two hundred years."

Her keen eyes took in every occupant of the conference room, finally resting on Tom. "This compound was originally a small Lombard castle, highly fortified, with a solid stone wall almost four stories high. The castle was converted to a monastery some two centuries later."

Princess Maria let this information sink in, then continued, "Desiderata was one of four daughters of Desiderius, king of the Lombards, and his queen, Ansa. She was married to Charlemagne in

770. More than likely, this was strictly a political alliance, designed to form a bond between the Franks and the Lombards."

She uttered a tiny sigh. "Unfortunately, things did not work out as planned. The marriage was annulled after only one year, and war broke out between the two kingdoms three years later. The Lombards lost that conflict and their kingdom was taken over by Charlemagne."

The princess paused in her tale, and Tom dared to venture a question. "What happened to Desiderata?"

"As far as we know, she never remarried and never produced any children. She retired first to the Monastary of Santa Giulia in Brescia and later spent much of her time right here, the home of the King of the Lombards."

Once again, those piercing eyes seemed to see right through Tom, causing him to come close to squirming in his seat. His mind began racing. *What is the point of this history lesson? Why did she invite me here? What does she really want of me and my family?*

CHAPTER THIRTY-TWO

A s Tom's mind became more agitated, Marie continued to speak. "I am the youngest of eleven brothers and sisters, and the last surviving one. These gentlemen—" she gave a graceful wave of her arm to the Lombardi security team—represent the very best in the children and grandchildren of my siblings."

The stern bodyguards could not help beaming at this show of recognition from the princess. "Make yourself at home," she told them. "In the meantime, I shall retire to my quarters with King Tom, Professor Lombardi, and the two generals, Miliot and Antony Rohan. My sunroom should be more than adequate for such a gathering."

Marie's sunroom did, indeed, prove to be "more than adequate," with a conference/dining table that would seat ten, a comfortable sofa, windows that allowed sunlight from the south to pour in, a profusion of potted, flowering plants, and walls lined with family photographs. When the party had settled in, Marie said, "This is my favorite room in the entire compound. I believe this was where Desiderata spent most of her time, too."

Tom's attention was drawn to a photograph of a lovely woman with flowing blonde hair and Marie's own keen eyes.

"Ah, I see you have discovered my daughter, Heidi," Marie said.

She went on to explain how Heidi had immigrated to the United States as a young girl, become a U.S. citizen, and held a top position in the State Department. She grew up on an abandoned U.S. Army weapons test site near Carmel, California, graduated at 19 from the University of California at Santa Cruz, and earned her PhD in International Studies from Stanford University at age 23. She served as an intelligence analyst for four years while simultaneously earning a law degree. Joining the State Department at the height of the Yugoslavia crisis, she was then, at age 32, the assistant secretary.

"Another over-achiever, just like my wife," Tom remarked. He looked at the photo closely, respectfully. "We all know Heidi is now the Secretary of Homeland Security. Wow, reporting directly to the President of the United States!"

"Indeed," Marie said with a smile. "Heidi was born in Milan so she holds dual citizenship, Italy and the United States. As her mother, I was the youngest sister of the Lombardi gang's top boss."

"Your daughter is a remarkable, outstanding woman," Tom said, still asking himself why Marie had invited him to meet with her.

As if reading Tom's mind, Marie said, "You must be wondering why I invited you and Professor Lombardi and the two generals to my private quarters. Soon, all will be made clear."

The four guests seated themselves on the large sofa, while Marie took a comfortable easy chair next to table holding a selection of rare orchids. "You are familiar with asceticism, am I correct?" she began.

"The abstinence from sensual pleasures," Tom replied. "Often for the purpose of pursuing spiritual goals."

"Very true," Marie said. "However, that is not the case for many of us here at this convent. We have sequestered ourselves to repent and to pursue redemption."

Tom said that he understood and leaned forward so as not to miss a single word.

"Ascetics may withdraw from the world," Marie said, "but we live in dual worlds, partly here and partly out in society. When we are at the convent, we adopt a frugal lifestyle, renouncing material possessions and physical pleasures. We fast and spend our time on reflection and enlightenment."

Focusing on Tom, she said, "I invited you here for two reasons. First, there is a lady you must meet, and second, I want to share a Lombardi family story."

Tom felt a shiver run up and down as spine at the mention of a lady. The quiver of fear and curiosity intensified when Marie said, "I spent many days convincing this particular lady that, after sixty-five years, it is time that she should be reunited with you."

Belle Orschwil! My first love. But how… and why?

Marie's demeanor remained placid, in sharp contrast to Tom's growing inner turmoil. To General Miliot, she said, "Would you be so kind to take Tom and Antony to your mother's quarters?"

Tom's agitation grew worse. *Mother? Belle is General Miliot's mother? Does that mean I am …?*

He allowed himself to be escorted to a door at the back of Marie's sunroom, Antony following. General Miliot gave the door a gentle rap and announced, "King Rohan and his elder son Antony are here to call on Lady Orschwil."

A soft, pleasant voice from within replied, "Please invite them in, Alexandre."

For the third time that morning, Tom felt chills and nervous tension flood his entire body. *Belle's voice!* Even after sixty-five years, he recognized it instantly.

The woman who was supposed to be my wife and the mother of my children. The woman for whom I spent three years searching around the world after she disappeared. The woman for whom I gave up the kingship.

But how could it be, Tom asked himself. Belle was one year older, which would make her 102 years old.

With great apprehension, Tom walked slowly into the room. A slender woman, plainly dressed in a simple skirt and blouse, and with hair pulled back and knotted in a bun atop her head, rose from an easy chair.

Tom could only stand and stare, shocked to his very core. This woman appeared to be only around fifty years old, not by any means a centenarian. Plus, the Belle of his memory had been a voluptuous woman, always dressed at the height of fashion and with black curls flowing luxuriously around her neck and shoulders.

In a soft, graceful and confident voice she said, "It's really me, Tom. I am Belle Orschwil."

Tom felt tears pool in his eyes. No woman on the planet had this natural charm and confidence. No woman but his Belle. Tom fell to one knee, took her outstretched hand in his own, and planted one tender and respectful kiss.

General Miliot, recognizing the magnitude of the moment,

attempted to intervene. Tom turned to this man who might be his son, his vision so blurred he could barely see.

Tears streamed down Belle's cheeks and she choked out between sobs, "No, no, he is not your son."

But Tom was too deep in his own emotions to fully understand what she was trying to tell him. *No wonder she disappeared. No wonder she went into hiding for sixty-five years.*

Adding to his turmoil, Antony and General Miliot were both exchanging comments along the same line. "It makes sense that he gave up the throne" and "Now I understand why he lived like a commoner for so long."

Belle wiped her face with a tissue and in a calm voice asked for a few moments of private time with Tom.

"As you wish, my lady," the two military men said in unison, excusing themselves from the room.

Ten minutes later, Tom and Belle returned to the sunroom, joining Marie, Antony, General Miliot and Bruna Lombardi. They found Marie in the middle of a discussion of the history of the convent as it related to the Lombardi family. "In this reclusive, small castle, hidden in the mountains, the Lombards have continued their traditions and heritage for more than fifteen centuries."

Looking at everyone in the room, Marie continued, "Some twelve hundred years ago, the Carolingian King Charlemagne needed help, so he entered into a marriage of convenience with one of the Lombard princesses. Only a year later, he had the marriage annulled and later conquered the Lombards. We became part of the Carolingian empire."

After a small pause in which those in the room considered the significance of this long-ago union, Marie said with a wise smile, "Life comes full circle. A Carolingian fell in love with a Lombard princess, but she would not marry him. He gave up his kingship and spent three years of his life searching around the world for her."

Once again, Tom's eyes filled with tears. "I never found her. Never saw her again until just now." He lowered his head and mumbled, "And I never knew she was a member of the Lombardi family."

"Perfectly understandable," Marie said kindly. "You were young and didn't have the wisdom you possess now.

Then to the assembled guests and with special emphasis on Tom, she said, "The Lombardi has protected you and your family for sixty-five years now. Do you know why?"

"I think I'm beginning to understand," Tom said with a rueful laugh.

Marie nodded with wisdom. "It was all Belle's doing. It was she who set up the program to have the Lombardi protect you for all those years. Meanwhile, your father arranged for the Carolingian Sacred Heart to look after your safety and security some forty years ago."

"Looks like I had the best of both worlds," Tom said.

"You were born with great blessings!" Marie said, her voice strong and fervent. "You were granted the freedom to accept the crown or not. You chose to devote your life to academic pursuits. You have always been protected by two powerful groups. When you bring the Lombardi and the Carolingian Sacred Heart together, no security force in the world is more effective."

Tom shook his head in wonder. "I could easily have been killed in Paris had it not been for the Lombardi. Now I know I owe my life to Belle. It was she who insisted that I be protected."

Marie's face took on a look that reminded Tom of a Mafia matriarch as she said, "Many sages tell us that life runs in cycles. Often the fates re-converge, but with different ends. You, a Carolingian prince, gave up everything for Belle. For a Lombard's daughter. So when Gabriel Monet arranged for a Lombardi hitman to take you out—" she laughed and raised two fingers into the air "—we sent our very best gunman to do the job. Not for money, but to protect you. Until today, they have no idea why we did so."

With another chuckle, she added, "As the Americans would say, we kicked ass that morning in front of your bank in Paris."

When the laughter died down, Maria fixed her gaze on General Miliot as she said, "Good will often runs as a cycle in life. Belle has stated that you are not Tom's son. But I am not sure that she is right." When a girlish giggle that seemed to come straight from her heart, Maria said, "If I had been in Belle's position, I don't think I could have said no to Tom's proposal. And everything would have turned out completely differently, wouldn't it."

The men responded to Maria's remark with stunned silence as they realized the power of this one-time top boss of the Mafia. Belle's face grew crimson with embarrassment.

Marie's expression became serious. "But that's not what happened," she said, looking first at Tom and then at Belle. "However, the details of that private discussion you just had behind closed doors should remain between the two of you for now."

"Let's just say we shared fond memories of a first romantic love and leave it at that," Belle said.

The others in the room sat in rapt silence, taking in every word and gesture of the two one-time lovers. Tom kept his attention fixed on Belle as he said, "I still don't understand why you had to just disappear like that."

Belle rose and put a hand on Tom's shoulder. "It was the only way, don't you see? A clean break. I don't know if I could have resisted your charms forever. In a moment of weakness, I might have accepted your proposal. You could be very persuasive, you know."

Tom managed a weak smile as he said to all in the room, "And all this time, while I was chasing around the world looking for Belle, she was sequestered right here in this very convent."

"But now you see how it all worked out the way it was supposed to," Belle said. "After all, if I had not removed myself from your life, you never would have met Antoinette."

Antoinette! At the mention of his dear wife's name, Tom was overcome with wave after wave of longing and homesickness, more powerful than he had ever before experienced. At that moment, he would have given anything to be able to issue a royal order and immediately transport himself to the little farmhouse in the Dijon countryside, and to see Antoinette's familiar face smiling at him from across the dining table. *Never to have met Antoinette! Never to bring into the world the seven children who had brought me so much joy!* The mere idea was simply unthinkable.

"You know I'm right," Belle continued with her gentle confidence. She finished by placing a quick kiss on Tom's cheek.

Tom could only nod, still overwhelmed with emotion. With that simple, chaste kiss, Belle's lips brushing his own skin, he realized he felt nothing. Nothing except a whisper of nostalgia for the young man he had once been. More than anything, he felt himself bursting with gratitude for the freedom that Belle had granted him, and the life that he had been privileged to make with Antoinette.

The room fell silent as everyone realized a moment of great profundity and meaning had just taken place. The only sound was the faint babbling of the fountain in the courtyard as each person contemplated his or her own youthful choices and consequences.

Marie finally broke the silence, saying to Tom, "It's not exactly a secret that you've been telling certain people that you want to renounce your kingship, and that you won't be holding the title for much longer."

"Apparently the walls have ears," Tom said humor.

Marie returned the smile and said, "It's likewise no secret in the business world that the Rohan finances are on the verge of collapse. It will take at least three months, if not three years, for the Rohan corporation to get itself back on its feet.:"

"So they say," Tom agreed, wondering where this amazing woman was leading him next.

"Now more than ever, Rohan needs a leader with integrity, courage, and vision" Marie said firmly. "I'm talking big picture, not just the financial and legal realm."

Now it was clear what Marie had on her mind. Tom braced himself for what he knew was coming.

With a point of one elegant finger, Marie said, "You are that person! You cannot walk away this time like you did before! Among other things, you have your Rohan heritage to uncover and to enlighten the world."

"I'm just a simple researcher and pharmacist," Tom protested.

Marie sat up straighter and her face grew stern, that Mafia matriarch look again. "My lord, your years as the King of Rohan are yet to come! You are the one to lead, to prevail, to glorify Rohan.

You could be the most important king in centuries of Rohan history. This is your destiny, Maximal Oto Thomas Rohan! It took sixty-five years of dormancy living in the ordinary world to groom a real king with the fullness of humanity, royal blood with the common touch. Only you can do this!"

Antony, General Miliot, Belle and Bruna leapt from their seats at this inspiring declaration and began a spontaneous round of applause for both Marie and Tom.

"There, you see?" Marie said when order had been restored. "More proof that good will runs in circles. You must not break that cycle."

Tom stood and drew himself up to his full height. "Very well. As you have said, what goes around, comes around. In less than a week, the Lombardi saved my life in Paris. Then Louis, a Carolingian, rescued me from sure death deep in the dungeon. The patterns of life recur in many ways."

Encouraged by the show of respect from the others in the room, Tom went on, "I never felt I 'owned' any of the huge wealth and historical archives bestowed upon me. But I do accept the responsibility of stewardship. I shall use these resources in a benevolent and compassionate manner for the betterment of all humankind."

He began to pace in front of the window with its view of Lake Lugano and the Swiss Alps as he thought out loud. "A cycle of a thousand years could be the same as one man's lifetime. My hope is to make it a cycle of benevolence and compassion. For example, Duke Michael's extensive donations to various charitable organizations. Unfortunately, I don't have the privilege to use the Rohan assets in that manner in this critical moment."

He stopped in a shaft of sunlight that poured through the window like a natural theatrical spotlight and said, "I shall use my own assets to break the negative cycle enacted by the most recent custodians of the Rohan finances. As most of you know, I own a small chain of drugstores. Four, to be exact."

The others in the room nodded.

"I shall sell three of them, and just keep the one in Dijon, nearest to home. The funds realized by the sale will be used in two areas: children and education. My goal is to help break the cycle of poverty, illiteracy and ill health."

As more ideas began to form in his mind, Tom's voice grew louder and he waved one arm in enthusiasm. "With my recent visit to the delightful town of Saint-Meyer, I have become aware of the dire straits facing many of our small towns and villages. I intend to do something to get them back on the path to economic sustainability. Then there's the vast Rohan holdings in art and historical artifacts, rare and irreplaceable—a tremendous responsibility, and one which I will accept."

He seated himself amid another round of applause. Belle said, "When I first met Tom, I was living a lavish lifestyle among the Paris elite. We took luxurious vacations every year, sometimes staying at a Rohan resort. Tom was there, working not in top management as you would expect, but as one of the common frontline wage-earners.

She faced Antony. "Young general!"

Tom saw his son visibly flinch at being so addressed, and half expected him to snap to attention and deliver a salute. Instead, he merely straightened in his seat and listened intently as Belle continued, "Even dressed in the uniform of a gardener or a porter, your father stood out. No amount of workingman's clothes could disguise his dignity, education and grace. In the humble circumstances that he chose for himself, he outshone all of us in the ranks of royalty and high society."

With a little smile playing on her lips at the memory, she said, "At the time, I was considered to be quite the beauty and had the finest education. Trust me, there were many handsome, wealthy men eager to place an engagement ring on my finger. And yet, when Tom invited me to tour his vegetable garden, I was simply swept away by his knowledge, grace and deep sense of humanity."

Tom, too, felt himself being swept away by Belle's story, at the memory of standing with this elegant, poised, and beautiful young woman while he held a shovel and wore dirt-stained overalls in the middle of a vegetable garden in the French Riviera.

Belle continued, "Two years later, I found out he was a professor at one of the top universities. So young to have attained such a lofty position! And what was he doing, spending his summers toiling among the working class?"

Another Mona Lisa smile played on her features. "Of course, I was intrigued. To my delight, he seemed to be intrigued by me. So, I used my Lombardi family connections to have him investigated— rank does have its privileges, you know—and discovered that he was of royal blood, next in line to the Rohan throne. Later, I learned that he had renounced the title in order to pursue my hand in marriage."

Marie interrupted the tale to remind the listeners that the King of Rohan is the highest royal title in France, on the same level as the British monarch and the Pope.

Turning to Antony once again, Belle said, "Please tell your mother, your siblings, and all the Rohan family: your father is very special. He possesses great integrity, kindness, intelligence compassion and courage. He is a giant among men and is more than worthy to wear the crown of Rohan."

Tom nodded to accept the compliment from his long-lost love. In this comfortable sunroom in an ancient Lombardi convent in Italy, his emotions no longer churned and his mind no longer raced. Instead, he felt a deep satisfaction and sense of peace, knowing that the cycle of life really did come around full circle.

EPILOGUE
ONE YEAR LATER

Tom sat in his study in the farmhouse in Dijon, studying the latest messages from the Rohan business units downloading to his computer. If he had lifted his head and looked out the window, he would have observed his carefully tended garden of medicinal herbs and Antoinette's beloved fields of lavender. But on this particular afternoon, he was immersed in answering emails—specifically, would he agree to be profiled by the prestigious American magazine, *Vanity Fair*?

This time, he did allow his attention to rest on the natural wonders that lay just outside his home office, as if sheer beauty would help him make the right decision. On the one hand, he detested all publicity and usually said no to all such requests. Inevitably, the reporters wanted to know Tom's secret of longevity. He usually managed to deflect their questions with vague references to his knowledge of Far Eastern medicine, healthy nutrition, moderate exercise, and the luck of good genes.

Having exhausted that topic, they would then probe into Tom's past and future—why did he give up the throne? What was he going to do to rescue the Rohan corporation from its dire financial straits? Then they would press him for details on the secret societies that he was supposedly associated with, the Lombardi and the Carolingian Sacred Heart. How long could he continue to put off the news media with "no comment"?

But before he composed his usual negative response, Tom reconsidered. The readers of *Vanity Fair*—society's foremost elite, powerful political figures, corporate titans—were exactly the type of people who might donate to his charitable causes, as well as support his efforts in preserving the Carolingian heritage.

True to his word, Tom had sold three of his drugstores, keeping just the one in Dijon. With André in charge of day-to-day operations, he expanded the Dijon pharmacy to include a pediatric clinic, a nursery and child care center, a continuing education facility, and a cafeteria serving low-cost nutritious meals. Many of the flowering plants in the gardens surrounding these facilities grew from seeds or cuttings from Castle Rohan.

In addition to selling the three drugstores, Tom had also dissolved his research facility. Antoinette had shifted the focus of her brilliant mind to Artificial Intelligence, developing apps for the corporate and educational sectors.

For now, Tom held onto the title of King of Rohan, even though he very much wanted to turn it over to one of his children. But Antony had flatly refused, insisting he was a military man through-and-through. Julia had likewise demurred, citing her responsibilities as a prosecutor in Paris. As for second eldest son Ronald, he had simply scoffed and said, "My greatest strength is in the classroom. All of you know that."

That left Philip, the fourth eldest and the smart, ambitious banker. Tom had put him in charge of the newly created Rohan Business Group, overseeing all Rohan deeds, real estate developments, and investments. But within a week, Philip was bored with living at the isolated castle. He returned to Paris and took Victor Monet with him as his chief-of-staff. Tom knew that someday in the not-to-distant future, Philip would accept the crown in order to leverage the prestige to become president of the French Republic—because more than anything, Philip craved power.

Tom, meanwhile, continued to wear the title of the 54th King of Rohan, albeit reluctantly. He devoted his efforts to preservation and conservation of the vast Rohan holdings in art and historical artifacts, dividing his time between Dijon and Castle Rohan. He was also heavily involved in reviving the village of Saint-Meyer and due to his efforts it was well on the path to economic stability. What little spare time he had remaining was devoted to organizing and improving the Rohan archive at Basel.

At the castle, he put Louis in overall charge of maintenance and security for the building and its gardens. Other key directors continued in their roles: Brigitte in charge of staff and operations, Sandy Montague as chief legal counsel, and Chloe Durand as director of art. He appointed retired General Miliot and Bruna Lombardi as his special assistants.

While Tom sat in his home office in Dijon and debated in his own mind whether to accept or deny the request from *Vanity Fair*, in an middle upper neighborhood near Castle Rohan, Brigitte and her second husband, Jacques, a retired police captain, were entertaining three special guests: Louis, General Miliot and Chef Jean, all key members of the Carolingian Sacred Heart. They were seated around a table laden with a sumptuous dinner and dessert.

Jacques refilled the champagne flutes. "I would like us all to toast to Brigitte. But first, I would like to disclose a grand secret plot of hers."

All leaned forward, eager to hear what Jacques would say next. He did not disappoint them. "A year ago, Duke Michael passed away. He left no heirs. No uncles, no brothers, no male or female offspring. The world thought the old family line had ended."

Jacques continued, "Brigitte knew all about the evidence required to prove a claim to the throne, as did Duchess Marie de Courcillon."

Louis interrupted, :"You're talking about the fifty Rohan coins and at least eleven land deeds, each with the proper Carolingian seals, and each over five hundred years old."

"That's correct," Jacques said. Brigitte knew that the Monets would be unable to provide the above evidence to make any claim as a Rohan heir. She knew the coins and deeds had disappeared along with Tom."

He smiled at his wife and said, "It was Brigitte who had the idea to issue an invitation to select students through the country, young people who more than likely could trace their lineage back to some branch of the Rohan family, to participate in a special tour of Castle Rohan. Her dream was that one of those students would possibly prove to be Lothair's heir and would bring the coins and deeds back to the Kingdom."

This brought murmurs of approval from around the table, with Jacques saying, "To our surprise, not only did Brigitte's plot bring back Lothair's descendants, but the King of Rohan himself. After disappearing for sixty-five years, he is still alive and well."

Jacquie stood up and raised his champagne glass in Brigitte's direction. The guest followed suit, cheering loudly as they drank a toast to Brigitte.

Brigitte now rose and with a demeanor of deep joy and grace, said, "Yes, it was my plot, my plan, among my many efforts over the years to locate a legitimate heir to the throne. No one was more surprised that I when not only did we locate the Rohan bloodlines, but we brought back the authentic 54th King, Maximal Oto Thomas Rohan!"

Very solemnly, Brigitte continued, "I have always deeply suspected that the Lombardi played a vital role in issuing that invitation directly to young Gilbert. And, they ensured that the youngest Rohan child would actually bring home the letter. They knew, once Tom heard the Rohan line had apparently ended, he could no longer ignore the call of his love for his parents to return to Rohan one day. Meanwhile, it was the Lombardi who deceived Gabriel Monet into carrying out the assassination plot to take Tom out on the Paris street. Instead, as we know now, the Lombardi have always been Tom's guardian—guardians of the 54th King of Rohan!

Brigitte raised her glass for another toast and round of cheers.

As for Tom back in Dijon, he was now keenly aware of the presence of the Lombardi bodyguards, and wondered how he could have been so oblivious to them for sixty-five years. Just too focused on his research and with raising a large family, he supposed. Now, it was impossible for him to move outside his home without being aware of Big Bobby and two or three of his large, black-suited men surrounding him. His frequent visits to the castle, Saint-Meyer and Basel always involved an armored limousine and similar vehicles leading and following.

As for Belle, Tom had had no contact with her since that momentous day at the convent. And yet, he was somehow aware of her presence. He'd overheard a conversation between General Miliot and Big Bobby dropping hints that she had moved to Dijon. Sometimes he could swear he caught a glimpse of her out of the corner of his eye, as if she were trailing him at a discreet distance, watching over him. But... more than likely, it was just his imagination.

With one more contemplative moment, Tom made his decision and tapped out instructions to Brigitte to go ahead and approve the request by *Vanity Fair* to conduct an interview, take photographs, and publish a profile of the King of Rohan. The greater good—charitable donations, historic preservation—would outweigh whatever discomfort it might cause him, he decided.

Tom closed the laptop and made his way to the dining room, where the tantalizing aromas of one of Antoinette's savory stews wafted. To his delight and surprise, he found seated at the table not only his beloved wife, but youngest son Gilbert, home on holiday from university.

"I couldn't miss this special occasion," Gilbert said when he noticed Tom's puzzled expression.

"What special occasion?"

"Don't you know, Papa?" Gilbert's round face broke out in a grin. "It was exactly one year ago to this very day that I came home from school with the news that I'd been chosen for a special trip to Castle Rohan."

Tom quickly reviewed the dates in his mind and realized his youngest son was absolutely correct. He'd been so immersed in business details that it had completely slipped his mind.

"If it hadn't been for me winning that trip, none of this would have happened," Gilbert crowed.

"You do realize that wasn't a coincidence, correct?" Tom said with gentle humor. "Obviously, other forces were at work."

"I'm not stupid, Papa. But still, if it hadn't been for me..."

The two paused in their loving banter as Antoinette ladled stew into bowls and passed around a salad made up of ingredients from their own garden and warm, thickly-sliced homemade bread. The dining room was almost exactly the same as it had appeared one year ago, when Tom and Antoinette had debated how they would raise the money so Gilbert and a chaperone could take the trip. The only change was the addition of a family photograph and three framed architectural drawings. The photograph was a copy of the one that Tom's parents had cherished for so many years, showing a young Tom and Antoinette holding baby Antony, while the drawings were copies of those created by King Raymond so that Tom could build an exact replica of the castle dining room. The originals were now being stored in climate-controlled conditions in the Rohan archives.

"I've made an important decision about my studies," Gilbert said as he slathered butter on a slice of bread.

"That's wonderful," Tom said, always eager to show interest in his children's academic pursuits.

"Yes, I'm going to major in history, but no, I don't want to be a history professor." His voice grew more rapid with his enthusiasm. "My goal is to be an archivist, or a curator, or a historic preservationist."

"You mean…?" Tom asked, hardly daring to hope.

"Yes!" Gilbert beamed. "Someday, when I have the knowledge and training, I'd like to take on the whole Rohan heritage thing, follow in your footsteps, continue your work. Write about it too, so all the world will know."

With a voice thick with emotion, Tom said, "Nothing would make me prouder, my son."

"There's more," Gilbert continued.

"And that would be, what, *bébé?*" Antoinette inquired when she realized Tom was to overcome to speak.

"I'm going to start right now," Gilbert said, his boyish eagerness apparent despite his nineteen years. "I'm writing a paper all about what happened to us last year: the trip to the castle, and discovering that Papa is actually a direct descendant of the Carolingian kings, and the coronation, and your explorations of the dungeons, and how Julia and Philip were attacked, and how Papa went on that Rohan Heritage Tour and… and… just everything."

Well, not quite everything, Tom said to himself, thinking of the gathering at the Lombardi convent and the great secret that was revealed.

"Maybe someday it will even be a book!" Gilbert said with triumph.

Tom sat back and studied the auspicious presence of the dragon that had watched over the Rohan family dining room for so many centuries. The benevolent mythical creature symbolized the blessings that he had inherited from his ancestors, as well as the blessings that he and Antoinette intended to pass down to their own children and grandchildren.

Once again, he was reminded that good will runs in cycles and that love, kindness, and acts of charity will be repaid a thousand times over. A feeling of great peace and satisfaction filled his heart.

THE END

Author's Note

I am often asked about my fiction creation process. Where do I get my ideas? How do I develop them into a story?

For the longest time, I didn't know how to answer those questions, even though I have now sketched out ideas and outlines for ten books. Upon reflection, I have come to realize that each one starts in a moment of enlightenment and elation, momentarily overwhelming. The process feels like a hurricane, slowly growing in size out in the ocean, gaining momentum and size, and finally making landfall as it arrives in the hands of the readers.

I have always been fascinated with enlightenment and the evolution of humanity. When I retired after forty years as a computer engineer and scientist, I had planned to write three books and to complete two science projects. I've always kept a book of world history at my bedside—the only book. Upon awakening, I would put my ideas on PowerPoint storyboards, complete with action, dialogue, pictures of characters and settings, maps and diagrams. Eventually, I had ideas for ten works of fiction.

French Legend is one of those books and the first to be published. For four nights in a row, the entire story unfolded right before my eyes. Initially, I had 55 slides of story and some 20 slides with details about character and setting.

Unfortunately, a health setback in 2016 forced me into a slow and long recovery path. It was a sober woke-up call for my second life. Fortunately, by the end of August, 2018, I was recovered sufficiently to take a trip to Denmark, Sweden, and the glaciers of Norway. I had concerns that my limited physical health might not able to cope with a trip undertaken mostly by myself. Very fortunately, the trip proved my physical recovery was over 90 percent, not the 40 percent I had thought.

One month after returning from the Denmark, Sweden, and Norway trip, I completed the French Legend outline, which had grown to 260 PowerPoint slides. I also defined the major plot points of Book II in the King Rohan saga. At this point, I involved a fellow writer, Joyce Krieg, to help turn the storyboards into an actual book. To continue the hurricane metaphor, of the 500-mile storm path, the last 150 miles is Ms. Krieg's. She brings the hurricane to you.

Now I have the chance to complete four books with a common link—the Lombards of Italy. The follow-up book to *French Legend* will be *Lombardy Slough*, with action set in an advance research facility in District 3 on Monterey Bay, exploring the super powers of bio-intelligence. *Maple Beach* is a story of redemption, benevolence and compassion. *Lombardi's Daughter* tells the story of a legendary woman from the Lombardi family, raised in District 3, California, who plays a key role in the top-secret mission in the Yugoslavia Crisis. Finally, we return to Europe for *King Rohan II*.

The Lombardi Family Saga
by Joe-Ming Cheng

BOOK I:
French Legend—The King of Rohan
(2019)

BOOK II:
Lombardy Slough
(SUMMER 2020)

BOOK III:
Maple Beach

BOOK IV:
Lombardi's Daughter

BOOK V:
French Legend—The King of Rohan II

THE LOMBARDI FAMILY SAGA CONTINUES...

CHAPTER ONE FROM THE UPCOMING
BOOK II: LOMBARDY SLOUGH

One hundred miles south of the metropolis of San Francisco, less than hour's drive from the worldwide headquarters of Apple, Facebook, Google and Tesla, lies a land of beauty and serenity, little changed since the arrival of European settlers to California some 250 years ago. Originally settled by immigrants from the Lombardy section of Italy, it is now the site of Hope Park, a farm and scientific research facility. This modern structure blends well with the natural environment and is the only sign of human activity among the fields of wildflowers and the estuary teeming with birds and sea life.

On one particular evening, the scene was anything but peaceful, the mood far from hopeful.

"Dale, you didn't tell me we were dealing with a South American drug cartel," Ron Ford shouted at Dale Forman. Every inch of Ron's rugged, six-foot and four-inch frame bristled with tension.

"Do I have to tell you everything?" Dale snapped back.

The two men, plus a third, Phil Winter, were dressed in camouflage and clustered around a rented SUV parked on the shoulder of a narrow road that skirted a saltwater marsh just outside the Hope Park premises. The three had been close friends, comrades in arms, ever since serving together as military contractors in Baghdad.

With a sigh of frustration, Dale said, "All I know is, it's Zpac's operation, not ours. All they want is Dr. Lee's laptop. A simple break-and-grab operation. If everyone cooperates, no one gets hurt."

None of the trio required a reminder of the stakes. Dr. Lee's laptop held quite possibility the most valuable intellectual property in the country, if not the world, formulations that could bring untold profits to anyone who possessed the secrets and knew how to use them.

But that was only half the story. Tonight, the stakes were much higher than mere scientific breakthroughs.

A convoy of SUVs and pickup trucks roared up the road, coming to a halt just behind Dale's SUV. Raul Zavala climbed out of the lead vehicle, followed in quick succession by eighteen other gunmen. The Zpac leader strutted with confidence and arrogance, with a crooked smile seemingly frozen on his cruel face.

"Good evening, gentlemen," Raul said with a sneer in the direction of Ron, Dale and Phil. "My eighteen brothers are ready to move in." The tough-looking men began unloading automatic assault rifles, semi-automatic handguns, grenades, four machine guns and two rocket launchers.

Ron's face turned pale. "Is all this really necessary?" he asked.

Raul uttered a short laugh, a sound wild and ruthless. "I make the decisions around here, not you."

"But there are innocent civilians inside," Ron insisted. "A female doctor, three scientists, two office staffers, five security guards, and one very sick little girl."

"They are of no importance to me," Raul replied.

"Have mercy!" Ron begged desperately. Tears began to pour down his cheeks. "For God's sake, show some mercy. Don't do this!"

Raul's eyes remained cold, the crooked smile frozen. "Thank you for the information," he said to Ron. "Now we know exactly who and what we're dealing with inside. That is all we require from you three."

Ron took another look at all the deadly armaments, now lying in neat piles next to the vehicles. "You have brought enough firepower to take down a professional army," he protested. "The people inside are civilians. One of them is a child! As for the security guards, their weapons are toys compared to his."

Raul responded with a look that chilled Ron to the very bone. He realized he was looking into the eyes of the very devil. Raul said, "Our plans are set. No room for discussion. We'll go in and in less than ten minutes take whatever we need. If anyone dares to stand in our way, we will show no mercy."

The Zpac leader then turned his attention to Dale. "We have known each other for many years," he said. "You are under notice—this is Zpac's operation from this moment going forward."

Ron and Phil had always looked to Dale as their leader, the man they trusted with their lives. Now Ron stared at Dale with disbelief. Was he actually willing to obey the orders of this ruthless killer?

Raul barked out orders to Dale with the precision of a drill sergeant. "Your men will stay behind the line. No questions! This is our operation. If you want to leave now, fine. If you want to stay and watch, fine. But do not attempt to interfere, or participate, or create the slightest inconvenience for me and my men. Understood?"

Ron was about to blurt out that he'd be damned if he'd stand by and watch innocent people put in danger. At the last second, Phil grabbed him by the arm and pulled him aside. "Not now," he whispered. "We can't afford to offend Zpac."

Dale, meanwhile, nodded humbly and said to Raul, "Yes, sir! We understand fully that it is your operation. You brought us in merely to provide surveillance on the Hope Park property. Anyway, we are unarmed, so what could we do? The operation is all yours."

This response seemed to be the correct one, because the Zpac leader's hard expression softened slightly. Nodding at Dale, Ron and Phil, he said, "You guys stay out and stay behind."

Raul turned to face the five-story Hope Park building. "Move in, men. Anyone gets in your way, send them straight to hell!" Two men stayed behind to guard the perimeter of the 40-acre property while Raul and the other sixteen marched on a path that ran along the marsh, crossed the employee parking lot, and faced the building. A glassed-in entryway at the left corner led to a reception area and research lab, where the Hope Park scientists conducted their experiments. A second door at the midway point of the building was the employee entrance, where the nine-to-five staff labored in a large hall. One security guard was position in this area, while four others guarded the lab.

The lights visible through the windows from inside the building suddenly went dark. A few dim lights appeared in various corners of Hope Farm as the back-up security system flickered to life.

Ron stood and watched helplessly as Raul and his men advanced across the parking lot and positioned themselves in front of the two entrances. He assumed they would break down the doors. Instead, he heard a terrific explosion that shook the ground under his feet. The Zpac men were using the grenade launcher!

Two gaping holes appeared in the walls of the building and black smoke poured out. The uniform of the security guard station at the employee entrance caught fire. He dropped to the ground and began to roll, screaming in pain. Two other security guards from the lab ran deeper into the building, presumably in the direction of their gun locker.

The Zpac men, wearing the very latest technology in night-vision goggles, entered Hope Park in two separate columns of military precision and with machine guns blazing. Raul donned a bullet-proof vest and ran to catch up behind the column entering what was left of the reception area at the left corner of the building.

The two men who'd cut the electric power emerged from the bush and positioned themselves between Dale's team and the surrounding farmland. Dale recognized them as Raul's two younger brothers.

Ron shook his head in frustration and agony. "Six civilians and a little girl are inside," he said to anyone who would listen. "Only five security guards to go up against a commando army. They are being put through hell because of us." He could no longer control the tears that fell freely.

Phil, looking equally grim, pulled Ron into their rented SUV. Dale, meanwhile, showed no emotion. He walked calmly to the back door of the vehicle and opened it. To Ron and Phil, he said, "We have a powerful sniper rifle and two sub-automatic guns, all with night-vision scopes and silencers. Plus handguns and night-vision goggles for each of us." His voice cold and confident, he concluded, "We have enough firepower. No one will be able to match us."

Not wanting to believe what he was hearing, Ron peered into the back storage area of the SUV. "You told Raul we have no weapons. Now look at this pile of armaments." He shook his head emphatically. "No way. I am not carrying a deadly weapon ever again."

"Me neither," Phil said, walking away. "You can count me out."

Dale acted as if he had heard neither of his friends. He donned a bulletproof vest, wrapped the automatic handgun around his right thigh, slung the semi-automatic rifle around his neck, put on the night-vision goggles and grabbed the high powered, precision sniper rifle. "I should be able to take care of this myself," he declared.

Ron's heart sunk. What could Dale possibly be planning? To take down all eighteen Zpac men, plus Raul? Then snatch the laptop for himself? And do what with the world's most valuable intellectual property?

While these thoughts ran through Ron's mind, the mayhem inside the Hope Park building grew louder and more intense. Explosions, shattering glass, shots from automatic rifles, screams of agony. From what Ron could tell, the security guards were putting up only a token resistance.

Feeling utterly helpless in the face of such carnage, Ron could only sink into a sitting position with his back against the side of the SUV. He buried his head in his hands as the tears continued to flow. "Lord, forgive me for any part I played in this massacre. Innocent civilians and security guards, and a six-year-old girl..." He was overcome, unable to go on.

Another burst of machine gun fire, more shattering of glass, and renewed cries of pain and terror. "This is a crime on humanity!" Ron moaned. "This is carnage. Lord, forgive my deep sin."

By now, Phil had joined Ron on the ground next to the SUV and appeared as upset and disbelieving. A pair of booted feet planted themselves in front of two men. Dale peered down at them, his expression sly and victorious.

Only four minutes had passed since the Zpac men had invaded the Hope Park building, yet to Ron the scene was more savage than anything he'd witnessed in the Middle East. Seventeen ruthless South American drug thugs with automatic weapons and grenade launchers against six civilians, a little girl, and five security guards.

"My Lord, show us your mercy," Ron cried out. "Save Hope Park, save the innocent victims."

He collapsed onto the ground and his voice grew hoarse as he continued to plead, "Lord, save your children. My Lord, have mercy and save all your children."

Find out what happens next in *Lombardy Slough*,
to be released in the summer of 2020.

Joe-Ming Cheng

Joe-Ming writes novels of contemporary suspense, creating stories in storyboard format. An accomplished IC, hardware system, algorithm developer and researcher for forty years, Dr. Cheng studied at CYCU, UCSB, ETH, and UCSC with a Ph.D. in Computer Engineering. He has written ten story outlines and plans to release five of them having the common link to Lothair I, a Holy Roman Empire co-emperor and to the land that once stretched from today's Holland, Alsace, and Switzerland to northern Italy's Lombardy region.

JOYCE KREIG

Joyce Krieg is the author of three mysteries published by St. Martin's Press: Murder Off Mike, Slip Cue and Riding Gain. She was the winner of St. Martin's "best first traditional mystery" contest and an Agatha nominee for best cozy mystery. She is the immediate past president of California Writers Club, with 22 branches and some 2,000 members throughout the state. Joyce is a former newspaper reporter and radio news announcer. She resides in Pacific Grove, California, where she works as a freelance editor and writer.

SETH D.J. FOLEY

Born and raised in San Jose, California, Seth has over 20 years of commissioned freelance art work. Has done illustrations for children books for authors Arlene Taylor, Ph.D. and Sharlet Briggs, Ph.D. Seth developed the passion for drawing since early grade. In college he learned industrial design. He likes to combine both industrial and creative art forms in his works when the opportunity arises. Seth is a graduate of California State University Long Beach.

Made in USA - Crawfordsville, IN
76873_9781950562220
02.17.2020 1533